DANGEROUS PASSION

Gabrielle eyed him doubtfully. "Would *you* teach me how to be a real woman?"

Cam sucked in his breath and exhaled slowly. Smiling, he said, "My dear, what else are husbands for? It shall be my pleasure."

His kiss was hot and sweetly erotic. She felt as if she were floating, and clutched the lapels of his coat as her head began to spin. She clung to Cam as if he were her lifeline.

His fingers dug into her hair, holding her steady as his lips sank into hers. He'd wanted women before. But never like this. He wanted her with a desperation that shocked him. She was his. He would make it so. The kiss became rougher, more urgent as his need to possess began to spiral out of control.

It was Gabrielle's first taste of physical desire. Some of the symptoms she had experienced before — the shortness of breath, the erratic heartbeat, the pounding in her ears. Danger. Her sixth sense came into play. He was the enemy. She should be taking to her heels. But all through her body she could feel a curious urge to surrender.

Cam lifted his head.

"For a novice, you did remarkably well." His tone was as matter-of-fact as he could make it. "With a little practice, you'll be quite proficient."

Scarlet Angel

ELIZABETH THORNTON

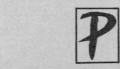

PINNACLE BOOKS
WINDSOR PUBLISHING CORP.

PINNACLE BOOKS

are published by

Windsor Publishing Corp.
475 Park Avenue South
New York, NY 10016

First printing: August, 1990

Printed in the United States of America

Prologue

Paris, September 2nd 1792
The Prison Massacres
The Abbaye

He stood transfixed at the small turret window overlooking one section of the prison courtyard, unable to drag his eyes from the appalling scene of slaughter. The latest batch of prisoners to be forcibly prised from their cells was dragged before their "judges." God, and what judges! The rabble of Paris, butchers in their red caps and leather aprons, their bare arms covered in blood; *sans-culottes,* those illiterate dregs of society; and *federés,* citizen-soldiers from the provinces, an undisciplined gang of cutthroats who would murder a man as soon as look at him.

The executions had been going on for hours. They'd known what was coming. Even in prison, word traveled fast. It had started in the afternoon when gangs of armed men had attacked several coaches of priests who were being conveyed to prison for, predictably, refusing to take the constitutional oath. From there, the mob had moved to Carmes prison and systematically murdered the total population imprisoned there. When night had fallen, and there was no one left to murder at Carmes, the same rabble, their ranks now swollen to two hundred or so, had surged *en masse* to the Abbaye. No one tried to stop them. And now the executions had become indiscriminate.

Sickened, his heart pounding in his chest, Cam closed his eyes to shut out the frightful spectacle made

11

all the more hideous by the presence of *poissardes* — fishwives and other market women who, on request, were feeding the executioners brandy mixed with gunpowder to aggravate their fury for the unending task. He had never before seen women in the throes of bloodlust, could not take in what his eyes told him — that they were totally immune to the growing pile of mutilated corpses and the suffering of those who were not yet ready to meet their end.

His turn was coming. He knew it. No one would be spared, except, pray God, the women and children. His stepmother and twelve-year-old sister were in another part of the building. He could not believe that even this *canaille* would stoop to murder such innocents.

Another man jostled him aside to take his place at the window. Cam moved to one of the filthy cots against the wall. How ironic, he thought, that when they had finally been captured and incarcerated — was it only a fortnight before? — he had been glad that they had been taken to the Abbaye and not to one of the other prisons, where his sickly sister might be shut up with women of the street or worse.

Three months in France, and two of those in hiding, and it had come to this! Oh God, how naïve they had been in England to welcome the first reports of the Revolution! They should have known from their lessons in history that moderation and restraint was not part of the human temperament once blood had been spilled. And France's bloody past did not bear thinking about.

Hindsight was a wonderful thing! And so was the English Channel! How could they know, how could they possibly imagine in England, what it was like to live in terror of the mob?

Shutting his ears to a bloodcurdling scream that came from below, he stretched full length on the cot and forced himself to think of anything but the fate that was rushing to meet him.

Recriminations pressed in to scourge him. He should never have allowed his stepmother to remove to her family in France on the death of his father five years before. He should have kept his sister with him in England, in spite of the doctors' advice that a more temperate climate would benefit her delicate health. He should have defied his guardians sooner, before he reached his majority, and come to France himself to see what was afoot. He should have insisted that they quit Paris in the first days of his arrival, even supposing his stepmother was right in averring that Marguerite would never survive the journey.

He stirred restlessly and turned his face to the wall. Oh God, how could he have done any of those things? He had been only a boy of sixteen when his father had died. There was no panic in England when the Revolution began. His stepmother's family was close to the French throne — God, and who knew what had become of them? — and therefore as powerful as any. His sister's health had completely broken down. There was no question that she would survive the rigors of the kind of journey they would be compelled to endure. What else could they have done but go into hiding until the worst of the storm had passed?

And who could have foreseen this sudden turn in events? It was the massacre of five hundred of the king's Swiss Guards at the Tuileries two months before, that and the appointment of their archenemy, George Jacques Danton, as minister of justice, that had finally convinced the French aristocracy that their days were numbered.

The royal family was now under heavy guard in the gloomy fortress of the Knights Templar. The atmosphere in Paris was suddenly transformed. Foreign governments had withdrawn their ambassadors. Embassies were closed. And the aristocrats, long since stripped of their titles, were leaving their houses in droves and going into hiding or making a dash for freedom across the Channel.

All Paris had been waiting for something to happen, for the bloodletting to begin. And it had started with reprisals against the defenseless populations of the overcrowded prisons. Most of the inmates were classified by the mob as dangerous opponents of the Revolution — priests, lawyers, journalists, ordinary citizens who had criticized the conduct of their new masters, and those unfortunate members of the aristocracy, men, women and children, whose hiding places had been discovered in the house-to-house searches.

"When they take us out, we should offer no resistance." The comment came from one of the Carmelite priests who had been hearing the confessions of some of the prisoners.

Cam raised himself to a sitting position and surveyed the shadowy figures of the other dozen or so occupants of the small cell, most of whom were priests on their knees, praying for the dying and for the suffering to come. He understood the priest's reference. Perhaps everyone did, for no one asked the old man to explain himself. The condemned prisoners who tried to protect themselves with their hands were first dismembered before being stabbed or decapitated. But there was no question in his mind of going docilely to his fate like a lamb to the slaughter. He could not do it.

The man he knew as Rodier, a lawyer by profession, joined him on the cot, and Cam made room for him.

"Good advice if you're an old man and already have one foot in the grave," said Rodier in an ironic undertone for Cam's ears only.

In the weeks since they had been incarcerated, the two men had developed something of a friendship, despite the disparity in their ages. Rodier was in his early thirties, eternally an optimist, and as ugly as sin, though he possessed a certain charisma that stood him

14

in good stead whatever the circumstances. He was also a member of the more moderate Girondist party, which, for the present, had been discredited. But on the morrow, who was to say which clique would hold the upper hand?

"You're not thinking of following the old man's advice?" asked Rodier, eyeing the younger man with a considering eye. He liked what he saw and knew of the young English aristocrat; approved of the ungallic, stoic reserve; admired the devotion to family that had propelled the youth to his present, perilous course of action; and, not least, was gratified by the boy's grasp of French language and letters. In his experience, the majority of the English nobility was a herd of ignorant asses, just like their French counterparts, and proud of it. But then, the boy had been raised by a French stepmother, an unhoped for happenstance, in Rodier's opinion.

Still, the boy sorely needed guidance, which was why Rodier had taken him under his wing from the moment they had been unceremoniously thrust behind the gloomy walls of the Abbaye. The youth had given his goalers his correct name, with no thought of subterfuge. Thankfully, many English surnames were French in origin. "Camille Colburne" had passed without comment. Thank God the boy had had enough sense not to reveal his title! It would never do to let the authorities know that they had a member of the English aristocracy, a duke no less, in their hands. And from the boy's appearance, apart from the intelligent, startlingly light-blue eyes, he was swarthy enough to pass for a Spaniard, let alone a Frenchman.

Those blue eyes had learned to be guarded in the weeks since Rodier had first befriended the boy. In that small, overcrowded cell with the only light coming from the pitch torches in the prison courtyard, it was too dark to read his expression. But his hesitation in answering the lawyer's question left no doubt in Ro-

15

dier's mind that the deep-set eyes would be cautiously half-hooded.

"You're not thinking of following the old man's advice," Rodier prodded.

"When hell freezes over," drawled the boy.

A laugh was startled out of Rodier. He clapped Cam on the shoulder, and several of the priests crossed themselves as if to protest some obscene profanity that had just been committed.

"Young men were ever hotheaded," said Rodier good-naturedly. "I like you, Camille." In a more serious vein, he went on, "Listen! If you perish, you will be of no use to your mother and sister. Use your head, man! Resistance will gain you nothing. There's always tomorrow if we survive this night's work."

"I mean to die happy," said the young man.

"What? By taking a couple of those *canaille* with you?"

"Then what do you suggest?"

"I make no promises, mind, but I suggest that you follow my lead. I'm not a lawyer for nothing, you know. Before they dispatch us, they're giving us a chance to defend ourselves."

"You're referring, I presume, to the makeshift tribunal presided over by that rabble-rouser, Maillard?"

A strange smile touched Rodier's lips. "Maillard may be their leader, but there is someone else who holds the real power."

"Oh? Who?"

"Someone who is keeping very much in the background. Danton's right-hand man. He's there in the shadows. You didn't notice him?"

"No. Who is he?"

"Mascaron."

"I've never heard of him."

"Few have. He doesn't want to be known."

A thought occurred to the boy, and he sat up straighter. "You said he was Danton's right-hand man!

Then if the authorities know what is going on, perhaps he's here to put a stop to these murders."

"You're jesting! Whatever his sentiments, Danton would never gainsay the mob. They might kick him out of office tomorrow, and then where would he be?"

"Where he deserves to be," said Cam with a betraying bitterness edging his voice.

Nothing was said for a full minute, then Rodier observed, "Mascaron must be here for a reason. I wonder what is so important to make him show his face when . . ."

Rodier stopped in mid-sentence. The rush of approaching feet could be heard coming from the circular stone staircase. Snatches of revolutionary songs hung on the air. The light that shined under the door grew brighter. Within, all conversation ceased. Only the drone of the priests' prayers continued unabated.

As the key grated in the lock, men rose to their feet.

"Are you with me?" asked Rodier.

"I'm with you," said Cam, rising to stand by the other man.

"You're my nephew," said Rodier. "Let me do all the talking. And try to look properly humble, if you can. Let them smell an *aristo* and we're both done for."

A rabble of fearsome *sans-culottes* came bursting into the cell. In their bloodied hands they brandished sabers, pikes, and butchers' hatchets. Rough hands were laid on the prisoners, and they were hauled with blows, kicks, and curses into the torchlit passageway, down the steep, narrow stone steps, and into the courtyard, where a rough and ready justice awaited them.

Cam could not help recoiling in horror at the scene of frightful carnage that met his eyes. Even the daredevil Rodier was momentarily stunned. The courtyard glowed like a red-hot furnace from two bonfires that had been lit to facilitate the fiendish work. To the right, in full view of the prisoners who were being in-

17

terrogated, the condemned were being hacked to pieces. Carts drawn by horses had arrived to carry away the mounting heaps of corpses. Women, some with human ears pinned to their aprons, were piling bodies on the carts and breaking off occasionally to dance the carmagnole. The uproar of the assassins and their victims was almost deafening. Hell could not be more frightening, thought Cam, as he tried to quell his heaving stomach.

The "judges," more drunk than sober, sat around a table. Rodier, making a rapid recovery, grabbed the sleeve of his "nephew" and pushed his way close to the front of the line.

Cam hung back in what he hoped was an attitude of terrified submission. Should Rodier lose in his gambit they would be no worse off. And he was determined that he would take one of the executioners with him when his time came. Preferably the leader, but which one?

Surreptitiously, his eyes roved over the throng of "judges." Maillard, that hero of the Bastille, his wire-rimmed spectacles perched on his thin nose, handed down a summary verdict if the prisoner had the misfortune to be an *aristo* or a priest. There were no exceptions here.

From time to time, Maillard's eyes flicked to a well set-up, handsome man of indeterminate years who sat in the shadows a little apart from the other judges, a long black cloak enveloping his broad shoulders. It might have been a trick of the light, but Cam was almost sure that a silent communication was taking place between the two men. He wondered if he was looking upon the man called Mascaron.

Before he had time to guard his expression, Cam found himself caught and held in the mesmerizing gaze of the judge he had been covertly scrutinizing. Eyes as brilliant as gemstones seemed to probe and capture his secret thoughts. He tried to break the older man's hold, to no avail. Incredibly, amusement gathered in those brilliant eyes a moment before they released him. *He knows,* thought Cam, *He knows who and what I am!*

He heard Rodier's confident tones address the tribunal and kept his eyes firmly on the flagstones.

"*Citoyens,* if you find my nephew and I enemies of the Revolution, then I, Marie-Gilbert Rodier, adjure you to do your duty and rid France of all traitors to our glorious cause."

"Why were you arrested?" asked Maillard, unimpressed by this rhetoric.

"I was denounced as a traitor," stated Rodier boldly and without prevarication.

Maillard's eyebrows rose. "By whom?" he asked.

"By enemies of my master."

Impatiently Maillard demanded, "And who is your master? Speak up man, we haven't got all night!"

Rodier said the words slowly, weighting each word with due care. "My master is General Dumouriez."

His stroke was masterly, thought Cam. For though at the moment Danton and the Cordeliers held sway, Dumouriez was a Gerondist and at that very moment at the head of the French army as it marched out to meet with hostile Prussian and Austrian forces under the command of the Duke of Brunswick. Sensible men were slow to pick a quarrel with either Danton or Dumouriez until one or the other was the clear leader.

"You can prove this?" asked Maillard.

Rodier shrugged philosophically. "I had papers, yes. But they were taken from me when I was brought here with my nephew. When General Dumouriez returns from the front, he will vouch for us both. We're only clerks, after all, in his service."

Maillard seemed to deliberate. It was no trick of the light now, thought Cam. It was evident to him that Maillard deferred to the older man who kept to the shadows.

"You are free to go," announced Maillard. "Next!"

"I would know the young man's name." The softly spoken command came from the judge called Mascaron.

At his side, Cam felt Rodier go rigid.

"Camille," said Cam before Rodier could answer for him. His eyes lifted challengingly to meet Mascaron's steady stare. He knew then how the untried David must have felt when first setting eyes on Goliath. "Camille Colburne," he answered truthfully.

"My sister's son," interposed Rodier quickly to explain the difference in their surnames.

But the *sans-culottes* were becoming restless with this idle chitchat. The men were jostled aside to make room for easier game. Cam felt Rodier's firm clasp on his elbow and he was propelled towards the massive iron gates that led to the Rue Saint Marguerite and freedom. Carts and horses coming and going, however, had choked the exits, and they were forced to turn aside as vociferous *poissardes* shouted curses at each other to clear the way.

Cam could not believe that he had escaped so easily when he had been so sure that Mascaron could denounce him with a word.

"Why is he here?" asked Rodier reflectively, looking back over his shoulder at the man shrouded in shadows.

"Why not?" asked Cam, shrugging off his vague and uneasy uncertainties. He had things of far greater import to consider than the enigma of Mascaron.

"Because it's out of character for that one. Mascaron prefers anonymity, and with good reason. The Revolution is a fickle mistress."

But Cam had lost interest in the conversation. His mind was racing ahead to ways and means of securing the release of his mother and sister. There must be something, someone . . .

"What's this?"

Rodier laid a restraining hand on his sleeve and Cam followed the direction of his companion's gaze. The doors to the women's section of the prison stood open and a score of women and children were being herded into the courtyard. Coarse catcalls and ribald jests greeted their appearance.

"No!" Cam felt the shock of this new development all through his body. "No!" he said again, and started forward, only to be brought up short by Rodier's vise-like grip on his arm.

"Mordieu, do you want to get us all killed? Hold, man, and bide your time! Mascaron is not a butcher of women and children. This may mean nothing at all!"

But it did mean something, that much was evident from the infuriated howls of the *poissardes* and other women who left their ghoulish work at the carts and surged toward the terrified band of newcomers, some clinging to each other, most weeping, and some too stunned to absorb the horror that met their eyes. At the very edge, toward the back of the crowd, Cam recognized the erect figure of his stepmother. Clasped in her arms and weeping uncontrollably against her breast was his sister, Marguerite.

"Tuez les aristocrates! Tuez! Tuez!"

Every muscle in Cam's body coiled for action. Without thinking, he shook off Rodier's hand.

It was Mascaron, the man of the shadows, however, who took action. In a flash, and before Cam could move, he had placed himself between the angry mob of women and their victims. In a voice like thunder he roared, "Back! Back! Kill all you want when the tribunal has done its work! Back, I say! There will be more than enough victims for you before the night is over!"

The mob of angry women, cowed by his air of authority, fell back a few paces, muttering among themselves.

After a moment, Mascaron returned to his place at

the table but remained standing.

Maillard, as if on cue, called out, "Madame de Brienne, step forward!"

At the name, an angry buzz went up from all round the courtyard. Count de Brienne, following in the footsteps of his friend General Lafayette, had attempted to defect to the Austrians only a week before. He had fallen foul of a band of *federés* who had given chase. The count had been executed on the spot and his wife and child brought back to Paris and lodged in the Abbaye. Feelings against Lafayette, who had succeeded in his defection, ran high and spilled over to his former friends. The de Briennes had the misfortune to be of their number. Moreover, Lafayette was beyond the power of the mob. The de Briennes were not.

"Madame de Brienne, step forward." Maillard's voice cut across the disconsolate murmurs of the angry women, who saw the easy prey being snatched from under their noses.

A child, a girl of no more than eight or nine years, clasping the hand of an ashen faced, curiously blank-eyed woman, pushed her way out of the tightly knit group of female prisoners.

"I am Gabrielle de Brienne, and this is my mother," said the child, not bold, not cowed, but strangely calm, as if somehow untouched by the heaps of bloodied corpses that lay strewn around and the cruelty of the jeering faces that confronted her.

Surely no one, thought Cam, could help but be stirred by the picture the child presented. Angelic by name, he thought, and angelic to all outward appearances. Her mane of gold hair picked up the glow from the bonfires and seemed to shine with an incandescent halo. Her heart-shaped face was dominated by a pair of enormous eyes. Her back was straight, her chin elevated a fraction, and she had stationed herself slightly in front of her mother in a gesture of protection. An

22

innocent in the inferno of hell, he thought, and was swamped with an almost overpowering urge to throw caution to the winds and call down heaven's wrath on the fiends who would desecrate her innocent beauty.

"Steady!" murmured Rodier at his elbow, as if reading his mind.

Maillard stepped forward. In a not unkindly tone he said, "Child, let your mother speak for herself."

"*Maman* cannot speak," said the child, betraying only a slight tremor in her voice. "Not since Clermont."

As everyone there knew, it was at Clermont that the *federés* had overtaken de Brienne and his family. The girl had seen her father cut down before her eyes.

The mood of the mob was becoming more ugly by the minute. If the mother could not be questioned how could she be condemned? And if she could not be condemned, what sport was there in that?

Momentarily stymied, Maillard's eyes flicked to the man who was clearly his superior.

"Gabrielle," said Mascaron stepping into the light, "Can you prove your loyalty to the Revolution?"

The eyes of the child wandered over the figures of the judges, finally coming to rest on the man who had spoken.

"Prove your loyalty to the Revolution," said Mascaron gently, "and you and your mother shall go free."

A howl of protest went up.

"Silence!" roared Mascaron. In a moment, a pistol appeared in his hand. No one doubted that it was primed and ready for instant use.

The mob fell silent. Cam did not doubt that beneath their forced compliance there smouldered hatreds and passions ready to erupt at any moment with the force of a volcano. Then nothing would hold back the tide of blood, not Mascaron, not Maillard, not even the silver-tongued oratory of Danton himself, should he be prevailed upon to defend these innocents.

He was stirred from his anguished reveries by the clear carrying tones of the young girl. She was singing one of the revolutionary songs: "Ça Ira!"

"What will be, will be!
People of our time keep on repeating
What will be, will be!
In spite of our enemies
We shall succeed in everything."

As the words fell from her lips, the refrain was taken up first by the *federés* and then by the *sans-culottes,* and finally by the coarse market women. Tears glistened on many a face that moments before had been contorted with bloodlust. The spectacle sickened Cam.

One or two of the prison women had fallen to their knees in an attitude of prayer. This stirring hymn of the Revolution boded no good for them. They were the "enemies" of whom the girl sang, the hated *aristos.* Deprived of their titles, their wealth confiscated, they had nothing of value left to lose but their lives. Before the song had ended, every single one of them had followed the example of the first of their group. Young mothers and their children, old women, heads bowed, lips moving, prayed for a miracle or the deliverance of a quick death.

"No! Oh God, no!" groaned Cam. In her innocence, the child had as good as signed a death warrant for the women at her back. But no, he could not, would not believe that it was possible. There were young children among them. Men could not be so bestial as to permit such a thing.

When the song came to an end, the revolutionaries began to cheer. It was Maillard who held up a hand to silence them.

"*Citoyenne* Brienne, Gabrielle Brienne," he said in a clear carrying tone, "you are free to go."

No "Madame de Brienne," now, thought Cam. The word *citoyenne* was just coming into use. It was as if the self-styled judge had paid the woman an extravagant compliment — and she who so shortly before proudly bore the title of countess!

The girl seemed unsure of what she should do next. Dumbly questioning, she looked to Mascaron. From nowhere, two men in the uniform of the Garde Nationale appeared and led her away in company of her mother. She passed so close to Cam that he could have reached out to touch her. At that moment she looked directly at him. Her eyes were glazed and brimming with tears. She brushed them away and moved quickly past him, but not before it registered with Cam that the girl's eyes were as brilliant as polished emeralds. Mascaron's eyes, he thought, and felt a rise of helpless rage, as if the child had somehow betrayed him.

His gaze traveled to his stepmother and sister. Like sheep for the slaughter, they awaited their fate. He began to edge his way toward them. Before he had taken many steps he became aware that Mascaron was shouldering his way from the courtyard, passing between stationary carts filled with the night's gruesome work.

With blinding clarity, Cam saw that with the release of Gabrielle de Brienne and her mother, Mascaron's purpose in coming to the Abbaye had been served. For the fate of the other prisoners — men, women, or children — the man was completely indifferent. The butcher Maillard was now left in sole command.

Almost faint with horror, Cam's eyes became riveted to the leader of the *sans-culottes*. Maillard's gaze was trained on the retreating figure of his superior. As soon as Mascaron had quit the courtyard, Maillard searched for a paper in his pocket.

Slowly, deliberately, he began to pronounce the sentence of death. There were no reprieves.

"No!" The strangled cry, torn from Cam's throat,

was drowned out by the roar of the rabble.

"Mort aux aristocrates! Death to the aristocrats!" Like a tidal wave, the crowd surged forward.

Cam had one glimpse of his sister as she was torn from his mother's arms before he was hit on the head from behind. Mercifully, darkness claimed him almost instantly.

1803

Eleven Years Later.

Chapter One

Lord Lansing, a young man of thirty summers or so, lolled comfortably in an oversized, stuffed armchair in the Duke of Dyson's bedchamber in his commodious house in Hanover Square. He was reflecting, rather gloomily, on Europe's future now that Napoleon Bonaparte had taken the reins of France's destiny into his hands.

"You'll find London rather thin of company, Cam," observed Lansing, toying absently with a lock of his blond hair.

Cam Colburne, the duke, ducked his dark head below the surface of his bath water and came up spluttering. "Shall I?" He shook his head vigorously, sending droplets of water flying. "Simon, be a good fellow and fetch me that towel."

From a rack in front of the blazing fire, Lord Lansing obediently plucked a warm towel and threw it at his friend's head.

Catching it with one hand as he emerged naked from the copper tub in which he had been bathing, Cam proceeded to dry himself briskly.

Some minutes were to pass before Lansing took up where he had left off. "It's because of the peace treaty, you see."

"What's because of the peace treaty?" asked Cam.

He had donned clean linen and was buttoning his white satin breeches.

"That London is thin of company," explained Lansing. To his friend's questioning look he answered, "Every man and his dog, it seems, is off to Paris to catch a glimpse of that Bonaparte fellow."

"That will soon change. In another month or so we shall be at war again."

Lansing snorted. "That's if Mr. Pitt can persuade the opposition to toe the line."

"Mr. Pitt is a very persuasive fellow," observed Cam mildly. "Where are my shoes? Oh, there they are." Over white silk stockings, Cam slipped on a pair of black patent pumps with silver buckles. He noticed a fleck of something on his right toe and swore softly.

"You don't much care for the leader of the opposition, do you, Cam?"

"Mr. Fox? I don't care for him at all. He's a true, dyed-in-the-wool Whig, for God's sake. They are the most dangerous kind. Where the devil is my neckcloth?"

"On the back of the chair, where you left it. More to the point, where the devil is your valet?"

"What? Oh, he remains at Dunraeden," answered Cam, referring to his seat in Cornwall, an isolated, impregnable fortress jutting into the English Channel.

"How long have you been on the road?"

"Three days. My thanks for the message, Simon. I wouldn't miss this meeting for the world."

"It was Mr. Pitt who particularly asked that you be present. He seems to think that if anyone can persuade Fox to temper his oratory in the House, that person is you."

"Does he?" Cam deftly tied his pristine white neckcloth with a skill that arrested the attention of his companion. "Did he say why?"

Coming to himself, Lansing responded, "He seems to think that you have made a study of Mr. Fox's worldview and will know what tack to take if we get into difficulties."

"Fox is an idealist and a liberal," said Cam. "That's all we need to know." Throwing his friend an imploring look he asked, "Would you mind acting the gentleman's gentleman, Simon?"

Lansing helped ease his friend into a tight-fitting, dark blue evening coat with silver buttons. "There! Brummel himself could not find fault with you in this getup." He stepped back to admire the cut of his friend's coat. "Who's your tailor?"

"Weston of Old Bond Street. Do you know him?"

"Good God, Cam! That's Brummel's tailor!"

"Is it?" Cam grimaced at his reflection in the long cheval mirror, then turned to face his friend. "Well? Do I pass muster, or does my valet have the right of it when he tells me that I'm as helpless as a babe without his ministrations?"

"You'll do," retorted Lansing. He was thinking, without envy, that his friend cut a glamorous figure. In addition to the title and fortune, the Duke of Dyson possessed uncommon good looks and the physique of an athlete. Moreover, he had about him a certain air, a solitude, that at one and the same time attracted overtures of friendship and repelled a presumptuous intimacy. Lansing counted himself the most fortunate of fellows that he was one of Cam's few intimates.

"Where do you Cornishmen come by those extraordinary blue eyes?" he asked.

"From our parents," answered Cam dryly, and carefully inserted a diamond pin in the knot of his neckcloth.

"What's the occasion for the formal wear?" asked Lansing.

"Louise. She's giving a reception for some of her compatriots. I'm going on there later, after we meet with Mr. Pitt and Mr. Fox. You're invited, if you care to attend."

31

"My French isn't up to it," offered Lansing hopefully.

"Nonsense. These French *immigrés* will be eager to practice their English on you. Besides, since we shall be in France by the end of the week, you yourself need the practice."

"How is Louise?"

Cam's hands momentarily stilled as he adjusted the lace on his cuffs. He looked a question at his friend. "Fine, as far as I know. Isn't she?"

Lansing's look was incredulous. "Cam, don't you know? Don't you care? The woman is your mistress, for God's sake, and has been these two years. How can you go off and leave her unattended for months on end? She's a beautiful, desirable creature. You're asking for trouble."

Cam's eyebrows rose. "What? Has she found another protector?"

"Not to my knowledge. That's not the point." Lansing shook his head at the note of indifference he detected in his friend's voice. He opened his mouth to remonstrate, then thought better of it. "It doesn't signify. I'm sorry I mentioned it."

"No, no! Truly! I want to hear what you have to say."

"I don't know what I want to say. Yes I do. I've been making a study of *your* worldview, Cam, and . . . ," Lansing hesitated.

"And?" encouraged Cam softly.

Shrugging helplessly, Lansing said, "Sometimes I wonder if you care for anything but your causes."

"So. We're not really talking about Louise, are we? Oh don't dissemble on my account. If you don't wish to come to France with me, just say so."

"You know it's not that. It's . . . well . . . don't fly off the handle, but the whole idea seems so farfetched."

When Cam had first proposed the daring scheme of holding one of Bonaparte's ministers to ransom for vital military information, Lansing had readily fallen in with his plans. That Mr. Pitt, the leader of their party, must not be taken into their confidence, did not sit well with Lansing. In some things, the Duke of Dyson was a law unto himself. Lord Lansing had occasion to be grateful for his friend's unorthodox methods. It was only as Cam revealed the full scope of his design that Lansing began to have second thoughts.

Cam filled two crystal glasses from a decanter of brandy and gave one into Lansing's hand. Seating himself in an adjacent chair, he said, "You know Mr. Pitt's mind. In spite of the threat Mr. Fox poses, by May the war with France will be resumed. That's only weeks away. Before the end of the year England may expect Napoleon Bonaparte to launch an armada for our invasion *and* subjugation. If we can be one step ahead of the French, it's worth any risk."

"I suppose, but . . ."

"Yes?"

"Must we involve the girl? She's so young."

"Gabrielle de Brienne is eighteen years old. Not so young by my reckoning."

Something flashed in Cam's eyes, so fleetingly that Lansing wondered if he had imagined it. He shook his head. "This Mascaron fellow, her grandfather . . ."

"The assistant minister of the Marine."

"Can't we find some other way to get the information from him? To abduct his granddaughter and hold her to ransom seems . . . ungentlemanly, if you want my opinion."

Cam made a harsh, derisory sound and set down his glass sharply. "Ungentlemanly?" he demanded. "Good God, man! This is war! Mascaron is in a privileged position! He can give us the disposition of the French fleet! Advise us where and when Bonaparte means to attack!" Moderating his tone, he went on, "In any event, it's too late to turn back. Everything is set. If you wish to withdraw, however, you may do so

33

with my goodwill."

Lansing's eyes fell before Cam's cool stare. He cleared his throat. "Do you really suppose that I shall not support you in this if your mind is set on it? You should know me better, Cam."

"I know that you are a very loyal fellow to your friends."

"My family owes you a debt that can never be repaid. When I think how you risked your political career to save the skin of that hotheaded brother of mine . . ."

Cam waved Lansing to silence. "That's old history, Simon, and best forgotten." He offered the decanter and, as he topped up both glasses, he asked, "How is Justin these days? You haven't mentioned him in an age."

Lansing grinned. "He's serving with the British army in an outpost called Fort York."

"In Upper Canada?" Lansing nodded, and Cam chuckled. "That should keep the young scapegrace out of hot water."

"I'm counting on it," averred Lansing.

Cam's expression turned grave. "Canada isn't Ireland, Simon. Put your mind at rest. I am persuaded that Justin's brush with those subversive elements is over."

"Yes. He seems to have learned a salutary lesson, thank God!" After an interval, he said carefully, "Cam, about the girl?"

"Gabrielle? What about her?"

"I give you fair warning. We're on our own in this. Pitt would never sanction the girl's abduction, and if Mr. Fox ever got wind of it, he would take great delight in ruining us both."

"Ruin *me*, you mean!" said Cam, grinning. He rose and indicated that it was time to go.

"Yes. I think he cares for you as little as you care for him."

"You worry too much, Simon. Since the girl will be hidden away at Dunraeden, it's not likely that anyone will get wind of it. But even supposing they do, I have a perfectly credible explanation for her presence. Besides, I have the advantage of Mr. Fox. I know how his mind works."

Cam led the way down the great cantilevered staircase. As they reached the front entrance a porter appeared with each man's hat and cane. Neither wore a topcoat, for the temperature was comfortable on that evening in late April.

"Then that gives you the advantage of almost everyone," said Lansing consideringly.

"Beg pardon?"

Cam waved over a hackney that was stationed in the square. Having given the driver directions to Mr. Pitt's rooms in Baker Street, he climbed in behind Lansing.

The coach swayed into motion, jolting its passengers as it rolled over the cobbled streets of Mayfair. In a matter of minutes, Mayfair was left behind as the hackney crossed the Oxford Road and entered the area known as Marylebone.

"You were saying?" asked Cam politely. His mind seemed to be miles away.

Lansing stifled a sigh. He had been on the point of saying that Cam had the advantage of almost everyone by virtue of the fact that no one could fathom the intricate workings of his mind. He thought better of it and offered instead some indifferent commonplace that was accepted at face value, and on the short drive to Baker Street no more contentious subjects were raised.

Five gentlemen were sitting at their ease around the table in Mr. Pitt's very elegantly appointed dining room in his rooms in Baker Street. A fine dinner had been consumed. In normal circumstances, they might have shared a dinner at any one of the gentlemen's clubs in St. James, though to be sure, eyebrows would have been raised and tongues would immediately begin to wag at the unprecedented spectacle of those long-standing political enemies, Charles Fox and William Pitt, breaking bread together at the same table. Closeted behind closed doors, this motley group of Whigs and Tories, men of enviable influence and stature, would have occasioned more than a little tongue-wagging. The suspicions of the whole world would have been roused against them, and rightly so.

It was Mr. William Pitt who had engineered the dinner. Though he had resigned from office only the year before as a protest against his sovereign's position on the Irish question, it was he, behind the scenes and with the same coterie of brilliant young men, two of whom, Cam and Lansing, were present that evening, who still led the Tories and steered England's course. The man who had stepped into his shoes as prime minister was a figurehead, and everyone at that table knew it.

Across the table from Mr. Pitt sat Charles James Fox, the leader of the opposition, in his mid-fifties and the oldest gentleman present. Fox's very good friend and colleague, Richard Sheridan, the playwright, occupied the chair on his right.

Fox adjusted his huge bulk in the less than capacious Sheraton shield-back chair, and calmly surveyed his companions. In an unguarded moment he thought, without conceit, that should some catastrophic event at that very moment blow Mr. Pitt's dining room and its occupants to kingdom come, it would be a sad day for England. He chanced to capture the Duke of Dyson's stare, and instantly he amended his opinion. No. It would be no sad thing for England, thought Fox, if Mr. Pitt's dining room blew up, but *after* he and Sheridan had effected an exit.

To cover the unholy smile that spread across his face, Fox raised his white linen table napkin to his lips. He settled himself to wait, with as much patience as he could contrive, until Mr. Pitt decided to reveal what profit there might be in this informal assembly of Whigs and Tories, who normally sat on opposite sides of the House, opposing each other adamantly and eloquently on almost every political issue.

His eyes brushed those of His Grace, and his mellow mood dissipated somewhat. Camille Colburne had proved to be one of Fox's bitterest enemies. Though never accepting any office from Mr. Pitt, he was there in the background, using his influence and well-articulated philosophy to shape Tory policies to his own designs. He was more than a brilliant orator. Every man at that table could claim that distinction. But Dyson was a thinker. His logic was faultless. His rhetoric in the House of Lords was always persuasive. He was indispensable to Pitt and a thorn in the flesh to Fox. Too many young Whigs, who would not give Pitt the time of day, had broken ranks because of this young man's clever tongue. Perhaps it was to be expected.

The fifth duke of Dyson attracted a wide following among both sexes. Young fribbles were known to copy his modes and manners to a ridiculous degree, and ton hostesses positively fell over themselves to ensure that the duke accepted an invitation to their parties. Not that Dyson cultivated his popularity. Far from it. There was a coolness there to which only a favoured few were not subjected.

Not unnaturally, few women could resist such appeal. But Dyson was no womanizer. If he had any vices, he kept them to himself. The man was an enigma. And Mr. Fox detested enigmas in politics. They were unpredictable, and therefore not to be trusted.

But his dislike of the duke went deeper. For a young

man, the duke lacked passion. He was too sanguine, too much in command of himself. Those Cornishman's blue eyes never betrayed what was going on behind their hooded expression. And Fox had never been so glad as the day when Lansing had persuaded the duke to go off with him to Ireland when their friend, the Viscount Castlereagh, had taken up his appointment as chief secretary. Fox had never cared much for Castlereagh either.

As Mr. Pitt began to speak, Fox's deceptively lazy eyes swept over the Tory leader's thin, ascetic figure. He heard him out without interruption, the straight line of his bushy black eyebrows the only indication that he was not gratified by what he heard.

When Mr. Pitt came to the end of his recital, Fox intoned, dangerously quiet, "You expect Whig support if England declares war on France? I presume, Mr. Pitt, you have some persuasive arguments for that rather forlorn hope?"

Mr. Pitt, a trifle nervously, started over, beginning with the advice that England's interests should supersede every other consideration, even loyalty to party.

Mr. Fox's lips tightened a little at this presumptuous and unwitting impertinence, but he let it pass. Many men had mistaken their man by judging him on his private life. He sipped his port slowly, inwardly seething as he came under a hail of advice from a man whose views he disdained. As if he needed to be told that his party would follow his lead if England were to declare war on France. As if he did not know that should the Treaty of Amiens be broken, the government might easily fall and the country be plunged into anarchy without his support. He scorned Pitt's facile reasoning, but he heard him out in silence, observing with some surprise that the duke had nothing to say for himself.

There was a pause.

Turning to Sheridan, who gave every evidence of

being sunk in his cups, Fox demanded, "Well, Sherry? What should I say to them?"

"Tell them to go to the devil!" said Sheridan without opening his eyes.

"You heard my friend," said Fox, scraping back his chair and rising. "Go to the devil or hold fast to the treaty. Break it, and I shall raise hell in the House."

"Oh, but we don't have to go to the devil," drawled Cam. They were the first words he had spoken in some time. Without haste, he stretched and rested his hands behind his neck.

"I beg your pardon?"

"The devil—he's coming for us."

Cam had Mr. Fox's full attention now. A light seemed to kindle in the older man's eyes. "Ah, now I comprehend," he said. "You're the one Mr. Pitt has been holding in reserve. Is this where you try to bugger me, Dyson?"

Mr. Fox delighted in shocking a reaction from friend and foe alike. His wits were rapier sharp and his tongue scathing, if not coarse to the point of objectionable.

On this occasion, Mr. Pitt flushed scarlet, Lansing was startled into laughter, and Cam's eyebrows rose drolly. Mr. Sheridan was heard to be snoring softly into his cravat.

"You'll be buggered soon enough," replied Cam easily, "if that devil gets on your back."

"What devil?" demanded Fox testily.

"Napoleon Bonaparte, first consul of France. I believe you met with him last year, just after the peace was signed? Paris has always been your favourite city, I've been given to understand. Why don't you sit down, and make yourself comfortable, Mr. Fox? In point of fact, no one here believes that you are open to persuasion. You are known to be a man of unshakable convictions. No, our purpose is this. You have met this . . . what is he? A benefactor to humanity? A dictator? A tyrant? And it goes without saying that you have formed some opinions to help guide us in our future conduct with France. It is we who are open to persuasion, Mr. Fox. Why don't you take your time and convince us that the man poses no threat to England? In other words, does Napoleon Bonaparte mean to rape England or does he not?"

Hours later, as Fox and Sheridan rose from the green baize tables at White's, pocketing the twenty thousand pounds that they had won from the Duke of Portland, Mr. Fox, still smarting from the scene in Mr. Pitt's dining room, complained bitterly to Sheridan that for once the fox had been outfoxed.

"I'm tired of that pun, and all its variations," objected Sheridan.

The two men found a quiet nook in one of the reading rooms and each ordered a bottle of burgundy.

"I feel cheated," said Fox morosely, adjusting his large bulk in a chair that was too delicate for comfort.

"You always feel cheated," pointed out Sheridan reasonably. "Let's face it, Charles, we've been kept out of office because we've made powerful enemies in our time. But, oh, didn't we have a grand time doing it?"

"Yes, but this one is only a cub."

"Who are we talking about?" asked Sheridan blankly.

"Dyson."

"Oh, you're back on that subject again, are you? Well, so he is, but a clever one. You thought he would try to argue you into a corner. And he knew that he could never match you in debate."

Slightly mollified, Fox asked, "D'you think so?"

"Indubitably. But he turned the tables on you good and proper just the same. Well, he understands that Napoleon Bonaparte is the antithesis of everything you've ever fought for."

"Strange that Dyson divined that, don't you think?" asked Fox, a grudging respect won from him. "Few others have done as much. God, Sherry, that jaunt to Paris was quite an eye-opener, I can tell you. They've all but forgotten the principles on which the Revolution was fought and won. The bloodshed . . . it's all been for nothing. Can you credit it, that hysterical megalomaniac, 'first consul' he calls himself now, actually thought that I would support his designs in England?"

"Why not? Everyone else thinks it."

"But Napoleon is an antirepublican. He is a betrayer of every principle on which the Revolution was founded!"

"Yes, which is why we radical Whigs will fight him if we must."

"While those conservative Tories will oppose him because he is a threat to the established order."

"Odd, isn't it? Lansing was right. What was it he said? 'Politics make strange allies?' "

"Something of the sort."

The two men imbibed slowly, each lost in private reflection. Suddenly, Sheridan chuckled.

"What?" asked Fox.

"That Dyson, he's very astute. Did you hear what he said?"

"About what?"

"He called us all liberals at heart, in spite of being in enemy camps."

Fox merely grunted.

"Don't you agree?" asked Sheridan.

"No, I don't agree. Who can say who or what Dyson is? The man is a closed book. Oh, he knows all the right words to mouth, I'll give you that. But I'd wager my last farthing that he's no liberal. I think he hates us with a passion. But he never gives himself away."

A footman in livery entered and the two men fell

silent as he removed old newspapers and empty bottles and glasses. As soon as he had quit the room, Fox and Sheridan picked up their conversation.

"Who is this Mascaron?" asked Sheridan. He was referring to a name that Fox had mentioned in passing during dinner in Mr. Pitt's house.

"He's a staunch supporter of Bonaparte. Didn't you hear me tell Pitt that the first consul has appointed him to the Admirality, or whatever they call it?"

"The Ministry of Marine?"

"Yes."

"What's his background?"

Fox permitted himself a small, derisory smile. "In these uncertain times in France, Sherry, no one inquires too closely into a man's background."

"Mmm. Well, Dyson and Lansing know him, or know of him."

"Do they indeed?" asked Fox interestedly.

"When you mentioned his name, Lansing threw Dyson such a look!"

Fox grinned. "Behind that somnolent pose, you're quite an observer of the human scene, aren't you, old boy?"

"I've found that it pays not to let my subjects know that I am studying them," admitted Sheridan.

"Your devotion to your art is commendable."

"No more than your devotion to duty. Which brings us back to this unpleasant business of Bonaparte. What do you intend to do, Charles?"

Mr. Fox took some few minutes before responding. Finally he said, "He's got to be stopped. There's no doubt in my mind that his ambition is to make himself master of all Europe. And I don't doubt that Dyson is right. Bonaparte is using the peace to build an armada for the invasion of England. Well, my own sources have told me as much. If we don't clip his wings soon, there will be no stopping him."

"Your own sources?" asked Sheridan interestedly.

Fox smiled, and Sheridan's brows rose. "Charles, are you saying that you are still corresponding with Talleyrand?"

"And if I am?"

"He's Bonaparte's man!"

"He's France's man," retorted Fox.

"I see," murmured Sheridan. "At all events, you'll never keep our party in line if England declares war on France. You've been preaching peace for years past."

"Peace with the revolutionaries, not with the likes of a Bonaparte," explained Fox patiently.

"Yes, but will our chaps see it that way?"

"Oh, I think so, Sherry. If we can back France into a corner and make it look as if she is forcing us to declare war on her."

"I don't imagine that the first consul would be so stupid."

"A man's ambitions very often outdistance his good sense. And Bonaparte is a man of overreaching ambition. What do you say we toddle off to Brooks?"

This sudden change in topic evidently confused the man of letters. "What books?" he asked.

"*Brooks,*" corrected Mr. Fox. "The night is young."

"Oh! You mean to game away your winnings? If you don't mind, Charles, I'll make my way to Cavendish Square. I promised Harry I'd look in on her party."

"*Chacun a son goût,*" said Fox softly.

"Yes," agreed Sheridan. "We each have our fatal weaknesses."

It was no secret that his own was the beautiful and erudite Countess of Bessborough, while for his companion it was a predilection to gaming. White's had never been Fox's favorite haunt. At Brooks, just across St. James Street, not only were the politics more to his taste, but also the character of the gambling. Play was deep and turned on the vagaries of chance rather than skill. Fox was a firm believer in luck.

43

"I wonder what Dyson's weakness is?" mused Fox idly.

"You don't much like him, do you?"

"Frankly, no. But then, by and large, I'm not over-fond of this younger generation."

The words brought a smile to the lips of both gentlemen. The younger generation was a topic that never failed to amuse them, in a manner of speaking.

Sheridan raised his glass. The toast had become almost obligatory between these two friends, "To the younger generation," he intoned dryly.

Fox gave the expected rejoinder. "What a drab, unadventurous lot!"

Both gentlemen drank with gusto.

After a moment, Fox observed, "We could teach them a thing or two about how to live, Sherry! God! They're such small-minded, shallow people."

Sheridan drained the last of his burgundy and set his glass on a side table. "You're wrong about Dyson."

Fox's bushy eyebrows shot up. "What makes you say so?"

Sheridan shrugged. "I can't put my finger on it. But there's something about him." He gazed thoughtfully into space. "It's my surmise that he's driven by his own devils."

"Piffle!" retorted Fox. "He's as cold as a fish, that one. It will be a sad day for England if Dyson ever steps into Pitt's shoes."

"You think it's possible?"

"In politics, anything is possible. But . . ."

"Yes?" prompted Sheridan.

"Oh, I was only going to say that hopefully, before that day arrives, the means will be put into my hands to force him out of politics altogether."

"That doesn't seem likely."

"No," agreed Mr. Fox. "I'll see you in the House tomorrow? I still can't believe I've promised my support to Pitt and his cronies. Dyson's clever, all right, and

44

that's about as much as I'm willing to concede to the man."

"Pitt owes you a favor now. Just be sure to get your due from him."

For some reason, the thought of Charles James Fox getting his due from Mr. Pitt tickled the fancy of both men. Moments later, these inseparable friends were seen to leave White's arm in arm and convulsed in laughter.

Chapter Two

The house that Cam rented for his mistress was in Gloucester Place, in the district of Marylebone, and only minutes away from the northern perimeter of the more exclusive Mayfair, where he had his own residence. In the last number of years, with the influx of French *immigrés*, Marylebone had changed character and was now something of a French quarter.

This circumstance could only find favour with Louise Pelletier. A French *immigrée* herself, she had arrived in England when she was a girl of twenty, almost eight years before, with her widowed mother, who had died shortly thereafter. With little more than the clothes on her back, and with no connections in England, the girl's choices had been limited. Within months of arriving in London she was offered two positions of employment. One was as governess to Lord Tuttle's children; the other, which offered far more in the way of remuneration, was as his mistress.

Louise had elected the latter and had never regretted the course she had chosen for herself. Though she'd had several protectors over the years, it was always she who had delivered their *congé*, and never before she had selected her next suitor. Nor were her choices based solely on avarice. Louise had standards. She was gracious, cultured, and a woman of discriminating tastes. In Cam Colburne, the Duke of Dyson, her expectations had been wildly exceeded.

On this night she captured his arm from the moment he crossed over her threshold. Not only was Louise more educated than most women, she was no fool, either. Those deceptively soft brown eyes could flash with sudden fire when confronted with the spectacle of another woman throwing out lures to the duke. And more than one lady present that evening knew what it was to come under the lash of her rapier tongue. Louise Pelletier had claws, when she cared to unsheath them. Cam saw nothing of this. His mistress was at some pains to conceal this unpleasant side of her character. The duke had no patience for jealous women.

The evening passed pleasantly enough. Though the company was not of the first stare, with the exception of those gentlemen of the ton who had the *entrée* to both *beau-* and *demi-mondes,* conversation was lively and, for the most part, of the first consul of France. Cam sifted everything carefully, but not a name was mentioned that was of any interest to him. He was not sorry when the guests finally began to take their leave.

With half-closed eyes, he watched Louise's graceful figure as she ushered the last knot of people through her front doors. Lansing's words came back to him. He wondered if she were playing him false. Though he put no such constraints on himself, in a mistress he expected fidelity. It was a privilege for which he was paying dearly.

He lounged languidly against the wrought iron stair rail as he waited for Louise to come to the end of her *adieux*. Like its mistress, the house oozed elegance, he thought. He looked about him with interest. In the months since he had been out of town, Louise had redone every room. He had given her *carte blanche* to spend as much as she pleased. He'd since seen the bills, and deemed every penny well spent. With its white and gilt French furniture, the house was a perfect setting for the lady.

His thoughts drifted to Dunraeden, his castle in Cornwall. In comparison to the setting Louise had created for herself, his domain was rustic. He admired elegance, but he set more store in preserving his heritage. He knew that given half a chance, Louise would make a clean sweep of Dunraeden's hopelessly old-fashioned furnishings. She had no patience with anything less than perfect. He thought of the water colors, pleasant but by no means exceptional, that his mother had executed and that held pride of place in Dunraeden's dining room. There were other things and bric-à-brac that he held equally estimable for no other reason than they were of some significance to former generations of Colburnes. *Oh no,* he thought. To let Louise loose in Dunraeden would be to invite a transformation that would add nothing to his comfort.

As the doors closed upon her departing guests, Louise swung to face him, pausing momentarily for effect.

And why not? thought Cam, allowing himself a small smile at the practised gesture. She was a beautiful creature, with a striking figure which was displayed to admiration in the new, high waisted, classical mode with its transparent gauzes.

She flung her arms wide and quickly crossed the distance separating them. "Cam," she said, "Oh Cam!" and slipped her arms around his neck, hugging him affectionately. "I have missed you dreadfully," she whispered against his chest.

"Have you so?" he murmured, his long fingers turning her face up for his slow inspection.

Her dark eyes looked steadily into his.

"I believe you have," he said, amusement threading his voice. He understood, then, that Lansing's words had been in the nature of a rebuke. Perhaps Louise *had* been lonely. Lansing, now that he remembered, had a soft heart.

He draped an arm over her shoulders and led the way to the upstairs bedroom.

His appetite was somewhat dulled. Three exhausting days on the road had taken its toll. He had meant to put Louise off, at least for another night. But Lansing's words were having an effect on him. He could not deny that he had neglected her abominably.

Louise was a skillful lover. As she did to everything, she brought her own stamp of finesse and style to their bed. Her knowing, practised caresses soon put his fatigue to flight.

In the last months, in the wilds of Cornwall, his few sexual partners had been lusty tavern wenches. They satisfied his carnal appetite but left something to be desired. Louise's skin was as soft as velvet and smelled faintly of violets. Cam approved of the way she pampered herself. She was everything a man could want in a mistress, both in the salon and in the boudoir — especially the boudoir.

He took her with slow sensuality, building the pleasure between them till she was gasping for release. Smiling, he raised himself over her and thrust smoothly. She climaxed almost immediately, and he gave himself up to his own pleasure.

But Louise was still greedy for him and was not sated until he had made love to her a second time. When he finally pulled from her, she protested softly.

"Cam?"

"Mmm?"

He had rolled to his feet and was already reaching for his discarded clothes.

"Just once, couldn't you stay the night?"

Her dark eyes feasted on the sight of him. Without the least pretense of modesty, her eyes roamed blatantly from the broad muscular chest covered with a profusion of black hair to the tight stomach and hips and the oak-hard, sinewed limbs. He had the physique

49

of an athlete, she thought, Spartan and honed for endurance.

The slow smile that gentled his ruggedly sculpted features did something devastating to her insides. Involuntarily, her breath became suspended in her throat.

"I can't stay," he said in the easy, quiet way he had about him. "Without my valet, I'm as helpless as a babe."

It was a lame excuse, but they both knew she would not press him. A mistress was paid to be accommodating. Once she had hoped that, in time, and given their mutual interests, she would be the woman to demolish that impenetrable wall of solitude. But even in that final act, when their bodies were blended as one, he kept something of himself in reserve. Camille Colburne was a man who safeguarded his privacy.

She knew that her hold on him was tenuous at best. It had occurred to her that if she were to become pregnant with his child there would be a bond between them that could never be broken. But she was not so rash as to go against his express wishes. From the very beginning he had made his sentiments known; had even gone so far as to give her lessons in birth control. As if she needed that! No. She dared not invoke his wrath by disobeying his clear instructions. Cam Colburne would not suffer such a flagrant betrayal without making his displeasure felt.

One day he would marry. Not that he had ever mentioned such a thing to her, but it was the way of their world. A man of his position must beget heirs. His bride would be some eligible, unexceptionable girl. Her one consolation was that, according to Lansing, the breed was not one that held any attraction for the duke. There would always be a place in his life for a woman of her particular talents. And she had no intention of allowing another woman to supplant her.

Forcing a smile to her lips, she asked, "How long

are you to be in town this time?"

"Till the end of the week." He found his buckled shoes and sat on the edge of the bed, slipping them over each silk-stockinged foot. "In point of fact, I wish to say something to you about that."

She came under the hard scrutiny of those brilliant blue eyes. "Oh?" she remarked cautiously.

"I have a ward, a young girl, in France. I intend to bring her out and install her at Dunraeden. She won't like it, so I'm afraid I'm going to have to make her something of a prisoner until she becomes reconciled to her fate. There are servants there, of course, but no female to offer companionship. I don't even know if the child speaks English. I thought perhaps you might consider befriending the girl."

Her jaw sagged. Thunderstruck, she asked, "You want me to go to Dunraeden?" It was a privilege, an honor, she had never thought to be offered. A gentleman, no, an aristocrat, the scion of a great and noble house, did not install his mistress in the centuries-old family seat, the prize of all his possessions. Nor did he introduce the ladies of his family to females from her social milieu. It was unheard of. Unless . . . For a fleeting moment, hope soared in her heart.

As if reading her mind, he chuckled. He touched a finger to her cheek. "No one must know that you are there," he said. "And no one must know that my ward is coming from France." To her questioning look, he replied, "Fortune hunters."

"I'd love to come," she replied quickly.

"Perhaps you should think about it. Dunraeden is very isolated. I'm afraid there can be no outings or entertainments of any description. You may begin to feel like something of a prisoner yourself after a week or two. And I can't remain there for long. But if you could see your way clear to helping me out of my predicament . . ."

"Of course I'll come!" she cut in.

"Louise," he cautioned, "this will be no picnic. My ward will not be there by choice. She may prove to be something of a watering-pot. She could sulk for weeks."

"How old is she?"

"Eighteen, I believe."

"I could handle a girl of eighteen. What is she like?"

"I don't know. I haven't seen her for more than ten years."

There was a pause, and Louise breathed a little more easily. "When do we go?" she asked.

"I'll send word to you." He was shrugging into his blue superfine, the one that fitted him like a glove and showed the breadth of his shoulders.

She had a million questions she wanted to ask, but before she could voice a single one his warm lips brushed her cheek and he was gone.

Once outside, Cam hailed a hackney. He would have preferred to walk the short distance from Gloucester Place to Hanover Square. In spite of the pleasant interlude with Louise he was possessed of a restless energy. But a light drizzle was falling, and he was not dressed for the vagaries of the English climate.

He was chafing at the bit, he decided. Now that everything was in place, he was eager to get underway. He was close, so very close, to fulfilling a sacred promise. God, revenge was sweet! He could almost taste it.

No. Not revenge, he cautioned himself. Justice. Men like Mascaron should not go scot-free while his victims' bones rotted in quicklime in unmarked graves. Danton, Marat, and Robespierre, those authors of the September massacres and the worse terror that had followed, they had paid the price for their sins. They had basked for a time in the spotlight. It was the men of the shadows who slipped through the net.

Mascaron and Maillard had escaped him for years.

One by one, the other "judges" at those mock tribunals had fallen to him. Not that his hand had struck the blow that had felled them. But just the same, it was he who had contrived their downfall with the help of Rodier and his agents. Only Mascaron and Maillard had escaped his long reach.

Maillard had shown more sense than his former master. Rodier had discovered him living in Paris under an assumed name and identity. Even the accession of Napoleon Bonaparte had not the power to reassure him.

How wise he had been, thought Cam, and how powerless to escape his retribution. It had been easily arranged. A word to the surviving relations of one of the victims of Maillard's mock tribunal, and justice was served. Maillard's body had been dragged from the Seine only the month before. His neck was broken.

Mascaron could not be dealt with so easily. Officially, he had been exonerated from any involvement in the prison massacres. And under Bonaparte his rise to power had been meteoric. His downfall would be no less so, Cam promised himself grimly.

And yet, Cam knew that Mascaron had already proved he had more lives than a cat. Time and again, even after he had gone to ground in the spring of '94, when Danton and his followers had gone to the guillotine, the man had slipped through his fingers. Rodier had picked up his trail a dozen or more times, only to lose it again. And the search for Gabrielle de Brienne, whom Cam was sure would lead them eventually to Mascaron, had proved fruitless. After the massacre at the Abbaye the girl seemed to have vanished off the face of the earth.

But shortly afterward, Rodier had been shocked to uncover one interesting fact. The girl was Mascaron's granddaughter. Cam could not find the same shock of discovery in himself. He had surmised something of the sort from the moment he'd looked into the child's emerald green eyes. Mascaron's eyes. At first, Rodier could not be persuaded to Cam's opinion. He had known of Mascaron for a number of years in pre-Revolution France. As lawyers in Paris, they'd moved in the same circles. If Mascaron had any surviving family, no one knew of it.

It took Rodier almost a year to piece together something of the story. Mascaron and his granddaughter, he had learned, were strangers to each other. The girl's mother had been raised by her maternal grandparents in the country. There was no love lost between Mascaron and his wife's family. In time, to all intents and purposes, he virtually abandoned his daughter. By the time she married de Brienne and gave birth to Gabrielle, the break was complete. It was as if they did not exist.

Until the night of the prison massacres, thought Cam. Even for someone as callous and calculating as Antoine Mascaron, it was inconceivable that he would not make the attempt to save his own flesh and blood. If Gabrielle and her mother had suffered the same fate as the other female prisoners, the irony would have been consummate. It was Mascaron and Danton who had permitted the rabble to wreak their vengeance on the defenseless prison population. It seemed probable that Mascaron had learned of Elise de Brienne's incarceration too late to avert the course of events that had already been set in motion.

With Mascaron's sudden reappearance on the scene as a leader in France's new society, another course of events had been set in motion, thought Cam with a fierce surge of elation. Soon, he promised himself, soon, retribution would catch up with him.

Cam paid off the hackney and slammed into the great empty house in Hanover Square, calling for servants to get a blaze going in the grate in his study and fetch a bottle of his best brandy from the cellars.

While he waited for them to do his bidding, he unlocked his desk drawer and withdrew a letter. Having smoothed it open on the flat of the desk, he fetched a candle and proceeded to devour the contents of the tightly scribbled pages as if he had not already memorized every word.

Gabrielle de Brienne, so Rodier had written, had finally been located. And though her whereabouts during the course of Mascaron's years in hiding still remained a mystery that he had yet to solve, there was not the slightest attempt at concealment now. The girl was openly acknowledged by Mascaron to be his granddaughter. For a short time, she had been with him recently in Paris. But for some unspecified reason, she had removed to the seclusion of a château on the Seine. Already, one of Rodier's agents was in place, posing as a gardener.

Château de Vrigonde near Gaillard, read Cam. Gaillard was the great fortress built by Richard I of England to subdue the French. Gaillard, thought Cam, and following the Seine, to Rouen and on to the coast of Normandy. And then—across the Channel to Cornwall. It was all so simple. It could be done. The girl could be abducted very easily.

He poured himself a generous splash of brandy and drained it in two gulps. He thought that he had not been so keyed up since the time he had helped some of Rodier's Girondist friends escape after Marie Antoinette's execution in the winter of '93. The world had been mad then. Forty thousand men, women, and children executed in ten years! And Charles Fox had the gall to preach of the Revolution's principles and ideals! And Lansing berated him for the life of one slip of a girl!

Gabrielle de Brienne, the scarlet angel, he thought. He sprawled inelegantly in the armchair flanking the blazing fire. He replenished his glass, stretched out his long legs, and imbibed slowly, savoring each swallow.

55

He had meant what he had told Simon. The girl would not be hurt by his design. She was merely a pawn in the game. His target was Mascaron. And he had plans for that devil that he had shared with no one but Rodier. Simon was soft-hearted but indispensable to his purposes just the same. To his friends, the man was loyal to a fault.

He must be getting soft himself, thought Cam, and gave a low, self-deprecating chuckle. What had possessed him to invite Louise to Cornwall? That had never been part of the plan. Simon again! In his own inimitable way, Simon could make rents in the fabric of a fellow's conscience.

Well, no harm done. Louise's presence at Dunraeden might be beneficial all round. The girl would be glad of female companionship, and he certainly wouldn't cavil at having Louise's sleek, perfumed body accessible when he had need of a woman. It would make a pleasant change from the country, Cornish girls who smelled distressingly of the pilchards that were the staple of their diet.

His thoughts turned to the girl. What kind of woman had she grown into? How much did she remember of the Abbaye? How had she been shaped by France's bloody history? Mascaron had missed going to the guillotine by the skin of his teeth. So had the girl.

She would be terrified once she realized she was being abducted. Regrettable, but unavoidable. He must impress upon her that she would be safe so long as she followed his orders. In a few months, her ordeal would be over. Surely it could not be longer? From all reports, Bonaparte was already amassing his flotilla for the invasion of England. Once Mascaron had given them the information they desperately needed, the girl would be returned to France. And then his hands would be free and he could deal with Mascaron as he deserved.

His thoughts lost focus, drifted, and pictures of his family in happier times flitted across his mind. Perhaps it was the result of ingesting too much brandy too quickly, but a lump rose in his throat, constricting his breathing.

In the next moment, he felt as if he had been transported back in time to the Abbaye. He could almost feel the heat of the bonfires, hear the screams of the victims, and worst of all, taste the anguish of the nineteen-year-old boy he had been then, helpless to save his family. He could go mad with remembering, he thought, and tried to suppress his unhappy reflections. They would not budge. He drained the brandy in his glass and poured himself another.

Gabrielle de Brienne, as he had first seen her, the angel of the Abbaye, filled his mind. His first instinct had been to worship her. Oh God, how wrong he had been! And how many times since he had damned her to hell for what she had done. One day, he thought, one day . . .

God, it was absurd! He could not possibly be holding *that* against the girl — a child of only seven years? But the brandy had released some demon in him that refused to be silenced.

The girl was not necessary to bring Mascaron to justice. Why involve her at all? Wearily, he passed a hand over his eyes. In vain he tried to marshal his defences to suppress the next disquieting thoughts.

He wanted her at his mercy, had secretly dreamed of holding her as his captive; was determined that she should suffer in some small part for what she had unleashed that night. At the very least he wanted to damn her to her face. And wasn't there an implied insult in putting her into the care of his mistress? Oh God, he was deranged to torture himself with such ludicrous fantasies!

Abruptly bolting to his feet, he flung his empty glass from his hand. It shattered against the marble

57

fireplace. Moments later a lackey came sprinting into the room.

"Your G-Grace?" the man stammered, coming to a sudden halt.

"Order the coach round," said Cam. He was already striding from the room. "We go to Richmond."

"Richmond, Your Grace?" It was four in the morning and Richmond was a good eight miles away. And even in these modern times, highwaymen were not unknown.

"I'll act as coachman. I'll take four grooms with me. They can act as outriders. Tell them to hitch my fastest team. Oh, and to be on the safe side, they had better arm themselves well."

"But, Your Grace?"

"Yes, man, what is it?"

They had moved out of his study, and Cam had one foot on the bottom step of the white marble staircase.

"What address shall I give Thomas?"

"No address. I simply mean to drive these blasted cobwebs from my mind."

But Cam was not to be so fortunate. The fantasies were too deep-seated to be so easily banished. They remained with him long after he had drifted into what he had hoped would be the oblivion of sleep.

Chapter Three

"*Sacre nom de Dieu!* You worry too much Rollo! Everyone at the château is occupied one way or another. We'll never be missed. And what Mascaron doesn't know can't hurt him. Now let's get this boat on the river before we miss the rendezvous."

The speaker, who appeared to be a slight youth of fifteen years or so, angled his shoulder against the prow of a small, flat-bottomed river craft and exerted every ounce of strength to help his companion ease the heavily laden vessel into the river.

Rollo was the first to heave himself on board. His next action was reflex. He grabbed for the seat of his companion's breeches and effortlessly lifted him over the rail.

Gabrielle de Brienne immediately made her displeasure known. Cursing softly under her breath, she slapped the offending hand away. "I can manage," she hissed. "By the holy virgin, I swear I don't now what's come over you."

Rollo laughed and grabbed for the oars in the center of the boat. Gabrielle climbed over wooden casks filled with Calvados and oilskins protecting their precious cargo of lace from nearby Tosny. She settled herself at the tiller.

They had made this trip scores of times before, but only in the last month had Rollo begun to treat her with the deference due a female. It infuriated her. For ten years they had been raised as brothers. There wasn't a thing Rollo could do that she could not do as well, if not better. Goliath, their tutor and Rollo's grandfather, had taught them everything they knew. She was sure that she could out-ride, out-shoot, out-fence, and out-*wit* any man alive. *Diable,* she could even out-spit her childhood companion. As if to prove her point, Gabrielle jerked her head, and spat into the dark, muddy waters of the Seine.

"That's not ladylike!" objected Rollo.

Though all that Gabrielle could see in the darkness was his shadowy outline, she could hear the frown in his voice.

"Ladylike!" she scoffed. "What do you know about ladies?"

Rollo's soft laughter seemed to roll across the slow-moving river to be caught and rolled back to them by the jagged escarpments on either side. "Not as little as you, it would seem," he answered. "Haven't you learned anything at all from Madame l'Anglaise? Good God, Gaby, she's been with you a whole month now."

Rollo, a young man of eighteen who looked to be in a fair way to inheriting his grandfather's powerful build, was referring to Mrs. Blackmore, an English widow who had been hired by Mascaron and given the thankless and near impossible task, in Rollo's opinion, of turning Gaby into a lady.

Gaby snorted indelicately, and Rollo gave himself up to the rhythm of the oars as they delved and skimmed through the smooth waters of the Seine.

Everything was changing, thought Gabrielle, a sudden tightness constricting her throat. Before Madame Blackmore had come on the scene, Rollo had treated her as an equal. But ever since she had been forced to don skirts and petticoats and those hideous stays and drawers, a new reserve had crept into their relationship. A month ago Rollo would have been grumbling that she was trying to shirk her share of the work. Now, he would not let her get near the oars. If this went on much longer she was sure that her muscles would turn soft and atrophy altogether. Even her hands were becoming soft. Worse! Horror of horrors, when she examined herself in the long cheval glass in her chamber before she donned her night rail, she would swear that a curse had been laid on her. Soft. She was getting soft everywhere. And it made no difference how many hours she practised with Goliath in the gallery improving her swordplay, or how many hours she spent in the saddle, or how often and how long she swam naked in the Seine. The softness seemed to be spreading like an insidious disease.

Everything was changing, and she was helpless to turn back the tide. Mascaron, she could never get used to calling him *grandpère,* had changed all the rules on her. For years she had been forced to forget that he was her grandfather; for years she had donned the disguise of a boy—and all to throw their pursuers off the scent. In those days, Mascaron had applauded her skill with foil and pistol. He'd been proud of her prowess and ability to take care of herself. But that had been during the uncertain days of the Revolution, when they had been hunted from pillar to post. A new era had dawned, and suddenly all the arts she had been at some pains to master just to please him had fallen out of favor. Oh, she had his permission to keep up her proficiency in the manly arts, for who could say what the morrow might bring to France? But things were so very different now. In short, Antoine Mascaron had decided that the time was ripe for his granddaughter to become a lady, whilst Gabrielle wanted things to remain as before.

Imbecile, she muttered softly under her breath. Things could not go on as before. She was a woman. Nothing could change that unpalatable fact. But a

61

lady was something else. A lady's skin stank of perfume. Ladies took small, mincing steps. And no wonder! thought Gabrielle. It was a miracle they could move at all, given the restrictions of female clothing. But ladies were not meant to move, she had discovered. They were like painted china dolls, the playthings of men. She scorned their narrow ambition. Men was all they ever thought about. But she'd rubbed shoulders with enough men to know that women played a very insignificant part in their lives. Men did the really important things. They went off to war or became smugglers. Men had adventures. Ladies stayed home and wept buckets of tears.

But she had tried, really tried, to be what Mascaron had wanted her to become. More than anything, she had wanted him to be proud of her. It was a forlorn hope. She had spent two months with him in Paris and she had been miserable. Not only had she felt like a fish out of water, but the women to whom she'd been introduced had looked down upon her as if she were some sort of freak. She had no small talk, no grace, no accomplishments she could name in polite society. Ladies had shunned her. And after that embarrassing incident at the Tuileries where Laporte had overstepped what was acceptable and she had laid him out flat on his back, (in front of the first consul, no less) with the practiced wrestler's moves she had learned from Goliath, she had become a laughingstock. Mascaron had relented and had sent her home to the Château de Vrigonde, but in the keeping of Madame Blackmore. For the last month Gabrielle's freedom had been somewhat curtailed, but never more so than in the last few days, when Mascaron himself had descended upon them.

The peace talks in Paris were not going well. The English, it seemed, refused to relinquish Malta. It was Lord Whitmore who had suggested to Mascaron that more might be accomplished if the negotiators assembled in a less formal setting. The parties concerned scarcely knew each other. Distrust and dissent were rife. A respite from the incessant haggling could only be beneficial. Not unnaturally, Mascaron had taken the hint and offered the Château de Vrigonde, placing it at the disposal of the English ambassador. Lord Whitmore had accepted the offer with alacrity. The château was ideally situated, only a day's drive from Paris, and in the most scenic section of the Seine. What could be more delightful?

Gabrielle grunted and tightened her hold on the tiller. Since his arrival, Mascaron had been in his element.

"Recognition!" he had told her jubilantly, "And of the sort that can only turn the tide of our family's fortunes. Respectability, Gaby. From now on, that's our motto."

But Gabrielle could not reconcile herself to this unhappy turn of events. Respectability was one thing, but recognition was something she shunned. She had no conception of how to go on in society. And to expect her to act as hostess to a set of men who were *au fait* with the manners and modes that prevailed in the highest social and diplomatic circles was the most absurd thing she had ever heard. Few things disturbed the cool nerve of Gabrielle de Brienne, but the thought of the role she was expected to play when Mascaron's guests arrived on the morrow was one of the most terrifying tests of courage she had ever faced in her life.

In comparison, thought Gabrielle, that night's enterprise was child's play. But she rather suspected that her smuggling days were over. Fate had not been kind to Gabrielle de Brienne. Necessity had forced her to adopt the disguise of a boy. It was ludicrous to suppose that she could suddenly transform herself into a well-bred lady. Nor had she any desire to follow that course, or so she tried to convince herself. She was supremely happy to be exactly as she was. *Which was a damn lie,* some inner voice immediately responded. But Gabrielle mercilessly squelched that voice.

"We're here!", said Rollo, and rested his oars.

Gabrielle moved the tiller to the right and the craft swung to port. In a moment, Rollo had jumped into the shallows and was dragging the boat ashore. Shapes detached themselves from the gloom and came to meet them. Gabrielle pulled the brim of her cap down to her eyebrows. With her collar turned up, she felt reasonably safe from detection. Moreover, to the *contrebandiers* she was known as William Hanriot, Rollo's younger brother. As far as they knew, Gabrielle de Brienne was as cloistered as a nun behind the stout, stone turrets of the Château de Vrigonde.

In the shadow of the great medieval fortress of Gaillard, their cargo was soon unloaded and their business concluded. Gabrielle and Rollo did not themselves deal directly with the English smugglers, Cornishmen all, who waited off Normandy's coast in their fast sailing ships. From as far as Paris, contraband was passed down the line until it reached Rouen. From there, the river Seine changed character. Only the most experienced and intrepid rivermen would chance their boats and their lives to the unpredictable bore that was created where the incoming tide and the Seine met and battled each other for supremacy of the estuary. Over the years many boats had foundered and many more men had found a watery grave. But no one thought to give up the lucrative trade. Even war made little impression on *les contrebandiers*. It was a way of life they had followed for centuries. Not the Revolution, not Bonaparte, not the devil himself, and certainly not the English excise men in their fast clippers could put a stop to it. Gabrielle and Rollo were a very small link in the chain. For them, it was an adventure, nothing more. For those whose livelihood depended upon it, it was a serious and dangerous business.

With money to burn in their pockets, they turned their footsteps towards the centre of the little town of Andely. Near the cathedral they came upon the tavern, Les Trois Freres, a known smugglers' den, a half-timbered wattle building that was typical of the area. They pushed inside and found a place for themselves at a table in one corner of the public room. The place was crowded. Most of the patrons were coarse-clad, rough-spoken men of the river. A few were clerks or shopkeepers or others of that class. The odd traveler, a cut above the regulars, was also there. And the ladies were not precisely ladies.

Gabrielle soaked up the atmosphere. The haze from the clay pipes, which most of the *habitués* were smoking, curled in a lazy arc, rising to hang like a cloud beneath the low, oak-beamed ceiling. At a table by one of the windows, a noisy game of cards was in progress. Someone was playing an accordion.

They ordered Calvados and sipped their drinks in companionable silence. Rollo hunted in his pocket and withdrew a pouch of tobacco and a clay pipe. Gabrielle stretched out her long legs and watched his careful movements as he lit the pipe from the flame of a candle that was positioned in the center of the table.

Without conscious thought she rubbed the back of her neck. A few minutes later she found herself repeating the gesture. She half turned in her chair to look over her shoulder.

One of the men whom she had taken for a stray traveler, a tall swarthy fellow with surprisingly light blue eyes, seemed to be studying her with more than a little interest. Gabrielle felt her skin prickle. She did not care for the look in his eyes. It was the kind of look a man usually reserved for a pretty woman. But unhappily, she had discovered, some men—and always the handsome ones, like the stranger who was eating her with his eyes—had a penchant for pretty, smooth-faced boys.

She blazed him such a look, then presented her back. Her hand came to rest on her scabbard. The feel of her weapon was vastly comforting. By degrees, her fingers stopped trembling.

It wasn't the first time she had been the recipient of such stares. In Paris, when she had been robed in the revealing fashions of the day, she had surprised that famished look on many a gentleman's face. It made her more afraid than if they had come at her with cold steel. But she'd learned that to betray her uneasiness was regarded as a provocation. She'd been pounced on and kissed and fondled more times than she cared to remember. In her boy's breeches and boots she had thought herself immune from that perverse masculine foible.

She allowed her eyes to travel over the throng of people, and casually steered them in the stranger's direction. Damn if his eyes weren't still trained on her! Her vague uneasiness flamed into fear.

She poked Rollo in the ribs and stretched out her hand, indicating that she wished to share his pipe. His eyebrows shot up, but he obediently handed it over. Gabrielle stuck it between her teeth and inhaled and exhaled expertly, like any of the rough river men. It had taken her hours to master the stinking ritual. Though Gabrielle loved the smell of tobacco, she hated smoking with a passion. But at that moment she rather desperately wanted to give anyone who chanced to be looking her way the impression that she was, in very truth, a man's man.

A tavern wench carrying a tray of tankards passed close by. As she deposited the tray on a nearby table, Gabrielle returned the pipe to her companion, spat deliberately on the sawdust-covered floor, and stretched out one hand to pinch the serving girl's ample backside. Rollo gave a startled bark of laughter. The girl wheeled, ready to do battle. When she saw who had pinched her she let out a squeal of delight and fell into Gabrielle's lap. Gabrielle's cheeks flamed scarlet.

Berthe, the serving girl, had had her eye on the smooth-faced young river man for some time past. Gabrielle was well aware of it and had done her best to avoid the girl's snares, not least because the girl already had a brute of a man who considered himself her protector. This, decided Gabrielle, was going from the fat into the fire. Nor could she dislodge the wriggling girl from her lap. Berthe was a good three stones heavier than the smaller girl. Though she had not meant to look near the stranger again, Gabrielle could not help darting a quick glance in his direction.

"What are you smiling at, Cam?"

The question came from Lord Lansing who was toying absently with the handle of a pewter tankard.

"The young stripling over there," answered Cam with a chuckle. "He's trying so hard to act the man. I'll wager he doesn't know what to do with the wench in his lap."

"You may say so," said Lansing, "but I doubt that the fellow over there shares your opinion."

Cam's eyes narrowed on a bull of a man who had slowly risen to his feet. By degrees, the room went silent. Heads turned to see what was afoot. Cam slowly uncoiled his long length and straightened in his chair.

"Easy, Cam," cautioned Lansing softly. "This fight has nothing to do with us. Remember why we are here."

Cam did not need reminding. From Le Havre on the coast of Normandy, upstream to Rouen and beyond, to Andely, they had looked over the lie of the land. Rodier was stationed in Rouen and already setting things in motion for their escape. They were due to arrive at the Château de Vrigonde that very night, ostensibly as aides to Lord Whitmore. It had taken no mean feat to pull off the invitation to the wily lion's lair.

In a few hours they would reach Mascaron's little fortress, the Château de Vrigonde, and very soon they would put their plan into operation. Even the ambassador had not been taken into their confidence. To his knowledge, Cam and Lansing were exactly as they appeared—Mr. Pitt's emissaries. And if he wondered why Cam had suggested that they hold the talks at Mascaron's château on the Seine, he had kept his ruminations to himself. For him, it was enough to know that the Duke of Dyson had Pitt's confidence.

Everything, thought Cam, must seem exactly as it appeared on the surface. Not a breath of the girl's abduction must travel beyond the walls of the château. As Lansing had said, Pitt would never sanction such an act, and if it reached the ears of the first consul, Mascaron would become useless for their purposes.

In less than a fortnight, Britain was to recall all her diplomats before declaring war on France. Cam had never been so close to fulfilling a long-standing ambition. Gabrielle de Brienne would be the bait to put Mascaron into his power. He had no intention of jeopardizing their careful preparations. Nevertheless, in spite of his thirst for revenge, and against all logic, he knew that there was no way on God's earth that he would abandon the young river urchin to the fate he had inadvertently invited. There was something about the boy that stirred an emotion in Cam he could not put a name to. He shrugged off his idle reflections. It was enough to know that he would not allow the urchin to come to harm.

The man nicknamed "le Taureau" took a few, unsteady steps toward the whelp who wriggled suggestively beneath the woman on his lap. From the corner of her eye, the tavern wench caught sight of him. With a strangled cry of fright, she jumped to her feet and cowered behind the boy's chair. The boy looked about him to see what had caused the girl's sudden defection. When his eyes fell on le Taureau he gave a start and the color drained from his face. Without haste, he rose to his feet. Cam did likewise.

With a roar of rage, le Taureau rushed upon his quarry. The boy sidestepped, quickly threw out one booted foot and sent the big man sprawling. He fell against a chair, overturning it.

"Get the hell out of here," shouted the boy's companion, and immediately fell upon le Taureau.

A roar went up. The boy hesitated, but his companion turned on him. Whatever he said next seemed to bring the boy to a decision. He took to his heels.

Men were on their feet in every part of the room, shouting encouragement to the two protagonists who were wrestling on the floor. Someone said something to which his neighbour took exception. Glasses and tankards went flying. Before long the contest had degenerated into a free-for-all brawl.

Cam caught a glimpse of the boy's back as he pushed through one of the exits. He did not think about what he was doing. He went after him.

Gabrielle was fast, but not nearly fast enough to evade Cam. Knowing that she could not outrun her pursuer, she darted into the livery stable and quickly fastened the door. His first kick smashed the stout wooden bar. Gabrielle unsheathed her rapier. On the second kick, he burst through the doors.

With foil extended, she backed away from him. "I don't want to hurt you," she said. "I just want you to leave me alone."

The only sounds were her own rapid breathing, and the soft whinnies of the horses, which had become restive when the man had kicked in the door. More pervasive than the familiar smells of horseflesh and liniment was the masculine cologne that assailed her nostrils. She decided that she liked the man's smell as little as she liked him.

"I don't want to hurt you," she repeated, and raised the point of her rapier threateningly as he advanced upon her.

She read the amusement in his eyes. He was not taking her seriously, and that frightened her more. She made several slashing, intimidating sweeps with her foil, and crouched in position, foil extended, the other arm curved behind her for balance.

"There's no need for this," he said softly, reassuringly. "I only want to talk to you."

She lunged, and Cam danced out of reach, at the same instant unsheathing his own weapon. He could not help laughing.

"I know how to use this," she warned him.

"So I see," he said conversationally. "What's your name?"

"I'm not that kind of boy," said Gabrielle in a wail of outrage. "Touch me and I'll slice your hand off."

"What?" Her answer astonished him.

"I saw the way you were looking at me."

"Good God! Is that what you think? I assure you, you are mistaken." Cam's jaw had hardened into granite.

Almost by instinct, they were circling each other, but their foils had yet to connect.

"I'm not a fool," said Gabrielle. "I know *that* look when I see it. And I'm warning you, I want nothing to do with you."

The words infuriated Cam. Suddenly, he lashed out with pounding force. Gabrielle was ready for him. She parried his lunge, but she felt the power of his sword arm all the way to her shoulder.

Though she might be his equal in skill, she knew that she could never hope to equal him in endurance and strength. It was not a new experience for Gabrielle and it did not trouble her overmuch. Rollo had long since outstripped her in that sphere. But he had yet to beat her in a match.

She lunged and lunged again in a double feint, disengaging her weapon smoothly and swiftly, dancing away before her powerful adversary could disarm her by sheer brute strength. At this point she wished merely to test his skill, gauge his speed and reactions. She came at him again. He parried each thrust with disconcerting ease.

She drew back and took silent stock of her enemy. He was lean and hard-muscled, and when he moved she could see those muscles bunch and ripple along his powerful thighs and shoulders. But it was that air of confidence that he so unconsciously projected which alarmed her more. This man was used to carrying off the victory. It showed in every arrogant line of his body.

"There's no need for this," he repeated softly. "And if you're not careful, you'll hurt yourself."

Gabrielle said nothing, but her lips tightened at the implied insult. He was the cat, or so he thought, and she was the mouse. She was determined to wipe that smirk from his face.

By sheer force of will, concentrating on all of Goliath's precepts, she lunged at him, making a series of calculated passes, inviting ripostes that would open his guard to her attack. She saw her chance and threw the full press of her weight into the thrust, aiming for his shoulder.

He sidestepped her neatly. She could not regain her balance fast enough to bounce away from his parry. In a flurry of circular motion he engaged her foil, wrenching it from her grasp with such ferocity that she thought her wrist would break. Her weapon went flying harmlessly to the earthen floor.

She was gasping for air, as if she had just run a mile. Her opponent showed no such distress from their encounter. He studied her blandly, calmly, but something dangerous glittered in the depths of those blue eyes.

Gabrielle took a quick step backwards and came hard against the stone wall. Putting her hands out in an imploring gesture, she said, "Please *monsieur,* let me go. I'm not the kind of boy you think I am."

He took a step closer, crowding her against the wall. Her eyes widened in alarm.

Gently, soothingly, he said, "Don't be afraid of me. I have no wish to hurt you. I just want to know who you are."

Her heart was pounding in her throat. "Please, *monsieur,*" she pleaded.

"You're no river urchin. Where did a boy like you learn to fence like that?"

He was standing too close to her, blotting out everything but the arrogant set of his shoulders and his dark head. She felt as if the walls were closing in on her and involuntarily, she inched away from him.

"Don't be afraid," he said again, and reached out with one hand to prop himself against the wall, preventing her from putting any distance between them. Gabrielle sucked in her breath in fear.

He smiled reassuringly. "Why won't you tell me your name?"

She warily assessed him. She thought that she had never seen eyes so startlingly blue, nor lashes so thick and curly, except on a female. But there was nothing feminine about the square jaw. It flawed what otherwise might have been a classically handsome face. His dark hair, rather long on the collar, was tousled, as if he had combed it with his fingers. Or perhaps he'd been on the river and the wind had played with it. It gave him a boyish appearance. But Gabrielle did not make the mistake of thinking he was anything like Rollo or any of the boys she was used to.

This man was too old for her to know how to manage, too experienced, too tall, too powerful, too much in command of the situation, and too ruthless to be trusted. She could see it in the set of his lips. He had a mouth that suggested singlemindedness of purpose as well as sensuality. She trembled violently. This man would never let her go till she had given him what he wanted.

"William," she said quickly. "My name is William Hanriot."

"That's a good Norman name," he said, smiling. "Now that wasn't so bad, was it? I like you William. There was something about you that appealed to me from the moment I set eyes on you."

Gabrielle swallowed convulsively. Her panic was starkly evident in her eyes.

Chuckling, he said, "I am not a lover of boys, William. We English are not so liberal as you are in France. No, really, you have nothing to fear on that score."

"Then what do you want with me?" she asked, pressing her hands flat against the wall behind her to stop their trembling. That he was English surprised her. From the looks of him, she would have taken him for a dark skinned Corsair, even supposing his French conveyed the polish of Paris.

He seemed to be considering her question. She jumped when he laughed. "Damned if I know!" he said. "No, that's not entirely true. In spite of your slight build, you have the heart of a lion. And yet there's something vulnerable about you. Well, look how your friend jumped in to fight your battle for you. Do you have this strange effect on many gentlemen?" Abruptly, brusquely, as if not liking the drift of his thoughts, the smile left his face and his voice took on a different color. "I could use a boy like you in my employ," he said. "You weren't afraid of that bull of a man in there, and see how you defended yourself against me."

"But you beat me," she pointed out. "And easily."

He smiled to hear the disappointment in the boy's voice. "If you come and work for me, I'll show you where you went wrong. You have the makings of a fine fencer."

73

"It's impossible," she answered quickly.

"Why? What is there to keep you here? You're how old? Fourteen? Fifteen? This isn't much of a life for a boy like you. You'll be better off with me."

"No!"

He did not know why it should matter to him. The fate of one boy was not so very important when one considered recent events in France. But there had been something about the boy that had stirred him as few things had in more years than he could remember. *Bravado,* he thought. He had recognized it the moment the boy had pushed into the tavern. It was there in the tilt of his head, the exaggerated swagger, and the slender shoulders that squared as if in readiness to take on the world. It was rather . . . he discarded the word *amusing* and substituted *touching.*

And yet, if it had been only that, he would never have come after him when he'd hared out of the tavern. He had no wish to frighten the boy. But how was he to explain something so nebulous he could scarcely explain it to himself? He had sensed that the finger of tragedy had touched the boy's life. He'd read it in those huge, expressive eyes, eyes that had dared the world—and him—to do its worst. The boy had not learned yet how to guard his expression. That would come in time.

The boy was something like himself, thought Cam—a younger Cam who had adopted a similar pose to protect himself from the buffets of an indifferent, capricious fate. He did not wish the boy to become hard and unfeeling. His innocence, for want of a better word, was worth saving.

Brave, innocent, vulnerable, thought Cam, who was again touched with the whisper of something that left him oddly disturbed. He was no lover of boys, but there was something about this particular boy that evoked feelings he was at a loss to explain.

His voice was almost harsh when he next addressed

the boy. "I'll take care of you, look out for you. You'll like Cornwall, I think. And I'll speak to your parents, if that's what is troubling you."

"No. I don't want to go with you."

Gabrielle sensed an imperceptible tensing of his jaw, and the rhythm of her heart picked up speed, beating wildly against her ribs. When this man made up his mind, nothing could shake him. She nervously moistened her dry lips with the tip of her tongue.

Cam's gaze narrowed on that unconscious, feminine gesture. His brows slashed together. His eyes lifted and caught and held hers in their inexorable depths. Something she could not name pulsed between them. Gabrielle was too terrified to draw breath.

Before she could stop him, he had whisked the cap from her head. A torrent of blond hair fell about her shoulders. He sucked in his breath. When his fingers threaded through her hair, drawing her head up, Gabrielle moaned in anguished terror.

"I should have known! Oh God, I should have known!", he murmured, his warm breath breaching her parted lips. He laughed, a sound distinctly self-mocking. "You little vixen! Is it any wonder that you had me so confused? You're a *girl*, for God's sake!" To Gabrielle's ears, it sounded as if he were relieved at the discovery. "A female! I must have recognized that fact without really knowing it." He shook his head, as if to clear the cobwebs from his mind. Gradually, the laughter left his eyes. Gabrielle felt as if he was looking right into her soul.

A voice from the courtyard shattered the moment.

"Cam? Cam? Where the devil are you?"

"In here, Simon!"

Gabrielle was released as the man called Cam moved to the open doors. Over his shoulder, he instructed, "Don't you dare move a muscle."

Feeling suddenly cold she crossed her arms over her rough woolen jacket. Her eyes went longingly to her discarded foil, but she made no move to retrieve it. What would be the point? To offer resistance was useless. And now there were two of them.

She decided that she liked the look of the man who filled the doorway. His hair was the color of ripe wheat and fell across his forehead, giving him a decidedly roguish aspect. She thought that he was a man who smiled often. He was smiling now, and dimples slashed deeply into his cheeks. Gabrielle breathed a little more easily, feeling inexplicably safer with the presence of the new arrival.

"The strangest thing, Cam. You know that lad . . ." Lansing's voice died altogether as his eyes swept over the boy from the tavern.

Gabrielle self-consciously threw her long hair back over her shoulders.

His eyes still on hers, Lansing continued, "There's a giant of a man out here who is looking for him. Only, it turns out, he's not a boy after all."

From behind Lansing came a roar that might have come from a wounded lion. "Angel!"

The "giant of a man" came looming out of the shadows. He thrust past Lansing and made for Gabrielle. In a flash, Cam had blocked his path.

"Goliath! Oh, Goliath," cried Gabrielle, and dodging past Cam, she flung herself into the giant's outstretched arms.

In a voice that Lansing scarcely recognized, Cam said, addressing the stranger, "If you don't take your hands off her, you can consider yourself a dead man."

Lansing was shocked into action. His hand closed about his friend's arm as Cam brought up his foil. "Cam, are you mad? This is the gentleman we have been waiting for. He is attached to Mascaron's household and is here to conduct us to the château. And as for the girl, don't you know, can't you tell who she is?"

The tension in that small space crackled like a summer storm. In spite of Lansing's warning, it looked as if Cam would go for the bigger man. Nor was the giant intimidated by the fire shooting from the younger man's eyes. He was coiled to repulse any move that might deprive him of the girl.

By slow degrees, Cam's challenging posture relaxed. His eyes shifted to Gabrielle. Some buried memory moved within him, but refused to surface.

"Who are you?" he asked at length.

She was afraid to give him her name and could not say why. Her lips trembled, her eyelashes lowered to veil her confusion. She moved closer to the shelter of Goliath's comforting form.

It was Lansing who answered his friend's question. "Cam, her name is Gabrielle de Brienne."

Gabrielle's eyelashes fluttered open. The sudden blaze from those flashing blue eyes reached out to scorch her. She flinched away in fear. Nor was that fear relieved when the blaze was slowly tempered by a rigid control. She had not seen such unfettered dislike since the dark days of the Revolution.

Something awful seemed to have been unleashed in the air. She shivered as Goliath picked her up in his arms. Neither Englishman tried to stop him as he strode through the doors.

That night, the old dreams came back to torment her.

Chapter Four

The scent of apple blossoms was carried on the air and seemed to permeate every corner of every room in the Château de Vrigonde. Cam was reflecting that, in future, whenever he thought of Normandy, the memory of this fresh and pleasant fragrance must fill his nostrils.

His eyes wandered from the open window and traveled the interior of the *grande salle*. For the moment, he ignored the occupants, the several gentlemen who were idling into the spacious chamber in twos and threes for the first session of the talks. His mind was calculating that Antoine Mascaron was a gentleman of considerable means. If he was not mistaken, many of Versaille's former treasures—paintings, tapestries, crystal chandeliers, tables and commodes in elaborate gilt designs and inlaid with porcelain and ivory—all had found a home in this opulent room.

But the treasure that Antoine Mascaron prized above all others was not in the *salle*. Nor was the room a fitting setting for the girl. It was too elegant, too refined. Gabrielle de Brienne, as Cam had last seen her, belonged in the stables. He'd had a few unquiet moments wondering if perhaps Rodier had been right all along, that Mascaron would not jeopardize his position to save the girl. Her appearance at Andely had suggested that she was no better than one of the servants. But that fear was soon laid to rest.

Within minutes of meeting his host the night before, Cam had made a casual reference to the girl. Those cat's eyes of Mascaron had darkened to jade. The polite host's smile had softened into something more genuine. And though the words that followed were restrained, the voice in which they were uttered held a betraying undertone. To hear Mascaron speak, one would have thought the girl as unexceptionable as a Bath miss.

And as the gentlemen had lingered over their wine, safely closeted in this same *grande salle,* the giant had smuggled the girl into the back of the house. *Bath miss, my foot!* thought Cam. She was a hoyden! A veritable hellion! But if her grandfather did not know it, he wasn't about to reveal what he knew. The last thing he wanted was for the girl to be kept under lock and key, as she deserved. Let Mascaron give her all the freedom in the world. It would make his task that much easier.

The taste of victory had been almost tangible on Cam's tongue, when Mascaron had introduced a jarring note. "We've met before, I think," he had said, studying his guest candidly.

"It's possible," said Cam, "though I don't remember."

He had made up his mind that if Mascaron were to ask him, point blank, if he had been present at the Abbaye all those years ago, he would admit to it at once. Nothing could be served by denying it. But someone else claimed Mascaron's attention, and the awkwardness was smoothed over.

What he had expected of the man he held to be one of the perpetrators of the prison massacres, Cam could not say with any assurance. Certainly not this urbane man of letters, whose charm was hard to resist. Not that Cam was seduced by it. He knew Mascaron for what he was. But he had expected something different, something more sinister, some evidence in the man's look or bearing or address of the monster that lurked beneath the surface. There was nothing.

On the contrary, Mascaron seemed to be untouched by the Abbaye and its aftermath. Cam knew that Mascaron's life had not been an easy one. He had made sure of it. But apart from a shock of silver hair, Mascaron had weathered his trials well. He must be nearing sixty, thought Cam. He might easily be taken for a man a good ten years younger. There was not an ounce of spare fat on his trim frame. And the intelligent green eyes that looked out at the world, though of a less brilliant hue than formerly, invited confidence. In some sort, Cam found this polish, this perfection, more than a little repugnant. It was obscene. And his revulsion for Mascaron only intensified.

From the corner of his eye, Cam caught a movement. Talleyrand, the leader of the French delegation, approached. He was surveying the *grande salle* with obvious admiration.

"Exquisite, n'est-ce-pas?" murmured Talleyrand. "Our host's taste is faultless."

"You've known Mascaron long?" asked Cam, more for politeness sake than any desire to hear the answer. Talleyrand and Mascaron, as he well knew, went back a long way, to the beginning of the Revolution.

"Mascaron and I knew each other once, a long time ago," answered Talleyrand. "But our paths diverged. Happily, we are now traveling the same highway. Have you seen the Titian?" Talleyrand limped off and beckoned for Cam to follow.

Cam paced himself to match the steps of France's minister of foreign affairs. He dutifully admired the girl in Titian's portrait. It was no hardship. The painting was magnificent.

"She is the daughter of Louis XV," explained Talleyrand.

"Then it does come from the Palace of Versailles?" Cam's question was more in the nature of a statement.

"Most certainly," said Talleyrand. "It was unfortunate that during the Revolution, Versaille's treasures were sold off. The hatred of anything with the taint of royalty was anathema to us in those days. Versailles took the brunt of our anger, I'm sorry to say."

"And the royals, themselves," said Cam dryly.

Talleyrand looked more closely at the younger man. His full lips turned up slightly. "You might say, Your Grace, that Louis XIV built Versailles, Louis XV enjoyed it, and poor Louis XVI paid for it. It is a lesson from history we would do well to remember."

"France's history," corrected Cam. His perusal of the portrait was unwavering.

"And you are of the opinion that the same thing could never happen in England?"

Cool blue eyes shifted to Talleyrand. "It's highly improbable," said Cam.

Frowning, Talleyrand observed, "You are persuaded, no doubt, that the English character is more stable than the French?"

"What I think," said Cam, "is that, in England, we are not so idealistic. You would be disappointed in us, Monsieur Talleyrand. We're rather a dull, uninteresting lot."

Talleyrand chuckled. It was evident that he had taken Cam's words as a compliment, as his next words proved. "You do your countrymen an injustice, Your Grace. I am acquainted with one Englishman, at least, who is no stranger to idealism. I refer to Mr. Charles Fox."

"How very true," murmured Cam ironically.

He had lost interest in the conversation, for his host, Antoine Mascaron, had at that moment entered the room with another gentleman, whom Cam recognized as Joseph Fouché.

"Well, well," said Cam in a soft undertone to Talleyrand. "This is a surprise. What is Fouché doing here?"

As everyone knew, Joseph Fouché had formerly held

the post of Minister of Police. Bonaparte had dismissed him the year before, a most popular move. Fouché was feared by almost everyone. His spies were everywhere and his methods were anything but above board.

Talleyrand's smiling expression betrayed little. "He's a useful man to know," he said. "And the first consul is beginning to realize just how useful Fouché may be in these uncertain times. We're all here. Gentlemen, shall we begin?"

Cam was to contribute very little to that first session of talks, which were ably led by Talleyrand and Lord Whitmore. His mind was occupied with sifting through only those matters that would aid or hinder him in his abduction of the girl. He wondered how easy it would be to win her confidence. He wondered if he wanted to. But most of all, his thoughts dwelled on Mascaron, and on how very soon retribution would catch up with him.

There was a time when Antoine Mascaron was accused of being a traitor to his class and blood. It was not always so. He had been born into a Norman family, that had some pretensions to gentility. At one time, the Mascarons had held a place on the periphery of the French court. But fate had not smiled on the Mascaron family. And as is often the case with the minor nobility who have slipped into genteel poverty, respectability had become a substitute for power.

By the time Mascaron reached his majority he had become disillusioned with the status quo. It was evident to him that his ambition could not be served by waiting for some great man to favor a petition on behalf of services rendered by his forebears. For a young man of his intelligence and drive there were few openings. Mascaron assessed them carefully. On reflection, he decided to enter the profession of law.

As he approached his mid-twenties, he gave into family pressure to find a suitable bride. He married the daughter of a neighboring family, a quiet girl of gentle birth whose beauty did not hold him for long. There were other women, but none of them of any significance. He had no time for emotional entanglements. He was too busy carving out a career for himself.

In due course, a daughter, Elise, was born. He became a widower. Elise was sent to live with her maternal grandparents. The older generation of Mascarons died out. These events made little impression on him. Antoine Mascaron concentrated all his energies on rising to the top of his profession.

The years slipped by. The occasional visits to his daughter ceased altogether. She married Conte Robert de Brienne, a minor nobleman and professional soldier who served in the French cavalry. Brienne, a Royalist, had no use for Mascaron or his politics. It was he who voiced the thought that Mascaron was a traitor to his blood and class. By the time children were born to Elise de Brienne — of whom only the youngest, a girl, survived — the break between Mascaron and the Briennes was final. Mascaron did not care.

The Revolution took France by storm in the summer of '89. Only the royal family and the French aristocracy were taken by surprise. Mascaron, and men like him, had long foreseen and prepared themselves for such a turn of events. The idealists among them threw themselves wholeheartedly into the power struggle. Idealism had never been the driving force in Mascaron's life. His ambition was totally self-centered. For as long as it was possible, he kept a foot in both camps, judiciously joining the revolutionary clubs that called for the overthrow of the aristocracy and at the same time, but only when it cost him nothing, using his influence to subvert the wrath of the revolutionaries from grateful aristocrats who might one day be restored to power.

Mascaron did not covet fame. Power was his goal. He was content to keep to the background. And as one clique followed another, without a ripple of conscience, he successively attached himself to whichever political party seemed most likely to advance his ambitions. He prospered.

The autumn of '92 found Mascaron a follower of Georges Jacques Danton. On his master's business, Mascaron journeyed to Toulon. On his return, Paris was buzzing with the news of Brienne's capture and execution at Claremont, and the incarceration of his wife and daughter at the Abbaye. That Mascaron was related to Elise de Brienne and her child was known to only a very few. It could not be otherwise. He deemed it prudent not to reveal the relationship when he procured a *carnet* for their release into his custody.

Mascaron, however, had no knowledge of any movement to exterminate the prison population. When the massacres began he was caught by surprise. He arrived at the Abbaye at the height of the carnage, at a time when the mob was in no mood to accept any rule but its own. Mascaron refused to be intimidated, for though he felt as yet no affection for the child who would one day fill his whole life, he discovered that it was not in his nature to countenance a threat to his own flesh and blood. He acted instinctively to protect his own.

In fear of reprisal, for the name of Brienne was still hated throughout Paris, Mascaron sent Gabrielle and her mother to live in a small farm in the suburbs with the Hanriots, men-at-arms to the Briennes for generations. Elise died soon after. She had never recovered from the shock of seeing her husband murdered before her eyes.

The following years were catastrophic for Mascaron. His fellow Dantonists were rounded up and tried in the spring of '94 and summarily executed. He had long since made overtures to the opposition. Robespierre would have welcomed the addition of Mascaron to his coterie of supporters. It was not to be. Three days after the execution of Danton, a broadsheet was circulated throughout Paris, blazoning Mascaron's career, including his aristocratic beginnings. The most damning piece of evidence against him was his involvement with les Septembriseurs, a name coined for all those who had participated in the prison massacres of '92.

This barbaric act, which had once found favor in the eyes of the general populace, was now roundly condemned by all and sundry. The broadsheet credited Mascaron, maliciously, as being the instigator of the massacres, and Maillard as the executioner.

Warned by Fouché, who owed him several favors, that his arrest was imminent and that his peers were in no mood to listen to his defense, Mascaron prepared to go into hiding.

There was no shortage of funds. Over the years, he had used his position to amass a considerable fortune. His first inclination was to make for England with Gabrielle.

Again, it was Fouché who warned him from the attempt. His agents had disclosed that there would be no refuge for Mascaron with either England or her allies. It was evident that somewhere in his career, Mascaron had made a fatal blunder. Perplexing as it was, it seemed that he had incurred the hatred of some powerful enemy who would be satisfied with nothing less than his blood.

For himself, Mascaron might have been tempted to brazen out the storm and take his chances on the floor of the Convention. But there was more to consider than his own skin. When it occurred to him that Gabrielle might become the means to effect his chastisement, he discarded the thought of defending himself before his peers. Only one course was left to them.

With assumed names and identities, they went into hiding.

Before long they were betrayed and forced to become fugitives. Over the years there were many close calls, so many that Mascaron now knew himself to be the victim of a personal vendetta. Fouché, to whom he had passed information that came his way on his travels, had never been able to uncover even a hint of who might be behind the relentless quest for revenge.

But all that was behind them. Bonaparte was indifferent to the old hatreds. Betrayal, in such circumstances, was no longer a threat. Eight years later, his star once more waxing strong, Mascaron ascended the great staircase of the Château de Vrigonde. He had everything he had ever desired—wealth, position, power. He was reflecting on the irony that, though it was gratifying to have achieved almost every ambition of his youth, those ambitions now paled into insignificance when compared to his fierce devotion to one slip of a girl.

Gabrielle. She was in her bedchamber, as nervous as a kitten, dressing for her first dinner party with the most exalted guests who had ever graced the *salles* of the château. One of the maids was putting the finishing touches to her toilette.

"There's no hurry," said Mascaron, waving his hand vaguely. "Our guests are assembling in the *grand-salle* for a pre-dinner Calvados. I'll wait for you in your sitting room."

He closed the door softly and stood for a moment looking about Gabrielle's private sanctuary. Smiling, he shook his head, and selected a comfortable upholstered armchair flanking the empty grate.

This room, though a trifle shabby, was exactly to Gabrielle's taste. Style, elegance, the treasures of Versailles—for these things his granddaughter could not have cared less. But here was her grandmother's high oak dresser, chairs with needlepoint cushions that had once been worked by her mother, and on the walls, miniatures of family members who were long gone and most of whom she had never met. Very little remained of what once had belonged to their family. And what there was, for the most part, had come to her from her paternal grandmother, Marie de Vrigonde.

With the advent of the Revolution, everything had been lost. It was he, Mascaron, who in later years had purchased the château when its current owner had run afoul of the law. His own preference would have been to settle in Paris, in the fashionable St. Germain quarter. But Gabrielle pined for Normandy. Norman blood ran in her veins. And any small thing, any relic that recalled the former era of security and happiness she had enjoyed as a child, was to be cherished.

His thoughts were interrupted as the door opened. On a rustle of skirts, Gabrielle entered. At the sight of her, pride, pleasure, and tenderness swept through Mascaron in quick succession. He studied her slender form as she crossed the distance between them. Her strides were long and awkward, like those of a young leggy colt. She had yet to learn to shorten her steps to accommodate the unfamiliar sweep of feminine skirts and petticoats. He could not help smiling.

A frown clouded her brow. "Well, Antoine? This is the frock you wanted me to wear tonight. Will I do?" Brilliant green eyes ringed with gold lashes gazed steadfastly at him as she waited anxiously for his answer.

The gown was of sheer white gauze, embroidered at the bodice in an intricate pattern worked in gold satin-stitch. The low, square neckline revealed the swell of her young breasts. Her mane of hair was tamed in several braids and pinned to the crown of her head. Her skin, in keeping with her blondness, should have been as pale as alabaster. It was glowing with health, and gold like ripe corn. The minx, thought Mascaron, had been up to her old tricks, sunbathing in the nude.

He rose to his feet and captured her wrists, throwing her arms wide. "You look like a princess," he assured her, and had the pleasure of seeing the gloomy look banished by a radiant smile. "Gabrielle," he said, turning suddenly serious, "I've decided that you are to come to Paris with me."

"I'm not ready for Paris," she protested. "You promised I could stay here until I'd accustomed myself to girl's clothes . . . and . . . and so on," she added with a helpless shrug of her shoulders. "Mrs. Blackmore has been here for only a month. I need more time. Please, Antoine?"

"Mrs. Blackmore is worse than useless. It was a mistake to think that she could manage you. I'm giving her notice."

The truth of the matter was that Mrs. Blackmore had no interest in any female but herself. He had met her in Paris, in one of Madame Récamier's famed salons, and had been instantly taken with her conversation and sense of style. It was what he wanted for Gabrielle. Unfortunately, though the impecunious young widow had accepted his offer of employment with alacrity, she had neither the inclination nor the aptitude to transmit her knowledge of clothes, manners, and conversation to Gabrielle. He was irritated with the woman. He had not been back a day but he had perceived already that Gabrielle heedlessly pursued her own course despite her presence.

Gabrielle shifted uncomfortably under Mascaron's keen scrutiny. "My English is improving," she offered feebly. "In another month or so . . ."

"No!"

For a moment she wondered if the Englishman had betrayed the fact that he had found her at Andely. She discarded that thought almost immediately. When she had descended the stairs that morning she was not sure what she might expect. But it was very evident

from her grandfather's smiles as he proudly introduced her to the gentlemen who made up the delegations that the Englishman had said nothing. If he had
done so, Mascaron's reception would have been far
different. Goliath's silence, she had known she could
count on. He was her man, not Mascaron's. But the
Englishman's silence had surprised her.

She bit her lip. "Antoine," she began imploringly.

"Is it too much to ask that you address me as *grandpère?*" he asked whimsically.

"Forgive me," said Gabrielle. "But sometimes I forget that there's no longer any necessity to pretend."

They were both remembering the straits that for
years had forced them to conceal their relationship.
Mascaron had been tormented by the fear that the unknown enemy who hounded him would not cavil at
wreaking his vengeance on Gabrielle, should he ever
discover her existence. It was for this reason that Gabrielle had assumed the identity of a boy. And given
the conditions of the rough and uncertain life they
were forced to lead, reflected Mascaron, her disguise
had simplified matters.

"I wonder if I did the right thing," he said, and
touched a hand to her cheek. "You have been cheated
of so much. I promise to make it up to you, Gaby."

She knew at once to what he referred. "Rollo thinks
it was all a grand adventure," she said, trying to
lighten his mood.

Mascaron laughed. "And you?" he asked.

"We survived, didn't we? Isn't that what matters?"

"Perhaps."

"Perhaps?" she repeated, her brows lifting.

"What I mean, Gaby, is that perhaps I should have
done things differently."

"What, for instance?"

He folded his arms across his chest and regarded
her with a half-serious, half-challenging expression.
"For a start," he said, "if I had known how difficult it

was going to be to part you from boy's breeches and bad language, I'm no longer certain that I would have permitted you to assume the identity of a boy."

"Oh?" said Gabrielle, pouting. "And I suppose I would have dashed on horseback all over France in petticoats and panniers?"

"There's something in that," agreed Mascaron, amused at the entirely feminine set to Gabrielle's lips.

She lowered her lashes. When she looked at him again the green of her eyes had gone cloudy. "I won't disgrace you," she said quietly. "If I learned to act and think like a boy, surely it can't be so difficult to learn how to act like a girl?"

"You *are* a girl, and a very beautiful one, too. All you lack is a little polish. A few months in Paris and you'll be the lady you were born to be."

Gabrielle was silent.

"Gaby, don't you *want* to be a lady?"

She framed her lips to say the word *non*, then thought better of it. She took a few paces around the room. "They all make fun of me," she said, peeking at him over her shoulder.

"Who makes fun of you?"

She was thinking of the Englishman. "Everyone!" She shrugged. "Let them laugh. I don't care."

Mascaron went to her then and put an arm around her shoulders. "You'll have the last laugh," he told her. "Mark my words, one of these days you'll bowl them off their feet."

Once again Gabrielle thought of the Englishman. A gleeful, mischievous smile transformed her face.

"Paris," he said softly, implacably. "In a few months you'll wonder why you made such a fuss. If you won't think of yourself, think of me. I'm an old man now, Gabrielle. I'm selfish. I want you with me for as long as possible in the time that remains to me."

Her eyes widened as the implication of what he was saying finally dawned. She had lost her father and mother in very short order. Rollo, she was about to lose to the military academy in Paris. Mascaron had always seemed to her to be the buttress that held them together. Without Mascaron, her world would fall apart, and she could not bear it.

With a small cry of protest, she threw herself into his arms, hugging him tightly. "Don't say such things!" she said into his shoulder. "Don't say such things! You're not old. Never! D'you hear? Never!" Her eyes swept up. By degrees, suspicion kindled in their turbulent depths. *"Sainte Vierge!"* she swore softly. "You're just saying this to get your own way."

Behind the jibe, he heard the anxiety. "You don't think sixty is old?" he asked, feigning incredulity.

She tried for a saucy smile. "You're still the handsomest man I know."

"Ah! That's the problem, Gabrielle. You don't know many gentlemen, or young people of your own age. I mean to rectify that omission. It's Paris for you, my girl, and I won't stand for any argument."

Her eyes assessed him slowly, carefully.

He read the unasked question. In a familiar, comforting gesture, he patted her shoulder. "I'll live to be a hundred," he told her.

There was so much more he wanted to say, but decided against it for the moment. "In a few weeks," he said, "you will leave the Château de Vrigonde to begin a new life. Agreed?"

She searched his face. There was no relenting in the steady look he gave her. Resigned, she nodded her assent.

He held her at arm's length. "It won't be so bad," he promised. "And the longer you hide yourself here, the more difficult it will become for you to take your place in society. It was a mistake to let you come back."

Silently, she allowed him to lead her down the great staircase, toward the salon where their guests were congregating. On the threshold she halted, her eyes

91

traveling over the several people who were standing about, imbibing a pre-dinner Calvados, the local drink for which Normandy was justly famous.

Her eyes brushed those of the Duke of Dyson and slid carefully away to touch briefly on his companions. Already Gabrielle could feel her tongue cleave to the roof of her mouth. Her hands began to sweat. She had nothing in common with these polished sophisticates. Mascaron's hand on her elbow had a steadying effect. She tilted her head, and took a step into the room.

Chapter Five

One day slipped into the next. As far as possible, Gabrielle kept her distance from her grandfather's guests. During the daylight hours, this was very easily accomplished. For the most part, the gentlemen kept to the *grande salle*, where the talks were in progress, while Gabrielle's time was equally divided between Mrs. Blackmore and Rollo.

In the mornings, her companion compelled her to work on her embroidery or practice walking with a pile of books on her head or apply herself to the scores of useless things deemed necessary accomplishments for a lady of fashion. In the afternoons, she and Rollo, to all intents and purposes, had the place to themselves. They whiled away the hours in their favorite occupations. They took long rides around the estate. When they were sure that they were unobserved, and well out of earshot of Mascaron's guests, they set up a target and practiced with pistols. Occasionally they went fishing. Gabrielle's one regret was that the fencing gallery was forbidden to her until the gentlemen were safely away.

The evenings were not so pleasant. It was then that she was obliged to dress up and act as Mascaron's hostess. The task unnerved her. She felt intimidated in the presence of Talleyrand and Fouché, men whose names had terrified her at the height of the Revolution. And then there was the Englishman.

The duke did not like her. She did not know why this should be so. They did not know each other. But she knew that in this she was not mistaken. And since the Englishman did not like her, she could not be comfortable with him. Adding to her difficulties was the fact that, as a courtesy to their guests, conversation tended to be conducted almost exclusively in English.

In the normal course of events, this was no hardship for Gabrielle. She had a fair fluency in that language. Mascaron had seen to it. He had never given up hope, during those dark days when they were fugitives, that there would come a time when they would find sanctuary in England. For that eventuality, which was no longer of any interest, he had been devout in tutoring his granddaughter. Gabrielle had learned quickly. But her fluency completely deserted her whenever the Englishman came into her line of vision. She would become flustered and would stutter her way into silence. To compensate for this humiliating failure, Gabrielle took to hanging on her companion's skirts. Mrs. Blackmore was never at a loss for something to say, and by sticking very close to the lady, Gabrielle was saved the trouble of saying more than two words.

"Mrs. Blackmore does enough talking for the two of us," she said, when Rollo commented upon Gabrielle's odd silences.

A gust of wind whipped at the folds of Gabrielle's habit, flattening it against her lean, boyish figure. Lost in thought, she gazed out over the edge of the escarpment, beyond the waters of the Seine, to the great ruined fortress of Gaillard.

Rollo was sprawled on a large rock, chewing idly on a blade of dried grass. Their mounts were tethered in a copse well back from the edge of the cliff.

"God, I'll say!" said Rollo with feeling. "No one can get a word in edgewise once she gets started. If she ever again mentions that place she comes from . . ."

"Bath," supplied Gabrielle helpfully.

"If she ever again mentions Bath and its infinite superiority to anything and everything French, I shall positively throttle the woman. Oh well, she'll be returning to Bath soon enough."

"Yes, when I join Mascaron in Paris." Gabrielle was saddened by the thought that she and Rollo had come to a crossroads and were fated to take different paths. He was bound for the military academy, and she was destined to take her place in France's new society.

"Sooner," said Rollo.

"Oh?"

"The peace talks have all but broken down, something to do with Malta. It's only a matter of time before our countries are at war again. Mrs. Blackmore won't wish to be caught behind enemy lines."

That the talks had broken down came as no surprise to Gabrielle. From the very first, Mascaron's hopes that the two delegations would reach an amicable settlement had been very slight.

"When do you leave?" asked Gabrielle, turning at last from her lookout.

"I expect we shall be leaving tomorrow, or the day after."

"So soon?"

"As I understand, Mascaron wants to be present when Talleyrand and Fouché make a report to the first consul. He'll send for you as soon as may be."

Gabrielle crossed to the rock and settled herself beside Rollo, leaning back on her elbows. She half-closed her eyes against the afternoon glare. High overhead a hawk, wings spread, soared in a lazy arc as if oblivious of the wood pigeons below, which foolishly ignored the presence of their natural enemy. Suddenly the hawk swooped. The pigeons scattered, but not before one of their number was caught in the ruthless talons.

Gabrielle sat bolt upright. Her nerves were on edge, *which was to be expected,* she thought. The old nightmares had come back to haunt her, and especially the one that had so terrified her as a child. She was dreaming of *him* again. He was on their trail, that faceless and hateful presence that had been the blight of their lives. His name had always remained a mystery. But there had never been any doubt about his purpose. He wanted their blood.

She was aware that for years Mascaron had puzzled over the enigma of this man's identity. He'd made many enemies, but no one he could think of who would be so tenacious in his hatred. They could never be safe in one place for long. Again and again they were betrayed to the authorities. Again and again they had escaped by the skin of their teeth. It was only when Bonaparte had come to power that the old quarrels no longer counted for anything. Gradually the nightmare had faded from Gabrielle's dreams. Until now.

Gabrielle sighed, and Rollo reached out to cover her hands in a comforting clasp. Feeling too close to tears for comfort, Gabrielle shook off Rollo's hand and sprang to her feet. "Military academy!" she scoffed. "You think that will give you the advantage? You'll never be half the man I am, Rollo Hanriot!"

"Oh won't I?" he said, rising to her bait and joining in the familiar mock battle. He towered over her. "I've said it once, and I'll say it again. You'll never outgrow being a puny female, Gabrielle de Brienne!"

They were both grinning, remembering a time when they were children and Gabrielle had knocked a chip from one of Rollo's front teeth for issuing the very same insult.

"Last one back to the château is a pig's bladder?" she challenged.

"You're on! No, wait! Mascaron won't like it!"

"Won't he?" asked Gabrielle. The glint in her eyes betrayed that they had gone too far now to turn back. Her long, athletic strides soon carried her to their tethered mounts.

Rollo laughed. "No. And he won't like it either if he sees that you're not riding sidesaddle."

"I can handle Mascaron," said Gabrielle with more bravado than conviction.

She swung herself into the saddle male fashion, and her booted feet unerringly found the stirrups. Her skirts were hiked halfway up her thighs.

Rollo followed suit. "You'll . . ."

But he wasn't given the chance to complete his sentence. With a taunting smile over her shoulder, Gabrielle dug in her heels and her horse shot forward. Rollo gave chase.

Cam caught sight of the riders as they came thundering over a rise towards the château. He was alone in the east turret, taking advantage of Mascaron's invitation to view the landscape from the best vantage point the château had to offer. At the spectacle of Gabrielle, hunched low in the saddle, her blond hair streaming behind her like a river of gold, his mouth tightened. Her laughter, clear and natural, rose on the air and lingered like a woman's fragrance. As she neared the stable a figure appeared at the entrance and began to walk toward her: Mascaron. Gabrielle reined in her mount and the gallop slowed to a decorous trot. She threw the reins to a boy who came running and lightly sprang down. A few strides took her to Mascaron's side. She catapulted herself into his arms.

As he turned from the window, Cam's lip curled. God, everything about the girl irritated him. She had

97

the looks of an angel and the manners of a ragamuffin. He tried to push the disturbing thoughts of their few encounters from his mind. Gabrielle's laughter reached him again through the open window, and his thoughts refused to obey his directions.

On the few occasions when he had absented himself from the talks, in his wanderings over the grounds, he'd occasionally come upon the girl. The boy, Rollo, was never far from her side. They were like two children at play, heedless of propriety and deportment. And their conversation, when they supposed themselves private, was liberally laced with the coarsest, most vulgar expressions.

Not that that signified. Cam's only interest was in discovering the lie of the land and whether or not the girl was ever left unprotected. He had his answer.

In some things, the girl was not very wise. She kept secrets from the very people who were set to guard her. He had discovered things about Gabrielle de Brienne that would make her abduction that much easier.

On two occasions, from his bedroom window, he had observed the girl stealing away from the house in the hour before dinner. The third time it had happened he had been lying in wait. Following at a safe distance, he had trailed her to a cove carved out of the rocky cliff where the stream that cut across Mascaron's property emptied into the Seine. The sun was low in the sky, though it was some hours before the light would fade altogether.

He knew at once what her purpose was. But he never thought to remove himself. He could not tear his eyes away.

Her movements were as unself-conscious as those of a child as she unhurriedly removed each layer of clothing to reveal her lithe, virginal form. With her curtain of gold hair streaming over her shoulders, she stood

98

motionless for a fleeting moment, like some pale, ivory statue, before slicing smoothly into the water. She could not know how her innocent, untouched beauty affected him, with what powerful, confused emotions he watched her cavort playfully in the water before she settled into a steady rhythmic stroke.

He had come away appalled at the way his senses had quickened at the mere sight of her nudity. He'd decided then that he'd been celibate too long. It was a woman he needed. Any woman would do. Any woman with the exception of Gabrielle de Brienne. She was a mere child.

The girl, Cam told himself, was the antithesis of everything he admired in a woman. In the *salon* she was gauche and without conversation. She smelled of horses. Her hands were calloused. She had no interest in cultivating the womanly virtues. And that was the best he could say about her. Released from the constrictions of her role as Mascaron's hostess, the girl became a hoyden.

He surmised that few things frightened Gabrielle de Brienne. She was afraid of him. Even in a crowd of people, he could sense her discomfort, see it in the way her eyes slid away from his whenever their glances touched. Perversely, her fear annoyed him, but at the same time he felt a base but powerful surge of satisfaction. He would not hesitate to use that fear to compel her obedience when the time came.

He said as much to Lansing when he found him alone in Mascaron's library.

"I think you're making a mistake," said Lansing. "In the first place, honey catches more flies than vinegar."

"And in the second place?" asked Cam dryly.

"Mmm? Oh, if Gabrielle is afraid of anything it's in the commonplaces we take for granted—you know what I mean—idle chitchat, drawing room conversation, flirting. She's out of her depth there and she knows it, poor girl."

"Flirting?" quizzed Cam, his brows raised. "With *that* spitfire?"

Lansing laughed, and darted a self-conscious look at his companion. "You've captured the attention of the only other female present, Cam. So what's a poor fellow to do?"

"It seems to me that Mrs. Blackmore is more taken with Talleyrand," pointed out Cam.

"You're hoaxing me," protested Lansing, making a grimace of distaste. "Besides, with the departure of the French delegation on the morrow, you will have a clear field, at least for another day."

"If things were different I might be tempted," agreed Cam amicably. "But there's no sense complicating matters with the girl's companion. The ambassador has inveigled an extra day at the château. I, for one, intend to make the most of it."

To the ears of an outsider, Cam's words would have sounded innocuous. To Lansing, they were heavy with meaning. Cam meant to check out the house and grounds one last time before the plan for the girl's abduction was set in motion.

By tacit consent, the two friends wandered through the French doors leading to the stone terrace. Cam produced two slim cheroots and offered one to Lansing. For some few minutes they smoked in silence, then idled their way further from the house. In the shade of a spreading chestnut tree they halted.

It was Lansing who finally broke the silence that had fallen between them. "What have you learned of Fouché?" he asked on a more serious vein.

That Fouché was to be a member of the French delegation for the duration of the talks had come as an unwelcome surprise to the English. To Cam and Lansing, his presence had seemed sinister. As a precaution, Cam had sent to Rodier in Rouen for any intelligence he could gather on the matter.

"The report is reassuring," answered Cam. "It's the merest bad luck that Fouché showed up at such an awkward time for us."

"What does that mean, precisely?"

"It means that the first consul's confidence in Talleyrand is not profound, to say the least. According to our sources, Fouché's presence is simply a precaution by Bonaparte to ensure that Talleyrand does not stray from the straight and narrow."

"In other words, Bonaparte does not trust his minister of foreign affairs?" asked Lansing, thunderstruck.

"No, and for the simple reason that Talleyrand really is set on this sham of a peace. He's the only one who doesn't seem to understand that we are just going through the motions for appearances' sake."

"And you think that's it?"

Cam shrugged, and drew on his cheroot. "I'm of the opinion that that's all there is to it. You've seen how Fouché dogs poor Talleyrand's heels. It is almost comical."

"I'm not laughing," said Lansing, "and for a very good reason. Have you considered that Fouché can put names and faces to us now?"

"I don't see that that's relevant," answered Cam.

"In the long run, it might be, if Fouché ever begins to suspect that Gabrielle has been abducted. He might put two and two together. He's clever, Cam. Don't underrate him."

"Yes, I can see that Mascaron's usefulness would come to an end in such circumstances. But trust me, Simon. Fouché will never get wind of what we're up to."

After a considering moment, Lansing said grudgingly, "I hope you know what you are doing."

Cam slowly exhaled a ring of smoke. "You like the girl, don't you?" he asked.

Lansing immediately responded, "As a matter of a fact, I do. She's a little unusual, I grant you . . ."

"Unusual!" Cam snorted. "Outrageous, more like. She runs wild with smugglers, and in breeches, for God's sake. Gabrielle de Brienne is positively *mauvais ton.*"

"Scarcely that!" retorted Lansing, surprise etching his voice. "Mascaron and her father were both well born, and I'm sure that Mascaron has no conception of what she gets up to."

"In different circumstances, it would have given me great pleasure to inform him of what transpired at Andely. Though I've no doubt the girl would get off scot-free. She has the man wrapped around her little finger."

"Yes, I've observed as much. But she is, after all, his granddaughter. It's to be expected."

Cam made a noncommittal sound and propped one shoulder against the trunk of the tree. He was the picture of indolence, a man with nothing more on his mind than enjoying a quiet smoke in convivial company.

Lansing squinted speculatively at his friend. "She's not exactly what we expected, is she?"

"Hardly!" said Cam. "She fences like a seasoned duelist, rides like the wind, and shoots like a musketeer. It's a lion-tamer who should be waiting for us at Dunraeden. Poor Louise."

Lansing's sudden rumble of laughter disturbed a flock of geese that had been happily foraging on the nearby lawns. They hissed their displeasure and gave him a wide berth.

When the sporadic laughter was under control, Lansing said, "Which is exactly my point, Cam. Gabrielle won't give in without a fight. You can count on it. You may think she's afraid of you, and perhaps she is. But Gabrielle won't let that deter her."

"Indeed," drawled Cam, studying his friend through half-closed lids, "You seem remarkably well-informed about the girl. Where did you come by your information, Simon, if you don't mind my asking?"

Lansing's gaze roamed over the expanse of groomed lawns, and beyond, to the stands of tall beech trees which marked the banks of the small stream which fed into the Seine. "It's only a feeling," he offered. "Just the odd word that some lackey or other has let slip." Smiling, he turned to face Cam. "When you were closeted with the ambassador, I fraternized with the natives. Her watchdog—what's his name, Goliath?—he's inordinately proud of the girl."

"The faithful watchdog," murmured Cam. "Where does he fit into the picture, I wonder?"

"I can tell you. He's not really Mascaron's man. He's an Hanriot, and there have been Hanriots serving the Briennes since feudal times, as near as I can make it. His loyalty is not to Mascaron but to the girl. His position is almost impossible to define with any assurance. On the one hand, he's a sort of manager of the estate. On the other hand, he takes a very proprietary interest in the girl. He stands in the role of a guardian, I should say. He's like family, and yet . . ." Lansing shook his head as he groped to put his thoughts in order. "He never mixes with Mascaron's guests, though he has the run of the place. With Rollo, it's quite different. To all intents and purposes, he *is* a member of the family. He and Gabrielle are like brother and sister."

"Interesting," said Cam. "Is Goliath an employee?"

"I can't say. But if he is, his employer is Gabrielle, not Mascaron."

"Ah," said Cam. "I had wondered at the man's conduct after finding her at Andely in such circumstances."

"You should be grateful to him," observed Lansing.

103

"Had he betrayed her to Mascaron her liberty might be curtailed and our plan made more difficult to execute. As it is, she's singularly well guarded, even supposing she has the run of the place."

"I've taken that into account."

"It's all set then?"

"Let's walk a ways, and I'll fill you in on the how and the when."

Cam was still thinking of Gabrielle when he took the last turn in the stairs that led to his chamber. The landing was lit by a small window, but with the sun beginning to set and the candles yet to be lit, they came face to face in semidarkness.

She jerked away from him. *"Pardon, monsieur,"* she said, her voice low and strangely breathless.

She made to move past him, but he blocked her progress by the simple expedient of resting one hand on the banister and the other flat against the opposite wall.

She drew back and assessed him cautiously, *"Monsieur?"*

In true Revolutionary form, she never addressed him by his title—another small annoyance. Slowly, deliberately, he levered himself onto the next step. She did not disappoint him. She stood her ground, though he could almost hear the rapid pounding of her heart.

"We were interrupted." He spoke in English. "In Andely."

Through the shield of her lashes she studied him carefully. The smile he angled her was surprisingly gentle. Even his cold eyes seemed to reflect its warmth. By degrees the tension left her.

She smiled at him shyly. "Andely," she repeated. And she wondered if it were possible to persuade the Englishman to reveal how he had contrived to disarm her so easily. His swordplay was something to be envied. In anticipation of learning his secrets, her lips parted.

"Does Simon flirt with you?" Cam asked, his eyes slowly roaming over her face. He caught glints of green through the thick sweep of her lashes.

She shook her head, then shrugged her shoulders. "Flirt? I don't know that word."

"It's the same word in both French and English. *Flirter,*" he added by way of explanation.

Not a spark of comprehension registered in her eyes.

"Shall I show you?" he asked softly.

A faint line appeared on her brow. "What is *flirt?*" she asked, her eyes meeting his directly and without guile.

His hand slid onto her nape. "*Doucement,*" he said when she flinched. Her skin was warm and as smooth as satin. "Easy. It's quite painless. *Il n'y a pas de la douleur.*"

At the first touch of his mouth, she froze. He could feel her breath fluttering at the back of her throat. Her hands came up to his shoulders and tightened. His lips skimmed over hers in an unthreatening, passionless caress. He drew back, but kept his hand cupped on her neck. "Flirt," he said. "Now that wasn't so bad, was it?"

She shook her head as if mesmerized.

Slowly, he lowered his mouth. This time he held nothing back. When she struggled to free herself he used his weight to pin her against the wall. He took his fill of her, without haste, deliberately crushing her small pliant body against his hard length. She was like warm wax in his hands, soft, feminine, yielding. He tasted cider on her tongue, sweet and heady. He sank his mouth into hers, swallowing her small cries of distress. When her fingers curled into his hair, he went wild for her.

It wasn't supposed to be like this. He'd wanted to teach her a lesson. She was supposed to fight him, hate him, fear him. He was losing control, fired by her innocent response. He'd never before felt such an instant explosion of passion for any woman.

When he pulled away from her, his breath was coming hard and fast. He was shocked at himself. A furious imprecation spilled from his mouth. Gabrielle didn't understand a word, but the message was clear. For some reason she could not fathom, the Englishman was blaming her for what had just happened.

She practically threw herself from him. She stumbled, then turned on him like a spitting wildcat. *"Cochon!"* she swore at him. "You son of a sow! If you ever lay your filthy hands on me again I'll cut off your manhood (she used the foulest, vilest word she could think of) and feed it to your relatives in the pigpens."

She was still swearing abuse at him when he slammed the door of his chamber. It was his laughter that silenced her.

Chapter Six

With a slow, graceful movement Gabrielle stretched and rolled to her side, dimly aware that the sun's rays were beginning to scorch the tender skin of her breasts. Raising one leg to cover the other, she adjusted her naked length to make herself more comfortable on the hard, granite boulder. Her unruly mane of gold hair blew about her face as it quickly dried in the fragrant breeze.

Sounds that scarcely ever registered lulled her like a soothing lullaby: the rhythmic lap of the water against the rock on which she sunbathed; the ripple cast by some small fish as it thrust above the surface in search of flies; the heavy drone of bees; the hum of legions of insects and the song of the wind as it restlessly played with the leaves overhead. Alone in Paradise, thought Gabrielle, sighing softly, for once content with herself and with the world.

Through lazy lids she surveyed the silhouette of a river craft, a yacht, and some rich man's toy, she surmised. She had noted it earlier when she had arrived at her secret cove for her daily swim. Its low, sleek lines won her approval. *Beautiful,* she thought, but was too drowsy to be more than slightly curious about the vessel's furled sails and its crew and cargo. It was enough to know that it was too far distant for prying eyes to detect her presence.

At her back, to her left, a twig snapped. In days gone by she would have been instantly alert. She tensed, then forced herself to relax. A fox, a rabbit, or one of the stable cats was no doubt curious about the strange antics of this hairless, naked specimen of the human species worshiping at the sun's altar. She smiled.

"Don't be alarmed. I won't hurt you."

His voice was low-pitched but easily recognizable. To Gabrielle's ears, it broke the silence like the crack of a pistol shot. Her heart lurched madly. It was a testament to Goliath's training that she controlled her first impulse to bolt like a terrified rabbit. Without haste she rolled to her knees, bringing her hair forward to cover her nakedness as best she might. She measured the distance between them carefully and felt reassured. Her discarded clothes, with a pistol concealed in their folds, were almost within arm's reach.

Shading her eyes against the sun, she demanded, "What are you doing here, Englishman?" That she was as naked as the day she was born was, in that moment, of no consequence to Gabrielle. Her mind was frantically sifting through a host of unconnected facts and impressions. The Englishman was dressed in the rough getup of a workman or a *contrebandier*. He should have been in Paris, or even back in England by now. No one of any significance remained at the château. Mascaron and Rollo had left for Paris several days since. And Goliath had gone to Tosny on some errand or other.

"Why are you here?" she asked, and slowly rose to her feet in a crouching position.

"Your grandfather sent me to fetch you," answered Cam easily.

"Mascaron?" She squinted up at him.

"He's been delayed in Paris with the first consul.

108

Since I had nothing better to do, I offered to escort you to him."

She considered his words carefully. There was no reason that she could think to doubt him. He hadn't made a move toward her. And she knew that this man, strangely, had Mascaron's confidence. Having convinced herself that she had nothing to fear, she became excruciatingly aware of the awkwardness of her position. Gabrielle flushed scarlet. The Englishman showed a flash of white teeth.

"Why don't you get dressed," said Cam, "and I'll explain everything to you as we walk back to the house?"

He retreated a few steps and gave her his back. Gabrielle set her teeth. It was evident to her that he purposely wished to embarrass her. Why else had he come in person to fetch her? When he saw her state of undress, he ought to have kept his distance. The thought that she had only boy's clothes with which to cover her nakedness did nothing to mollify her rising temper.

Embarrassed and angry by turns, she reached for her clothes and began to dress. She had donned only her chemise and drawers when the Englishman again addressed her.

"That will do for my purpose," he said.

Like a doe scenting danger, Gabrielle lifted her head. Caution came back in full force. The disturbing impressions she had shrugged off crowded in on her all at once. Her eyes narrowed on the Englishman's strangely motionless figure. She had enough experience to know when an adversary was tensed for action.

Her next move was reflex. She dropped to her knees and frantically felt for her pistol. She could not find it. Her heart was hammering in her throat.

"Is this what you are looking for?" drawled that

hateful voice from only a few feet away. Holding Gabrielle's pistol in his hand, Cam cocked it and pointed it straight at her. "Hold still," he said, deadly serious, "and no harm will come to you."

Gabrielle slowly straightened, her eyes never leaving the barrel of the pistol that was aimed at her heart. "I don't know why you want me," she said, her voice uncommonly hoarse and unsteady, "but I warrant you don't want me dead."

The words were scarcely out of her mouth before she was leaping away from him. With a muffled curse, Cam was after her.

At this point on the river, the escarpment, sheer and formidable, soared above them like the battlements of some great fortress. The Englishman had cut off the easy escape route that led to the château. Gabrielle hared along the narrow strip of shoreline that came to a dead end at an outcrop of granite. Needle-sharp stones and gravel tore at her bare feet. In her panic, Gabrielle scarcely felt them.

Like a surefooted deer, she leaped to her first foothold. She scrambled higher. A viselike grip closed around her ankle. She kicked out, trying to free herself, and dug in her nails to keep herself steady.

"Get down or I'll drag you down," ordered Cam.

Gabrielle's struggles became wilder. She was wrenched from the rock. Cam braced himself to catch the falling girl. But Gabrielle instinctively twisted away to evade her captor's arms. She went flying. When she hit the ground, her momentum carried her along. If she'd had any breath left in her body, she would have screamed as grit and small stones became embedded in her face and torso before she finally came to rest.

"Gabrielle!" The Englishman was on her in an instant, turning her over, straddling her with his powerful thighs. His face was grim as he tested for broken bones. She had not the strength to shake him off and she lay there like a stone, suffering the indignity of those hateful hands learning her intimately. Tears welled in her eyes and, despite her best efforts, spilled over.

When he spoke, his voice was sober and unrevealing. "You're not hurt in any way that counts. I'll help you. Just come quietly and nothing will happen to you. I swear it." As he spoke, his hands moved to his throat to untie his kerchief.

She could see what was coming. He meant to gag her. She wanted to scream, but did not think she could summon enough breath to utter a hoarse whisper. But one thing she could do. With the last of her strength, she brought her head up. She sank her small, sharp teeth into the fleshy part of his hand and held on. Too late to draw back, she saw the raised fist as it came at her. Pain exploded in her head the moment before she went limp.

Cam was shaking. He had never before hit a woman in his life. He cursed himself for being overconfident. He'd never expected that, deprived of foil and pistol, the girl would put up such a fight. It was inconceivable that such a little thing should even think of pitting her puny strength against his. What the hell was the matter with her? Didn't she have enough sense to know when she was beaten?

She looked pathetic, thought Cam, and felt a flood of remorse as he studied the lacerations that covered her face and shoulders. Her thin lawn undergarments were ripped to shreds. He was angry with her, and more furious with himself. He tried not to think of the bruise that would show on her jaw before many hours had passed.

He used his kerchief to wipe the worst of the dirt from her face. The task was hopeless.

111

"Damn you, Gabrielle," he said under his breath, and stripped off his coarse seaman's jacket. He went down on both knees and wrapped it around her as if she were a sleeping baby. "Damn you," he said again, before he cradled her in his arms and rose to his feet.

It took only a few minutes to retrace his steps to the rock where he had found her. In a clump of bushes close by, he uncovered Rollo's small rowing boat. He'd come across it earlier in the week before the peace talks had broken down. He laid Gabrielle carefully in the stern and climbed in beside her. When her people found her clothes and the abandoned boat, they would know what to think, thought Cam.

The river was relatively quiet. It was in the dark of night that the *contrebandiers* transacted most of their business. The sun was still hours from setting. No one made a move toward them, nor did Cam expect trouble. With Rodier's help, he had sent Goliath on a wild-goose chase to Tosny, upstream. By the time the girl's watchdog returned they would be long gone.

When he reached his yacht, which was anchored close to the opposite shore, it was Lansing's hands that reached down to take the girl from him. He said nothing at the girl's condition, but his eyes spoke volumes. Cam clenched his jaw.

"Where do you think you're taking her?" he demanded as Lansing took a step away from him.

"Below. She badly needs attention."

"Give her to me." Cam's dispassionate tone belied the storm in his eyes.

Lansing knew better than to argue. Wordlessly, he placed the inert girl in his friend's outstretched arms.

"Send Will to me with hot water," said Cam.

"And let's get the hell out of here." On an after-thought, he turned back. "She's not to be trusted under any circumstance. D'you understand?" His steely eyes traversed the silent members of his crew, daring them to say one word in challenge. Satisfied with what he read in their expressions, he turned on his heel and went below.

Cam pushed through the door to his cabin and set Gabrielle on the small bunk. With trembling fingers, he removed the coarse jacket that covered the unconscious girl. His eyes swept over her, taking stock of her injuries.

She didn't look a bit like the snarling wildcat who had fought him with tooth and claw. She looked like a child, a waif of the street, the property of some callous monster who had abused her mercilessly. He was sickened at the violence he'd felt compelled to use against her. Making war on women was not his way.

A knock at the door announced the presence of the cabin boy. White-lipped and silent, Cam accepted the basin of warm water and shut the door in the boy's face. He was grateful that the girl had not roused from her stupor. He did not know how he would tend to her if she tried to fight him now.

Striving for impassivity, he began to strip off the shreds of her undergarments, shutting his mind to everything but the deeply embedded scratches and bruises that disfigured her skin. He squeezed out a washcloth, soaped it, and carefully began to clean each raw looking abrasion, scrubbing gently to remove the embedded grit and dirt.

Gabrielle moaned and moved restlessly. She felt the gentle touch of his hands, the soothing comfort of unintelligible words.

"Goliath?" she queried softly, and then on a whisper, "Did we lose them?"

113

When no one answered, her eyelashes fluttered. She grew more restless. "Did we lose them?" she asked again, her breath wheezing painfully in her chest.

"Yes. We lost them," Cam replied. By degrees, the girl relaxed and made no objection as he continued to doctor her. On the underside of her left breast he came upon old scar tissue. There was a similar mark on her thigh. When he came upon another longer scar on one golden shoulder blade, his hands stilled as the full realization of what he had uncovered hit him with the force of an exploding shell. The girl had sustained a number of injuries that could only have been caused by the sharp point of steel. He reeled with the knowledge, and a thousand questions coursed through his mind all at once.

He gazed at her for several long minutes, his fingers tracing the evidence of . . . what? He could not begin to imagine who had done such a thing. The thought of someone, anyone, hurting her made him want to do murder. The irony was not lost on him. A crooked, derisory smile briefly touched his lips.

Gabrielle made a sudden, spasmodic movement and began to whimper like a child. "Goliath. Please. I hurt." Her voice was low and throbbing. Dry, rasping sobs shook her thin shoulders.

Swallowing a knot of something that had become lodged in his throat, Cam moved to a chest at the foot of the bunk. In a moment, he returned with a glass of laudanum mixed with water.

He held her head and instructed her to drink, knowing perfectly well that she obeyed merely because she was too disoriented to recognize who held the glass to her lips. He gave her a few minutes to get settled before he started on the ugly red abrasions on her face.

His first touch brought an anguished moan, low in her throat, as she winced with the pain. He did not know where the soft, soothing words came from, nor was he fully conscious of what he was saying. They spilled from his mouth as naturally as he drew breath.

"It's all right, Angel. I'm here. Go to sleep. I'll take care of you. I swear, no one and nothing will ever hurt you again as long as I have breath in my body."

Either his words or the laudanum was having its effect. She became quiet beneath his ministrations. He finished quickly and smeared a soothing ointment into several of the rawest, angriest welts. Last of all, he fetched a clean linen shirt from the chest and drew it down over her head, smoothing it over her inert limbs. When he pulled the covers up to her chin, he became aware that he was covered in a fine sheen of perspiration.

He grew impatient with the thoughts that tried to force themselves into his mind. Gabrielle de Brienne was the bait to lure Mascaron into his trap and nothing more, he reminded himself forcefully. She was his prisoner. To think of her as anything else was madness. It was sheerest folly for him to have taken her in his arms in the dimly lit staircase of the Château de Vrigonde merely to prove that he, and he alone, could awaken everything that was female in her nature.

That he had succeeded in his design gave him no comfort. For the desire to go one step further, to handle her possessively, to know her intimately, had been born in him from the moment he had felt her yielding beneath the pressure of his kiss.

That kiss! *Forget it,* he admonished himself. He'd kissed scores of women in his time. And the only reason he could think that *that* kiss was the most memorable was because he'd been the first man to bring Gabrielle de Brienne to an awareness of her femininity. He'd never been first with any woman before. It was the novelty that appealed to him. There could be no other explanation. For Gabrielle de Brienne was definitely, indisputably, incontrovertibly, not in his style.

In only a few days they would reach Cornwall. Louise would be waiting for him. It could not come too soon for his peace of mind. He would lose himself in Louise. Her accomplished lovemaking would soon banish this wayward longing to possess such a young, inexperienced girl. With Louise's ripe body accessible to him all thoughts of Gabrielle would be easily stifled.

He took a step back and his eyes swept over her. She looked so small and helpless. But he knew that when she woke up he would have a spitting tigress on his hands. The whole situation suddenly struck him as unbelievable. God, he didn't know what he was letting himself in for. Hopefully, the laudanum would keep her under for some hours to come, at least until he had time to decide how best to handle her. And himself.

Before quitting the cabin he gave in to one last impulse. He brushed her halo of tangled hair back from her face, spreading it out on the pillow.

She moaned, her jaw working spasmodically.

A responsive flicker came and went in Cam's eyes. When she woke up, she would hate him. He took that thought with him as he went on deck.

Moaning softly, Gabrielle came slowly awake. She struggled against the blackness that threatened to drag her down into forgetfulness. Think. She must think. They were on the run again. She had been hurt, but Goliath's gentle hands had tended her wounds. She was safe, even though her head throbbed and every bone in her body jarred with each shallow breath she drew.

"Goliath?" she breathed softly, willing her eyes to open as unfamiliar sounds and scents invaded her senses.

There was no answer. Her eyelashes drooped as she tried to remember. Perhaps it was the smell of him in her nostrils that brought the flood of memories rushing back.

Despite the blazing pain in her head and the dull ache in her ribs, she rose on her elbows.

He was seated at a table against the wall, watching her with those hooded, fathomless eyes of his, eyes that never gave anything away. Her gaze moved to take in the small confines of the cabin, and she remembered the unfamiliar vessel that had been anchored on the Seine.

With a gasping cry she threw back the covers and attempted to rise. Waves of dizziness and nausea swept through her.

He reached her in two swift strides. As he pushed her back into the mattress, she tried to fight him off. Desperate, frightened, she flayed at him with wild blows with no force behind them. When her meager store of strength was depleted, she fell back, panting.

"Gabrielle, that's enough! No one wants to hurt you."

The unexpected gentleness in his voice momentarily surprised her into stillness. His hands hovered over her. And then she remembered everything. She would have bitten him again, but the effort of baring her teeth sent waves of pain racing through every muscle in her face. Sobbing as much in anger as in pain, she dragged herself across the small width of the bunk, as far from him as possible, and huddled against the corner. She made no attempt to shade the intense hatred that blazed from her eyes.

Soberly he met her stare. On reflection, Cam had decided that his best hope of subduing the girl was to reveal all the salient facts behind her abduction. If she could be persuaded that her confinement was to be temporary and painless, she might see the logic of obeying him, however reluctantly.

"You're my prisoner," he said flatly. "I'm taking you back to England. If all goes well, you'll be released within a month or two. You'll be back in France before you know it." He waited for some response. When none came, he forced himself to finish what he had begun to say. "It's not you we want, Gabrielle. It's information. If your grandfather cooperates, you'll be returned to him as soon as may be. There's nothing to be frightened of. I swear it."

Though Gabrielle put no stock in what the Englishman swore to, there was never any doubt in her mind that her own person was of little worth to anyone. She let his words slowly revolve in her mind. Mascaron had information the Englishman wanted. She was to be the currency of exchange. That much she did believe. She could have wept for the pity of it. After everything he had been through, and with recognition finally within his grasp, Mascaron did not deserve this. She swayed weakly.

Cam's voice — warm, persuasive — cut across her thoughts. "I swear you won't be hurt if you don't resist me."

To conceal her murderous thoughts she dropped her eyelashes. "Where are we?" she asked abruptly.

Relieved at her quiet acceptance of the inevitable,

Cam breathed a little more easily. "You're on my yacht. We are approaching Rouen. I'm taking you to my home in Cornwall."

A shaft of pure jubilation lit up her eyes. "You'll never make it!" she said scornfully. "If Goliath doesn't get you, the bore will. Your yacht will be smashed to smithereens by the tide." If she could have curled her lip in contempt without cracking her bruised jaw she would have done so with pleasure.

"No one will come looking for you, Gabrielle," he said gravely. "To think otherwise is to indulge in fantasy."

She was very quick to catch his meaning. "You think Mascaron and Goliath will think I have drowned because of the clothes I've left behind?" She made a derisory sound. "They're not such fools! Until they find my body, they won't stop looking for me."

"Even when they find Rollo's smashed boat?"

Her green eyes glowed like polished emeralds. "I thought," she said thoughtfully, "that you wished to trade me for information. If Mascaron thinks I'm dead, how will that profit you?"

Smiling, he answered, "For a girl, you're very bright."

She mimicked his tone and manner exactly when she replied, "For an Englishman, I presume you are running true to form."

The smile left Cam's eyes. He took an intimidating step toward her, and Gabrielle scrambled frantically to her feet. There was barely room to crouch, and she had to duck her head when it grazed the low ceiling. Everything swam before her eyes and she bit back a moan of pain. If the wall hadn't been at her back, she would have slumped in a heap. And still, Cam noted, defiance flashed from her eyes.

"For God's sake!" He combed his fingers through his hair. "What the devil do you think I'm going to do to you?"

She tried to laugh, but the sound came out a pathetic gasp. He had hurt her, badly. When he had dragged her from the cliff face, she could have been maimed for life. She would never forget the rough handling she had taken from those powerful, masculine hands. More than anything, she wished he would go away and leave her in peace. She could scarcely sustain this proud and defiant posture, spitting her hatred at him. She was frightened and alone with a stranger who did not care whether she lived or died, except as it affected his plans for Mascaron. The pain was coming at her in waves. She was weary to the bone. And he had the gall to ask what she thought he was going to do to her.

He put out his hands in a placating gesture. "Sit down before you fall down, all right? I've brought something for you to eat."

He backed up a step and Gabrielle allowed her legs to buckle under her. Slowly, she slid down the wall to a sitting position. Through half-lidded eyes she watched him warily as he proffered a cup of some liquid. She accepted it without thinking and brought it to her lips. After a few sips of the weak broth her stomach began to heave.

"I can't," she said, and tried to lay the cup aside.

Without saying anything he took it from her and set it on the small table. Restlessly, he took a few paces around the tiny cabin and came to a halt at the foot of the bunk. A muscle tensed in his jaw. "When I dragged you from the cliff, I meant to catch you in my arms. You shouldn't have twisted away from me."

No response.

120

"You wouldn't come quietly. I had to hit you, don't you see? I'm sorry that you made that necessary. I had no wish to hurt you."

Her stony silence rekindled the ashes of his anger . . . and his shame. "If you act like a man, you may expect to be treated like one. I give you fair warning—if you try to thwart me, you'll be punished."

His threat stung her. "I'm not afraid of you!" she cried out.

She flinched when Cam suddenly raised his hand to rub the back of his neck. He caught the slight, fearful movement and smiled grimly. She was afraid of him, he thought, but she would fight him every inch of the way. A reluctant admiration was won from him.

"Look, if you don't care about your own fate, think of your grandfather."

"He, at least, is beyond your reach!"

"Is he?"

Her head came up the merest fraction.

"What do you think would happen to him if it ever got out that you had been captured by the British? Just for argument's sake, let's say you managed to escape me and made it back to France on your own. I'll tell you what would happen. The authorities would immediately jump to the conclusion that your grandfather had passed information along to France's enemies in order to save your life. Surely I don't have to tell you what they would do to him under those circumstances?"

He gave her a few minutes to assimilate the full threat of his words before he added for effect, "Officially, of course, we would deny it. But unofficially, our sources in France would let it be known that Mascaron was one of our agents, however unwillingly."

"Spies!" she spat at him.

Her venom seemed to amuse him. He inclined his head gravely. When it became evident that she meant to preserve her silence, Cam's tone turned hard.

"In a few days we'll be in Cornwall. You're to pass yourself off as Gabrielle de Valcour, my ward, whom I've rescued from France. We're distant kin. D'you understand what I'm saying?"

She didn't, but she nodded just the same, then grimaced as needles of pain shot through her head.

"I've brought you some boy's clothes to wear. It's all I could find." He picked up a bundle of garments that was lying on a chair and threw them on the bunk at Gabrielle's feet. "You're more at home in these than you are in a woman's garb, anyway. I knew you wouldn't mind."

For the first time she became conscious that her only clothing was a man's shirt. She touched it gingerly. Her eyes flew to his and read the answer to her unasked question. Color heated her cheekbones, and she lowered her lashes as if to blot out the sight of him.

"There was no woman on board to attend you," he explained quietly. "It was necessary for someone to doctor your wounds. I did not think you would wish strangers to see you as you were."

"*You* are a stranger," she said, but with so little force that the words were scarcely audible. Her eyes remained closed.

Cam had to fight against the impulse to gather her in his arms and soothe her as if she were a hurt child. That she would as soon murder him as look at him, he never doubted for an instant.

In the same patient tone, he said, "When you are dressed, I'll take you up on deck. The fresh air will do you good. We'll be going through the bore in a day or so. Cheer up. You may have your wish. Perhaps my vessel will founder."

"I'll pray for it," said Gabrielle, opening her eyes to give him a direct look. They both knew she meant it.

Chapter Seven

It was during their brief stopover at Rouen that Gabrielle was instructed to copy a letter to Mascaron at Cam's dictation. She was happy to do it, though no look or gesture of hers betrayed her state of mind. She believed what she had told the Englishman, that neither Mascaron nor Goliath would accept her death without incontrovertible proof. Nevertheless, she could not bear to think of the distress they must suffer when they found her missing. Though everything in her rebelled at adopting the role of the docile hostage, she put a rein on her temper so that her own designs might be accomplished. She wrote the short epistle without a word of protest.

Relieved at this unhoped-for capitulation, Cam took the single page from her hand and glanced over it.

"That's all you want me to say?" asked Gabrielle, frowning. There was very little in the letter except the intelligence that she was alive and well.

Cam folded the sheet carefully and slipped it into the inside pocket of his jerkin. "My emissary will deliver it. He'll give your grandfather a fuller accounting of what he may expect."

"And if Mascaron doesn't accept your terms, Englishman? What then?" Her words were couched as an insult.

Eyes blazing, he responded, "My name is Cam. You'd better get used to saying it. You're my ward, remember?"

She was too tired or too sick to argue the point with him. Even breathing was difficult. Though she was sure that no bones had broken when she had taken the fall, her ribcage protested at the slightest movement.

Inclining her head in the barest acquiescence, she persisted, "What happens to me if Mascaron refuses your terms?"

"You don't want to know," he said and smiled grimly as her head snapped back and her eyes, wide with shock, met his.

Pride stiffened her back. She looked at him coldly, but said nothing.

Cam felt like the veriest bully. Gabrielle de Brienne might be only a slip of a girl, but she could incite a temper he had not known he possessed until he met her. He combed one hand through his hair. Relenting, he said, "Nothing will happen to you if you do as you are told. All right?"

She met his look with bitter disdain. "You expect me to believe that, after everything you've already done to me?"

Refusing to be drawn into useless argument, he pulled back her chair. "You've sulked in the cabin too long as it is. It's time you got some fresh air."

Dressed as she was in boy's clothing, and in her sorry condition she was reluctant to show herself to the crew. But one look at the unrelenting set of Cam's jaw and she thought better of the almost irresistible temptation to fight him at every turn. As she allowed him to escort her on deck she consoled herself with the thought that once she had fully re-

125

covered from the injuries he had inflicted he would not have everything his own way, not by a long shot.

Once on deck, Gabrielle came face to face with Lord Lansing. Color washed out of her cheeks. She ought to have been prepared for Lansing's involvement in her abduction. She was not, and could not conceal her start of surprise before she schooled her features to indifference.

Cam observed the awkwardness between Gabrielle and his friend, and he experienced a keen and inexplicable stab of satisfaction. Whistling, he left Gabrielle in Lansing's custody as he descended to the quay that would take him to his rendezvous with Rodier.

Several minutes were to pass before Lord Lansing broke the strained silence that had fallen between them. "I'm sorry we had to meet under these circumstances," he said by way of apology.

Gabrielle darted him a reproachful look then looked away again. With pretended idleness she watched the progress of a small boat and began mentally to take stock of her position. With the Englishman gone she felt that her chances of escape had never stood higher. True, his yacht was anchored at the far end of the quay. But Rouen was a busport. There were plenty of other small craft about to give her sanctuary, if she could only find the stamina to get to them.

Her eyes roamed the rigging and decks. With the exception of Lansing, none of the crew was paying her the least attention.

Again Lansing made a stab at ending the frigid silence which had fallen between them.

Gabrielle ruthlessly crushed the bile that rose to her lips and returned some suitable rejoinder. Feigning an interest in the far shore, she moved away from him.

His hand closed over her elbow, halting her in her tracks. "Gabrielle, please. I have my orders. You don't have the run of the ship. It's more than my life is worth to let you attempt anything foolish."

"It never occurred to me to . . ."

"Didn't it? Then you won't mind if I hang on to your arm. No, don't look at me like that. If you escaped, Cam would have my hide."

Like a furious spitting kitten, she rounded on him. The smile on Lansing's face died. Her French was too quick, too impatient for his untutored ear, but he grasped the gist of what she was saying. If Cam was going to have his hide, by the time this was over, she was going to have his . . . Lansing flushed scarlet. Such words! He'd only heard them before from the mouths of coarse sailors on the docks of Calais and Marseilles. And while he was still standing there, stunned into immobility, the next thing he knew she was diving for the rail.

He thought he had lost her, but as she tried to hoist herself over the side, she gave a gasp of pain and collapsed in a heap. By this time, Lansing had caught up to her, and he gathered her unresisting form into his arms.

"Gaby, what is it?"

She was wheezing, and fighting for breath. "My ribs," she finally got out. "I think I must have . . ." Without warning, she went limp against him.

For a moment, he thought it might be a trick. Cam had advised him in no uncertain terms that this girl would resist them to the point of folly. But one look at her ashen face, and he knew she was not shamming.

As Cam had done before, Lansing carried the unconscious girl below. Before she came out of her faint, he had bound her ribs securely with the strips of a torn sheet. When Gabrielle opened her eyes, Lansing was ready with a glass of brandy. He, too, had found the old scar tissue and was avidly curious about what had caused it.

"You look awful," he said, and tipped the glass back till brandy dribbled into her mouth. She took the glass from his hand and Lansing sat down on the edge of the bunk. "Drink it," he said, and Gabrielle obediently took a few short swallows.

By degrees, the color washed back into her cheeks. Lansing studied her carefully and decided that he'd seen pugilists come off better in a prize fight.

"Why didn't you tell Cam about the ribs?" he asked.

"What need? They're not broken."

"With the pain you are suffering, you can say that?"

"I've had broken ribs before. I know the difference."

Not for the first time, Lansing realized that beneath that fragile exterior the girl hid the heart and will of a warrior. Just to look at her filled his mind with visions of the ancient British queen, Boadicea, who had uselessly pitted herself against the invincible Romans. The thought of Gabrielle pitting herself against Cam filled him with foreboding.

His voice was very sober when next he spoke. "I'm telling you this for your own good, Gabrielle. Don't fight Cam. You'll only come to grief if you do. And it won't matter to him that you're a female."

Something in either his voice or words arrested her attention. Her eyes, which had been making a more thorough inventory of the cabin, narrowed on him speculatively. She pulled herself to a sitting position.

"Then let me go before he returns."

"No."

"You've seen what he did to me." She touched her fingers to her jaw and the scrapes on her face. "He hates me. He won't be satisfied until . . ."

"No!"

"But why?" she pleaded. "I'm not asking you to do anything. Just turn your back for a few minutes, that's all, just a few minutes, and—"

Lansing shot to his feet. "For the last time, no!"

Almost despairing, she cried out, "What kind of hold does he have over you?"

"The best kind. I *owe* him my loyalty! And don't ever ask me to betray him again."

"I see," she said faintly, sinking back against the pillows.

"Do you? I wonder." He removed the glass from her fingers. "There's one thing you should understand, Gabrielle. There isn't a man on this vessel or at Dunraeden who would entertain what you have just suggested. In one degree or another, Cam has *earned* our respect and loyalty. You might say we're hand picked. Do you understand what I'm saying?"

She shook her head wearily.

"No one will take your part against Cam. You'll come to grief if you try that tack at Dunraeden. Cam rules there as if he were king. Do you see what I am saying? *His* law stands, not the laws of England." At the door he turned back. His voice not ungentle, he said, "No one wants to see you get hurt Gabrielle, but there's more at stake here than the life of one girl. Give in gracefully, and Cam will deal justly with you."

He waited for her reply. When none was forthcoming, he exited quietly. He was very careful to lock the door behind him and to pocket the key.

Rouen, like Chester in England, thought Cam, retained much of its medieval character. Its tortuous, cobbled streets were lined on both sides with the familiar, half-timbered wattle buildings, giving Cam the impression that he had stepped back into another century.

He struck out along the Rue de Gros-Horloge, until he came to the famous clock in the arch that spanned the narrow street and gave it its name. He loitered and turned as if to read the time from the face of the centuries-old monument. Satisfied that no one was following, he ducked into the door of a cobbler's shop. An exchange of greeting using the correct formula was all it took before he was ushered into the back corridor. In a moment he had traversed the width of the house and had entered the outside courtyard.

A workman, crouched over a bundle of dyed leathers, looked up at his entrance. He wiped his hands against the legs of his breeches and came toward Cam.

Gilbert Rodier was a man of many disguises, and in the eleven years since Cam had first been thrown together with him, he'd had time and enough to perfect them all. It was his wonderfully mobile face and that uncanny talent for mimicry, thought Cam, that could deceive the keenest eye. Dressed in the appropriate getup, Rodier could pass himself off as a simpering, aging *roué* or the roughest, coarsest jetsam of the dregs of human society. Even the man's own agents could not identify him with any certainty, a circumstance that had saved Rodier's skin on several occasions.

130

Grins were exchanged and hands taken in a firm handclasp.

"You made good time," said Rodier, motioning for Cam to take one of the benches against the wall. "No trouble?"

Cam's jaw tightened imperceptibly before he replied, "Nothing I couldn't handle. Everything went like clockwork."

He extracted Gabrielle's letter from his pocket and handed it to Rodier. There was no need to go into explanations. Their plan of action had been decided on weeks before.

"What news?" asked Cam as Rodier pocketed the letter and joined him on the bench.

"It's almost certain the first consul will be emperor by the end of the year. You've heard that the Tribunate voted in favour of the proposal?"

"I've heard." Cam smiled.

"That pleases you?"

"Of course. That intelligence will stick in the craw of Mr. Charles James Fox and all liberals like him. And the Americans won't take kindly to the idea either. Bonaparte is not very wise, thank God."

"No. He doesn't think he needs to be. His confidence resides in destiny, or fate, or whatever you wish to call it. With his star in the ascendancy, he thinks he is invincible. He won't cavil at taking on the whole world if it comes down to it."

"That may be our salvation," said Cam reflectively.

For an interval nothing was said as the two friends contemplated what might be in store for their respective homelands in the coming years. In both their minds, the picture was bleak.

Finally Rodier said, "I like your Mr. Fox. I wish we had more like him in France."

131

They'd had this argument scores of times before, and Cam refused to rise to the bait. Rodier could never be persuaded that the Revolution in France had been wrong in principle and that, given time, the power of the aristocracy would have been gradually transferred to a wider base. Like Fox, Rodier was an idealist. It was this idealism that set him against the tyranny of absolute power, whether it resided in the throne or in the right of the majority. It was this idealism that led him to pursue a course that others would have roundly condemned as traitorous. Fortunately, however, thought Cam wryly, Rodier was also blessed with a modicum of Gallic realism. Otherwise, he would not have lent his support to the abduction of Gabrielle de Brienne.

To change the subject, Cam asked, "Have you learned anything more of the girl's background?"

Rodier shot his companion a commiserating look. "As it happens, I've picked up quite a bit of information on the girl, though there are still gaps that I don't suppose will ever be filled in." He slapped Cam on the shoulder. "I hope you have not bitten off more than you can chew. It's not a lass you've captured, Cam, but a soldier, and one, moreover, who's earned her spurs in the thick of combat." And Rodier launched into a description of Gabrielle's years between her release from the Abbaye until her reappearance in French society.

His information was very sketchy, but by the time he had reached the end of his recital, Cam had a fair idea of the kind of life Gabrielle had endured. Gradually his incredulity gave way to a slow, simmering anger, but neither voice nor expression betrayed what he was feeling.

"What was Mascaron thinking of?" he demanded. "If he feared for her safety, why not simply hide her away?" He was thinking of the scars he had discovered when he had tended to Gabrielle aboard his yacht. "Other females managed to come through the Revolution unscathed. Why was it necessary for her to take the identity of a boy? Why did Mascaron insist that she go with him?"

Rodier studied his friend with frank curiosity. "Who's to say?" he asked at length. "It's possible that Mascaron was influenced by the fate of other innocent women whose male relations were denounced. Have you forgotten how many of those followed fathers, husbands, and brothers to the guillotine? The girl had two blots against her. Her father was Robert de Brienne and her grandfather was a hunted man."

Both men fell silent, remembering that though Rodier had escaped Madame Guillotine, his family and friends had not been so fortunate.

Cam shrugged philosophically. "It's regrettable that the girl's destiny was so closely tied to Mascaron's."

"It still is," remarked Rodier.

Cam said nothing.

Rising, Rodier held out his hand. "You'd best get going. The tide waits for no man. What will you do, Cam, when this is all over?"

"When this is all over?" asked Cam. He got to his feet and clasped Rodier's extended hand.

"For more than ten years you've been driven by your thirst for revenge. I was just thinking that without Mascaron to occupy your thoughts, your life will lack focus."

"You think too much," said Cam, laughing.

But as Cam retraced his steps to Rouen's busy quays he considered Rodier's parting shot. Would his life lack focus? He conceded that his old friend might have a point, for though he had committed

133

himself to any number of political causes over the years and had made himself indispensable to Pitt, it was his determination to bring his family's murderers to justice that had been the driving force in his life. What was in his future? he wondered.

He reflected that it might be the opportune moment to consider the next generation of Colburnes. A man in his position must beget heirs. He was thirty years old and the last of his line. His family tree could be traced back to the Norman conquest. He had always accepted the inevitability of matrimony sooner or later.

For some reason, Gabrielle de Brienne came into his mind. He snorted derisively at his errant thoughts. Gabrielle de Brienne was certainly not the stuff of a duchess. As far as he could tell, she did not have it in her to be a woman, let alone the mother of his children. And it irritated him to find himself so intrigued by imagining himself in the role of her first lover.

Fortunately, that role would never fall to his lot. The girl hated him. He was her abductor. She regarded him as an unfeeling monster. And Rodier's words had given him pause. Without his connivance, Mascaron would never have become a hunted man and Gabrielle might have been spared the rough and ready life into which she had been thrust.

Mascaron. That name would forever stand between them. They would always be enemies. He must remember that. For whether he would or no, Gabrielle de Brienne was beginning to occupy his waking and sleeping hours to a disturbing degree.

He made a conscious effort to rout her from his mind with the image of his mistress. When that failed, Cam turned, almost in desperation, to memories of his stepmother and half sister. This time he succeeded.

Of his own mother, he had no recollection. She had died giving birth to him. And for his sins, Cam had been punished by his father's abandonment, or so it had seemed to the young boy. Raised by a succession of nurses and governesses who did not long withstand the isolation of Dunraeden, he had been a lonely, withdrawn child. It was only when his father remarried that he'd had his first taste of family life.

Initially he had distrusted the young woman with the infectious laughter who had breezed into his solitary domain, adjuring him to call her *Maman*. At six years old, he was a shy child with more than his share of the proverbial Colburne coldness. But this young woman had come to fascinate him. Her warmth had gradually melted his reserve. No one could long remain immune to her charm, least of all a boy who was starved of affection.

For the first time that he could remember, Dunraeden had taken on the aspect of a home. And when Marguerite, his sister, was born, there had been no happier boy in the whole of England. Like one of the knights of old, he was to be his sister's champion, or so *Maman* had told him. She had fired his imagination with all sorts of nonsense. And he had loved it, adored her, worshiped his sister, and had gradually come to accept the forbidding man who, until then, had been a shadowy figure on the periphery of his life.

It was salutary to remember what he owed his stepmother, thought Cam, as he approached the quay where his yacht was docked. *Marguerite*. He had named his yacht for his sister. Before he could suppress the memory, he had a vivid impression of his stepmother and sister as he had last seen them. His hands fisted at his sides.

135

Mascaron. He had plucked from his young life the only two people who had meant anything to him. Cam refused to feel even a twinge of remorse for what Gabrielle had been forced to endure. She had survived. And if she ever discovered the part he had played in her grandfather's downfall, she would think nothing of dispatching him with blade or pistol. Destiny had set them against each other. So be it. His face was expressionless as he boarded the *Marguerite* and gave the order to set sail for Caudebec, their next safe harbor on their journey down the Seine.

At Caudebec, the bore was spectacular. The incoming tide met the waters of the Seine with such velocity that the river was thrown back upon itself. And they were still miles from the mouth of the estuary.

For more than twenty-four hours, Gabrielle had been confined to the small cabin under lock and key. She had seen nothing of the Englishman, nor did she want to. She thought of him in the way she thought of cockroaches and dead rats. He was to be avoided like the plague.

As the vessel edged its way into the stream, she was sent for. It was the cabin boy who came with the message that the captain requested her presence on deck.

"What does he want now?" she asked Will, not bothering to conceal her rancor.

"The tide has turned, miss," answered Will respectfully. He could not quite keep the excitement from his voice. "We'll be entering the bore any minute now."

"So?" she said in a creditably bored drawl.

"If the *Marguerite* founders, it's best not to be caught below decks. Captain's order, miss."

She went on deck without argument, for between

Caudebec and the coast lay her last chance of escaping her captors. Yet when she looked down into the boiling waters of the Seine, her hopes vanished. To throw herself into the bore at that point was to invite certain drowning, even for a strong swimmer like herself. And her encounter with the Englishman had left her well below par.

He scarcely spared her a glance, but it was evident that Will had been ordered to guard her. She was herded into a doorway near the stern of the ship and told to hang on for dear life. Above the roar of the churning spray she could hear Cam's voice shouting orders. Sails were unfurled as men moved quickly to do his bidding. Her eyes were inexorably drawn to him.

He was in his element. Wind, spray, and the pitch of the small fragile craft—he seemed to exult in the danger. Gabrielle had never seen him look more alive. There was nothing now to be seen of the indolent aristocrat. It was as if he absorbed his energy from the very elements he meant to subdue. The spectacle disturbed her. She did not think that he would consider one small girl so very great a challenge.

Suddenly the vessel righted itself. A calm descended. A roar went up from the crew. The yacht shot forward.

"What is it?" Gabrielle cried out.

Will turned a smiling face towards her. "We go with the tide, miss. There's nothing on God's earth can stop us until we're into the Channel. And then, God willing, home to Cornwall."

Home. She tried to voice the word, but it lodged in her throat like a broken blade. In that moment, she chanced to look in the Englishman's direction. He was staring straight at her. She read the challenge in the blaze of his posture. *I've won,* he was telling her.

A moment before, she had been ready to concede defeat. That one supercilious, masculine look touched a raw nerve. She bristled. With studied insolence, she spat on the deck. As his face darkened, she smothered the small flame of fear and smiled.

Cam threw back his head and laughed.

Chapter Eight

Dunraeden. Standing high on a rocky promontory, it loomed out over the English Channel like a sentinel standing guard over Cornwall's southern shores. Gabrielle watched with fearful fascination from the deck of the *Marguerite,* as they approached the forbidding walls of the fortress. Perhaps it was the bite of the wind that made her shiver, she thought. No, it wasn't the wind, it was Dunraeden. Without conscious thought, she crossed herself.

Lansing joined her at the rail. "Don't let the exterior put you off," he said in an attempt to ease the tension that seemed to radiate from the girl. "Cam has modernized the place, from dungeons to turrets. Dunraeden has all the comforts of home. You may take my word for it, Gabrielle. Everything has been done to make your stay comfortable."

"It's still a prison," she said.

Reasonably, placatingly, Lansing observed, "Only if you make it so. I'll be there to keep you company."

"Naturally," she replied dully. "Prisoners must have gaolers."

She glanced over his shoulder and her eyes locked with Cam's. She wished she knew what the Englishman was thinking, but his half-hooded expression gave very little away.

Lansing said something and she turned obediently to follow the direction in which he was pointing. In other circumstances, she would have admired the striking landscape, with its towering red cliffs and long ribbons of sandy beaches. But now all she could think was that even if Mascaron was to discover her whereabouts, any escape attempt from the sea was doomed to failure.

"It doesn't look so formidable when the tide is out," said Lansing. "You'll see miles upon miles of sandy beaches. There's a whole warren of caves along the shoreline that can only be reached at low tide. As you may expect, our Cornish smugglers make good use of them."

"Oh?" Now that was interesting. Her eyes scanned the base of the cliffs but could detect nothing from that distance. She sensed the Englishman's presence behind her and stiffened.

"It may not look so formidable," said Cam in her ear, "but when the tide is out, that's when the beaches are most treacherous. Many a foolhardy stranger has found himself caught in no-man's land. The speed with which the waters return is staggering. It's what has kept Dunraeden safe from sea attack in the last number of centuries. But all this is only of academic interest." A long look passed between Cam and Lansing. "For as long as Gabrielle is my guest, she is to remain within Dunraeden's walls."

"Of course," answered Lansing quickly. "I did not mean to suggest anything else."

The *Marguerite* anchored in the lee of a great stony promontory, and they were rowed to shore in small boats. A narrow path led them round the base of the cliff to the landward approach to the castle.

Impressive, thought Gabrielle as she noted the deep

140

natural cleft in the rock formation that separated Dunraeden from the mainland of Cornwall. There could be no hope of rescue from that direction either. Her hands grew cold and clammy. When they passed through the two sets of great doors that gave entrance to the bailey and she heard the resounding thunder as they were closed at her back, her sense of panic flared out of control.

It was so reminiscent, so very reminiscent of that other time when she had been incarcerated with her mother in the Abbaye. Who would have believed the horror that awaited them behind its walls? *Maman*. She suddenly wondered if she'd screamed the word aloud, just as she had done then. In her brief life she had faced a mob of enraged *federés;* had swum the Loire with a broken rib; had dived from the walls of Valence onto a moving cart. But nothing, *nothing* terrified her more than the thought of prison walls closing in on her. Like a wild thing looking for escape she scanned the battlements and towers that hedged her in.

"Gaby! What is it?"

His touch on her shoulder electrified her. She spun to face him. Her shoulders were heaving as she tried to draw in air.

"Gaby!" said Cam again, and his eyes anxiously traveled over her. She looked as if she'd seen a ghost. He didn't think about what he was doing. In one deft movement he had swept her into his arms and was hugging her against his chest. Long strides carried him across the bailey and up the narrow stairs that led to the great hall.

"Brandy," he shouted as a footman came running. He dropped into an oversize chair, and cradled her gently, the fingers of one hand sweeping back the tangle of fine hair from her face. "Sweetheart, don't take on so. I'm here. You're safe. I promise you."

141

His lips skimmed over her fluttering lashes, brushed the scrapes and abrasions on one cheek and feathered lightly against her lips. She turned her face up, a faint line furrowing her brow. He read the uncertainty in her eyes. Almost by instinct he began to knead the taut muscles in her neck and shoulders. "Gaby," he said, and the word seemed to catch in his throat. "Gaby."

Her lips parted and her eyes dropped to his mouth.

"Cam! You're home!"

Louise Pelletier slowly descended the stone staircase, her eyes widening at the unprecedented spectacle of the Duke of Dyson nursing a stable boy in his lap. Cam moved slightly and a fall of fair hair cascaded over one arm. He looked up to meet Louise's shocked stare, and grinned sheepishly.

"My ward," he said, indicating the slight form that was sprawled against him. "The crossing was wretched. The poor child has yet to find her land legs." He accepted a tot glass of brandy from the lackey who had run to do his bidding and forced Gabrielle to drink the whole of it.

"Good God! Whatever happened to her?" asked Louise. Unvoiced was the thought that this young slip of a girl who looked as though she had been thrown from a horse could not possibly pose any threat to her place in Cam's affections. And yet there was something in the way he was holding the girl, something in the way he was looking at her, that roused Louise's worst suspicions. Nothing of what she was thinking, however, showed in her voice or expression when she said, "You should have told me, Cam, that the girl was a mere child. I'm not sure that the wardrobe you ordered for her is at all suitable."

The effects of the brandy or the woman's voice

penetrated the warm cocoon that Cam had woven around Gabrielle. She struggled free of him and stumbled to her feet. Cam rose in a more leisurely fashion.

"Make your curtsey, Gabrielle, to your companion and compatriot, Mademoiselle Louise Pelletier. Louise, may I present my ward, Gabrielle de Valcour?"

Without thinking, Gabrielle closed her fingers around the legs of her boy's breeches and bobbed a curtsy. When the other woman broke into a trill of laughter, she flushed scarlet, realizing how ridiculous the gesture must appear in her boy's getup.

She stood awkwardly, clasping her hands together, as the lady who smelled like a tropical garden brushed by her and went into the Englishman's arms in a rustle of silks. The embrace was short, and Gabrielle knew intuitively that Louise was disappointed when Cam set her away from him. She smelled a romance in the air. Possibly a betrothal. She told herself that it was only natural to experience a sudden rush of curiosity about the woman who displayed such a proprietary interest in her gaoler.

As her companions embarked on a conversation that she vaguely recognized was domestic in content, Gabrielle studied Louise through lowered lashes. Louise Pelletier, Gabrielle decided, was the epitome of everything she admired in a woman—beautiful, stylish, confident of her femininity, and even more confident of her ability to converse easily with the enigma that was the male of the species. As she watched Louise dimple and flutter her eyelashes, the word *flirt* crossed Gabrielle's mind unbidden. After the Englishman had kissed her at Vrigonde, she had looked up the word in the dictionary. There was never any question in her mind that Louise Pelletier knew all that there was to know about flirting, and that she considered the Englishman worthy of her attention.

That surprising thought moved Gabrielle to direct a long, sideways glance at Cam. The man was handsome, she conceded. She had never denied it. But from the moment of their first encounter at Andely she had been conscious of some unspecified threat he had posed to her person. And she had been right to fear him, as subsequent events had proved. In his own setting, that threat seemed muted almost to the point of absurdity. He was laughing at something Louise had said and was more relaxed than Gabrielle had ever seen him. She felt her own lips begin to turn up and quickly stifled the half-formed smile, telling herself that although he had shown some kindness to her when he had held her in his arms moments before, he had also shown a ruthlessness that she would be a fool to forget. She was his prisoner, not his reluctant ward, as he had just indicated to the beautiful lady at his side.

Gabrielle became conscious that two pairs of eyes were studying her reflectively. When Louise walked slowly in a circle around her, she stiffened.

"Impossible!" disclaimed Louise.

"That word doesn't exist in my vocabulary," replied Cam easily. "If you can't do it, my dear, I'll find someone who can."

Louise gave a small, deprecating laugh. "Cam, you mistake my meaning. All I meant was that it won't be easy. Well, look at her." She captured Gabrielle's wrist and turned her hand over.

Confused, unsure of the direction the conversation had taken while she had been only half listening, Gabrielle stood as rigid as a statue. Her eyes dropped to the hand Louise displayed for Cam's inspection. When she saw her dirty, broken fingernails and calloused palms, she jerked out of Louise's grasp and quickly thrust her hands behind her back.

"It's not only the boy's garb," mused Louise, her eyes sweeping over Gabrielle's stiff posture. "It's the way the girl moves and holds herself. Well just look at the way she's stationed herself."

Three pairs of eyes dropped to Gabrielle's splayed, booted feet. Color heated Gabrielle's cheekbones. It was sheer bravado that brought her chin up. She'd met cruel remarks and stares in the *salons* of Paris. Nothing had ever shamed her as much as this cold, unfeeling appraisal. She blinked back the hot sting of incipient tears.

"And that stench!" Louise averted her nose. "What is it?"

"Sea spray and fish scales, I shouldn't wonder," said Cam and sniffed the sleeve of his rough, woolen jerkin. "A bath and a change of clothes will soon cure that particular failing."

He laughed and Louise laughed with him. Gabrielle stared at them both unblinkingly.

"Does she have any conversation worth mentioning?" asked Louise, smothering yet another giggle.

Belatedly Cam realized that Gabrielle was not party to their shared mirth. Too late he saw the sparks that flashed to green fire in her eyes. He had only time to grab her wrist and take a step in the general direction of the staircase before she let loose with a long and abusive description of her companions' physical and mental attributes, a description that would have shamed the sensibilities of a hardened soldier.

Louise's mouth gaped open. Cam's ears burned scarlet. He cupped a hand over Gabrielle's snarling mouth, clamped one arm around her waist and half dragged, half carried the struggling fury up two flights of stairs.

She knew as soon as he dumped her over the threshold why she was to be given that particular chamber. It was at the very top of the south tower, circular, and with impressive views over the Channel. It was also a prison from which she could foresee little hope of escape.

Pretending an indifference she was far from feeling, she sauntered to the great tester bed with its blue velvet hangings, and plumped herself, boylike, down on the soft feather mattress.

"Your maid is called Betsy," said Cam.

"Fine." Her eyes roved the interior, pointedly evading Cam's stare. She noted the three Brussels tapestries against the walls and the upholstered armchairs flanking the stone fireplace. It was evident to Gabrielle that someone had taken the trouble to make the room comfortable. It was no less of a prison for all that.

"I'll send Betsy to you to help you bathe and choose something suitable to wear for dinner."

"Fine." She did not deign to so much as glance in his direction.

Cam folded his arms and propped himself against the closed door, waiting for Gabrielle to notice him. After an interval, he began to lose patience.

"We intended no insult," he began diffidently.

Hostile eyes collided with his.

He began over. "Gabrielle, you take too much to heart. You are supposed to be my ward, for God's sake. It's the most natural thing in the world for a guardian to take an interest in his ward's dress and deportment. I was only playing a part."

She said nothing.

Cam's patience wore thinner. "You'd better make up your mind to it, Gabrielle. Over the next few weeks, you are going to learn to dress and conduct yourself like a lady. And if you ever, *ever*, use language like that again in my hearing, I shall wash your mouth out with soap and water, and that's a promise."

She was off the bed in a flash and standing toe to toe with him. He had to admire her courage.

"A lady!" she challenged. "I'm to become a lady! Like Louise Pelletier, I suppose?"

"Yes," said Cam cautiously.

"You want me to emulate her example?"

"Why not? If you really wanted to, you could learn to be like Louise."

She took a quick backward step and her eyes, insulting, baiting, swept over him. Cam's arms dropped to his sides and he came away from the door.

"You stink," she told him.

"What?" His frown was thunderous.

"Sea spray and fish scales I shouldn't wonder," she drawled. She placed thumb and forefinger to the bridge of her nose and pinched delicately.

"Gabrielle," warned Cam, and stopped when he suddenly realized what she was doing.

She grabbed his wrist and held it in front of her as if she had picked up a dead rat. "Tut tut," she said. "Englishman, I do believe you need a manicure."

"My name is Cam. Cam! It's about time you learned to say it."

She threw his hand from her. "I may yet call you Cam," she said scathingly. "But I'll never call you a gentleman! No more than I'd call that woman a lady! You think I don't recognize quality when I see it? If anything, she's worse than you are. Save your breath, and your energies, Englishman. I may not be much. But the last thing I want is to be like her, or you, for that matter."

She would have pivoted away, but he caught her shoulders and dragged her back to face him. His anger was equal to hers when he spoke. "You're right about one thing. You'll never be the equal of Louise. You haven't got it in you to be a woman, let alone a lady. But by God, you're going to give it a try. And my name is Cam, damn you, Cam! Now say it."

"Pig!" she spat at him.

He was furious at her defiance and would have shaken some sense into her. It was the sniff that froze him, a pathetic sound that pierced his anger. He suddenly saw himself as he must look to Gabrielle. He did not wish her to think of him as an unfeeling monster.

A tear squeezed from beneath the fans of her lowered lashes. "Gaby! No! I didn't mean it. Not one word of it!" He made a soft sound of protest when she tried to pull away from him. "Why do you persist in fighting me? If you would only give in! Give in, Gaby."

What he was demanding that she surrender was not clear to him. He gathered her close, easily subduing her slight show of resistance. His hands moved over her, possessively, fitting themselves to her shoulders, the valley of her waist, the soft flare of her hips, molding her closer, closer, as if he could protect her by making her one with his body. The thought sliced through the sensual fog that had begun to cloud his logic, startling him into immobility.

Gabrielle turned up her head. The uncertainty was back in her eyes.

He was still trying to decide what he should do about her, when the sounds of a commotion in the bailey reached them through the opened window.

And still Cam hesitated.

Lansing's voice rose on the air. "Cam! Cam! It's war!"

It was Gabrielle who put an end to his dilemma. She wrenched herself out of his arms and raced to the windows. She flung it wide.

"Where's Cam?" shouted Lansing.

All about him men were throwing their hats and caps in the air and cheering wildly.

Cam set Gabrielle away from the window and leaned out over the sill.

Catching sight of him, Lansing shouted, "It's war, Cam! His Majesty declared war on France two days since. It's war!" He did not try to hide his jubilation.

Cam shut the window, then looked toward Gabrielle. There was no uncertainty in her eyes now. She was as cold as a block of marble.

"I'm not your enemy," said Cam quietly.

"And I'm not your prisoner, I suppose?" Her voice was bitter with sarcasm.

"It doesn't have to be that way."

She forced a laugh. "You mean you want me to enjoy my captivity? I'm sorry to disoblige you, *Englishman,* but I owe you no loyalty. You are an enemy of France. That makes you my enemy, too."

She had needled him deliberately and was not sorry when he slammed out of the room. The scrape of the key in the lock was no less than she expected. She eased herself onto the bed and stared hard at the canopy overhead.

She hated those looks he gave her, when the blue in his eyes clouded and went dark. She didn't know how to read those glances. But there was something there, something totally masculine and predatory that frightened her almost as much as his unbridled anger. Violence, she thought. In her experience, it was the distinguishing mark of the male animal. She wished she could lay her hand to foil or pistol. A weapon. She needed a weapon to force the Englishman to keep his distance. But what?

Soon she would grow strong and think of some way she could return to France without bringing catastrophe down on Mascaron's head. But not now. She was too shaken, too confused, too tired to think of anything but sleep. Closing her eyes, she let her thoughts drift to Normandy.

It was well past midnight when Cam finally made his way along the gallery to Louise's chamber. The great hall was in shadow, the only light to illumine his way coming from the long windows high in the walls that overlooked the bailey, where he had set guards.

He was restless, he decided, and in a strange humor. She was the cause of it . . . that impossible child-woman who had turned his first night home into a disaster of the first magnitude. He grunted and thought viciously that whoever coined the ridiculous axiom that an Englishman's home was his castle should be forced to sit at dinner in Gabrielle de Brienne's company.

A shudder passed over him as the events of the last few hours came vividly to mind. He remembered the tureen of soup that had slipped from her fingers; the scoop of mashed potatoes that had come to rest on his shoulder, missing his face by inches; the glass of wine that had inauspiciously tipped into Louise's lap, occasioning a swift and vociferous exit of the poor lady; and the irreparable rent to Gabrielle's new gown, one for which he had paid a not inconsiderable sum, when she had caught the hem beneath the legs of her chair. But what angered him most was that when he had first caught sight of her as she had descended the turn in the stairs, he had been struck speechless. *His angel,* he'd thought then. Witch! he swore under his breath.

All of it was deliberate. He was sure of it. And he would have put a swift end to this veiled defiance if Simon had not pleaded on the girl's behalf. The poor child was still suffering the effects of her injuries, he had sworn, not least the damage that had been done to her ribs.

"Ribs?" asked Cam.

It was the first he had heard of it. His eyes flashed to Gabrielle. She gave him a pained smile and pressed her hand to her side, beneath the swell of her breasts. His conscience smote him. It was only later that he realized the girl was a born actress. She was thumbing her nose at him. Or punishing him. Or warning him in no uncertain terms to keep his distance.

He was grateful for the lesson. God knows what foolish fancies he'd begun to weave about the girl. Not for the first time he found himself fervently wishing that he had never set eyes on Gabrielle de Brienne.

Thank God he was to be given a respite. In the morning he would remove to London for the inevitable debate in the House now that war with France had been declared. Gabrielle was to be left in Lansing's custody for the fortnight Cam expected to be away. He ought to feel sorry for his friend. He searched his conscience and could not find it in himself to pity Lansing's plight. Lansing had a soft spot for the girl. But after the events of the evening Louise did not. He was counting on Louise to take some of the starch out of Gabrielle de Brienne. At the thought, Cam smiled.

When he came to Louise's door, Cam knocked

softly and entered. He was expected. She was dressed in a gauzy silk robe that revealed far more than it concealed. She welcomed him with a warm smile and outstretched arms. Cam's appreciative gaze slid slowly over her lush figure. He flashed her one of his lazy, intimate smiles. Here was a woman who knew how to be a woman. The scent from her hair filled his nostrils. Her skin was smooth and pampered. His dour humor lifted.

He stopped her mouth with hard, demanding kisses. He didn't want to talk. He didn't want to think. He wanted to lose himself in pleasure. He wanted to sate himself till the image of Gabrielle de Brienne was consigned to oblivion. Desire rose in him, hot and fast. He groaned and pulled Louise to the bed.

Chapter Nine

On May 18th, 1803, His Majesty, George III, in one of his more lucid moments, declared war on France. Five days later the House of Commons assembled to debate the position Britain had adopted. It was expected that those longtime parliamentary adversaries, William Pitt and Charles James Fox, Tory and Whig leaders respectively, would give the speeches of their lives. The gentlemen's clubs in St. James were deserted as all London hot-footed it to Westminster to gain admittance to the few seats reserved for the populace at large.

Cam's bored eyes traversed the packed galleries and he nodded occasionally in acknowledgement of the odd salute. There was not a space to be had. It was even rumored that parliamentary reporters who were tardy in finding their places had been unable to gain admittance. And no one could be persuaded to give up his place merely to ensure that the text of Pitt's speech reached the press for publication in the morrow's newspapers.

The debate had been going on for more than an hour, and Pitt had yet to put in an appearance. Cam stifled another yawn. He found it hard to share in the general excitement as the House waited for Mr. Pitt to arrive. He'd had more than his share of excitement in the last month or so. He wondered if anything of any note was happening in Dunraeden and decided it was better not to know.

His head was beginning to drop when he as awakened by shouts of "Mr. Pitt! Mr. Pitt!"

On the floor below, Cam watched Pitt stride to his usual seat on the third row behind the ministerial bench, next to one of the pillars. The House was impatient for him to take the floor. The speaker who held sway brought his argument to a summary conclusion and sat down. When Pitt rose to speak, he received a tumultuous cheer.

For all that Pitt's arguments for resumption of hostilities were predictable, Cam found himself hanging on every word in company with everyone else. Mr. Pitt never lost himself in the passion of his rhetoric. And yet a word here, a turn of phrase there, and all wedded to a logic that was irrefutable, and the man could convert almost anyone to his persuasion. Anyone, that is, but Mr. Fox, amended Cam as his eyes found that portly gentleman on the other side of the chamber, in the front row of His Majesty's opposition benches. And where Mr. Fox was, predictably, Richard Sheridan was to be found also.

An hour into Mr. Pitt's speech, and Cam could sense the seething indignation that gripped the spectators as Pitt catalogued a long list of grievances against the first consul of France. Not least among Bonaparte's transgressions were his methods of clandestinely obtaining information of a military nature. "Commercial agents," Pitt euphemistically called them. "Damn spies!" was the murmur that was taken up on both sides of the House. It was the one item in that long catalog of grievances that Pitt imbued with all the passion of which he was capable. Cam's conscience troubled him not one jot, though he was forcibly reminded that Mr. Pitt was some-times overnice in his notions and would never un-derstand, let alone sanction, his own unorthodox methods of influencing events.

Pitt spoke without interruption for almost two hours, with only a cursory look at his notes. He concluded by urging his listeners to recognize that the decision to renew the war was a solemn one, and that it should be waged not merely defensively, to stave off invasion, but offensively, to rid the world of a tyrant. When he sat down, the applause was tremendous.

All eyes now turned to Mr. Fox. But Fox, who had never, in anyone's memory, hesitated to follow a two-hour speech with a two-hour rebuttal, elected not to speak that evening. A motion to adjourn the debate until the following day was quickly agreed to, and the House adjourned early, shortly after ten o'clock.

In the lobby, Cam came face to face with Rich-ard Sheridan.

"Well, Dyson," said Sheridan, "I take it you fel-lows are feeling very pleased with yourselves after this night's work?"

"Very," agreed Cam.

The eyes of both men traveled to the figure of Mr. Pitt. He was mobbed by a host of admirers who were tendering their congratulations.

Sheridan continued, "Though it goes against the grain, I'll give the dog his due. I don't think I've heard Mr. Pitt in better form. Splendid oratory! Simply splendid!"

"My sentiments exactly," responded Cam. He caught sight of Castlereagh in the crush and made his excuses.

Sheridan detained him. "Shall you be in the House tomorrow to hear Mr. Fox?"

"I wouldn't miss it for the world."

From the pocket of his vest, Sheridan withdrew a gold-plated watch and made a show of studying the hands. "I'd best be off," he said. "Bad business, this. You have my sympathies." And with a bland smile he moved off, leaving Cam staring.

Outside the House, Cam was still mulling over Sheridan's cryptic remarks when he was joined by Castlereagh and Canning. Their talk was all of Pitt's incomparable speech. A hackney was found to take them to Pitt's residence on Baker Street, where Pitt was to join them as soon as he could get away.

It was Canning who doled out the drinks once they were shown into Pitt's study. "Nothing but port!" he said disparagingly, lifting the stopper of first one decanter, then another.

"Port will do fine," said Cam. It was generally known that Mr. Pitt rationed himself to two or three bottles of port daily. His friends gave out that it was for medicinal purposes. Pitt's health had never been very robust. Personally, Cam thought that Pitt's constitution was remarkable. There were few gentlemen of his acquaintance who could down a bottle of port and minutes afterward hold sway on the floor of the House and no one the wiser.

Talk was desultory until Mr. Pitt bustled in. One of his rare smiles suffused his face. For some few minutes, the conversation turned to Pitt's performance that evening. But Mr. Pitt was never comfortable with praise, however well deserved.

Accepting a glass of port from Canning's hand, he cut off Castlereagh by saying, "Gentlemen, good news from France." He drank deeply, and his colleagues waited patiently until his empty glass had been replenished. Finally, he said, "In spite of Bonaparte's posturings, the threat of imminent invasion is so remote as to be nonexistent. Though it

156

goes without saying that our vigilance will not relax one whit, information has been received that exactly pinpoints the disposition of the French fleet. Gentlemen," he looked from one to the other, gauging their reactions, "Gentlemen, we have it on unimpeachable authority that the French fleet is scattered to the four corners of the earth."

"What does 'unimpeachable authority' mean?" asked Canning, grinning from ear to ear. He already knew the answer.

"Spies," said Cam flatly.

"Delta, to be precise," responded Mr. Pitt.

Only Cam knew that Delta was the code name Rodier went by in England.

Castlereagh feigned disbelief. "What about that show you put on in the House earlier this evening, sir?"

Smiling, Pitt responded, "You are referring, I presume, to those remarks I made in passing about the French use of spies?"

"Harangue, more like," struck in Canning.

"My heart was just about busting with indignation and patriotic fervor mixed in equal parts," said the Viscount Castlereagh.

"As it was meant to," observed Cam. "As orators, we're all familiar with the ploy. Within minutes, Mr. Pitt had us all but eating out of his hand."

"Filthy business, spies," said Mr. Pitt with a deprecatory shrug of his shoulders. "But a necessary tool in times like these. Now, gentlemen, if you've had your fun? There's more to tell."

There was no doubt in Cam's mind that Rodier's informant was Mascaron. Only someone highly placed in the Ministry of Marine could have access to the sort of information that was passed along. From Rodier's report, it was obvious that the British declaration of war had caught Bonaparte napping, in spite of the arsenal and flotilla he had been assembling in the months before the truce was broken. Not only was the French fleet scattered, it was also numerically inferior to the British; its crews were inexperienced; and after the beatings they'd taken in the last number of years, an atmosphere of defeatism pervaded all ranks.

But Bonaparte was making up for his previous inertia. An army of workers was employed to build transports and invasion craft that could ferry more than a hundred thousand men across the Channel. There were plans for vast basins and artificial ports along the coast, some of them already under construction. Before the year was out, Bonaparte was determined that he would launch his invasion fleet against Britain.

"Things look grim, indeed," commented Canning when Mr. Pitt came to the end of his recital.

"Agreed," he responded. "But there are two things in our favor."

"Which are?"

"Admiral Nelson, for one. The French can't match him, and they know it. And of course," again he gave his companions one of his rare smiles, "the vagaries of the English climate. That typically filthy weather in the Channel that we normally deplore may yet turn out to be England's salvation."

From there, the conversation veered to Mr. Fox's speech slated for the following day. A month before it had appeared crucial to have Mr. Fox's support for the war with France. But in a few weeks much had happened to change the tenor of public opinion, not least Bonaparte's bid to have himself declared emperor. By that injudicious act he had forfeited much of the goodwill he had once generated among England's lower classes. A hereditary monarchy, though far from perfect, was infinitely more preferable to out-and-out dictatorship.

Cam listened idly as his colleagues speculated on what tack Fox was likely to pursue on the morrow's debate, and what their course should be if he endeavoured to disrupt the prosecution of the war. Inwardly, he was reflecting that he very much regretted that the final confrontation between the French and British navies was to be delayed, even for a few months. That circumstance necessitated Gabrielle de Brienne's remaining in his custody when, so he told himself, he could barely suppress his impatience to be rid of the chit. Perhaps then, when his plans came to fruition and he had returned her to France, he would be free to concentrate on other, more important matters.

As the conversation around him droned on, Cam began seriously to consider for the first time what Gabrielle's life would be like once she was restored to her homeland. By such time, of course, Mascaron would have paid the penalty for the part he had played in the September massacres. There would be no one there to guide the girl, no one to look out for her interests. And if anyone needed someone to look out for her and ease her way in society, thought Cam, that person was Gabrielle de Brienne.

Cam was unprepared for the shock of self-recrimination that suddenly swamped him. The girl would be bereft at the loss of her grandfather and would have no one to turn to. Goliath, her watch dog, he completely discounted. The man was without influence. Loyalty had its place, but all the loyalty in the world would not save Gabrielle de Brienne if some powerful figure in French society decided to make her his prey. In all likelihood she would once again become a fugitive.

The drift of his thoughts made him uncomfortable and restless. In no time at all he had taken an absentminded leave of his companions and was striking out for Hanover Square, the problem of what to do about Gabrielle de Brienne still revolving in his mind. That the problem would be solved if he spared Mascaron never once occurred to him. That plan had been too long in the making, was too close to his heart, for Cam to question its wisdom. His thought ran more on the lines of keeping Gabrielle with him, making her his ward in very truth, fitting her to take her place not in French society but in his own circles.

The more he thought of it, the more merit the enterprise seemed to gain. He was not some monster without conscience who could set the girl adrift to face an uncertain future back in France. She was innocent of any wrongdoing, and he was not one to shirk an obligation, however unpleasant. True, Gabrielle would not thank him for his pains. But then, he had no intention of taking her into his confidence. And by the time she divined his purpose, perhaps she would be more reconciled to her fate.

For the first time since Gabrielle's abduction, Cam felt as if a dead weight had been lifted from his heart. He was going to make everything right, he promised himself: the loss of her homeland, those moments of terror she had been forced to endure when Rodier's agents had been hounding Mascaron.

His mind raced ahead to the time when he would be finally relieved of responsibility for the girl. That day would come with a brilliant match to some titled gentleman, thought Cam. Lord Lansing's name immediately came to mind and was instantly rejected. Though Cam was aware that Simon was attracted to Gabrielle, he did not see, in all conscience, how he could permit Simon to take on such a termagant. Gabrielle, he was persuaded, would run rings round his friend. The man who would be lord and master of Gabrielle de Brienne must be made of sterner stuff than poor, softhearted Simon. The girl needed a firm hand and a will stronger than her own. He was sure he did not know where he was to find such a paragon.

As was to be expected, the Commons was packed to the rafters the following evening when Charles Fox rose to address the House. Though other members of parliament had contributed to the debate, everyone there knew that it was the contest between Pitt and Fox that was the drawing-card. This time, the parliamentary reporters were on hand, their pencils poised over their notebooks as Fox made his opening remarks.

Cam was sure he had never heard a better speech. It was at once lucid yet full of subtleties, scathing yet outrageously witty, and above all, elevated in scope. Where Mr. Pitt had taken the narrow view, Fox addressed himself to universal principles. Where Pitt advocated an unrelenting aggression, Fox advocated inexhaustible negotiation, but he left the door open for armed conflict when absolutely necessary.

Cam's respect for the man increased apace. Without alienating his supporters or rousing their suspicions, Fox was charting a new course for the Whigs. It was, thought Cam with something like a sneer, a rather unscrupulous though brilliant stratagem for a man who professed an unshakable commitment to the lofty ideals he preached. But Cam had never underestimated Mr. Fox's ability to use whatever means were necessary to pursue his own goals. In that one respect they were not dissimilar.

Fox spoke for three hours. When the House divided, the Tories carried the day by a massive margin. But no one felt sorry for Fox. On all sides, the man was acclaimed as a genius. The principles he had espoused in his speech, so some said, would be a lasting legacy to the nation. In short, thought Cam, though Mr. Fox had lost the vote, he had won the debate with Pitt hands down.

Cam was one of the first on hand outside the Chamber to congratulate Mr. Fox on his brilliant address.

"Oh, don't run away, Dyson," said Fox as Cam edged away to make room for a mill of well-wishers. "There's someone who is quite anxious to have a few words with you about the girl you abducted from France." He was distracted momentarily by the crush of his admirers. "We can't talk here," he said. "I'll be in my rooms later this evening. You know where to find me. It's in your own best interests to be there, Your Grace."

To say that Cam was thunderstruck would be an understatement. He was shocked speechless, though by no means at a loss as to how he should explain Gabrielle's reluctant presence at Dunraeden if called to account. Against that eventuality, he already had a story prepared. But so great was his surprise in that moment that he momentarily lost his bearings. When he came to himself, Mr. Fox had turned away.

It was, thought Cam, an invitation he would be a fool to refuse. It was imperative that he discover how much Fox knew about Gabrielle. Not for one moment did he suppose that Fox knew the whole of it. If he had, Cam did not doubt that he would have used that knowledge not only to ruin him but to embarrass all of Pitt's Tories as well. But Fox knew something. And the source of that information was something Cam was hopeful of discovering.

When Cam presented himself at Fox's rooms in Clarges Street he was shown into a small anteroom. Sounds of what gave every evidence of being a victory party wafted on the air. Within minutes of his arrival, the door opened to admit Mr. Fox. He stepped aside to permit another portly gentleman to proceed him into the room. It was George, Prince of Wales.

"Your Royal Highness," said Cam, rising to his feet.

"Dyson," acknowledged the prince affably.

The heir to the throne seated himself and languidly motioned the other gentlemen to follow his example. A few pleasantries were exchanged, but the prince could never be comfortable with men of Dyson's stamp, and it showed in his restless gestures and shifting eyes.

The Duke of Dyson was no friend to him, thought the prince, which was why he had consented to lend his support to Charles Fox's designs. Dyson was a Tory and was to be lumped with Mr. Pitt and all his troublesome disciples. George, Prince of Wales, was not forgetting that it was the Tories who for years had refused to vote sufficient funds to keep him in a style befitting one in his position. They could not conceive the expenses he had incurred to make his palace, Carlton House, a showplace for the nation. Extravagant, they called him. Grim-faced, unimaginative boors, he thought them, with their noses always to the grindstone. They had no notion of how to indulge in the things that made life so eminently worthwhile and satisfying.

Nor could he forgive Mr. Pitt for keeping the Regency from him when His Majesty, George III, was almost totally incapacitated by fits of madness. One day there would be a reckoning. And if he had anything to say about it, Pitt and his disciples would be booted out of office and he would install those who had proved their friendships for him. Charles Fox and Richard Sheridan came immediately to mind.

The smile that lit up the prince's childishly plump face was just short of gloating, thought Cam, and he waited patiently for the cat and mouse game to begin. His own views of the prince could be summed up in few words. "A fribble with no substance to him." His Royal Highness was easily led, however, and it was Charles James Fox who pulled on the leash. Though his posture was relaxed to the point of indolence, Cam was as alert as he had ever been.

It was Mr. Fox who opened the game. "The strangest story has reached my ears, Dyson," he said, breaking the silence.

"So I surmise from the remarks you made in the lobby of the House," answered Cam, deliberately taking the initiative out of Fox's hands. "Respecting my ward, from what you said."

"Your . . . ward?" intoned the prince politely.

"Yes, my ward, Gabrielle de Valcour," said Cam, and immediately launched into the story he had rehearsed. Gabrielle de Valcour, he began, was the last surviving member of his stepmother's family. When he'd been in France, he'd discovered, sadly, that the rest of the Valcours had perished during the Revolution. The girl had been raised in the direst poverty by strangers. Her plight had moved him to pity. In other circumstances, lawyers would have arranged for the transfer of the girl to his custody. As it was, with the outbreak of hostilities threatening, he'd followed the only course open to him. He'd abducted her in his yacht and made haste for Cornwall.

"Abducted," mused Fox. "That much I believe, at

least. From all reports, you treated the girl abominably."

"Strange as it may seem," said Cam imperturbably, "Gabrielle had no wish to leave France. I was sorry to have to use a minimum of force to compel her obedience."

"Minimum," scoffed Fox. "My sources say otherwise."

"Give me the names of these sources," said Cam, "and I'll confront them in person."

Fox laughed. "I'd wager you would, too! But I wonder what the girl has to say for herself?"

"She'll say what I've already told you."

"Terrified into submission, is she?"

The prince's languid drawl interrupted, "All this is beside the point, gentlemen, surely?"

"Yes," said Cam, "I was hoping we would get to the point before very long. What exactly *is* the point, Mr. Fox?"

It was the prince who replied. "Dyson," he said, "at the very least you've compromised a girl of gentle birth."

"I beg your pardon?" said Cam, taken aback. This was one ripple that had never occurred to him.

The prince looked a question at Mr. Fox.

"My dear sir," said that gentleman, uncrossing one grotesquely plump, silk-stockinged leg and crossing the other over it, "There's a witness to what transpired aboard your yacht. It is known that you shared a cabin with the lady for four nights in a row."

"And for a very good reason," said Cam. "As I've already told you, Gabrielle did not wish to be rescued. And if I did stay with her in the cabin, it was to prevent her from escaping."

"My dear Dyson," reproved the prince mildly, "I

believe you. But facts are facts."

"What you don't seem to understand is that your abduction of this French girl has placed England in a most delicate position."

"England!" exclaimed Cam on a startled bark of laughter. "You'll forgive me, Mr. Fox, if I say I take leave to doubt that."

"Look at it this way," said Fox. "Whether or not the girl is your ward, you have abducted a citizen of France. Did you force the girl to become your mistress?"

Cam almost laughed in relief. It was evident that Fox had no conception of who Gabrielle was or what her significance was to him. Still, he sobered almost instantly. He was beginning to discern the stakes in Fox's game. Gabrielle was to be used as leverage to force him to do something he did not wish to do. But what? he wondered. Calmly, dispassionately, he stated, "The girl is my ward, not my mistress."

The prince was on his feet. His companions were obliged to follow suit. In a bored voice, he said, "This is easily settled. Is the girl French or is she not?"

"She is," answered Cam at once.

"Then you leave me no option. I demand that you give the girl into my custody as soon as may be. From this moment on she will be under my protection."

"Your . . . protection?" murmured Cam. "I scarcely think that proper, Your Highness."

The Prince of Wales stiffened. "I meant, of course, as a temporary measure. When we are satisfied that there is no foundation to these rumors, then your . . . *ward* . . . will be returned to you forthwith. Should you balk at this, Dyson, speculation must become more vicious than it already is."

Cam's eyes were mere slits. "I have no objection," he said mildly.

"Then that's settled, then."

Cam snapped to attention and bowed gravely. "Your Highness," he intoned. His smile was patently ironic.

With a curt nod of dismissal, the prince quit the room.

"England, Mr. Fox?" Cam murmured softly. "I would never have guessed that you were addicted to hyperbole."

"Don't be a poor loser, Dyson," said Fox easily. "And I promise you, I'm not exaggerating. A few questions raised in the House and this could quite easily turn into an international incident of the first magnitude. And you know Pitt won't take kindly to the Whigs breathing down his neck, not when England is about to prosecute the war with France."

"Correct me if I am wrong, but I take it that I may count on your discretion if . . . what exactly are you after, Mr. Fox?"

"I think it's time you took a holiday."

"A holiday?"

"From politics."

"Ah!" said Cam, smiling. "I'm flattered that you see me as such a threat to your party."

"Oh, not to my party, to England. You'll observe I don't underestimate your talents."

Fox's hand was on the door handle, as he too prepared to quit the room.

"A moment, Mr. Fox, if you would be so kind," drawled Cam. "Should I decide to follow your advice and take a holiday from politics, what is to be my reward?"

"Reward?"

"What happens to Gabrielle?"

"Oh, her fate rests with the prince now. But rest

167

assured, no harm will come to her. As for yourself, you've estates in Yorkshire as well as Cornwall, as I remember. You'll have all the time in the world now to make them a showplace. Do what you like, sir, as long as you retire from politics, and I give you my word that we Whigs shall hold our peace on the matter. I'll give you a few minutes to recover your equilibrium."

Fox smiled and shut the door softly as he exited. He caught up with the prince in his study.

"Well?" asked His Royal Highness, raising a glass of ruby red liquid to his lips. Before imbibing, he inhaled slowly, savouring the bouquet of the burgundy.

Fox grinned. "I've got him this time, if I'm not mistaken. Thank you, Your Highness, for your intervention."

"A trifle," demurred the prince. "I was happy to be of service. You don't think Dyson will marry the girl and bring your hopes to ruination?"

Fox's bushy eyebrows shot up. "The girl may be of gentle birth, but she's anything but gently bred. From all reports, she's a veritable Hun. She may do very well in the role of mistress, if one has a taste for a rough ride, but as Dyson's duchess? I think not. The man has too much conceit to shackle himself to such an ineligible connection."

"You may be right, Charles," allowed the prince. He was far from sharing Mr. Fox's convictions, however. He was thinking that he and Fox had both formed ineligible connections in their time. Mr. Fox had married his mistress, an actress whose sexual favors at one time they had both shared. He thought of his own dear Maria, Mrs. Fitzherbert, his secret, morganatic wife whom he had discarded, more or less, when that coarse, obscene sloven, Caroline of Brunswick, had been forced upon him.

168

Tears filled his eyes, and a shudder or revulsion passed over him.

It was Pitt's doing. The marriage was to have brought him money. And so it had. But Pitt and his Tories had given with one hand and taken away with the other. Half a million pounds in debt and all of it to be repaid, and at four percent! He, the Prince of Wales, heir to the British throne, had tottered on the brink of financial ruin for years. Fortunately, Parliament had finally bailed him out of his difficulties, but again the Tories had dragged their heels. Pitt! The man was his nemesis.

The prince let out a long sigh and asked morosely, "What exactly do we hope to gain, Charles, if we are forced to discredit Dyson?"

"I beg your pardon, Your Highness?"

It was evident that Fox, no less than himself, had been lost in his own reveries, and the prince remembered that Pitt was Fox's nemesis also. He repeated the question.

Fox shifted his great bulk, and the prince could not help remarking inwardly that though he himself had put on a few stone in the last number of years, in comparison to his old friend he was as thin as a reed. The thought cheered him materially, until he remembered Dyson's spare muscular physique. He noted that two of the buttons on his waistcoat were straining in their buttonholes. He frowned and sucked in his stomach.

"If I know anything of Mr. Pitt," answered Fox, "Dyson's influence will be at an end. He'll be an embarrassment, a millstone to his party. They'll drop him."

"I thought it was Pitt you were after."

Mr. Fox evinced some surprise. He gave a low laugh and topped up the prince's half empty glass. "Mr. Pitt is a devil I know. He holds no surprises for me. No, Your Highness. It's Dyson who is my quarry this time."

The prince sipped thoughtfully. After an interval he asked, "What has Dyson ever done to you?"

"To me? Nothing that I know of. It's the broad view I'm taking. He can't be much more than thirty, wouldn't you say?"

"What of it?" asked the prince.

"It's my considered opinion that the man is something of a fanatic. He's close to the center of power as it is. He has years ahead of him in which to shape Parliament and government policies to suit his own ends."

The prince had a vision of Dyson standing in Pitt's place for the next twenty or thirty years, and in particular, for the duration of his own reign as England's next monarch. "Good God!" he exclaimed. The picture terrified him. He bolted his drink without thinking. "Charles," he said with feeling, "you're a farseeing man."

Fox laughed. "Shall we return to my guests, Your Highness?"

"Beg pardon?"

"The party expects me to do my duty," droned Fox.

The prince looked at him blankly. A burst of laughter, followed by several resounding cheers, split the air. "Oh *that* party!" said the prince, shaking his head. "You and your puns, Charles!"

Mr. Fox swallowed a sigh and followed his prince from the room.

Chapter Ten

The Englishman was back, and at the sight of him Gabrielle felt the familiar quiver of unease deep inside. She and Lord Lansing, Simon as she now called him, were taking a turn around the castle battlements when he came in through the north gate. She did not know how she knew, but she sensed, when he looked up and caught sight of her, that he was in a towering temper. His eyes, she thought, would have flared to that dangerous hue that always betrayed the turbulence of his emotions. Shivering, she drew closer to Lansing.

"He's back," she said, "and he's in a foul temper."

"Who's back?" asked Lansing. "Not Cam, surely?" Lansing turned to the inside wall that overlooked the bailey. "By Jove, it is Cam! I wonder what's brought him back so early?"

The pleasure that Lansing so obviously experienced at the duke's return was not shared by his companion. The blissful interlude she had enjoyed in the Englishman's absence was about to end. Gabrielle thought of the liberties Lord Lansing had allowed her in the past number of days and stifled a sigh of regret. She did not think that the Englishman would prove so lenient a gaoler.

When she entered the great hall on Lansing's

arm, his first words to Lansing confirmed her conjecture.

"Am I to understand that Gabrielle has been given the run of the place in my absence?"

Not for a moment was Gabrielle misled by the deliberately casual tone. It was otherwise with Lord Lansing.

Before answering, he clapped Cam on the back and greeted him effusively. Gabrielle was surreptitiously edging her way to the stairs that led to her chamber when Lansing caught her wrist and drew her forward.

"Gabrielle was bored to tears with her confinement, Cam. She's not much of a reader and she's never had the leisure to learn how to do embroidery and such like. She was going out of her mind stuck away in that tower chamber until I had the notion to show her Dunraeden."

Gabrielle shifted uneasily under Cam's unwavering stare. It had been no great feat to have Lord Lansing fall in with her designs and deceive him into thinking that it was she who was falling in with his. For a full week, she had familiarized herself with every nook and cranny of the great fortress. Her purpose in learning everything there was to know about how Dunraeden was supplied and managed was far from innocent. Escape was her object. She looked into Cam's eyes and hoped that her game had not been divined.

"Has she been outside the walls?" asked Cam. He held Gabrielle in his inflexible stare.

"Not yet," answered Lansing.

"Not ever," said Cam. There was a slight relaxation in his stance. His lips turned up in a parody of a smile. "Gabrielle," he said, "I scarce would have known you," and his gaze traveled the length of her, from the unexceptional white muslin, with

172

its low, square neckline and puff sleeves, to the satin ribbons atop her cluster of gold ringlets.

"Your Grace," she said, and curtsied so deeply that the gesture was almost an insult. She noted the slight clenching of the Englishman's jaw and wondered at the turn in her nature that provoked her to such recklessness.

Lansing was oblivious to these hostile undercurrents. He gazed fondly at Gabrielle. "As you see, Cam, we've made remarkable progress. Gabrielle is as fine a lady as you'll ever find . . . when she wants to be," he added with a chuckle.

Gabrielle fluttered her eyelashes and Cam grunted.

"Where's Louise?" he demanded, and pivoted away from them to stalk to the staircase.

"She's about somewhere," said Lansing.

Cam took the stairs two at a time. From the gallery above he called down, "Find her, Gabrielle, and have her wait for me in the library. And Simon, I'll see you in my chamber directly. *Now,* Simon, if you please."

Lansing turned a puzzled look upon Gabrielle. "What's got into him, I wonder?"

"I told you he was in a temper," said Gabrielle.

"Cam? In a temper? You must be mistaken. I've never seen him shaken from his habitual sangfroid."

"He's shaken now," said Gabrielle, nodding her head wisely.

Lansing's smile was slightly superior. "When you know him better, Gabrielle, you'll understand how absurd that comment is. Cam is as solid as the rock of Gibralter. He's a stranger to the volatile emotions that plague us lesser mortals."

Gabrielle's eyes widened at Lansing's words, but she thought better of contradicting him. On the subject of the Englishman's character, she had dis-

173

covered that she and Lord Lansing could never agree.

"Simon," roared the voice of the man who never lost his temper.

"I'd best go to him," said Lansing and hastened to answer the impatient summons.

Gabrielle wandered up to find Louise. She came face to face with her on the last set of stairs.

"You're wanted in the library," said Gabrielle. "The Englishman's come back."

"Cam's home?" asked Louise, for once her cold and haughty demeanour warming at the edges.

Gabrielle was under no illusion that the warmth was for her benefit. In the week since the Englishman had absented himself, Louise Pelletier had made no attempt to disguise her dislike. Nor had Gabrielle's subsequent behaviour endeared her to that lady. Since she was considered farouche to the point of barbaric, Gabrielle had taken every opportunity to ensure that Louise's expectations were not disappointed. In this, at least, she was consistent. For with Lord Lansing, whose expectations were so diametrically different from Louise's, she had conducted herself in an exemplary fashion.

"He's in a filthy temper," offered Gabrielle. She wasn't warning the other woman of what she might expect. In some way she was testing the waters, trying to discover if she were the only one in the whole of Dunraeden who had the knack of interpreting the Englishman's moods. Evidently she was.

"How little you know him!" scoffed Louise, and swept by her.

Gabrielle shrugged philosophically and mounted the stairs. She wasn't sorry to see the Englishman in a pucker, just so long as he kept his distance from her. Without volition she shivered, remembering that there were other incomprehensible moods that seemed to come upon him that she found infinitely more menacing than a mere display of temper.

In her chamber she found Betsy, the maid who had been assigned to her. Gabrielle had developed a fondness for Betsy, not least because Betsy lavished her with an unquestioning affection. Like a mother hen with her chick, Betsy cajoled, ordered, and, when all else failed, shamed her young charge into doing her bidding. Gabrielle was not averse to the rough mothering Betsy administered.

As Betsy bustled about readying towels and arranging a screen in front of a huge copper tub, Gabrielle lowered her brows. "I had a bath yesterday," she protested.

"Ye stink of fish," answered Betsy without a glance in Gabrielle's direction. She tested the bath water with her elbow.

Lifting one bare arm to her nose, Gabrielle sniffed delicately. "Only faintly," she said. "What of it?" and remembered this time not to shrug her shoulders. "It was you, yourself, who smothered me in that foul smelling salve." Grinning, she offered, "I may not smell very wholesome close to, but my skin is as soft as a baby's bottom. Even my hands are losing their callouses." It was that more than anything that made her persist, every night, with Betsy's foul-smelling salve. It took hours to air her chamber in the morning, so strong and lingering was the stench of fish oil.

"That's as may be," said Betsy, her eyes twinkling, "but the master is home now. He'll not take kindly to his ward smelling like a barrel of fish."

She advanced upon her charge and in a no-nonsense manner relieved Gabrielle of her garments. Her eyes carefully scrutinized Gabrielle's bare skin, as if, thought Gabrielle, she were selecting a plump

175

goose for Christmas dinner.

"Ye're healing nicely," she observed, and urged Gabrielle into the tub. "We'll leave off the salve until it's time for bed. But mind, in the morning, when ye're at your ablutions, wash every last lick of it off your skin."

"Can't I at least rub it into my hands?" asked Gabrielle, studying that portion of her anatomy. "Look, Betsy," she said, holding out her hands for the maid's inspection. "They're getting to be as white and as soft as flounders."

"Aye, and they stink like them, too! Now mind my words. Ye're to leave off that salve until it's time for your bed."

For the next few minutes, Gabrielle gave herself up to the sensual pleasures of the fragrant bath water.

"He's in a towering temper, you know," she remarked at length.

"Who?"

"The Englishman."

Betsy's brows drew together.

"The duke," amended Gabrielle quickly.

"The master never loses his temper," said Betsy in the voice of one who is well versed in such matters.

Gabrielle slipped into a meditative silence, remembering each and every occasion when the Englishman had displayed a ferocity that would have shamed a bear with a sore tooth.

Her ablutions completed, Gabrielle obediently allowed herself to be helped out of the tub. A voluminous towel was wrapped around her and she was led to the bed, where once again Betsy examined the many cuts and abrasions that Gabrielle had sustained in her fall from the cliff. As she waited patiently for the older woman to satisfy herself, Ga-

176

brielle made her own appraisal.

Betsy was, as close as Gabrielle could make it, something over forty, but not so old as Mascaron—she had never had an aptitude for estimating ages. Her skin was sallow but not as swarthy as the Englishman's, and her dark hair under her mob cap was shot liberally with silver. As servants went, she was a law unto herself. There was only one person whose word carried any weight with Betsy, and that was her master. The other servants went a little in awe of her by virtue of the fact that Betsy held the longest tenure of any of Dunraeden's retainers. As Gabrielle heard tell, as a young girl, Betsy had helped bring the Englishman into the world. There was an affection there that Gabrielle had discovered would not permit of anyone to say one word to her master's disparagement. And Gabrielle was far too wise a girl to make an enemy of one of the few friendly faces she had found at Dunraeden. Nevertheless, she was too curious about this blind devotion to maintain her silence.

"Why do you say that the master never loses his temper?" she asked, careful to couch her question as inoffensively as possible.

Satisfied that all was well with her charge, Betsy slapped Gabrielle on the bare buttocks and bade her get dressed. She surveyed Gabrielle thoughtfully. "I wish he would lose his temper," she said. "It's years since he's shown his real feelings about anything."

Gabrielle presented her back so that Betsy could do up the long row of tiny buttons on her gown. "I don't think I understand," she said over her shoulder.

Betsy sighed. "There was a time when he was more like the rest of us. But he closed himself off after he lost his mother and sister."

Cam had told Gabrielle very little of his French stepmother and half sister. She knew only that it was this connection that was to explain her own presence at Dunraeden. She was his ward, so he gave out, because she was the last surviving Valcour. Every other member of the family had perished during the Revolution. Betsy's words made her curious to discover more.

"What happened to his stepmother and sister?" she asked.

"No one knows." Betsy moved about the chamber, folding wet towels and putting Gabrielle's things away. "He went to France in '92 to bring them home. They were murdered in those prison massacres. He stayed on. When he came back to Dunraeden I scarcely recognized him. He never smiled, never laughed, never lost his temper. It was like it used to be when he was a lad."

Gabrielle thoughtfully absorbed Betsy's words. "What was he like when he was a lad?" she encouraged.

"Lonely." And slowly, haltingly, Betsy began to relate the events of Cam's childhood.

The picture her words evoked touched Gabrielle's heart. She wasn't thinking of the Englishman. She was thinking of a small, motherless boy who had reconciled himself to his father's frequent absences and a long string of governesses by withdrawing into himself. Her own early years with parents who lavished her with affection seemed blissful in comparison.

"What a cruel, unfeeling man his father must have been!" she struck in at one point.

"Not cruel," corrected Betsy, "at least, not deliberately. And when the old duke remarried, everything changed."

A moment later, Gabrielle found herself laughing

178

as Betsy recounted the gift the boy's stepmother had used to breach his reserve.

"A monkey!" she exclaimed.

"Aye," said Betsy. "A monkey, no less. And I tell ye, that creature was as near human as makes no difference. And as wicked." Her eyes gleamed with the recollection of it. "Lucifer by name, and Lucifer by nature. He led the young master a merry chase. He followed that devil o' a monkey from one scrape to another."

"And was that good?" asked Gabrielle, smiling.

"Oh aye," said Betsy. "Boys should be boys, and no paragons o' propriety."

"Somehow I can't imagine him as anything but a very proper person, even as a boy." She was remembering how easy it was to provoke him with curse words and a disregard for the niceties.

Betsy sighed. "Aye," she admitted sadly. "When he lost his mother and sister in France, it was as if the years between had never been."

"Of course," said Gabrielle with a flash of insight. "How could it be otherwise? Once again, he had lost the only people who meant anything to him." She could only guess at what the Englishman must have endured, for though she could remember vividly the loss of her own parents, Mascaron and Goliath had been there to fill the void.

"You're very fond of him, aren't you?" asked Gabrielle absently. She was wondering what sort of man the Englishman might have become if the circumstances of his life had been different.

"Fond isn't the word," said Betsy gruffly. "I want what's best for him, 'tis all." She eyed Gabrielle consideringly. "She was your aunt, wasn't she?"

"Who?"

"The master's stepmother. You have the same name."

Gabrielle became involved in arranging her hair. Studiously avoiding Betsy's scrutiny she replied, "Yes, we have the same name. But I never knew her." She was embarrassed to deceive someone who had shown her nothing but kindness, but the Englishman had warned her that if she once deviated from the story he had fabricated, she might well be endangering Mascaron's life.

"Ye're like her in some ways," observed Betsy, taking over the task of taming Gabrielle's wayward ringlets. "There, that should do it." She studied Gabrielle's reflection in the looking glass before stepping away. "D'ye know what I think?"

"What?" asked Gabrielle.

The oddest smile creased Betsy's plump cheeks. "I think ye may be like yon monkey. Aye. Ye'll lead the master a merry chase if I know anything."

Surprise held Gabrielle silent, and by the time her lips had framed the questions that jostled her thoughts, Betsy had slipped away.

As might be expected, Betsy's confidences respecting Cam caused a rent in Gabrielle's determined dislike of her captor, and she was left to wonder if Betsy had contrived that very end. If so, she had been remarkably successful, for Gabrielle could not now think of him without experiencing a very natural regret for all that he had endured as a child and for the catastrophic events that had overtaken him as a young man. When she found herself conjecturing how she might breach the shell he had constructed around himself, she pulled herself up short. The man was her enemy. He wasted no sympathy on her unhappy plight. And she would be a fool not to extend to him the very same courtesy.

Such were her thoughts when she received a summons to attend His Grace in the library. She encountered Lord Lansing on the gallery.

"God, I don't know what's got into him," he said.

"What happened?" she asked.

"You don't have to do anything you don't wish to do. Remember that. I'll support you, whatever you decide."

The terse words alarmed her. "Simon, what. . . ?"

"Gabrielle!" Her heart lurched. She looked over the balustrade. The Englishman stood framed in the open door of the library.

"Come down, Gabrielle. I want a word with you," he commanded.

"You'd best go on down," advised Lord Lansing, and brushed by her.

Squaring her shoulders, she slowly descended, her hand lightly skimming the stair rail. At the bottom, she halted. Louise Pelletier, eyes flashing with some emotion, retreated from the library. Not a word was exchanged as Louise pushed past her and ran up the stairs.

Gabrielle's steps became even slower as she approached the tall figure who held the door for her. She drew level with him and resisted the impulse to scoot by. As if she were practicing with a stack of books on her head, she sailed into the library and turned to face him. She wished that Betsy could see how those eyes smoldered when they were trained on her. She swallowed, thinking herself a deranged woman for the flight of fancy she had previously entertained. The man who towered over her so intimidatingly had never been a boy, she decided. Her sympathies should be all for herself.

"Sit down," he said curtly.

She was happy to oblige, for she felt her legs buckling beneath her. When he moved to sit behind the enormous desk, some of the tension went

181

out of her.

Leaning on his elbows, his long fingers clasped in front of him, he regarded her steadily. Very slowly and deliberately he said, "Circumstances make it imperative for us to wed as soon as possible."

Her mind made the connection instantly. The duke and Louise Pelletier were about to be married. She wasn't surprised. From the first moment she had seen them together, she had sensed a romance. She waited expectantly.

"What?" he asked in an amused tone. "You've nothing to say on the matter?"

Cautiously, she said, "My felicitations."

There was a silence. "Flippancy does not become you," said Cam coldly.

Gabrielle shifted restlessly. By and large, she managed to converse in English with fair fluency. Occasionally, as at the present moment, certain nuances in the language escaped her. She tried another tack "What's the matter with Louise?" she asked.

He went as stiff as a poker. "We shall leave that lady out of this discussion, if you please."

Gabrielle signified, rather wonderingly, that she was very pleased to leave Louise out of the discussion, and waited for him to continue.

"It shall be a marriage of convenience, naturally," said Cam.

"Naturally," replied Gabrielle. She'd heard, of course, that the English followed very strange customs. And who was she to correct them? She was sure it was none of her business.

"An annulment should be very easily procured, say in a few months or so."

He was waiting for her to make some suitable reply. "An annulment sounds . . . lovely," she answered. Not for the world was she going to quarrel with him about something that was of no significance to herself.

"I've found a cleric who will perform the service."

"A cleric," she repeated, trying to look intelligent.

Cam smiled. "He's Church of England, but in the circumstances, I don't suppose it signifies to which dogma the priest subscribes. Do you?"

"No," she readily agreed. "Church of England sounds most . . . appropriate." Unless, of course, Louise was a Catholic. But Gabrielle discreetly chose not to voice that objection. Louise could take care of herself.

"He's to arrive later this evening. I took the liberty of procuring a special license."

His last observation was beyond her, but she fastened on the one thing she did understand. "So soon?" she asked for something to say.

"The sooner the better. As I told you, circumstances make it imperative for us to marry at once." He looked at her consideringly for some few minutes. Very gently, he asked, "Gabrielle, don't you wish to know what those circumstances are?"

"No," she replied. "It . . . it doesn't signify." It wasn't disappointment she was experiencing, she assured herself. The Englishman could marry Louise or Betsy or anyone else, for that matter, if he had a mind to, and with her blessings. But she did not think that she could sit in silence while he extolled the surpassing virtues of the lady of his choice. It was of no moment to her that Louise Pelletier's beauty was incomparable, her conversation unexceptionable, and her breeding beyond reproach. And she did not know why tears were beginning to burn the back of her eyes. "Shall . . . shall I wear something different for the occasion?"

He looked at her oddly, shook his head, then

183

pressed one hand to his temples. "What an unpredictable girl you are!" he said. "No. You don't need to change. What you are wearing will do fine."

Gabrielle was more than a little relieved to have escaped so lightly. She had expected to be taken to task for making so free of his domain in his absence. But during the long and silent dinner that followed it was evident that Lansing and Louise had not been as fortunate as she. Killing looks and terse monosyllables were the order of the day. Gabrielle deemed it politic to be on her best behaviour, and not even a spoon slipped from her fingers.

It was Betsy who came to fetch her when it was time for the ceremony. Gabrielle halted on the threshold of the chapel. Her eyes were immediately drawn to the handsome figure of the duke. He and Lansing were at the altar with their backs to her. In front of them stood the cleric in his black robes. Of the bride, there was nary a sign.

"Where's Louise?" Gabrielle asked Betsy, and hung back for some vaguely disturbing reason.

"Gone," she thought Betsy answered, and knew she must be mistaken.

Betsy urged Gabrielle forward, and she looked around with interest. Gabrielle had rarely seen the inside of a church. During the Revolution there had been religious persecutions, and churches were closed. Like everything else, her knowledge of the faith had come largely from Goliath. As she moved slowly forward, her eyes traveled from the stained glass windows to the arched roof, and finally lighted upon the candles and flowers at the altar. For one of the few times in her short life Gabrielle sensed a Presence. She was filled with awe.

When she went on her knees at the altar it was

184

not done as a matter of form. She wanted to pray, but no words came to her. It didn't matter. She was where she was supposed to be. Nothing, in that moment, could have persuaded her otherwise.

She was raised to her feet by the black-robed cleric. Smiling, he placed her hand in the hand of the man who stood, soberly and silently, waiting for her to notice him. She stood transfixed, staring deeply into his eyes.

The priest began. "Dearly beloved . . ."

As the words continued, everything became suddenly clear to her. She sucked in her breath and released it slowly. It was inevitable. The thought held her captive far more than the strong fingers which closed around hers so securely.

"Why did you marry me?" Gabrielle was furiously pacing in front of Cam. The gold ring on her finger felt like a leaden weight. The thing was done. And she still could not credit that she had allowed it to happen.

"As I told you, circumstances . . ."

"What circumstances?"

Cam eased himself back in his chair, and studied his wife calmly. For the sake of appearances she had been moved to the bedchamber that adjoined his own. He had been stunned speechless when the knock had come at his door and he had been invited to join her. He wasn't sure what to expect. His eyes roved the room and went unerringly to the portrait of Héloise de Valcour that hung above the stone mantle. As always, the lady in the portrait was smiling at him. He had a sense of benediction, and wondered at his fanciful turn of mind.

As if soothing a fractious child, he began a recital of the events that had forced his hand. On another level, he was thinking that he liked the way Gabrielle's long strides ate up distances. He liked the way her hair was unbound and flowed loosely about her shoulders. When he looked at her, he thought of thoroughbred racehorses, high-strung and restive. The jockey who meant to ride this little filly would need a firm hand on the reins. His eyes drifted slowly down her sleek length. He could not help remembering that beneath the loose-flowing wrapper her skin was tanned by the sun, her female contours as soft as butter. He wondered what it would be like to have those long legs wrap around him and hold him securely at the moment of crisis. Belatedly he reminded himself that he would never find out. Gabrielle de Brienne, now Gabrielle, Duchess of Dyson, thought of him the way she thought of sharks and man-eating tigers. But his thoughts had wandered too far to prevent the sudden tightening in his body.

"I can see how you save your own skin by this hastily contrived marriage. But how, pray tell, can this marriage of convenience possibly protect my grandfather?" She had stopped pacing and her eyes were boring into his as if she would see right into his soul.

Cam's lids drooped lower. "Use your head," he said. "If it ever becomes known that Mascaron's granddaughter is in England, and believe me, it will, if Charles Fox ever gets his hands on you, your compatriots will turn their attention to your grandfather. Not only will he become useless for my purposes, but his life won't be worth a fig."

His answer would have satisfied her except for one thing. "Why was it necessary to use my own name during that sham of a wedding ceremony? Why not simply marry me as Gabrielle de Val-

186

cour?"

Cam, himself, had been wondering about the very same thing. He had no satisfactory explanation to hand, but he wasn't about to reveal as much to Gabrielle. "There was no need not to use your own name," he said. "Only Lansing, Betsy, and the priest who performed the ceremony were present. I can count on their discretion. Of that you may be sure."

She looked to be unconvinced, and he said with some heat, "Good God! You surely don't think I want *you* for my duchess? How many times do I have to tell you? This is a marriage of convenience. As soon as your usefulness to me is over, the marriage will be annulled."

That much she did believe, but far from being reassured, she felt a pang of something she could not quite name. Not regret, of course, but an awareness of something in herself that a man of the duke's cultured tastes would always find repellent. She understood now why he had been in such a towering temper when he returned to Dunraeden. The thought of marriage to her must have been very hard to stomach. That thought led to another.

Swallowing painfully, she said, "I'm sorry about Louise."

"We shall keep Louise out of this conversation," he said, his tone as discouraging as he could make it. The problem of Louise had already been dealt with.

She chose to ignore his advice. "How much does she know?"

He did not wish to speak about Louise, especially not to Gabrielle. "Nothing," he said harshly. "And as I've told you, we shall keep Louise out of this conversation."

"You've told her *nothing?*" She was aghast, incred-

187

ulous. "How can you be so cruel?"

"Cruel?" It was Cam's turn to be incredulous.

"Haven't you explained to her that in a few months you'll be free to wed her?"

Thunderstruck, he stared at her. "Wed Louise? Are you mad?"

"But I thought . . ." She faltered.

"What did you think?"

Their eyes held. Unspoken messages seemed to blaze between them. Invisible currents eddied in the silence.

Softly, he observed, "There was never any question of my marrying Louise. Never! Do you understand?"

She didn't, and shook her head.

"Gabrielle?" Before he knew what he was doing, Cam held out his hand in a gesture of appeal. "Gabrielle?" he repeated more softly, his voice taking on a persuasively sensual color.

Gabrielle flinched away. Her eyes dropped. "I don't know what I thought," she said, backing away from him. "Forgive me. It's none of my business. How soon do you think it will be before I can go home to France?"

Jaw tensing, Cam snapped, "Not soon enough for my liking."

"Good. As long as we understand each other."

Cam rose to his feet slowly. He knew a dismissal when he heard it. He bowed gravely. "Sleep well, duchess," he said, and muttering an oath under his breath, he strode for the door to his own chamber.

It took a good hour and almost half a decanter of brandy before he had himself in hand. He did not know what was the matter with him, why he should be plagued by these vague feelings of disappointment. Everything had gone off much better than he had expected. Gabrielle had fallen in with his plans without so much as a murmur of protest. It was Lansing and Louise who had tried to deflect him from his purpose.

His interview with Lansing had started out well enough. After relating the details of his meeting with Mr. Fox and the Prince of Wales in London, they deliberated on how these gentlemen had come by their knowledge of Gabrielle.

"It could be anyone who was aboard your yacht," said Lansing finally. "Unfortunately, most of the men have dispersed or gone back to France to pursue their trade."

"My men don't carry tales," said Cam with unshakable conviction.

"No. Not as a rule. But . . ."

"But what?"

Lord Lansing gave his friend a very direct stare. "Perhaps someone took a disgust of you, Cam. Gabrielle was not a pretty sight when you hauled her on board."

A dark tide of color rose in Cam's neck. "Not by my design," he answered levelly. "She brought it on herself. At all events, I'd be obliged if you would question the men, discreetly, of course, and see what you can find out. In the meantime, we are left with the problem of what to do about Gabrielle."

Damn Lansing! thought Cam, stretching out his long legs and closing his eyes, reliving the scene in the library. Would he ever forget the shock of that moment when Lansing had offered to solve the problem of Gabrielle by marrying her himself?

"You're smitten with the girl," Cam accused, his voice edged with the bite of ridicule.

Grinning, Simon answered, "I plead guilty. And if I'm not mistaken, Gabrielle is not averse to me, either."

189

Very softly, Cam said, "Simon, it's out of the question."

"Why is it?"

"Because I say so."

The argument that followed had been ferocious on Lansing's part, restrained on Cam's, but inflexible for all that.

"Why does it have to be you?" demanded Lansing. "Could it be, Cam, that you're in love with the girl yourself?"

Cam smiled lazily. "It's because I'm not in love with the girl that it falls to my lot to marry her. She'd have you twisted around her little finger within hours of the ceremony."

They had not parted the best of friends, but Cam was adamantly determined to have his way in this. The man who put his ring on Gabrielle's finger would be the one to call the shots. And in the game he was playing, the stakes were too high to involve a third party. Lansing, if he were to become Gabrielle's husband, might easily change the game plan. Intolerable!

After the interview with Simon he'd wandered down to the library, where Louise was waiting for him.

Calmly, dispassionately, he gave Louise an expurgated version of the circumstances that forced him to take Gabrielle to wife, namely that his enemies were threatening to end his political career unless he did right by the girl.

Her face as white as a sheet, she stuttered, "But . . . but, oh no! You can't! Tell me it isn't true!"

"I must. And it is."

"But she's your ward! You did nothing wrong."

"True. But Mr. Fox and his cronies don't see it that way. And neither will Mr. Pitt."

He watched her through half-lowered lashes as

she flung herself away from him. When she turned to face him again her bosom was heaving.

"Marry her!" she exclaimed. "I don't believe it!" She forced a laugh, and shook her head. "You're not saying that you mean to make her your duchess, surely?"

Almost humorously, he replied, "I thought I just did."

"She'll make you a laughingstock!"

Cam said nothing, but his brows lifted.

Shock and temper overcame Louise's natural caution. Unchecked, the words spilled from her lips. "The girl is farouche! A hoyden! The sorriest excuse for a woman it's ever been my misfortune to encounter. I tell you, Cam, I can do nothing with her! The language she employs! The way she comports herself! And the stench of her is enough to empty any roomful of people whenever she enters."

Smiling faintly, Cam offered, "Simon does not share your opinion. But all this is beside the point. I've told you that I mean to marry the girl. That much I owe you. But I don't discuss my future wife with anyone."

His unperturbable manner as much as his words gave her pause. Her next thought sobered her. If she was not careful, she could lose him altogether. She dredged up a weak smile. "Forgive me," she said. "The last thing I expected to hear from you when I came into this room was that you meant to marry. I was taken by surprise, 'tis all."

A fleeting smile that did not quite reach his eyes touched his lips. "In the circumstances," he said with brutal frankness, "it's impossible for you to remain at Dunraeden."

Concealing her anger as best she might, she managed in a calm tone, "Naturally, I shall do whatever you wish."

The short of it was that she was to remove from Dunraeden that very day, and not even in the duke's fine carriage but in a hired vehicle so that no breath of scandal would attach to his nuptials. Only one thing mitigated Louise's disappointment. It was evident that Cam was entering a loveless marriage of convenience. Her place in his life might still be secure. That thought gave her confidence to make a small suggestion.

"I have friends at Falmouth I haven't seen in an age. It was my intention to visit them when the season was over. Until you invited me here, that is. If it's all the same to you, I should like to be conveyed to whatever suitable inn or hostelry may be found in Falmouth. From there, I can find my own way to my friends' place of residence."

As they both knew, Falmouth was only hours away from Dunraeden. Their liaison could continue discreetly and with scarcely a break. If she returned to London, it might be weeks, months, before Cam was free to join her.

He considered her silently for a long moment. "Why not?" he said at last, as if speaking to himself. "I have no wish to arbitrarily order your life. But, my dear, are you certain that you won't be bored to tears with what Falmouth has to offer? The shops, the entertainments are not what you are used to."

Whether or not he was warning her that she could not count on his visits was not clear. "My friends' society is all that I require," she answered, lowering her lashes. And the matter was left at that.

Remembering their conversation, Cam filled his empty glass from the brandy decanter and sat glaring into its amber depths. Meticulously he went over everything that Louise had said about Gabrielle. He'd wanted to throttle her for her venomous remarks. A ridiculous notion, he admitted, when he himself subscribed to the same views. Gabrielle was barely civilized and indubitably not the stuff of which duchesses were made. And she didn't want him. That much was obvious.

Morosely, he raised the glass to his lips and took a long swallow. He sat back in his brocade armchair and closed his eyes. There were times when it had seemed to him that Gabrielle was not unaffected by his presence. If that were true, then what it amounted to was that she didn't *want* to want him, any more than he wanted to want her. By degrees, his eyes opened. He inhaled deeply. Setting aside the glass in his hand, he rose unsteadily to his feet. A few strides took him to the adjoining door. He hesitated for only a moment, before opening it and passing through.

A lone candle guttered in its sprocket. She was sound asleep, her hair spread about her pillow in glorious disarray, one white arm drooping over the edge of the bed. She looked like an angel, thought Cam, and shut the door soundlessly behind him. He took a few steps into the room, his eyes taking in great vases of lilacs that he'd ordered Betsy to arrange for the occasion. He smiled and inhaled their scent.

His nose twitched, and he inhaled again. Fish! And pilchards, if he was not mistaken! As he approached the bed, the odor intensified. He looked down at Gabrielle and his teeth snapped together. Wordlessly, he lifted her drooping hand to his nostrils. The stench of fish almost gagged him. She had done this deliberately to keep him at bay!

He dropped her hand as if it were a hot poker and turned on his heel. A simple no would have sufficed, he thought savagely as he pushed into his own chamber. There was no necessity to go to such lengths to turn him away. Not only had he never had to force a woman into his bed, but he had never stooped to seduction, either. A woman came to him willingly, or she came not at all.

Woman!? What woman? he demanded of himself hotly. His wife was a mere child! And he was very glad that a *real* woman was waiting to welcome him with open arms only a short distance away. With quick, impatient movements, Cam quickly dressed himself as he thought of Louise. Within half an hour, he was making for Falmouth.

Chapter Eleven

In the Rue de Richelieu, just off the Rue de St. Honoré, in an upstairs chamber in one of the many coffee houses that proliferated in the area, two gentlemen sat at their ease sharing a bottle of Claret. One of those gentlemen was Joseph Fouché, Napoleon Bonaparte's former minister of police. The other gentleman, younger than his companion by a score of years or more, was one of his newer recruits, a certain Gervais Dessins. They were discussing recent events in London, where Dessins had his field of operations. For some time past, their conversation had revolved around Mr. Charles Fox, and in particular the debate between Fox and Pitt that had taken place some weeks before.

"A strange speech from a gentleman who has always been devoted to France's interests," observed Fouché. In his hand he held the text of Fox's speech, which he had been carefully studying. "One would almost believe that Mr. Fox has changed sides." He looked questionly at his companion.

Dessins uncoiled his long legs and stretched them out in front of him. Fouché's eyes absently observed the movement, but behind that negligent stare his mind was at work absorbing everything about his subordinate, from the tips of his immaculate topboots to the elegant tailoring of his dark cutaway

195

coat and the snowy neckcloth that was arrayed to perfection. Dessins, Fouché noted approvingly, had adopted the mode of an English gentleman. That he was also incredibly handsome and a bit of a rogue with the ladies was no detriment in his present assignment. Dessins had no equal as a gatherer of information on the upper echelons of the English aristocracy. Few doors were closed to him. His breeding, his manners, and not least the touching though entirely fictitious background he assumed when in England, won him a ready sympathy, if not the confidence, of everyone he met. In point of fact, Dessins was an actor by profession, with no claim to the exalted position that Fouché himself had invented for him. His one failing, in Fouché's opinion, was that he had virtually no political acumen. Fouché, however, never put much stock in the opinions of others. His agents gathered information. The interpretation of the facts they passed along was his province and no one else's. But it amused him to solicit advice that he had never any intention of heeding.

"What do you make of this?" he prompted, holding up the text of Fox's speech.

"It's a careful speech," answered Dessins thoughtfully. "But you will note, Monsieur Fouché, that the sentiments he expresses are still favorable to France. And in the present climate of opinion in England, he has said as much as any man dare."

"In point of fact, he has said very little," pointed out Fouché.

Dessins shot a quick glance at his superior. Fouché was known to be an uncommonly subtle man. Hidden behind the habitually bland mask of his ascetic features, Fouché's thoughts remained impossible to fathom.

With assumed confidence, Dessins offered, "It is

my opinion that Mr. Fox is of the same mind as ever he was."

"Ah," said Fouché, his smile faintly ingratiating, "you have been admitted to his inner circle of intimates, I take it?"

Dessins straightened in his chair. "Not precisely the inner circle, but I think I may say, without conceit, that I am in Mr. Fox's confidence to some extent."

"The first consul will be gratified to hear it," said Fouché, and replenished his companion's empty glass.

The younger man regarded his superior doubtfully for a moment. Fouché's next words reassured him.

"You've done remarkably well to have got so far with Mr. Fox. I don't mind telling you now, that I sent two of my best agents on the very same assignment. You are the only one who has managed to do more than strike up a friendship with the man. How was it done, I wonder?"

Visibly relaxing, Dessins took a long swallow from the glass in his hand. Finally he responded, "I was in a position to render Mr. Fox a small service. After that, it was plain sailing."

"I'm all ears," said Fouché, settling back in his chair.

Dessins's smile verged on the self-congratulatory. "It's no secret that Mr. Fox nourishes a marked antipathy to the Duke of Dyson."

"And vice versa." To Dessins's questioning look, Fouché elaborated, "I had the pleasure of meeting the duke during the peace talks. A most interesting fellow. Pray continue."

Dessins absorbed his companion's words before obeying. "Dyson's mistress is a certain Louise Pelletier. As near as I understand, she fled to England not so much to escape the Revolution as to make her fortune." The two gentlemen exchanged a look of amused comprehension. After a moment, Dessins continued, "I made it my business to cultivate Mademoiselle Pelletier's friendship. From her own lips, I was told in the strictest confidence that her protector, Dyson, was bringing out of France a girl whom he regards as his ward, Gabrielle de Valcour. Do you know of her?"

"The name is familiar," allowed Fouché, storing it away for future reference. "What then?"

"You might say that I was grasping at straws," allowed Dessins. "Mr. Fox was proving elusive. It seemed I had nothing to lose by following up my lead on Dyson. I gave Louise Pelletier escort to his estate in Cornwall and then repaired to Falmouth, which is only hours away. I was on the point of giving up and going back to London when his yacht returned from France. Beautiful vessel," he mused. "It's berthed in Falmouth."

"And?"

"I struck lucky."

Dessins smiled as he began to describe that scene in the taproom of Falmouth's intolerable hostelry, when he'd finally run to earth someone who was willing to talk of the duke. It had been Dyson's cabin boy. It was evident that the young lad worshiped his master. And by carefully playing his cards, Dessins had discovered not only that Dyson's ward had come unwillingly but that she had put up a fight with her guardian and suffered some injuries.

"She's virtually a prisoner in Dyson's fortress," remarked Dessins.

"And the boy trusted you enough to disclose as much?" asked Fouché, surprise etching his voice.

"Certainly. I posed as a devout Bourbonist with

198

no sympathies for a foolish chit who did not recognize her good fortune in being offered sanctuary in England. I went so far as to chastise his master for being too lenient with the girl. The boy's defense was most eloquent. He told me far more than he realized."

"What you have told me is all very interesting, but you've yet to tell me how this could possibly ingratiate you with Mr. Fox."

"Frankly, I wondered at it myself. But I returned to London the very next day and wrote a note advising Mr. Fox of what I had found out. I was careful to couch my words in slightly indignant language, you know: 'Much as I deplore recent events in France, I regret to see a compatriot treated with so little respect or dignity,' and so forth. He called on me that very day so that I might give him a fuller account of the circumstances surrounding the girl's abduction. He was most gratified by what I told him. And since then he has counted me among his friends."

Fouché's brow pleated in a frown. "And?" he prodded. "To what use did Mr. Fox put the information you had passed along?"

"I can't say. On that, he did not take me into his confidence. But the strangest thing . . ."

"Yes?"

"Shortly afterward, Dyson married his ward. There was an announcement in the papers. And Fox was most displeased, to say the least."

"Indeed? And how did this displeasure manifest itself?" Fouché's languid tone masked an impatience he was at some pains to conceal. Dessins, he had discovered, could not be hurried. He swallowed a sigh and imbibed slowly.

Dessins's eyes were fixed on the intricate carvings on the mantel. "I was there when he read the announcement in the *Gazette*."

"Where, exactly, were you?"

"Mm? Oh. In Brooks. That's one of the gentle-men's clubs, by the by. A Whig stronghold. Though the *cuisine* leaves much to be desired, the company . . ."

"Yes, yes. I'm aware of all that. Just describe how Mr. Fox's displeasure at the announcement of Dyson's nuptials manifested itself, if you would be so kind."

"As near as I remember, he tossed the newspaper to a table and said something like, 'Damn and blast the man! I never expected him to go so far. But I'm a long way from done with him, make no mistake about it, Sherry.' "

"Sherry?"

"Richard Sheridan, the playwright."

"Interesting," mused Fouché, absently caressing his chin with his index finger. "And what do you con-clude from what you've just told me?"

"I don't know what to think, except perhaps that Fox hoped to embarrass the duke, and the duke forestalled him."

"Brilliant," muttered Fouché under his breath, but since a benevolent smile was pinned to his thin lips, Dessins decided, wisely, not to take umbrage.

In crisper tones, Fouché continued, "Pursue that matter until you get to the bottom of it. Also, there may be some merit in continuing your friendship with Louise Pelletier. She might be very useful to us one way or another." He looked at his watch. "It's about time for your interview with the first consul. He's most anxious to hear your assessment of Mr. Fox."

Fouché bit back a laugh when he observed the self-important grin that graced Dessins's handsome face. The young jackanapes was preening. It was to

200

be expected, he supposed. Bonaparte had expressed a desire to meet in person the agent who had contrived to become one of Charles Fox's intimates. The first consul was hopeful that in the event of the French invasion of England, Fox would tender his support. Bonaparte was not very wise in some things, thought Fouché. Unfortunately, the first consul had, from the very beginning, mistaken the character of his man. That any sane Englishman would regard Bonaparte as a liberator if he came at the head of an invading army was, in Fouché's opinion, an insane notion. Bonaparte, it seemed, was taking his own rhetoric seriously.

Not that he, Joseph Fouché, would take it upon himself to correct the error of his logic. Talleyrand, his minister of foreign affairs, could do that, if he had a mind to. Fouché was intent only in reestablishing himself as titular head of the police.

At the thought of Talleyrand, Fouché's thoughts took a less pleasant turn. There had been a second plot against the life of the first consul, and this time it was Talleyrand, acting on information received from England, who had foiled the attempt. Fouché wondered who the informant might be. He suspected that Charles Fox might have had a hand in it. His own agents had given him the intelligence that Talleyrand and Fox kept up a clandestine correspondence. Fox, he thought. The man was an enigma. He didn't approve of Bonaparte, but at the same time he would not see him assassinated. Fouché supposed it was something to do with the gentleman's code of honor to which all Englishmen seemed to subscribe. A more absurd logic he had yet to encounter.

Coming out of his reverie, he became aware that Dessins was staring at him. "I'll walk with you to the Tuileries," he said, rising to his feet.

At the gates to the Tuileries gardens they parted. A more sensitive man than Fouché would have given at least a passing thought to the irony of the situation: the new dictator of France had installed himself in the former Bourbonist palace. Fouché's mind, however, was already racing ahead to reports from his agents that were accumulating on his desk. It was weeks before he set in motion the investigation of the Valcour family in France, and as long again before he remembered to approach his friend, Mascaron, to quiz him about the man who had been a guest at the Château de Vrigonde for the ill-fated peace talks.

Mascaron stood by one of the long windows in his study in the Château de Vrigonde overlooking the south lawns. His mind was filled with pictures of Gabrielle. He could have sworn that the sound of her laughter still lingered, carried on the wind to the open window. Even the scent of the apple blossoms seemed to fill his nostrils.

Two months had slipped by since her abduction. Two months during which he had publicly assumed the role of grieving relative while privately pursuing every avenue open to him to uncover her whereabouts. Two months of chafing at the bit. His hands had been tied, as her abductors knew they would be. There was no one in authority he dared approach for assistance, least of all his old friend, Fouché.

But, incredibly, it was Fouché who had come to him. And at last, he had a name: Dyson. The coincidence of two abductions taking place simultaneously was too farfetched to be credible. Not that he had said as much to Fouché. With a flair born of desperation he had lied in his teeth. As a matter of fact, he said, the Englishman had mentioned in passing that there was a relative in France, a young girl whom he intended to remove to England. No, he did not know her name or any of the circumstances connected with her. And Fouché went away believing him, or so he hoped.

Dyson. The name stirred him to fury. His teeth ground together and his hands clenched at his sides. Never, not once, had it entered his head that Gabrielle's abductor would be English, and least of all, a member of the English aristocracy whom he had entertained in his own home. The rigid code of honor to which all English gentlemen subscribed was almost held to be a joke in France. He had assumed that her abductors were French royalists who were passing on information to the English, and that she would be held somewhere in France until such time as she was released.

God, he could not credit how blind he had been! And while he had secretly sent men to follow a false trail that began in Tosny and ended in Paris, Dyson had carried her off in his yacht under his very nose. The man had run rings round him! But no more. He had a name. He had a place. And he had the genesis of a plan.

That was important. There could be no question now of waiting until the English and French fleets finally engaged. That day might be months away, *years* away, and he could not take the chance that Fouché would not discover the whole truth. The man might be a friend, but he was also ambitious. There was little he would not do to regain his former position as minister of police. Friendship in such circumstances counted for nothing. Not that he cared for his own fate. But Gabrielle . . .

He put a hand to his eyes, momentarily overcome with emotion. Helpless. He was helpless, forced to depend on others to set his plan in motion, for it was imperative that he continue at the Ministry of Marine as if there was nothing on his mind but French mastery of the seas. He was being watched by Gabrielle's abductors, so he had been given to understand. And now Fouché had begun an investigation of the Englishman. Time was running out. He had to act quickly.

The soft click of the door brought his head up. Goliath stood watching him, just inside the threshold. Mascaron wondered fleetingly what the Norman was thinking. He had known the man at close quarters for more than a decade, and still they were strangers to each other. They had only one bond that held them together. Gabrielle. He would trust her safety to no one else.

"Everything is set?" he asked, moving to his desk.

"I leave tonight."

"No one must suspect . . ."

"No one will."

They stood silently staring at each other.

At length, Mascaron said, "Then there's nothing more to say but good luck and bring her back to us."

"I mean to," answered Goliath.

But each man was thinking that Dunraeden was a formidable fortress to penetrate.

Chapter Twelve

The weeks and months that followed the wedding ceremony fell into a curious pattern. Ostensibly, Gabrielle was Cam's duchess, the chatelaine and mistress of Dunraeden. In point of fact, she was still a prisoner, and her movements curtailed by Cam's order to an unnerving degree. Though a stranger coming among them would have observed nothing amiss, Gabrielle was never comfortable and excruciatingly aware of the guards who manned the castle walls and entrances. Cam gave out that they were posted to watch the Channel for the approach of an invasion fleet. Gabrielle tested the truth of that statement by slipping away to the chapel one evening when the guards were changing and their vigilance was relaxed. Within half an hour the alarm was given. In less time than that her hiding place was discovered.

"The pulpit screen?" Cam drawled, studying his wife laconically from beneath raised brows.

"Certainly," said Gabrielle. "Carvings are my hobby. The woodwork in your chapel is exquisite. I could not resist taking a closer look. I trust I was not trespassing?" And she met his eyes boldly.

"Trespassing?" murmured Cam, and patted her carelessly on the cheek. "My dear, how can you trespass? This is your home. You are free to come and go as you please. But in these dangerous times, it is more prudent to keep me informed of your movements. Do I make myself clear?"

"Perfectly," said Gabrielle, biting back the spate of curses she longed to fling in his smiling face.

In this exchange, Cam was following the pattern which he had followed since the night of their hastily contrived marriage. On the surface, all was serene and untroubled. Not an uncivil word passed his lips. But behind that chilly and safe politeness, Gabrielle sensed that dangerous, unpredictable emotions were barely held in check.

For all his civility, she was still afraid of him in a way that she had never been afraid of anyone in her life. When she tried to analyze her feelings, she came no nearer to discovering why this should be so. In the months that she had been at Dunraeden, there had been no overt threats to her person. On the contrary, the Englishman had treated her with deference and had seemed to go out of his way to ensure that everything was done to make her stay a comfortable one. And if Betsy and Lord Lansing were to be believed, the man was a paragon of every virtue imaginable.

Both had proved to have a fund of stories and anecdotes about her captor. She'd listened to them in silence and with something like suspended belief. It was impossible to recognize the warm, attractive character they portrayed in the cold, unfeeling man she knew. The change had come upon him, so she was given to understand, in that failed attempt, when he'd gone to France as a young man of nineteen summers, to rescue his mother and sister. Gabrielle drew her own conclusions. Having lost his mother and sister to the Revolution, he hated everything remotely French.

She could see it in his eyes when they touched

206

upon her, in the way he stiffened when she came into a room. There was violence there, the look of a lean and hungry caged tiger. It was a relief when she became conscious that he was deliberately keeping his distance. Fortunately, there seemed to be much to occupy him in and around Dunraeden.

Her own days were no less busy. The Englishman had taken it into his head that she was to play the part of his duchess and chatelaine as if their marriage had been genuine instead of a sham to mislead his enemies. When she had demanded, frigidly, why she should put herself to so much trouble when her stay at Dunraeden was to be of short duration, he had shrugged negligently and remarked that it was what everyone expected.

With irrefutable logic, he had added, "To do anything less would not only occasion gossip, but might also create a climate of antagonism toward you, that is, if you persist in flaunting your antipathy to the situation in which we find ourselves."

Inwardly, she was forced to concede that he spoke no less than the truth. Only the Englishman and Lord Lansing knew all the circumstances surrounding her abduction and incarceration at Dunraeden. To the servants, she was the most fortunate of girls. Having stolen her out of France, their master had bestowed his name and title upon her. They could not conceive, now, that she would wish to escape her fate. And if His Grace set guards to watch over her and never permitted her to go beyond Dunraeden's walls, it was done with the best will in the world. For who could say what those dastardly French might not attempt to have her back in their clutches? And she was known to be careless about her own safety, as the episode in the chapel had proved beyond the shadow of a doubt. For the moment Gabrielle had their sympathies. They may have had their suspicions that the marriage was not a love match, but since their master, by their lights, had done right by her, they expected Gabrielle to reciprocate. It was for these reasons, she persuaded herself, that she conceded to the Englishman's wishes.

By degrees she became more comfortable with everyone at Dunraeden, with the exception of its master. The servants offered a deferential friendliness and Lord Lansing and Betsy hovered over her like a pair of swans with a lone cygnet. Sometimes she had to forcibly remind herself that, in spite of appearances, she was a prisoner with a different life awaiting her once she was returned to France.

As one month slipped into the next with no word of when she would be released, she began to think more seriously of an escape attempt, though the enterprise seemed doomed to failure. Even if she managed to escape Dunraeden's walls, she was left with the problem of how to make her way across the Channel. The only answer that came to her was that she should stow away on some vessel bound for France. She knew there were smugglers in the area. Lansing had let slip that the warren of caves along the cliffs was a known rendezvous. And it was possible that the French *contrebandiers* themselves crossed the Channel to Cornwall. Gabrielle decided that it was foolish not to explore every avenue of escape should the opportunity ever present itself.

As it turned out, she soon perceived the advantages of pursuing her role as Dunraeden's chatelaine. Not only was the boredom that had begun to set in during her first weeks of captivity kept at bay, but under Betsy's tutelage she became familiar with every room and cellar, every stick of furniture, every piece of string and scrap of paper that fell to her domain. Regrettably, however, she did not have the run of the place. The armory was off limits, and the Englishman himself kept the key to that interesting locked door. Nothing daunted, Gabrielle made capital of what she regarded as a fatal blunder in the Englishman's strategy. She began to hoard anything that might assist her to escape. In the space of several weeks the cache she had hidden under the mattress in her chamber came to comprise one blunt carving knife and a set of boy's clothes. When a long coil of hemp rope finally came into her possession, she decided that it was time to put the first part of her plan to the test. Escape was not yet her object. At this point, it was enough if she could make it to the other side of her prison walls.

She chose her moment with care. Over her months of confinement she had become aware that the Englishman did not spend every night within the castle walls. Long after she had retired to her bed, she could hear the low murmur of voices as he dismissed his valet in the adjoining room. Shortly afterward, she heard his footfalls as he let himself out of his chamber and went stealthily along the corridor. He returned just before dawn. It never once entered Gabrielle's head that Cam was stealing away to meet with a woman. She knew him for a spy. It was to be expected, she thought, that spies would be involved in clandestine meetings under cover of darkness.

She was beginning to despair that the Englishman had given up his nocturnal activities, so long a time had slipped by since he had last spent the night away from Dunraeden. But her patience was finally rewarded.

They'd had words one afternoon for the first time in an age, and Gabrielle was lying awake, staring into space, retracing in her mind the substance of

209

their heated exchange. It had begun when she'd been called to the library and instructed to copy a letter to her grandfather that the Englishman had already set down. There was nothing new in this. At regular intervals her letters were carried to Mascaron, proof that she was alive and well and still in her abductors' power. This time she balked.

"It's more than two months since you brought me here," she said as she wrote the date at the top of the page.

"What of it?" asked Cam, propping one hip against the desk and folding his arms across his chest.

Gabrielle's eyes brushed over him and slid away. She had never denied that the Englishman was a handsome creature. It was almost inevitable, given her blondness, that his dark good looks would find more favor in her eyes than Lord Lansing's fairness. He had the build of an athlete or a warrior, lean and well muscled. She could appreciate that, that and the tests of endurance she knew were necessary to produce such sleek strength. As a prime specimen of masculinity, she gave him his due. But she had no difficulty in detesting the ironic slant to his sensual mouth, the baiting glint that flickered at the back of those intelligent blue eyes, and most of all, the air of condescension he adopted when there was no one present to observe how he dealt with her.

"How much longer am I to remain at Dunraeden?" she demanded.

He tipped her chin up with one long finger. "What? Bored with my company already, Angel? And you only a bride of two months?"

She shook herself free of him. "I'm your prisoner," she stated unequivocally.

"Prisoner?" He feigned incredulity. "You're my duchess. You have the run of the place. You want

210

for nothing." His voice changed color, became darker, harsher. "Do you know how many women would give everything they possess to be in your shoes?"

"Duchess!" She spat the word as if it were the foulest oath she could think of. "I have no interest in being your duchess."

His teeth snapped together. "No. And for a very good reason. The task is beyond you."

An angry flush heated her cheeks. "I'm as good as you are," she declared.

His lips curved in a sneer. "If the height of your ambition is to be the match of any man, then by all means, let us agree that there are few to equal you. But as a real woman you leave much to be desired on all counts."

She shook her head slightly. What she had meant to say was that by birth she was his equal. His words gave her thoughts a new direction. "I wear the clothes you choose for me. I watch my language. Lord Lansing says my manners and deportment are irreproachable. I've accepted the role you've set for me. What more do you want?" Her throat worked convulsively, and she did not know why his scorn should matter to her.

"What more should I want?" He had risen to his feet and was towering over her. She didn't like the set of his jaw, didn't trust the storm in his eyes. "From you, I want nothing. How could I?" His eyes swept over her, insulting, damning. "You're just a child playing at being grown up. Now write that letter like a good little girl."

Shamed, trembling, furious at the injustice of his venom, she pulled herself to her feet. In the months since she had been held at Dunraeden, she had been a veritable pattern card of propriety, the epitome of respectability, her manners, her language, her deportment faultless to a degree. In that moment it struck her forcibly that, inexplicably, and against all reason, she had been trying to win the Englishman's esteem. His words, his whole demeanor convinced her that the task was hopeless. She was an object of ridicule and was sorry that she had ever put herself to so much trouble. Mortification converted to a heedless anger. Caution was thrown to the winds. She wanted only to show him how little she cared for his good opinion.

Casting around in her mind for the vilest, most shocking curse word of her extensive vocabulary, she finally said, "Write your own f—ing letter." She hoped that the English word she'd picked up from his crew on their flight from Normandy was as coarse as any she knew in her native tongue.

He bared his teeth in a ferocious grin. Before she could push past him, he had grabbed her by the shoulders. "I'll wager you never use such language in Lansing's hearing. Is it just he who brings out the female in you? You are a woman, I suppose, Gabrielle? You can feel like other women, can't you? D'you think I don't know that you reserve all your smiles and soft words for him?" He administered a rough shake. "By God, you're my wife! You'd better not be giving him what you're refusing me."

Shocked, she stared at him, not knowing what to make of this outburst. His hands dropped from her shoulders and he spun away from her. His fingers combed through his dark hair.

"For God's sake, get out of here!" he said savagely. "Just get out of here before I do something we'll both regret."

She didn't need a second telling. Rashly, she had opened the door to the tiger's cage. She lifted her skirts and fled.

Gabrielle kept to her chamber for the remainder of the evening, too shaken to attempt to pass off what had taken place in the library as if it were of no moment. By turns weepy and blazing with anger, she paced back and forth in front of the great tester bed, venting her displeasure by shredding a silk stocking she'd left carelessly lying on the floor. She twisted it in knots, wishing all the while that she could do as much to the Englishman's thick head.

"As a woman, on all counts, you leave much to be desired," she muttered under her breath, mimicking Cam's voice exactly. "You're just a child playing at being grown up," she repeated, and savagely twisted the stocking in her hand. She felt a stab of satisfaction as she heard it rend. She threw it from her in disgust and stalked to the long cheval mirror.

The girl who looked back at her was as unexceptionable as any she had known in the *salons* of Paris. It was all so unjust. She'd given her very best effort to being a woman. Lord Lansing did not find fault with her. Why on God's earth did the Englishman have to be so beyond pleasing? She was sure she did not care.

"Is it just Lansing who brings out the female in you?" Now what the devil did he mean by that? She was a female, wasn't she? Couldn't he see that she had breasts and long hair?

The girl in the mirror brushed her hands over her breasts, then shook out her long mane of tresses. They fell about her shoulders in voluptuous abandon. The Englishman was blind, Gabrielle decided viciously. She was sure she was no different from any other female. Or perhaps there was more to being a female than she'd ever dreamed. She had always suspected as much. She thought of Louise Pelletier and the Englishman's words came back to her. *Now there's a woman who knows how to be a woman.*

Again she assured herself she did not care. She was sorry that she'd ever taken into her head to pass herself off as something to which she could never aspire. She took that thought to bed with her and between bouts of weeping persuaded herself that she was very happy to be exactly as she was — though she could not say with any certainty what she was exactly.

It was a long time before she heard the Englishman move about in his own chamber. When he dismissed his valet, she stirred and pulled herself to her elbows. Moments later, a knock came on the adjoining door.

"Gabrielle?"

Her heart skipped a beat.

"Gabrielle?" His voice was louder, more insistent.

She held her breath. After a moment's silence, she could hear him cursing softly on the other side of the door.

Evidently, it was one of those nights she'd been waiting for, one of those nights when he was engaged in his clandestine activities. But where before he had moved about with stealth, now he slammed around his room as if he wished to waken the dead. He was angry, and that made her smile.

She waited a good half hour after she heard him stomp along the corridor before she stirred from her bed. Within minutes she had donned the boy's garb and had the coil of rope draped over one shoulder and under one arm. Though she was as nervous as a thoroughbred, she could not help grinning when she saw herself in the looking glass. This was the Gabrielle de Brienne she recognized. She wished the Englishman could see her now. *Female,* she snorted. *I'll give him female.* And she snuffed out the candles

214

one by one.

As a matter of course, she tried both doors to her chamber. As always, she was locked in for the night. She padded to the window and cautiously eased herself over the sill and onto a narrow stone ledge that she had previously observed ran the length of the west wall. By ill luck or design, the window of her chamber overlooked the bailey. It was necessary to get to one of the towers before she could lower her rope over an outside wall. With slow, agonizing steps, her back pressed hard against the wall, she inched her way to the west tower. Far below, in the uncertain light of the few pitch torches, she could just make out the shadowy figures of men moving about in the bailey. She was still for some few minutes, but not one of them thought to check the sheer-faced walls.

Her worst moment came when she lowered herself over the tower ramparts. Gabrielle had always had the agility of a monkey, but either her ribs had not healed properly or the inactive life of a lady had made her as weak as a kitten. As she strained against the rope she felt the pull on every muscle and bone in her body. She could not take the chance that, having reached the rocks below, she would be able to haul herself up again. Recognizing that what she needed was more practice, she contented herself with hanging in midair, her feet braced against the wall.

Over the next several weeks she scarcely saw the Englishman for more than a few minutes at a time. He was up with the dawn and rarely returned before she had retired to bed. Lord Lansing explained, rather apologetically, that the Englishman's estates were extensive and that he spent the better part of each day visiting tenants and overseeing some project of an experimental nature.

The arrangement suited Gabrielle admirably. She had no more desire for the Englishman's company than he had for hers. And if Betsy and Dunraeden's other servants (who had a very romantic turn of mind) were somewhat disappointed at this lack of devotion on their master's part to his new bride, she herself was vastly pleased. The pity of it was, he did not stay away all night long.

For whatever reason, those stealthy nocturnal excursions had ceased altogether, and she had given up depending on the Englishman to oblige her by spending his nights away from home. As it was evident to her that she would never make it to the other side of the castle ramparts unless she submitted her body daily to some vigorous form of exercise, she had decided that she must be the one to take up nocturnal rambling. The Englishman never suspected what she was up to, and as the days slipped into weeks, she tested herself to the limits of her endurance. Gradually her former strength and agility returned. Only one thing occasioned her some disquietude. Fresh calluses began to form on her palms. During the daylight hours she was careful to keep her hands covered or hidden, and every night she conscientiously smoothed them with Betsy's miraculous salve. No one remarked upon them.

She was beginning to feel increasingly confident of her ability to control her own destiny. It showed, unbeknownst to Gabrielle, in the small secretive smile that curved her lips whenever her eyes came to rest on Cam. Soon she would be beyond his power, she thought. Nothing could stop her.

But then he found her with Lansing. And everything changed.

Lord Lansing was not in love with Gabrielle, no matter what Cam might have conjectured, but he was devoted to her, and moved by her unhappy plight. He had never been in favor of using an innocent pawn in the dangerous game in which Cam was engaged. And having met Gabrielle, and having come to understand something of her circumstances, he was more sorry than ever that he had not been more vigorous in dissuading his friend from the course on which they had embarked.

It had never been his intention to stay on at Dunraeden. He was a young man, and single to boot. The fleshpots of London held an allure for him that any gentleman of his acquaintance would have condoned. But when he thought of leaving Gabrielle to fend for herself with only Cam for company, he could not bring himself to do it. He knew his friend to be reserved, but in Cam's manner with Gabrielle he had detected a callousness that troubled him greatly. On several occasions he had tried to broach the subject of Gabrielle with Cam, only to be met by cold stares and short rejoinders that amounted to a warning to let sleeping dogs lie. The Duchess of Dyson was one subject on which, he was given to understand, her husband refused to be drawn.

Duchess! Lansing never thought of Gabrielle as Cam's duchess. She was Gabrielle de Brienne, an innocent hostage who had been cruelly wrenched from everything that was dear to her. And as one week slipped into the next, it began to be borne in upon him that to return Gabrielle to her former life as if nothing had happened was no longer possible. In France, it was generally presumed that she had drowned. How was it possible, then, to return her to Mascaron without occasioning suspicion? At the very least, the girl would be ruined.

217

True, Cam had wed her out of hand for his own purposes. But the marriage was to be dissolved when Gabrielle's usefulness was at an end. For all Cam's reticence in discussing Gabrielle's future, it had gradually become evident to Lansing that his friend had no *tendre* for the girl. His liaison with his mistress continued unabated, though to be sure, he had belatedly begun to exercise a modicum of discretion now that he was promoting the fiction that he was a married man. In Lansing's opinion, there was only one thing to be done. Since Cam seemed intent on having the marriage annulled, some other eligible gentleman must be found who would step into the breach. And since he was one of the perpetrators of her abduction, his own conscience constrained him to make the supreme sacrifice.

Such were Lansing's thoughts as he wandered through state rooms and private apartments in search of Gabrielle. She had deserted her usual haunts. One of the footmen directed him to the tower chamber that she had once occupied. He found her alone, seated at one of the window embrasures, looking out to the English Channel and beyond. In her white muslin gown with its green satin ribbons she looked as fragile as the first snowdrop of spring. Lost in private reflection, she was not aware of his presence until he said her name. The face she turned up to him before she had the presence of mind to school her features into a semblance of welcome was hauntingly beautiful, thought Lansing, and achingly sad.

"Thinking of home?" he quizzed, accepting the place she indicated on the window seat beside her.

Home. For days past she had thought of little else but Normandy. A plethora of unrelated thoughts continually chased themselves through her head. She wondered where old Roland, the leader of the local

218

contrebandiers, was getting his supply of Calvados. She thought of Goliath constantly, and wondered how he was passing the hours he had formerly devoted to improving her swordplay. Mascaron she could not remember with anything resembling equanimity. And at the recollection of Rollo as she had last seen him, handsome and debonair in his dress regimentals, a lump would invariably form in her throat. It was best not to think of home at all, she was coming to realize.

"One of our dairy maids was to have been married the very week I was brought here," she offered at length.

"And that makes you unhappy?"

"No. Why should it? I'm very happy for her. Minette snared a young man, one of our gardeners, whom all the girls were mad for."

"I see," said Lansing, his eyes regarding her thoughtfully.

Gabrielle's fingers were busily smoothing the ends of the green satin ribbons that adorned her frock. "How was it done, I wonder?"

"Beg pardon?"

"Minette." Gabrielle's huge eyes were turned upon him.

As green as grass, thought Lansing inconsequentially, and forced himself to concentrate on what she was saying.

"Even Rollo was partial to her." She waited a little breathlessly and then continued, "He said that Minette was a real woman. What . . . what did he mean, I wonder?"

With the greatest difficulty, Lansing swallowed a chortle of laughter. It was a moment before he could bring himself to say, with a semblance of gravity, "I expect the girl was a bit of a flirt, 'tis all."

"Flirt!" exclaimed Gabrielle, her tone disparaging. "I don't like flirting!" She was remembering Cam's kiss at the Château de Vrigonde. Just thinking about it made her go hot all over.

"Not like flirting!" Lansing was caught between laughter and shock. "My dear girl, in our society, flirting is *de rigueur*. It's an accomplishment of which every well-bred gentleman and lady should know the rudiments, to say the least."

She considered his words carefully. "D'you mean like pistol shooting and fencing and so on?"

Though his lips twitched, he managed in a neutral tone, "In a manner of speaking, yes."

"And . . . and might one improve with practice?"

"Of course."

Her smile was by turns dubious, tremulous, and finally dazzling. "Oh Simon," she breathed. "Could you, would you, be my tutor?"

Simon shrugged off a flleeting unease. There could be no harm in it. Cam, Lansing was persuaded, was too wise, too sensible, too urbane to resent this innocent game of dalliance. Besides, Cam was not here.

"I'd be delighted," he said, smiling.

Gabrielle sighed, turned up her head and pursed her lips. Her eyes were closed.

Lansing's smile deepened. "Oh *that* kind of flirting," he said, chuckling. "Gabrielle, haven't you ever been kissed before?"

She opened her eyes. "Yes, but I didn't like it."

"Not like kissing? Why that is positively . . . tragic! Here, let me show you how nice it can be."

His hands closed around her arms. "Come closer," he said softly.

She leaned into him, and trustingly angled her head back.

His lips, as cool as melting snow, brushed over

220

her in the faintest caress.

He pulled back slightly. "Open your mouth for me," he murmured.

"I wouldn't advise it!"

Cam's voice from the threshold cut the silence like the crack of a pistol shot. The couple on the window seat separated with a guilty start. When Cam slammed into the chamber, they both shot to their feet.

"Cam, what you are doing here?" said Lansing. "I thought you were inspecting the beacons along the cliff."

Cam smiled unpleasantly. "That would explain this cozy *tête à tête*."

Taken aback by his friend's hostile demeanor, Lansing stared at Cam. Recovering quickly, he exclaimed, "Oh no! Cam, you've got it all wrong! I was merely instructing Gabrielle in the finer points of flirting. You know, for when she goes into society."

He glanced uneasily at Gabrielle, who was affecting an interest in the strings of her white kid shoes. Cam's eyes, he noted, were riveted on his wife. Lansing was beginning to get the picture. He would have laughed out loud if he had not been so acutely aware of the jeopardy in which he stood. Preserving a grave face, he offered generously, "Well, now that you're here, Cam, perhaps you wouldn't mind going on with the lessons?"

He looked from Cam to Gabrielle. He might not have existed for all the attention they paid to him. He cleared his throat. "I'll be toddling along then." He waited.

Silence.

Lansing made an elegant bow to Gabrielle, shrugged negligently, and sauntered from the room.

It was a moment before Cam spoke. "Flirting?"

he said, and moved closer.

Gabrielle's chin lifted. He was close enough so that she could see that his eyes were not of a uniform color. Chips of a lighter blue ringed the irises. She wondered fleetingly if she was observing the phenomenon that the English called "sparks flying." She sensed that the Englishman was in a very unpleasant humor.

"He was teaching me how to be a real woman," she explained in her own defense.

If anything the specs around his irises grew brighter. "A real woman," he repeated between his teeth. "What does that mean, precisely?"

"You know." She could not sustain his hard scrutiny, and glanced longingly at the half-open door.

"Refresh my memory, if you would be so kind."

"It's what you said." She chanced a quick look at him. "You said I should become more like Louise."

Her answer seemed to floor him. "Did I say that?"

She nodded.

"You want to become a real woman?"

She was conscious that there was a change in him. If she hadn't known better, she might have thought that she read tenderness in his expression. "I don't know," she said, shrugging her shoulders. "Perhaps the task is beyond me. I've only had one lesson."

"Those lessons should come more properly from a husband," said Cam softly. "You'll come to me if you want to know anything."

Gabrielle eyed him doubtfully. "Would *you* teach me how to be a real woman?"

Cam sucked in his breath and exhaled slowly. Smiling, he said, "My dear, what else are husbands for? It shall be my pleasure."

He moved closer. "Now where were you with Simon? Oh, yes, now I remember." He grinned lazily. "Open your mouth for me."

Gabrielle felt his hands cup her shoulders. His touch jolted her. The heat of his body seemed to be overwhelming her. She began to have second thoughts. "I don't think . . ."

"Easy. *Doucement,*" whispered Cam. "This won't hurt a bit. I promise."

His lips, warm, strangely compelling, feathered along the arch of her eyebrows, her eyelids, heating her skin wherever they touched. He seemed to be fascinated with her chin, enthralled with her earlobes, charmed with the curve of her cheek, the slope of her throat. Gabrielle's lips followed his, trying to connect with them.

"Please," she whispered.

When he gave into her, his kiss was as soft as swansdown, as gentle as a summer breeze.

It was Cam who pulled back. "How was it?"

Gabrielle's eyelashes slowly fluttered open. She crowded a little closer. "Nice," she said. "Am I doing it right?"

Cam murmured something indistinct before taking her lips again. This time his kiss was hot and sweetly erotic. She felt as if she were floating, and clutched the lapels of his coat as her head began to spin. He took her deeper. The sensation resembled the one she had experienced before she learned to swim, when she had stepped into deep water. She was being sucked into dark turbulent depths. She clung to Cam as if he were her lifeline.

He only meant to taste and savor, Cam told himself. And yet as the kiss lingered he had to fight to hang onto his control. For weeks, months, he had struggled against his own devils. Gabrielle had become an obsession with him. Over and over he'd told himself that she was out of bounds, that there

223

were a score of cogent reasons for him to keep his distance. He could not even explain her attraction. But of one thing he was never in any doubt. She had spoiled him for other women.

Louise sensed that there was something amiss, had hinted coyly that she suspected him of taking up with other women. He'd found excuses not to visit her. A pall had fallen over what had formerly been a most satisfactory arrangement. His mistress was an undeniably sensual creature. It wasn't her fault that her skillful, practiced lovemaking left him longing for the unawakened passion of one innocent girl. Gabrielle. She wanted to be a real woman. To him she was the original Eve, mysterious, dangerous, an ingenuous siren, a scarlet angel. His mind, soul, senses were filled with her. She was his obsession, and he was done with fighting the inexorable magnetism that drew him to her.

His fingers dug into her hair, holding her steady as his lips sank into hers. He'd wanted women before, but never like this. He wanted her with a desperation that shocked him. If he'd found her with any other man than Simon, there was no question in his mind but that he would have resorted to brute force. She was his. He would make it so. The kiss became rougher, more urgent, and his need to possess began to spiral out of control.

It was Gabrielle's first taste of physical desire. Some of the symptoms she had experienced before—the shortness of breath, the erratic heartbeat, the pounding in her ears. Danger. Her sixth sense came into play. He was the enemy. She should be taking to her heels. But all through her body she could feel a curious urge to surrender. Aroused, confused, afraid of the unfamiliar sensations that were heating her blood, sensitizing her skin, she moved restlessly in his arms. Small animal cries of

4 FREE BOOKS

FREE BOOKS

TO GET YOUR 4 FREE BOOKS WORTH $18.00 — MAIL IN THE FREE BOOK CERTIFICATE T O D A Y

Fill in the Free Book Certificate below, and we'll send your FREE BOOKS to you as soon as we receive it.

If the certificate is missing below, write to: Zebra Home Subscription Service, Inc., P.O. Box 5214, 120 Brighton Road, Clifton, New Jersey 07015-5214.

FREE BOOK CERTIFICATE

4 FREE BOOKS

ZEBRA HOME SUBSCRIPTION SERVICE, INC.

YES! Please start my subscription to Zebra Historical Romances and send me my first 4 books absolutely FREE. I understand that each month I may preview four new Zebra Historical Romances free for 10 days. If I'm not satisfied with them, I may return the four books within 10 days and owe nothing. Otherwise, I will pay the low preferred subscriber's price of just $3.75 each; a total of $15.00, *a savings off the publisher's price of $3.00*. I may return any shipment and I may cancel this subscription at any time. There is no obligation to buy any shipment and there are no shipping, handling or other hidden charges. Regardless of what I decide, the four free books are mine to keep.

NAME _____

ADDRESS _____ APT _____

CITY _____ STATE ____ ZIP _____

TELEPHONE ( ) _____

SIGNATURE _____ (if under 18, parent or guardian must sign)

Terms, offer and prices subject to change without notice. Subscription subject to acceptance by Zebra Books. Zebra Books reserves the right to reject any order or cancel any subscription.   ZBMS02

GET
FOUR
FREE
BOOKS

(AN $18.00 VALUE)

ZEBRA HOME SUBSCRIPTION
SERVICE, INC.
P.O. Box 5214
120 BRIGHTON ROAD
CLIFTON, NEW JERSEY 07015-5214

distress caught at the back of her throat.

Cam lifted his head. Her green eyes were cloudy with desire. He knew he could take her very easily. He hadn't even touched her in any way that counted. And he could feel her arousal in every pore of his body. But he could also sense her panic. It was that, more than anything, that helped him find the strength to check the impulse to savage her lips and crush her warm willing body to his until she surrendered everything to him. It was too soon to take her the way he wanted.

Summoning the remnants of his control, he took a step back. He managed a laugh, but even to his own ears it sounded shaky. He didn't like what she was doing to him. Calm. Restraint. Finesse. He had to search to find his habitual balance. He gave her a moment to come to herself.

"For a novice, you did remarkably well." His tone was as matter-of-fact as he could make it.

She touched her fingers to her burning lips. The fear had faded, Cam noted, and she gazed at him with something like awe.

"With a little practice, you'll be quite proficient," Cam observed.

The look of awe changed to a look of horror. And still she said nothing.

Desire had receded, and Cam felt more in command of himself. "Oh yes," he said quietly, brushing one finger over her swollen lips. "We're not finished with each other, Gabrielle. Not by a long shot."

Chapter Thirteen

He was prepared to be very generous. For one thing, he had always indulged her expensive tastes. And for another, as mistresses went, Louise Pelletier was without par. He had no quarrel with her. To his knowledge she had never played him false. She was not given to fits of jealousy or sulks or outbursts of temper. In bed, she knew how to both give and take pleasure. She possessed a certain style that he could not help but admire. He knew himself to be the envy of many of his peers. And he could not wait to be shot of her.

He must be mad, thought Cam, as he unlocked the door to the little house in Falmouth that he had leased for Louise on Church Street. A rosy-faced maid accepted his hat and gloves with a shy smile and left him to find his own way to her mistress's bedchamber.

"Darling." She was at her dressing table, performing her toilette. A copper tub, fragrant with water, sat in the middle of the floor. It was evident Louise had come from her bath moments before.

Never once had he ever caught Louise looking anything less than stunning. Whether she was dressed to the nines or in the most blatant *dishabille,* she preserved the mode of a woman who cared about herself. Her fragrance filled the room.

Cam thought of Gabrielle and felt vaguely irritated.

He went to her at once and pressed a warm kiss to her welcoming mouth. She melted against him and he was enveloped in a swath of pink gauze and net. After a moment he disengaged himself from the passionate embrace and held her at arm's length. She wore nothing beneath the wrapper. Her bare skin glowed like satin.

"You must be bored to tears, waiting on my convenience," he murmured, and pressed a kiss to her fingers before moving away.

He strolled around the room, touching first one object, then another, as if he had never been there before. The room was a statement in femininity, thought Cam. Again he thought of Gabrielle, but this time with something close to exasperation.

She watched him for a moment, then went back to brushing her hair. "I don't expect you to be at my beck and call," she murmured.

A crooked smile played about Cam's lips. "Ah, no," he responded. "A married man must never call his time his own."

She arched one eyebrow, and continued with her task. Cam draped himself inelegantly in a fragile gilt chair of French design and regarded her steadily.

"Do we go out this evening, or are we getting ready to retire?" he asked.

She laid the brush aside and turned to face him. "Which would you prefer? You have only to state your preference."

"I'm afraid I can't stay," he answered easily. "There are a million things at Dunraeden that beg my attention."

Her lips curved, but her eyes remained cold. "Do you know Cam, I've been thinking that you were right about Falmouth."

"Was I?" he drawled.

She inhaled slowly. "To be perfectly frank, I'm bored." It was the closest she would come to complaining of his neglect, and they both knew it.

"That doesn't surprise me," said Cam, coming to his feet. "I'm a boring sort of a fellow. I'm surprised you've stayed with me so long."

She knew, of course, where his conversation was leading. His visits in the last weeks had dwindled to next to nothing, and long before that, his ardor had cooled. It only remained for the relationship to be severed. And ever the gentleman, he was hinting her into taking the lead.

"Many of my friends are removing to Brighton," she finally remarked. "I was thinking I might join them."

Suddenly grave, he said, "That sounds like a capital idea. There'll be no end of amusements with the Prince of Wales in residence."

He reached in his coat pocket and removed a small packet, which he tossed into her lap. Her brows lifted.

"To tide you over," he answered to that questioning look. "I'll be fixed in Cornwall for some time to come. There's no saying when we'll meet again."

She smiled faintly and deposited the packet in a rosewood coffer that sat on the flat of her dressing table. There was no question in her mind that the gift would be more than generous.

Glancing sideways at him, she said, "Am I permitted to know who my rival is?"

He came up to her and with one finger edged her wrapper aside. Pressing a kiss to her bare shoulder, he murmured in an amused tone. "Rival? My dear, you're peerless, an incomparable. I know of no lady who can claim the distinction of being named your rival." He straightened, and when she

228

made to answer him, brushed his thumb over her lips. Almost regretfully he said, "No, don't say anything. You knew at the outset that sooner or later this day would come."

She gazed at him steadfastly for a long moment, then something flashed at the back of her eyes. Shrugging him off, she closed her negligee and belted it tightly. "Marriage agrees with you, if I'm not mistaken," she ventured.

He looked at her with a curious expression. "Marriage? What has that to say to anything?"

Her eyes never left his. "A foolish notion," she agreed, then continued more deliberately. "Would you believe, Cam, I thought for a moment that you were enamored of the chit?" She gave a convincing laugh. "I should have known that your tastes don't run to the outlandish." Her voice dropped, became more dulcet. "Tell me, have you found a governess for the child yet?"

Though Cam's expression remained pleasant, something ugly seemed to have crept into the room, and Louise was sorry she had given in to the impulse to bait him. She flinched when he captured her wrist.

He raised her hand to his lips. "Shall we agree to consider those last remarks unsaid?" he suggested politely. His eyes were ice cold as he waited for her reply.

"I never meant . . . ," she began unsteadily.

"Of course not." He patted her on the cheek. "The lease on the house in town has a year to run. You know my man of business. If you need anything, I'd prefer if you would deal through him."

She watched in silence as he strolled from the room. When she heard the front door close behind him, she opened the coffer and examined the contents of the packet he had given her. As she had

229

expected, the settlement was generous, but it in no wise mitigated the insult she felt had been inflicted. To lose Cam to some dazzling high flyer lately come on the scene would have occasioned her some annoyance, certainly, but the thought that she was to be displaced by a farouche hoyden who was as graceless as she was ignorant was beyond anything. She would be a laughingstock, and that was not to be borne.

She glanced at the ornate clock on the mantelpiece. After a moment's reflection she went to the bell pull and rang for her maid. She was soon dressed to receive callers. A glance in the looking glass reassured her. She was a woman in her prime. The Duke of Dyson had sadly underrated her if he thought he could treat her so shabbily.

Having dashed off a quick note, she sent a footman to deliver it, reflecting that, in her experience, no severance settlement was ever sufficient to long maintain the style to which she had become accustomed. An hour passed before her visitor arrived. She received him in the ground floor parlor.

"Gervais," she said, offering him both hands. The look in the young man's eyes, which spoke so eloquently of his admiration, was like balm to a festering sore. "How good of you to come at once."

Gervais Dessins made an elegant bow and moved to take the chair nearest the one she had selected for herself.

Gervais Dessins was to some extent in Louise Pelletier's confidence. He had descended on Falmouth some weeks ago and had taken up residence with mutual friends, refugees like themselves. And since Louise had been left very much to her own devices, and as Dessins had proved to be an amusing and attentive companion, their friendship had blossomed. In truth, Louise had been at some pains to cultivate the acquaintance. Dessins was on terms of familiarity with the Prince of Wales. A lady in her circumstances would be foolish beyond permission to neglect any avenue of advancement that presented itself.

"Do you go to Brighton still?" she asked, coming directly to the point.

"On the morrow, as I think I mentioned." He flashed her a keen, comprehensive look.

"I wonder if I might impose upon you for escort?"

His handsome features were etched in surprise. "With pleasure, my dear. But what has brought about this change of heart?"

She gave a light laugh, and shook her head. "*Ennui*, Gervais. It will be the death of me if I'm not careful. Besides, you've painted such a portrait of Brighton that I was suddenly overcome with the notion to pay it a visit." She pouted prettily. "Or perhaps you were hoaxing me when you promised to introduce me to your circle of friends?"

Dessins smiled gravely. "You do me an injustice. But what of Dyson? Does His Grace join you later?"

There was not the least necessity for the lady to pretend to a virtue she neither merited nor desired. It was common knowledge that she was the Duke of Dyson's mistress.

She sighed mournfully. "Unhappily, 'tis not possible for Cam to leave Dunraeden at the present moment. I may have mentioned that the child he wed requires constant supervision?"

Louise had told Dessins very little of Cam's bride, though she sensed an avid curiosity behind the occasional question he had put to her. Now, having been given her *congé* with so little regard for her sensibilities, she saw no reason to maintain her former reticence. She feigned a smile at some private reflection, and a moment later smothered a laugh behind her hand. Soon, with a little encouragement, she embarked on a flow of anecdotes about Gabrielle, which kept her companion convulsed in laughter for some minutes to come.

But behind the charmed expression that Dessins affected a calculating mind was at work. It was becoming evident to him that Louise Pelletier was a discarded mistress, though she was at some pains to paint a picture that was significantly more flattering to herself. That she was becoming disenchanted with her present protector was a fiction Dessins did not entertain for a moment, though he was careful not to betray his scepticism.

As he took his leave of her and walked the short distance to his own lodgings, he was considering how best he might make capital of what he had learned. Any intelligence respecting the Duke of Dyson could only further ingratiate him with Mr. Fox and the Prince of Wales. And a woman scorned, if pointed in the right direction, could prove a very useful tool.

As for the duke's bride, he digested what little he had learned of her from the woman she had displaced. His master, Fouché, he decided, would be interested in this latest turn in events. He would expect him, no doubt, to cultivate the girl's acquaintance. But how was it to be done? By degrees, a plan took shape in his mind. To broach the subject with Mr. Fox would require a most delicate touch. His own interest in the Duchess of Dyson must never be suspected.

Escape. It was all she could think of. To be sure, the thought of striking out on her own terrified her. But the thought of remaining at Dunraeden as *his* captive terrified her even more. If only, she thought with something close to hysteria, she had quashed that insane curiosity that had led to her present predicament. She was sorry, now, that she had ever toyed with the idea of becoming a *real* woman, and was even more sorry that she had not been born a boy. Then the Englishman would not have kissed her. And that hungry look that she surprised more and more frequently in his half-hooded expression would be directed toward a different lady. She was sure she could not comprehend what perversity in her nature recoiled at the thought of the Englishman kissing another lady. Sainte Vierge, what was the matter with her?

Gabrielle adjusted the length of rope at her shoulder and pulled on a pair of stout leather gauntlets before climbing over the windowsill in her chamber. The blunt carving knife she regretfully left behind. It had almost slipped from the waistband of her breeches on her last practice, and she could not take the chance, now that she was escaping in earnest, of a repeat performance. Besides, as a weapon or a tool, the knife was a useless article. It had not even sawed half through the length of rope when she had attempted to shorten it. The rope was bulky and made her progress along the west wall more perilous than necessary.

Step by slow step, Gabrielle edged her way along the stone pediment, her back pressed to the wall. It was now or never. The Englishman was gone for the night. Lord Lansing had bid her a fond farewell some days since. The vigilance of the servants was more relaxed than it had ever been. She would never be handed a better opportunity than the present to escape her captors. And she was in the peak of physical condition. Then what the devil ailed her? How was she to account for this incomprehensible reluctance to leave behind the grim fortress that had been her prison?

The tides, she thought. *That must be it.* Naturally, she was reluctant to step outside the safety of Dunraeden's invincible stone walls where the treacherous tides threatened to sweep all before them. She'd been making a study, and knew to the minute how rapidly the incoming tide raced landward to dash at the very walls of the castle, turning Dunraeden into a veritable island amid the churning brine. The bore at Caudebec was not more alarming, in her opinion.

The pediment ended a good number of feet above the lower tier of the west tower. Like the athlete she was, Gabrielle dropped down lightly on the balls of her feet, finding her balance unerringly. She quickly knotted the length of hemp around one of the abutments and was soon lowering herself, hand over fist, to the rocks below. Not a twinge of pain or discomfort slowed her progress. She might have taken an animal pleasure in the sleek response of muscle and tendon honed for speed and endurance. But her thoughts were flying ahead to the perilous course she had set for herself.

The caves. She had caught sight of them only once, from a distance, the day she had arrived at Dunraeden. Since then, her captors had unobtrusively ensured that she was never in a position to spy out the lie of the land. Lansing occasionally invited her to walk on the south battlements. The only view from that vantage point was out to sea, or below, to the castle bailey. She had never been permitted to walk the other walls. *How far to the caves?* she wondered, and felt the blood pump fast and hot to every pulse point in her body. Every sense came alive to the jeopardy of her position. If she had miscalculated the distance, she would find a watery grave before the night was over. A cloud covered the moon and she shivered.

The rocks beneath her feet were covered in seaweed or slime. She crouched down, keeping her balance with her hands. There wasn't a minute to lose. Once her feet touched the wet sands she would be running the race of her life. And then she heard it — the roar of the breakers, like the roar of a predator that catches the scent of its prey. And she was off and running.

Though the darkness about her was velvet, when she turned landward she could make out the silhouette of the dark cliffs. They towered into the lighter vault of the heavens. *How far? How far? How far?* Her steps kept pace with the litany that drummed in her brain. Her boots sank into a quagmire and she stumbled. Sobbing, she pulled herself to her feet. Water swirled around her and filled her boots. Oh God, already the tide was catching up to her. She kicked off her boots and stumbled forward, the fear that clawed at her throat far more palpable than the stitch that clawed at her side. Moments later water swirled around her bare ankles. The tide was outstripping her, and the cliffs seemed no nearer. *Oh Cam,* she sobbed. *Oh Cam.*

At that very moment, Cam was slowly approaching Dunraeden from the landward side. Mounted on his prize bay, Caesar, he gave little thought to the treacherous track that dipped low between the towering escarpments. Both mount and master had made the journey in every sort of weather, at every hour of the day or night. They could have found their way to the great scarred doors which barred entry to Cam's domain blindfolded.

Big droplets of rain began to fall. Cam turned

up the collar of his mantle and brought the reins up, at the same time gently tightening his knees to urge Caesar to a faster walk. He was scarcely aware of these involuntary actions, so lost in thought was he.

It had been the strangest week, he was thinking. The closer he had tried to come to Gabrielle, the more she had shied away. Simon had become the buffer she had employed to keep him at arm's length. He had been wishing Simon at Jericho when Simon himself had suggested that he remove to town. He had accepted his friend's departure with a show of reluctance that fooled nobody.

God, he didn't know what he wanted from Gabrielle. And if he did, he refused to countenance it. In his weaker moments he had given in to a very understandable temptation to flirt with the chit. He was playing with fire and he knew it. Given their circumstances, there could never be anything between them but hostility and mistrust.

The girl was wiser than he. In the week since he had found her in Simon's arms she had reverted to her former ill-bred manners—striding about as if she were wearing her boy's breeches, letting dishes and cutlery slip from her fingers, falling against furniture, dropping food on her lap. And those English curse words! Where had she learned them if not at Dunraeden, as she had so scrupulously pointed out when he'd attempted to reprimand her. But worst of all was the stench that clung to her skin. Pilchards! He was so revolted he'd given up eating them. All of it was a deliberate attempt, of course, to keep him from her. And he did not know why he was laughing.

He felt lighthearted, as if a great weight had been lifted from his shoulders. He'd parted company with Louise, and if he had a modicum of honesty in his character, he would admit that he never would have done so if it had not been for Gabrielle. The chit had made him damn near impotent! He chuckled. That was not precisely true. Around Gabrielle his virility was never in question.

A wind was getting up. Cam pulled his cloak more securely around him. A cloud obscured the moon. With a touch on the reins, he checked his mount as they came onto the causeway that led to Dunraeden's rocky promontory. He could hear the whoosh of the tide as it surged landward. The moon came out. And then he saw her.

With head down, hair flying behind her, she raced like an arrow across the sands, the white breakers hard at her heels. In that instant he knew that she would never make it, that she had miscalculated the distance to shore. He let out a bellow and at the same moment dug in his spurs. Caesar reared up and obediently vaulted a rise of razor-sharp rocks. He hit the sands with a thud and faltered. Cam kept his mount's head up. The bay regained his footing, his hooves barely touching the wet sands as he shot forward.

Gabrielle fell full length and the breakers submerged her. Panting, she rose to her knees, then to her feet. And still those cliffs seemed no nearer. She had been running for miles. Fear lent urgency to her limbs, which were leaden with exhaustion. She struck out blindly, dragging air painfully into her lungs with each faltering step. Suddenly the water came up to her waist, and she cried out. She felt the pull of the undertow as it lifted her clear off her feet. As she was dragged under, she held her breath. She came up sputtering and gulping. The tide played with her, tossing her first one way, then another, as if she were a piece of flotsam. She went under again and thought that her lungs would burst. Invisible fingers seemed to clutch at her hair, dragging her under. She was too exhausted to fight.

Cam wound one hand round that rope of hair and held on for dear life. With his free arm, he encircled her waist. When she came up choking and coughing, relief exploded through him in shock waves. He called her name, but the wind whipped the cry from his lips. There wasn't a minute to lose, no time to check her condition. She was alive, and that was all that mattered. Later there would be leisure to consider the paralyzing sense of despair that had held him in its grip when he'd lost sight of her as he'd ridden into the churning foam. Later he would remember that night in the Abbaye courtyard, and the same annihilating sense of loss he'd experienced then. For the present, his mind was filled with Gabrielle as he hauled her across the back of his mount and into the cradle of his arms. A touch with his heels on the bay's flanks, and the nervous animal wheeled, whinnying softly before stretching out its long legs to eat up the distance to the causeway, each smooth stride carrying them farther away from the predatory waters.

Gabrielle felt the familiar motions of the horse beneath her and sobbed her relief. By degrees, she became aware of the strong arms holding her. *Cam's arms*, she thought, and burrowed closer as if she could crawl inside him. He tightened his arms around her protectively, and she began to weep silently into his chest.

It was a long time before she raised her head. The motions of the bay had slowed and finally halted altogether. Cam's eyes glittered down at her.

"I . . . I had to escape," she said weakly.

"Why?" There was no give, no gentleness in him. She shook her head. "I had to try."

"Why?"

She had no answer. "I . . . I don't know."

"Is this why, Gabrielle?" he asked viciously. "Is this why you wanted to get away from me?" and he covered her mouth with his own.

She was aware of the rain beating down upon them. She felt the motions of the horse as it shifted restlessly. She heard the roar of the breakers. She tasted the salt of the spray. And then she was aware of nothing but Cam and the heat of his body as the darkness pressed in upon them.

He'd lost his restraint the moment he'd thought he had lost her. He knew he would find it again. But not yet. He didn't want to find it just yet. He didn't care if he frightened her half to death. She deserved to be frightened. She'd put him through hell. Didn't she know what she was doing to him?

Rage and desire ripped through him, making him tremble. He savaged her lips, crushed her small, shivering body with arms of steel. He felt her hands at his nape, stroking, gentling him of his pent-up emotions. She was afraid for him. Good. He'd give her something else to fear. He angled her head back and slanted his mouth across hers, unleashing the full force of his passion against her. A man's passion, his kiss told her, full-fledged and insatiable. And by God, he intended her to meet it.

He wasn't gentle. But not for a moment was she misled by his rough wooing. He was at breaking point. She understood that. She tasted the desperation on his tongue, as well as the longing. And though she was innocent of a man's passions, the raw desire on his lips did not threaten her but rather stirred some hidden spring within her that had been waiting for this moment. He was dragging her into those dark sensual depths she'd read

239

in the promise of his eyes from the moment of their first encounter. He was drowning her in sensation. Strangely, she wasn't afraid. If only for a few minutes she wanted to answer the demand in his kiss, offer herself as consolation for the turbulent emotions she had provoked by her rash escapade.

Surrender. She was giving into him. He wanted to take her there, on the sands. He didn't care about the rain or the fury of the wind as it whipped itself into a mad dervish. He didn't want to give her time to think. He wasn't about to let her change her mind.

He released her lips and covered her face with urgent kisses. It was only then that he became aware that she was shivering uncontrollably. His conscience scourged him. "My God, what am I doing? You're in shock," he breathed raggedly, and gathered her closer to the shelter of his body. Without another word, he urged his mount forward.

She didn't correct his misapprehension. It was enough to be held comfortingly in his arms. Her heart was pounding, her pulse racing. She was beginning to recognize the symptoms. Not danger, but Cam. Or were they one and the same thing? she wondered. And when had she begun to think of the Englishman as Cam? He was the enemy. Her mind told her so. But her heart flatly rejected that piece of logic.

When they entered the bailey, Betsy was roused from her bed and Gabrielle was given into her care. And then the servants and guards saw a side of their master they had never before witnessed. The duke went on the rampage, blistering their ears with threats and reproaches for their blatant disregard for Her Grace's safety. Serving maids and lackeys who had wonderingly answered the late summons to the great hall miraculously disappeared into cracks in the walls as they came under a hail of vituperation from a master whose forbearance was practically legendary.

Round-eyed, Betsy supported Gabrielle to her chamber. A bath was soon drawn and Gabrielle readied for bed. She scarcely exchanged a word with her maid. She felt wretched, believing herself to have forfeited the goodwill of everyone at Dunraeden. If Cam's people had been watchful before, after this night's work she could be certain that they would never let her out of their sight.

She was curled up in the huge wing armchair flanking the empty grate, obediently sipping brandy from the tumbler Betsy had placed in her hands, when Cam entered. He was soaked to the skin, and in his hand he held a length of hemp.

"Leave us," he curtly instructed.

There was a glitter in his eyes that forbade argument. Betsy clutched the wet towels to her bosom, bobbed a curtsy and made for the door.

"A moment!" Cam said, and pointed to the sodden heap of boy's clothes that lay discarded on the floor. "Dispose of these, Betsy. Her Grace has no further need of them."

When Betsy left, Cam turned the key in the lock. He propped himself casually against the door. "And just where do you think you were off to?" he asked carelessly, holding the length of rope in front of him.

Shakily, Gabrielle rose to her feet. The moment when she had wanted to surrender everything to him was long gone. Then, she had been laboring under a sense of gratitude, she told herself. There'd been time for reflection since. True, he had saved her life, but if he had not abducted her in the first place, she would not have been forced to take such extraordinary risks to escape.

"I'm waiting for an answer," he said, exaggerated politeness in his voice.

This was the Cam she knew. The Englishman. Her gaoler. *Her enemy,* she reminded herself forcefully.

"France," she answered, tilting her head back.

"France," he mimicked. "Forgive me. I had not known that you were such an accomplished swimmer. Or perhaps you were aiming to grow wings and fly the twenty or so miles of water that separate our two countries? Of course," he said, throwing the rope from him, "angels have wings. Now why didn't I think of that?" He drew in a long shuddering breath. His eyes locked on hers. All amusement wiped from his voice, he said, "It's only fair to warn you. I intend to clip your wings, Angel."

The promise was back in his eyes; the sensual slant to his mouth was unmistakable. Gabrielle didn't think of the wisdom of what she was doing. Her action was purely reflex. She made a dive for the bed, her fingers frantically groping under the mattress. When she whirled to face him, she was holding the kitchen knife she had hidden away for just such an occasion. She raised it threateningly.

Cam had not moved from his position at the door. His response was not what she expected. He covered his eyes with one hand, shook his head, and gave out a theatrical sigh.

"Gabrielle, it's not working," he said softly. When he raised his head to look at her, his expression was grave.

She swore at him, and lifted the knife fractionally.

He forced a laugh. "What a terrifying spectacle,

242

to be sure," he cajoled, his eyes sweeping over her. His voice gentled. "Gabrielle, I tell you, it's not working—the boy's clothes, the manly gait, the urchin's manners, the bad language, even the stench of fish on your skin . . ." His voice dropped, became husky, almost caressing. "Love, it's not working. It never did. It never could. What made you think it would?"

Though he hadn't taken a step, she retreated, her eyes as big as saucers. She shook her head.

Patiently, softly, as if he were gentling a skittish mare, he promised, "I don't want to hurt you. I *never* wanted to hurt you."

"Words!" she said, finding her voice. "Empty words! You hurt me and you didn't care."

He closed his eyes momentarily. When he opened them they were cloudy with regret. "No, love. You're wrong. I've never wanted to hurt you. I do care. And I'll prove it to you, if you'll let me."

His shoulders came away from the door. Though he made the move as careful and as unthreatening as he could make it, he saw the flare of fear in her eyes. "I won't hurt you. Trust me," he soothed.

He didn't know where the soothing words were coming from. He'd never seduced a woman in his life. He knew that he was going against his own principles. He'd always considered seduction a ploy of the unscrupulous. His women came to him willingly. But he had never wanted a woman as much as he wanted Gabrielle. He didn't think he could survive another night without her. Perhaps if he hadn't tasted the surrender on her lips an hour before he might have been able to let her go. He did not know. But he wouldn't let her turn him away now, not unless she could convince him that her refusal was final.

God, he was sure he did not know what was

driving him. Not lust. Not pleasure. Not the need for the ease of a woman's body. Gabrielle. Only Gabrielle. He wanted to care for her, protect her, have some small say in the ordering of her life. Not as a captor, but with her full and willing consent. Oh God, when had he taken to gammoning himself? He wanted to possess her, claim her irrevocably in the most primitive way known to man. She was his mate. If she did not know that, she soon would. And he was done deferring to her virginal scruples.

Slowly, carefully, he took another step toward her.

"You're my enemy," she cried out. "It's my duty to fight you."

"No, love, I'm your husband. It's your duty to love me."

"A marriage of convenience! You promised the marriage would be annulled."

He was only a step away from her now. "I'm not going to force you," he said. "But if you don't want me, you're going to have to use that knife."

"I'm not afraid to use it," she warned, and aimed it straight at his heart. But they could both see that her hand was shaking.

His eyes searched hers, questioning, and at the same time offering reassurance. "Your choice, love," he said with a crooked smile. "Kiss me or use the knife."

"Cam . . . please . . . no," she whispered.

It was the first time, the very first time she had given him his Christian name. Until that moment, he had perfect control of his breathing. A shudder passed over him. He murmured her name and reached for her. She stiffened. For one paralyzing moment of doubt he thought she meant to use the knife on him. But it slipped from her fingers to fall

244

with a soft thud on the carpeted floor. Gabrielle gave a little whimper of protest, but when he captured her in his arms he felt her resistance begin to melt.

"Don't fight me," he breathed into her mouth. "Please. Don't fight me. Not on this. It's too late, don't you see? Fight me on anything else you choose, but not on this." And he glued his lips to hers.

Chapter Fourteen

He had never been any woman's first lover, had never wanted to be. Unlike some gentlemen he could name, he had never been attracted to virgins. And though one part of his brain was fiercely glad that Gabrielle was coming to him untouched, another part wished that she were a woman of experience. His need for her was so overpowering that he wanted to take her, there, on the floor, without any preliminaries.

Restraint, control, gentleness—he had to fight himself to find them. Later he would remember that fact and be appalled at how closely the battle was fought. He'd never before lost his head over any woman. He came very close to losing it over Gabrielle.

He'd known, of course, that one day he would be obliged to marry, if only to secure the succession. He'd never expected his bride to do more than tolerate the intimacies of married life. There was another class of women to whom gentlemen resorted to indulge that dark and frankly sensual aspect of the male animal. There was never any question in his mind that he intended Gabrielle to be far more to him than a conventional wife.

When he lifted his lips from hers she was shaking like a leaf; he was trembling like a boy in the throes of first love. He closed his eyes until he regained a small portion of his equilibrium. *Slowly, carefully, easily,* he told himself, before taking her lips again.

She had never suspected that there was such gentleness in him. And then she remembered the stories that Betsy and Simon had told her. This was the Cam they had described, the warm and compassionate man. He had never shown her more than a glimpse of this side of his character. And yet he was as familiar to her as if she had known him all her life.

"Cam," she murmured against his lips, and she touched her hands wonderingly to the hard planes of his face. She could scarcely credit that she had ever likened this man to a tiger. She had never felt safer in her life.

She had no conception of the subtleties of his strategy. She scarcely noted when her wrapper was slipped from her shoulders to fall in a pool of silk at her feet. The brush of his lips against her cheeks, her eyes, her throat, was little more than a whisper. The stroke of his hands at her back, urging her closer, was the most comforting touch she'd ever experienced in her life. And when he brought his lips back to hers, molding them softly, she sighed her contentment into his mouth.

His kiss changed so slowly that she was barely aware of it. It was curiosity that made her open her lips to the playful urging of his. *English kisses,* she thought dreamily, as his tongue surged and receded and explored the inside of her mouth. She'd heard tell of this odd English preference. It was common knowledge, of course, that the English were a strange race.

Desire crept up on her stealthily. It was the brandy, she decided, that was making her skin heat; the near tragedy she'd been snatched from that was making her tremble. And when she was overcome with dizziness and swayed into Cam she was suddenly grateful that he had the presence of mind to sweep her into his arms and carry her to the bed.

But when he straightened, and she thought that he meant to quit her chamber, she knew exactly what she was doing when she whispered, "Cam, don't leave me. Please."

He peeled out of his wet garments with a speed and efficiency that had her smiling. But the smile died on her lips when he stood there, naked at last, giving her a moment to drink in the sight of him.

He was a magnificent specimen of masculinity. Broad shoulders tapered to a trim waist; lean hips and flanks. She almost envied him those sleek muscles that rippled along his athletic arms and thighs. *He'd make a formidable enemy in any test of strength,* she reflected. His powerful chest was covered in a profusion of dark hair that narrowed at the waist before flaring down to his groin. She'd never seen an aroused male before. Her own desire flamed and then began to ebb.

When she could find her breath, she stammered, "You're . . . beautiful. But . . . Cam . . . I don't think . . . this isn't possible, surely?"

He'd been so damn careful not to frighten her. He should have known that her first sight of an aroused male would be overwhelming. For a moment, he'd considered snuffing out the candles. But he wasn't about to be cheated out of taking her the way he had fantasied so many times, awake and sleeping. He'd seen her naked when he couldn't do a damn thing about it. Things were different now.

Carefully, without haste, he stretched out beside her. "Your body was made for mine," he told her. He saw the doubt flickering at the back of her eyes, and he couldn't help smiling. And then, for the first time, it occurred to him that he was going to be the source of some pain to her. He couldn't let that deter him, he decided. And to his shame he resolved not to tell her till it was too late to draw back.

Slowly he slipped her nightrail from her, and spread her glorious hair over the pillows, draping one lock over her shoulder to fan across her breasts. His fingers smoothed that swath of gold, skimming over her breasts, unhurriedly tracing every valley and contour, calmly taking possession of what no man before him had ever claimed.

She was exactly as he expected, and at the same time, infinitely more. He should have known that she would feel like this, svelte, smooth to the touch, and incredibly soft. He lowered himself over her and opened his mouth on her bared shoulder, tasting the faint and surprising flavor of rosewater. She could have immersed herself in a whole barrel of fish oil and it wouldn't have made a jot of difference. The thought made him smile.

He wasn't smiling when his mouth closed over one coral-tipped nipple. When he sucked greedily, Gabrielle jerked. Her whole body went rigid and by degrees went lax beneath him. She moaned, and Cam almost stopped breathing altogether. He had to fight to drag air into his lungs.

So this was what she'd read in the promise of his eyes these past weeks, thought Gabrielle. She was languidly drifting with the current, immersed in sensation, helpless to turn away from the tide of his passion. He was dragging her down to those dark depths where her only safety lay in clinging fast to him. Her last coherent thought was that if she was about to drown, she was going to take him with her.

Their bodies seemed to flow together. Skin rubbed against skin and heated; breath mingled;

249

lips skimmed and tasted; lovers' words tumbled from their lips. When Cam slipped a finger inside her, passion exploded between them.

He resisted the press of her hands on his shoulders, urging him to cover her body. With one powerful leg he anchored her bucking hips, trying to soothe her with words he could never remember afterward. He didn't want to hurt her. Oh God, the last thing he wanted to do was hurt her! She didn't understand. She was on fire and he was being sucked into the conflagration. And then she begged him once too often, and it was too late to draw back.

He took her shocked cry of pain into his mouth. She went as still as a statue. He raised his head and waited till she opened her eyes. When her eyelashes lifted, he recognized the building anger in the green fire. His lips swooped down and he swallowed the long string of curses he guessed were gathering on her tongue, waiting to lash him. Her nails dug mercilessly into his shoulders trying to dislodge him where before she had urged him to take her. Her tears were a silent bitter reproach. With infinite tenderness he kissed them away.

"You're a woman now," he whispered hoarsely. "My woman. My wife," and he coaxed her back to passion with open-mouthed kisses and endless lingering caresses till she was shuddering with the same mindless desire that raced through him. Only then did he begin to move.

There was a moment when she resisted him. His hands slid under her hips, lifting her, teaching her the age-old rhythm. His blood sang when she followed his urging. And when she crested the peak, dragging him with her, and he took her keening cry of pleasure into his mouth, he thought his heart would burst.

His face was buried against her hair, one arm draped around her waist. He didn't want to know what he was feeling. He knew he was humbled. No woman had ever given herself so freely to him before. He didn't expect it. One way or another, he was used to paying for sexual favors. To his knowledge, no woman had ever wanted him for himself. It was so like Gabrielle not to count the cost, he was thinking.

She had been staring into space since he'd pulled from her. In the aftermath of their spent passion, not one word had passed her lips. It made him nervous. He dragged her closer to the shelter of his body.

"What are you thinking?" he asked softly.

Her head shifted on the pillow as she turned into him. He loved the look in her eyes, dazed and love-sleepy. Though the touch of her palm on his bare chest was whisper soft, he felt the force of it all the way to his loins.

"This changes everything," she said.

"Yes." His lips brushed over her eyes and feathered her mouth.

"Why?"

"I'm not sending you back to France." His mind searched for answers that she would accept. "Simon has convinced me that it's the worst thing I could do to you. How would you explain your absence all these months?"

"You should have thought of that before."

"It didn't matter to me one way or the other when I first brought you here."

She waited for him to continue, and when he remained silent, she said, "You're not thinking, Englishman. Don't you suppose that *I* had given the

251

matter some thought?"

He loved the way she said *Englishman*, as if it were a caress. Smiling, he asked, "And what solution presented itself?"

Musingly, she replied, "I'm sure Rollo would have been more than happy to marry me. We could have circulated a rumor that my grandfather refused his permission, so we eloped."

He didn't know that his hand had tightened to such a degree around her wrist that she thought her bones would snap. "You're my wife," he said. "Even now you could be pregnant with my child." Her lashes swept down and fear flamed through him. "Gabrielle!" He captured her face with both hands. "Is that so bad?"

A secretive smile turned up the corners of her lips. "Is that what you want?" Her eyes were sparkling.

"Yes. Oh God, yes!" And he brought her head up, kissing her ruthlessly, passionately, showing her with the force of his ardor what he daren't reveal with words, not even to himself.

For the first time since she'd passed inside Dunraeden's formidable walls, Gabrielle was offered the privilege of leaving by its front doors. In a spanking tan and black riding habit with matching bonnet perched perilously over one eyebrow, she came into the bailey to bright sunshine. Cam was already astride his magnificent bay.

She smiled at him shyly, thinking how handsome and grave he looked. And then she remembered the tender, careful lover of the night before and a becoming blush stole over her cheeks. When her eyes lit on the docile animal the groom led forward, however a tiny frown appeared on her brow. She missed the fleeting smile that came and went on Cam's face. Rambler was the slug of Dunraeden's extensive stables, and he looked it. Gabrielle shot Cam a suspicious glance, but the smile was carefully wiped from his lips. The groom assisted her to mount.

"Sidesaddle," she disparaged, but she could not prevent the smile. Since she had wakened that morning, smiles had never been far from her lips; laughter bubbled up and spilled over. She had no idea how happy and beautiful she looked, or how Cam's heart had constricted at his first sight of her.

Cam led the way. The first hour was given over to what was evidently to be an object lesson. They walked their mounts across the wet sands to the tower walls down which Gabrielle had lowered herself the night before. The rocks below, in the bright sunlight, had a frightening, ferocious aspect.

Cam was very grim when he said, "If you had slipped, or the rope had broken . . ."

"Pooh!" Gabrielle interjected forcefully. "That part was child's play!"

Anger flamed in his eyes. "You'll take it a mite more seriously than that!"

The change in him shocked her. Her gaze faltered and dropped away.

His voice gentled, bringing her eyes up. "Gabrielle. Please. I want your promise that you won't attempt anything so foolish again. Is that too much for a husband to ask of his wife?"

She colored a little and said in an earnest tone. "But Cam, I wouldn't. Not now."

She meant what she said. Though she could not have explained herself adequately, she was deeply conscious that what had passed between them during the night had bound her irrevocably to the man who had claimed her, and he to her. She had yet to think through all the implications of her surrender, but she was in love. She believed that Cam loved her too, though the words had not been spoken. Her confidence in their willingness and ability to solve their differences was, at that moment, unshakable.

Still, she was a little disappointed to see how quickly Cam had reverted to his former forbidding personality. In the dark of the night, the man who had initiated her so painstakingly, so passionately into love had been as tender and as affectionate a lover as she could have wished. With the confidence of youth, she made up her mind that she could not allow Cam to reestablish distance between them. The English were known to be an undemonstrative lot. That did not sit well with her, not when she had lost her heart to one of them. She wanted, needed the same closeness that they had shared in that long night of love. She wanted intimacy at every level.

With love shining from her eyes, she glanced up at him. "No," she said emphatically, "I won't try that again."

"I want your word on it."

"You have it," she answered at once.

Their eyes held, and Cam rewarded her with a devastating smile. "Good girl."

He read everything he had hoped to see in her eyes. She was so utterly transparent. And still he was not satisfied. He had taken the first step to bind her to him, but she had other loyalties, more enduring ones, that could easily break the tenuous hold he had established. He could not keep her a prisoner forever. Though he took her again and again, would it be enough? he wondered. With an unscrupulousness that formerly he would have eschewed in his dealings with women, he wished that he had taken her months before when he had first wanted to. By this time it was entirely possible that he would have fathered his child on her. At the thought, his eyes flared.

That bond would tie her to him forever. She would never wish to return to France then. His mind raced ahead to what was to be the culmination of years of patient intriguing. Mascaron. He had only to give the word to Rodier and Mascaron's treasonable activities would be quietly revealed to French authorities. True, his intelligence on the strength and disposition of the French fleet would come to an end, but that aspect of the plan had always been of secondary importance. It was Mascaron himself that Cam wanted. And though he had him in the palm of his hand for the first time, he held off for only one reason. Gabrielle. Because of Gabrielle, he was toying with the idea of subverting a course of action to which he'd been committed for years.

"Cam, what is it? What's wrong?" She saw that the cold, distant look was back in his eyes, and something inside her shriveled. And then, as quickly as it was there, it was gone.

"We're not finished yet," he said.

Evidently it was not to be the end of the lesson. They cantered toward the shore, where they dismounted. Garielle obediently followed as Cam led the way up the steep, narrow track that joined Dunraeden to the mainland. Near the top he turned aside to a sheltered outcrop of rock, where they might see the force of the tide as it raced to shore.

"One mile as the crow flies," he said. "But you turned due west. In the dark, it's almost impossible to find one's bearings."

Gabrielle shivered, but she could not say whether it was because of the chill in Cam's voice or because of the close call she'd had the previous night. Almost stubbornly she said, "I'm the proverbial cat with nine lives. I haven't used them up yet."

The velvet in his voice was underlaid with hard steel. "A more stupid remark I've yet to hear you make."

Her chin lifted. "Is it stupid for a prisoner to attempt to escape?"

"Is that what you want? Escape?"

She shielded her eyes against the sun, trying to read his expression. In one stride he was towering over her, cutting out her view of everything but him. He had her by the shoulders.

"Why didn't you use the knife on me if you wanted to escape?" His voice was rougher, fiercer than she had ever heard it. "Last night, why didn't you use the knife?"

"Cam, please, you're hurting me." She tried to shake free of his ruthless grip.

"I know why," he said.

His lips swept over hers, then sank in to take their fill. She could not have stopped him even if she had wanted to. Her body had a new awareness of itself, seemed to recognize the lips and hands that pulled at her senses so ceaselessly.

He dragged her to her knees. Her spencer was peeled from her before she was aware that the buttons had been slipped from their buttonholes. Through the fabric of her frock, teeth and lips raced over her breasts. At the first pull on her nipples, she collapsed against him.

"Cam. Not here." Her protest was weak, but he might have heeded it if she had not arched into him, offering him more.

He had the smoothest, nimblest fingers she'd ever encountered. Her breasts were spilling into his hands before she knew that he had even opened her

256

"You could teach me those passes you used in Andely, don't you remember?"

"The answer is no." His voice was clipped. He rose swiftly and strode to their tethered mounts.

"But why?" She scrambled to her feet and ran after him. "Why, Cam? Can't you just see Goliath's face when I beat him at his own game? I've never won a contest of skill with him yet." The laughter bubbled up but froze on her lips when Cam spun to face her.

Coldly furious, he said, "And I've no desire to be beaten at my own game. D'you suppose that I'm fool enough to put a foil in your hand and teach you how to win a contest of skill against me?"

It was her careless reference to Goliath that had brought his temper to boiling point. Her heart was still in France, he thought furiously. She would leave him if the chance ever presented itself. Hadn't he known it?

"Cam, no," she said softly, and laid a hand on his sleeve. He shook her off. Undeterred, she continued calmly, "Cam, I could never hurt you. That's why I couldn't use the knife when I had the chance."

Yet he did not trust her, and in the days and weeks that followed, that unpalatable truth was brought home to her cruelly. She was as much a prisoner as she had ever been, more so, if it were possible. For now, not only was she watched during the daylight hours, but her nights belonged to Cam.

She went into his arms willingly. There, in the privacy of their chamber, she had the man she had fallen in love with. She gave him everything he demanded of her and more. It was easy to give him the freedom of her body when her response to his slightest touch flamed out of control. It was harder to force him to meet her own needs. She demanded genuine intimacy, an intimacy in which they could share the secrets of their hearts. She was aware that Cam struggled to keep her at a distance, but she would not permit it. In the aftermath of passion she shared things about herself, fears and dreams, that she had never before shared with anyone. Love-sleepy and sated, Cam reciprocated to some extent.

Gabrielle absorbed everything he confided to her. For all her youth, she possessed an uncanny insight. It came to her gradually that he was afraid to trust himself to love. Everyone he had ever loved had been taken away from him. Some memories he refused to share with her. The circumstances of his stepmother's and sister's tragic end was a subject that could not be broached. Patiently, with every particle of her generous nature, she tried to gentle him of his deep-seated and unspoken fears. With womanly intuition, she knew that she had long since captured his heart. It was his trust that she courted. It was not to be so easily won. He thought to hold her by building the walls of her prison stouter and higher. It was love that chained her to him. He was too blind to see it.

She could not always be patient with him, of course. Sometimes she came very close to losing her temper. The night that she first suspected that she might be pregnant was just such an occasion.

It was Betsy who put the thought into her head. Gabrielle was undressing for bed when the maid re-marked, "You should have had your courses by now."

Startled, Gabrielle's eyes flew to Betsy's. "Should I?"

"A week since," answered Betsy, looking very pleased with herself for some obscure reason. "You've never been late in all the time you've been at Dunraeden." She looked a question at her young mistress.

"No, I've never been late in my life."

The click of the doorlatch alerted them to Cam's presence. Gabrielle's lips pursed in displeasure. Betsy's widened in a smile.

His blue eyes flared to a strange brilliance as they quickly scanned Gabrielle. She wondered how much he had heard. When Betsy excused herself and Cam followed her into the corridor, she surmised that he'd overheard everything.

When he came back into the room and lounged in the doorway, Gabrielle's eyes were flaming. His were dancing.

"You shamed me," she accused, and stalked to the bed where she proceeded to beat out her frustration on the feather pillows.

"I would never do such a thing deliberately," he replied.

Before he could take her into his arms, she spun away from him. Bosom heaving, she faced him. "I'm not a child. I'm a grown woman."

"I can't argue with that." His lips were grave, but his eyes betrayed him. "I thought we both agreed that you were more than comfortable in that role." He was referring to her confession, made in the deep of the night and in the security of his arms, that she feared she could never be a real woman. He'd convinced her otherwise in a most primitive fashion.

Coloring at the memory, she retreated as he began to stalk her.

His smile deepened. "In point of fact, as I remember, we agreed that you exceeded my wildest expectations."

"You don't take me seriously." She stamped her foot, and stood her ground as he approached. "You should have asked *me* what you wished to know, not my maid."

His grin dissolved and he offered a smile that was half contrite, half cozening. "I'm sorry. It was wrong of me. But I thought you might not wish me to know."

"Of course I don't wish you to know," she said with a burst of impatience. "It's only a week, for heaven's sake. It may mean nothing at all."

Eyes gleaming, he reminded her, "But you've never been late in your life."

She could not like his levity. Passionately, she cried out, "It would suit your purposes if I were pregnant, would it not? Then I could not scale walls and fence and . . . and so on."

His hands closed over her shoulders, kneading, caressing. "Hush, love," he chided. "You're getting into a state about nothing. You're not going any-where. Now come to bed."

She resisted the pull of his hands. "Be damned to you, Englishman! If I decided to leave you, nothing would stop me. D'you hear? Nothing!"

"No, love," he corrected, "I would stop you. If you went to the ends of the earth, I would find you and bring you back. Now come to bed."

He swept her off her feet and into his arms. She saw tenderness smiling in his eyes, but also an im-placability that made her shudder. Waves of hope-lessness washed over her. He would never understand what kept her with him. She began to cry in earnest. Hiccuping, sniffing, she muddled through a long and disjointed explanation, half in English, half in French, of why it would be a kind-ness to society in general, and to herself in particu-lar, if someone were to lock him up in Bedlam. Her words were liberally laced with curses and oaths.

Though she was sure she was inconsolable and could not respond to his lovemaking, he proved himself relentless even in that most intimate of all

262

acts. With a patience that was almost torture to her, he soothed her. Banking his own passion, he lavished her with slow, intimate caresses. He stole her breath with soft kisses and promises of the pleasure to come, breathed into her mouth. Sighs became interspersed with moans; hearts raced erratically; each breath became more difficult than the last.

Here she would show him, she thought. Here, where they were both at their most vulnerable. She turned into him. With artless passion, she pressed frantic kisses over his throat and shoulders, skimming every bare inch of exposed skin her lips could find. Her hands splayed out, and with the sensitive pads of her fingers she stroked slowly down the length of his hard body. She became bolder. Shamelessly, wantonly, she touched him as she had never touched him before, glorying in the hot silky shaft he thrust into her cupped hands.

The love in her heart spilled over. "I love you, love you, love you," she whispered into his mouth, and showed him with increasing abandon how wide, how generous was the scope of what she felt for him.

Cam went wild. She was rocked back into the mattress. He reared over her and pushed her knees high. He spoke the only words she wanted to hear the moment before he entered her. As she locked her arms and legs around him, waves of pleasure burst through him. For a moment he almost regained control. But she moved sinuously, voluptuously beneath him and he was lost. He wasn't gentle. She'd taken that away from him. Rhythmically, rapidly, straining to delay their pleasure, he rode her till they lay shuddering in each others arms.

When he tried to pull from her she stayed him with her hand on the back of his neck.

"I won't let you take back those words," she told him, and slowly, lovingly, pressed wet kisses to his chin. "You love me. You told me so."

He smiled down at her. "And I won't let you forget how skilled you've become in bed."

Her cheeks bloomed, but more in pleasure at his praise than embarrassment. "Is . . . is what we do in bed a skill?" she asked.

"You're getting to be quite an expert," he teased, and couldn't resist covering those adorable blushes with the brush of his lips.

Her eyes were wide and guileless as they stared into his. Solemnly she said, "I think you've had a mite more practice than I, if I'm not mistaken."

With great difficulty, he managed to bite back a smile, "I've never been in love before," he pointed out in his own defense.

Her eyes warmed the moment before her lips curved. "Let's practice some more," she suggested.

He was about to give her a lecture in masculine physiology when she made a sudden movement beneath him. Then her hands swept down from his shoulders to his flanks, leaving a trail of sensual heat wherever she touched him. Every muscle in his body tensed. He was gulping for air by the time she dragged his head down for her embrace.

Slowly, he promised himself. This time he would take her slowly and with all the care and skill of which he was capable. But it was Gabrielle who set the pace. She was just beginning to discover the power she had over him. *Ruthless, quite ruthless,* he thought, as she began to exploit that power to its limits.

Chapter Fifteen

With September came a welcome relief from the hot, humid days of that lingering Cornish summer. Inland, the countryside wore its autumn colors. Wheat and fruit ripened, and farmers labored to bring in their rich harvests. Gabrielle saw nothing of this. For all that she had been in Cornwall for four months, she had never been permitted to venture farther than the top of the cliffs overlooking Dunraeden, and never without Cam in attendance. There were no outings of any note. No visitors came to call. There was no fencing practice in the gallery as she'd been accustomed to in Normandy, no horseback rides to explore the countryside, and no adventures with the *contrebandiers*. In short, there was nothing to break the tedium of those long summer days when the sun never set before ten o'clock.

She missed Lansing. Even Louise would have been a welcome addition, though Gabrielle could not think of her without experiencing a twinge of conscience. In some way she felt that she had, in all innocence, lured Cam away from a lady whom he might very well have married. For the few days she had been in Dunraeden before Louise had taken her leave of them, Gabrielle had sensed an intimacy between Cam and the older woman that she could not dismiss. She'd been almost certain that an engagement was in the offing. And though she had never taken to Louise Pelletier, she was coming to regret that she had not tried harder to make a friend of the lady. Had she done so, she reflected, Louise might have stayed on, and she would not be so alone.

She was lonely. She was bored. Her role as chatelaine, for which she felt she had not the slightest aptitude, was severely circumscribed by virtue of the fact that there were no parties or amusements to arrange, no guests to entertain, only a monotonous inventory of bed linens, china, and cutlery, and lists of duties to oversee for Cam's army of servants. And really, she thought, she could not find it in herself to care one way or the other whether the domestics turned out the rooms in the west wing first, or whether it was more urgent to begin cleaning the silver or the crystal. Her own preference would have been to start on the armory or possibly the stables. But that was Cam's domain, and he never invited her into it.

Cam's time was occupied with estate business. Occasionally he left her for short stretches when matters of state called him to London. He was her husband. He was her lover. But more than anything, she wished he would be her friend. She hated the distance he successfully maintained between them during the daylight hours. It was a different man who came into her arms at night.

Not unnaturally, she became quarrelsome. She wanted more liberties as a demonstration of his good faith. She complained that she was completely cut off from any news of the outside world. The war might be over for all he told her. It was the servants who kept her informed. She begged for any intelligence of her grandfather. Cam was polite but uninformative. She knew that he wanted her to be happy. She was close to despair.

She conceived the notion that she would have to prove her trustworthiness in some extraordinary fashion, since her spoken assurance weighed little or nothing with him. Her imagination ran riot. The more far fetched of her schemes she reluctantly rejected. She did not see how she could contrive at one and the same time to put her husband's life in jeopardy, save it in the nick of time, and manage to do herself grievous bodily injury (not mortal, of course), which would bring him to his knees (and senses) in abject repentance. The plan she finally hit upon was much simpler, though to her regret, lacking in drama. She would leave Dunraeden and return of her own free will. The more she thought of it the more merit the scheme gained. He would be devastated when he found her gone. She was sorry to put him to so much pain, but the rewards when she demanded entry at Dunraeden's front doors would more than compensate for what he would suffer. The proofs of her commitment to him, in these circumstances, would be indisputable. But how was it to be done?

There could be no repetition of the last escape attempt. For one thing, guards were now posted at every tower, and for another, it was almost certain that she was with child. She would not dare provoke Cam's wrath by putting herself and her precious burden at unnecessary risk. It must be easily contrived or she would not do it at all. As for her promise to Cam that she would never again make any attempt to escape, her conscience was clear. A mock escape was no escape at all, at least by her lights.

A less resourceful girl would have agonized for weeks on how the whole enterprise was to be pulled off. Given Gabrielle's background, it was not to be surprised that she came up with a creditable plan in a matter of days. In point of fact, she'd considered and rejected this route once before. Though there was not the least threat to life or limb, the chances of successfully evading detection were hazardous.

She set her plan in motion by announcing to Betsy one wet and dreary morning that she intended personally to make inventory of the servants' livery. At Dunraeden the servants changed their livery every autumn and spring. It was no great labor, by the end of that morning, to have concealed in a pillow case one of the brown and beige suits worn by the young pages. When Betsy's back was turned, Gabrielle hared up to her chamber and stuffed her trophy at the back of her clothes press. When she idled down to the great hall moments later, eyes bright, cheeks flushed, she found Cam waiting for her.

He removed a piece of lint from her nose before leading her to his study. Smiling, he remarked, "Pregnancy must agree with you. You're positively blooming."

"I wish you would not speak so," she chided, allowing him to seat her at his desk. "It's too soon to say with any certainty."

The thought died as her eyes scanned the single sheet of paper she had idly picked up. It was in Cam's writing and addressed to her grandfather, and was similar to many she had copied for him in the past.

"I've asked a local physician to look in on us before the end of the week," she heard him say. The words made no impression on her.

When she looked up at him, her eyes were burningly intense. "I won't copy this, so don't ask me."

His smile faded. He gave her a calm, measured look. Cooly, he said, "It's necessary to ensure Mas-

268

caron's compliance, or I would not ask it of you."

"Why can't I tell him the truth? Surely now that our marriage is a real one, there's no necessity to go on with the game?"

"You're mistaken," he said. "Our marriage makes no difference. What made you think it would?"

The quarrel that ensued was ferocious and left them both shaken. At one point, having no clear idea of what she was saying, Gabrielle struck in, "Nothing can make me believe you are doing this for your country. This is personal. It's my grandfather. You hate him! You hate him, don't you?"

The truth was written on his face for anyone to read. White-faced, tight-lipped, he compelled her, by sheer force of will, to comply with his instructions.

She copied his letter and rose to her feet. Her voice was trembling when she said, "I wish you would tell me why you hate my grandfather."

He remained silent as he turned away from her.

Goaded, she cried out, "I love him. Doesn't that make a difference to you?"

She shrank from the look he turned on her. She flinched from the jeer in his voice. "You give your love too easily," he said.

Gabrielle gave a little cry and backed to the door. He said her name once but it did not check her. She slipped away before he could make a move to prevent it, before he had made up his mind that he wanted to prevent it.

He remained standing perfectly still, staring at the closed door. After a moment, he moved to the window and looked out blindly. The rain that had begun to fall hours before was unrelenting, and a fine mist was creeping in from the Channel.

In the past, whenever Gabrielle had written a letter to her grandfather, Cam had absented himself for several hours at a time. It seemed probable that the letter had to be taken to its point of departure, to some port close by, to some messenger who would make the journey to France. She hovered in the upstairs gallery till she heard his voice calling to one of the footmen to have his horse brought round. When the porters closed the front doors behind him, she turned on her heel and made for her chamber.

Timing was of the essence if she was to make her escape undetected. She ordered dinner on a tray to be sent to her chamber. As soon as she had shut the door on the maid who had delivered it, she was on the move.

Thirty minutes later, one of Dunraeden's young pages slowly descended the great staircase with Her Grace's almost untouched dinner tray. The few servants who were going about their business noticed nothing worthy of comment. Nor did they remark that the page made a detour to the library. Most of their number were already at board in the servants' hall, and the few who remained on duty were impatient to be relieved so that they might join them.

In the library, Gabrielle deposited the heavy salver on a chair. Quickly walking to the bookcases, she selected a slim volume and returned to the hall. She hoped that anyone observing would think that Her Grace had sent a page on an errand. She loitered in the great hall for a moment or two then slipped unobserved into a saloon that overlooked the bailey. Moving to the window, she looked out. Perfect. Fog as thick as a broth and unremitting rain.

She did not have long to wait. Guards at the gates and on the towers were calling out to each other. It was past time for the change of watch, and men were becoming more and more impatient to be relieved of their irksome duty and to take shelter from the hostile elements.

Gabrielle opened the sash window and climbed over the sill. It was only a ten-foot drop to the ground. With a practiced movement she turned onto her stomach and eased herself down the outside wall till only her fingertips curled round the window frame. She uncurled her fingers and landed on her feet, crouched over. Dragging her long, plaited hair free of her coat collar, she bundled it into a cap that she had removed from her pocket.

Though it was still some hours to go before dusk, the fog was so thick that lanterns had been lit in the bailey. They winked at her through the swirls of mist. When she heard the great outside doors begin to creak on their hinges, she straightened. With a little prayer on her lips, she moved purposefully toward the sound of voices, keeping her head down.

She had never expected it to be so easy. No one challenged her. Every man was too intent on getting out of the rain to pay much heed to his neighbor. And the dark livery she had donned might, in that uncertain light, have passed for the nondescript garb of any of the men.

For months she had carefully observed these regular changes in the watch. Not all the men lived inside the walls of the castle. Many of them had other occupations or had homes to go to nearby. Gabrielle had questioned Betsy in as offhand a manner as she could manage. From the little that Betsy had told her she surmised that the majority of them were involved to some extent in the lucrative smuggling trade.

As men jostled each other coming and going, Gabrielle ducked through the great arch, turning her collar up and her face into the wall. Her luck held

271

until, on the other side, and just when she thought she had got clear away, she ran smack into a rock-hard shape that suddenly loomed up in front of her out of the fog.

"Excusez-moi." The softly spoken, unthinking words were out before she could stop them. She sucked in her breath and tried to step to the side. A scream rose in her throat as a hand clamped over her mouth and she was dragged into the shelter of the wall.

Blinking rapidly, her fear-crazed eyes looked up at her assailant. The eyes widened. The hand was removed from her mouth. "Goliath," she breathed. *"Quel . . ."* And then her voice became too thick, her throat too choked for speech, and her body shook spasmodically. Weeping, she threw herself into his arms.

He was a big man, bigger than she remembered. She felt the scrape of his beard against her cheek and felt a familiar comfort wash through her. She burrowed deeper, remembering other times and places when he had been there, like a shield, to protect her. He smelled of leather and tobacco and . . . Calvados. She didn't know why a picture of apple trees laden with blossom should come into her mind. Normandy, she thought despairingly, and hiccuped.

He said something low and urgent and administered a rough shake. She came to herself gradually and made a pathetic attempt to speak. Goliath shook his head and gave her a smile that was both cautionary and encouraging. When he saw that she had herself under control, he gestured that she was to follow him.

The moment they turned off the well-trodden path that led to the top of the cliffs, Gabrielle was lost. She kept hard on Goliath's heels, wondering a little how he came to know the terrain so well. Before she had run into him she had meant to take cover in the sheltered outcrop of rock where Cam had once taken her. Soaked to the skin, hungry and miserably cold, she began to see how foolhardy her plan had been.

"Where are we?"

The darkness covered them like a wet blanket, but thankfully they were sheltered from the elements. She stayed perfectly still as Goliath felt his way further into what she realized must be a cave. Within moments, flint was struck and a lantern was lit.

"Come," he instructed, and led the way deeper into the bowels of the earth.

Gabrielle drew in a steadying breath, and followed obediently. There was no question in her mind that Goliath had come to take her back to France. She did not know what she wanted, but she knew she could not go with him. For good or ill, her place was with the man who had made her his wife. She wondered what words she might find to persuade Goliath to leave her behind. Numb with misery, she stumbled after him.

An hour later, gorged on dry bread and cheese and fortified with Calvados, she felt considerably more comfortable. Stripped of her wet jacket, she sat huddled on a wooden cask, wrapped in a coarse woolen blanket. From time to time she flicked an uncertain look at Goliath. He had heard her out in silence and had given her enough information about home to ease her mind. It only remained for him to reveal what he intended to do.

Goliath watched her consideringly. He had yet to make up his mind which course he would follow. It had taken him weeks to spy out the lay of the land. To the locals he was the leader of a band of French smugglers, more than tolerated for the quality of the cheap cognac he ferried across the Channel. By degrees he had won their confidence, so much so that they had allowed him the use of one of the caves for himself and his men in the event that overzealous excise men might come upon the scene before they could rid themselves of their contraband and put to sea. He had stumbled upon Gabrielle at the worst possible moment. He had no means of effecting an escape until his boat returned with a fresh cargo from France. And with no letup in the fog, it could be days before that happened. And now she had just told him a story that absolutely confounded him.

He probed gently, "Why would you want to remain here when I can tell by your face that you're not happy?"

She lifted her head and gave him her attention. "As I told you, I'm his wife now."

"Do you love him?"

She thought of Cam as she had last seen him. The man was a study of leashed violence. He was cruel, cold, and vindictive. His promises of love made only in that act of supreme intimacy were empty in light of his subsequent behavior. She could not possibly love such a man.

"What has love got to do with it?" she asked evasively.

"In that case, there's only one solution once we land on French soil."

"What does that mean?"

"Divorce." He was watching her carefully. "Normally, I wouldn't suggest it. But in this case . . ." He shrugged.

Color washed out of Gabrielle's face. She knew as well as Goliath that divorce in France had become a commonplace since the Revolution. "He would come

274

after me," she said earnestly. "He told me so."

"Then I'll take care of him before we sail."

"What?"

With a wicked grin, Goliath made a chopping motion with his hand against his throat. Gabrielle sprang to her feet.

"Oh, Goliath, no! I . . . perhaps I do love him a little," she confessed, shamefaced.

Having discovered what he wished to know, Goliath adroitly changed the subject. "What were you doing, dressed like a page and sneaking out of the Englishman's castle on a wild night like this?"

Gabrielle frowned down at her scratched boots. What *was* she doing out on a wild night like this? Oh yes. Something to do with showing her slowtop of a husband that love made her a prisoner, not the stout walls and towers of his invincible keep. When she looked up, she was grinning. "Teaching the Englishman a lesson, 'tis all. Now it's your turn. Were you seriously thinking of calmly walking into the lion's den?"

"I was doing a bit of scouting," he explained. "There's a game of cards, so I believe, that habitually takes place in the guard room of an evening. I inveigled an invitation to it. Does he love you?"

Caught off balance, Gabrielle stammered, "Not in the way I wish to be loved." Her eyelashes lowered and she sank back onto the wooden cask.

Goliath combed his fingers through his grizzled beard. He did not know what to make of the Englishman. He had half a mind to knock him on the head and carry him off to Normandy until such time as Gabrielle had decided what she wanted done with him.

"You're no longer a girl, Angel," he said idly.

"Was I ever one?"

Goliath's brow pleated in a frown. He glanced

sideways at Gabrielle's forlorn figure. She was a woman, he thought, and he was not sure if he wished to kill the Englishman or congratulate him for the transformation he detected in her.

Coming to a decision, he said, "I should get you back before they send out a search party."

"Then you'll let me stay in England?"

He grunted. "For the moment."

"And you'll tell Mascaron that the Englishman has no hold over him? Cam won't hurt me, you know. I swear it, Goliath. You see . . . I'm . . . we're . . . ," on a rush, she blurted out, "I think I'm with child."

Anger flared in Goliath's eyes. Now he would murder the Englishman.

Observing that fierce look and recognizing what it might portend, Gabrielle said, placatingly, "I'm happy about the babe. Really. And I wouldn't take it kindly if you did away with the father of my child." She gave him a rueful smile.

He offered her his hand and drew her to her feet. In his mind he had already decided that he wasn't going to leave her to the Englishman completely un-protected. Somehow he would contrive to be there in the background until he had some answers to the questions that had been raised in his mind.

"Let's go," he said, and led the way out of the cave.

They had not taken a dozen steps when Goliath came to a sudden halt. There was the sound of movement in the mouth of the cave they had just left. Goliath tensed and held up his hand, alerting Gabrielle to their danger. She looked around anx-iously, but could see no further than the dense fog that concealed everything more than a few inches in front of her face.

Goliath withdrew a broad bladed knife from the

waistband of his breeches. Around them, in a circle, came the unmistakable sound of pistols cocking.

A strident masculine voice shouted, "In the name of our sovereign, King George, I command you to surrender!"

"Cam's found us!" expelled Gabrielle on a ragged breath.

"Worse," answered Goliath, raising his hands high in the air. "English excise men."

Slowly, Gabrielle followed Goliath's example. Out of the fog, primed and ready, emerged several wicked looking pistols. One of them poked Gabrielle in the ribs. On command, she raised her hands higher.

"Falmouth?" repeated Cam with a sardonic lift of his eyebrows. "My page is confined at His Majesty's pleasure in the tollbooth at Falmouth?" His eyes fell to the paper in his hand. His voice grew more silky. "Who exactly is this French smuggler who was captured with him?"

Ned Hoverley, the man who had brought the page's message, began to shake in his boots. The reward the young lad had offered for carrying his letter to his master paled into insignificance beside the magnitude of the peril he had placed him in. Ned never suspected that the lad meant him to come face to face with the duke. He'd expected the page's master to be the butler or one of the footmen. "Cam" was the name he'd written on the outside of the single folded sheet of paper. The page had played a filthy trick on him, Ned decided, and as soon as he'd made his escape, he was going straight back to Falmouth to wring his scrawny neck. Observing the sparks kindling in the duke's impatient eyes, he stammered out, "There's been some mistake, Your Grace."

The duke's control visibly slipped. "Who the hell is this Frenchman he was captured with?" he roared.

"G . . . Goliath, he called him."

The duke went rigid. The temperature in that warm, book-lined chamber seemed to become suddenly arctic. "Goliath," repeated the duke, his voice pleasantly modulated. The messenger shivered. Cam reached into his desk and tossed a coin to the man who had brought Gabrielle's message. "For your trouble," he said dismissively.

Ned looked at the guinea in his hand, a small fortune, to his way of thinking. He thought of how he might double it. "Shall I carry a message back, Your Grace?"

"Mmm?" Cam's eyes focused on the man as if he could not remember why he was there. Coming to himself, he said, "That won't be necessary. A night in the tollbooth might prove very salutary for . . . my page. Who's in charge down there, by the by? Is it still Claverley?"

"No, Your Grace." Ned shifted uncomfortably.

"Not Claverley? Oh, now I remember. He was dismissed for . . . smuggling, wasn't it?"

Ned said nothing.

"Then it's Penhanley," suggested Cam.

"Aye," said Ned. He wondered what the duke would say if he knew that Mistress Penhanley had a penchant for French lace.

"Then I don't foresee any problems," the duke said musingly.

Neither did Ned. In his neck of the woods, the Duke of Dyson was the law, not the mad German Geordie who sat on the throne of England.

For two hours after Gabrielle's letter was delivered, Cam managed to convince himself that he

278

could not care less how distraught his wife might be or how primitive the conditions of Falmouth's tollbooth. She deserved to suffer the consequences of her rash behavior. Nor could he trust himself to come face to face with her with anything resembling equanimity. She had deserted him. And he had not even suspected that she was out of the house until her messenger brought her letter. God, how could she do this to him?

She was pregnant with his child. She'd given him a solemn undertaking that she would not try to escape. He had been so sure that she was coming to accept that her place was with him, and in England. It was what he had wanted to believe, what she wanted him to think. She'd lulled him into complacency with her artless confidences, her demonstrations of affection, her uninhibited response to his lovemaking. He tried to suppress the recollection of Gabrielle's soft body molding so eagerly to his when he came to her bed at night. He swore then that he would never touch the deceitful bitch again.

The acrid flavour of betrayal was on his tongue. With appalling self-disgust he saw himself as her lovesick slave. It galled him to think that such was her power over him that only moments before he had discovered her gone, he had been on his way to find her to apologize for the unfeeling way he had spoken to her earlier. He had not even handed over to his courier the letter he had forced her to copy, having all but made up his mind to forgo his revenge on Mascaron. He could not bear to think what she must suffer when justice finally caught up with that knave.

My God, when he caught up with her she would know the justice of an outraged husband! He would teach her the full measure of a wife's submission or he would break her in the attempt. If she thought herself ill-used before this open act of defiance, she would come to recognize how much forbearance, how much indulgence and generosity, he had thus far exercised in his dealings with her.

For more than an hour Cam nursed his fury to keep it at boiling point. By degrees, as was natural, the fury dissipated, leaving him spent and empty of emotion. With the return to a more stable frame of mind came a softening in his resolve to leave Gabrielle to her fate. Though he tried to shut his mind to her plight, he was tormented with thoughts that in such a place she might be prey to rough handling and gross insult. From there his thoughts became more fanciful, and more of a torture to him. When he finally rode out with a company of men to fetch her back he was assuring himself that his only motivation was a natural concern for his unborn child.

When Gabrielle was released into Cam's custody, she saw at once that he had placed the worst possible interpretation on her flight from Dunraeden. Her first leap of joy on seeing the familiar figure as she was led out of her cell instantly subsided when he turned his stony profile away from her. And before she had the chance to stammer more than a few words of thanks or to inquire about Goliath's fate, she was whisked into a waiting carriage.

It was ironic, she thought, that in the only time she had ever been in a position to see anything of Cornwall, fog and unremitting darkness were all that she could see out of the carriage windows. Their progress was slow, and with no one to keep her company to divert her unhappy reflections, she sank into a deep despondency. She did not see how she could persuade Cam that she had meant to return to him of her own volition. She had been captured. He was bound to think the worst. The one unshakable conviction that consoled her was that Goliath's safety, though not liberty, was assured with Cam taking a hand in matters.

When the coach finally rolled to a stop and she was assisted to alight, she eagerly scanned the faces of the half-dozen outriders who had accompanied the carriage.

"Where is His Grace? And . . . and my friend?" she asked one of the men.

His eyes slid away from hers. "The duke will be along directly," he answered noncommittally.

A moment later, becoming aware that they were not yet at Dunraeden, she asked, "Where are we?"

A groom came forward leading a mount and cupped his hands to throw her into the saddle. "The coach house, Your Grace," the man answered. "No carriages can make it down the steep incline to the castle."

She heard the subdued roar of the sea, and realized that they must be near the top of the cliffs. In other circumstances she would have been interested in learning more about the layout of her husband's coach house. As it was, she was more than a little anxious about what might be transpiring between the absent Cam and Goliath.

At Dunraeden, she found the servants subdued and distant. She could not wonder at it, she thought, for what they must think of her dressed in the livery of a page was more than she was willing to contemplate. Only Betsy seemed to be her usual cheerful self.

"It was only a thrush," said Gabrielle, by way of explanation, hoping that Betsy would not probe further.

"A thrush?" queried Betsy, disrobing her mistress

quickly and efficiently.

"A game, a hoax."

"A lark," corrected Betsy with sudden enlightenment. Then very sagely and incomprehensibly to Gabrielle's ears she added, "It's what he's been missing these many years, only he don't know it."

After Betsy withdrew, Gabrielle waited in some trepidation for the sounds of Cam's return. It was some time before she heard his tread outside her door. He hesitated for a moment, then went on to his own chamber. With as much composure as she could summon, she held herself in readiness for the moment he would come through the door that adjoined their two chambers. Thirty minutes were to pass before it registered that he had retired for the night.

The first wash of relief soon gave way to unbridled vexation. He was punishing her, and she was sure she did not care if he ever listened to her explanations. She doused the candles in a flurry of activity and stalked to the big empty bed. Having arranged the pillows to suit her own taste, she slipped under the covers.

Resolutely, she composed herself for sleep. Within minutes she was reflecting that she had not known the bed was so large. She edged into the middle and gave a sniff. Large and cold, she decided, and thumped her pillows in a most vicious manner. A moment later she set one of the pillows at her back, under the covers, and wriggled into it. The bed seemed less lonely. She shivered. Her feet were like blocks of ice. She was sure that by morning she would be frozen solid and that there was not a soul in Dunraeden who would lament her fate. A tear rolled down her cheek. Perhaps Betsy would, she thought. And Goliath, certainly, if she only knew where he was.

She pulled herself to a sitting position and stared morosely into space. Sighing, she pulled back the covers and rose to her feet. Someone had to swallow her pride and make the first move. And it seemed that that someone had to be her. She padded to the adjoining door and hesitated. Gathering her courage as if to take a fence, she turned the handle and pushed into Cam's bedchamber.

Chapter Sixteen

The room was in semidarkness, but she could make out shadowy shapes and forms. Her steps slowed as she neared the bed. As quickly as it had come over her, her confidence slipped away. Quietly, surreptitiously, she began to retrace her steps when, from the corner of her eye, she caught the glow of a light at the window. Cam drew heavily on the cheroot in his hand. She heard the rush of his breath as he slowly exhaled. The faint odor of tobacco smoke wafted over to her. He was watching her.

His voice was so soft, so dispassionate, that it took her a moment to feel the bite of his words. "It would be wiser if we deferred our quarrel until I am more in command of my temper," he said.

He had not spoken to her in that tone of voice in an age. Her heart constricted. "Cam," she whispered, "it is not as you think. You must know I would never leave you, and especially not when I am carrying your child."

Soft laughter mocked her.

Without thinking, she moved toward him. She said imploringly, "I meant to teach you a lesson. I was going to come back, only Goliath found me, and before I could return we were arrested."

He swore under his breath and turned his back on her. His voice unsteady, he said, "Spare me the lies!

Now leave me. I can't answer for myself if you provoke me further."

Guilt and remorse washed over her. She had hurt him and she could not bear it. "I love you," she said, and tears welled in her eyes. She blinked them back. "I was going to prove it to you."

"For God's sake!" Viciously, he ground the stub of his cigar into the cigar stand. "Don't, Gaby!" His voice was sharp as he evaded her outstretched hand.

She hesitated. "I'm sorry," she murmured, not knowing what else to say.

Through gritted teeth he said, "Leave me while I can still offer you the choice. I'm not myself. Please. I don't want to hurt you."

"You needn't think you can frighten me, Cam."

Her calm assurance mocked him more than she could possibly have known. While there was nothing he could do to frighten *her*, at every turn he was made to endure unspeakable agonies. He thought of the risks she ran, the danger she courted, and his patience came to an explosive end.

He was sure he was going to lay his hand to her bare backside when he caught hold of her. "You were going to prove that you loved me," he raged.

"Y . . . yes."

His mouth came down on hers with such force that her head snapped back. With lightning speed, his hands skimmed over her, freeing her of the impediment of her nightclothes. She was on her back on the bed, his weight pressing her into the mattress, before she could get her bearings.

Never had she tasted such desperation on his lips; never had his hands moved over her with such urgency. He sucked her into his passion with such speed that her senses reeled. She discovered that desire flamed from desire. He demanded, she answered, holding nothing in reserve.

With a lover's knowledge, he exploited her most vulnerable sensitive pleasure points — the hollow of her throat, the underside of her breast, the small of her back, the inside of her thigh — driving her to a fever of anticipation for the moment he would possess her fully. He held back, exulting in every gasp, every moan of pleasure, every plea for deliverance he won from her.

Heat danced along skin; movements became more rhythmic as they edged closer to the precipice; words disintegrated into soft cries and groans; voluptuous scents and flavors pushed them higher.

He drove into her with such ferocity that they both gasped. He had to grit his teeth to fight back the waves of pleasure. His eyes held hers as he raised to his hands, straightening his arms, making his penetration of her body as deep as he could make it. He stilled, savoring the feel of the mindless shudders that had begun to sweep over her.

Here he would have her submission, he promised himself. Here in that most ancient and primitive of all rituals, where a man proved his virility to his mate. He tried to tell her so. "I love you," he said, surprising himself. She arched beneath him and he could no longer restrain himself. He moved rapidly, forcing her to match his rhythm. As he took her over the crest, hearts beating as one, limbs straining, breath mingling, he knew that it was he who was surrendering everything. And then he knew only Gabrielle . . .

They lay still, locked in each others arms, breathless and stunned. It was Cam who recovered first. Frowning, he eased his weight away from her and pulled back to a sitting position. Gabrielle lay panting softly in the aftermath of love. Cam lit the candle beside the bed and turned back to study her.

She hadn't a shred of modesty, he decided. She

hadn't moved a muscle since he had pulled away from her, hadn't made the least attempt to cover herself. She lay there naked as the day she was born, wanton, skin flushed, eyes dazed, hair in silky disarray, looking beautiful and more desirable than any woman had a right to look. It wasn't fair that she should be sated and he greedy for more. He lowered his head and took her lips in a possessive kiss.

She raised a limp hand and touched it to his chest. "Cam, we must talk," she murmured, turning her head away to evade him.

"No." With one hand wrapped around her hair he brought her head up and kissed her again.

She pushed out of his arms and rose on her elbows. "Cam, you must believe me. I was going to come back by myself. I swear it."

"And Goliath just happened to come along." He couldn't keep the sneer from his voice.

"Yes! No! What I mean to say is, I didn't know he was here in Cornwall. I just happened to bump into him." Holy Mother of God, even to her own ears she was beginning to sound crazy. "What have you done with him?" she demanded, her alarm growing apace as the sparks in Cam's eyes began to kindle.

"He's in the dungeon," said Cam nastily. He could tell by her face what was going through her mind — shackles and thumbscrews, the rack and boiling oil, if he was not mistaken. He damned himself for a fool for having incarcerated Goliath in the south tower, in the chamber Gabrielle had once occupied, replete with all the comforts of home, to boot.

Her eyes searched his face and her alarm gradually abated. "Oh, well that's all right, then," she said. "I thought for a minute you might be treating him unkindly."

Cam slammed his clenched fist against the bedpost and Gabrielle fell back, her eyes as big as saucers.

"I could have him hanged as a spy," he roared.

Her lower lip trembled. "But you wouldn't, would you, Cam? Goliath is no spy and you know it. He came into Cornwall to take me home to Normandy. Nothing more."

He thought of the interview he'd had with Goliath after Gabrielle had been spirited away from the tollbooth in his coach. Damn if the man hadn't put *him* on the defensive, calling him to account for his brutal treatment of Gabrielle. She was an innocent, he was sternly reminded, before she'd been abducted from her home in Normandy. And like a callow youth, Cam had flushed scarlet at the accusation in Goliath's tone. He'd answered, rather savagely, that she was now a bloody duchess and in a fair way to becoming the mother of the next in line to the title. She couldn't go any higher unless she were to marry Napoleon Bonaparte or the Prince of Wales. And since both these gentlemen had been spoken for, Gabrielle was to be congratulated in snatching one of England's most eligible bachelors.

The fierce gleam in Goliath's eyes had muted to something suspiciously like a twinkle. Only then had he agreed to answer Cam's questions about how much Mascaron knew and what Goliath's purpose was in coming to Cornwall. He'd exonerated Gabrielle, of course, but that was only to be expected.

He couldn't trust her, Cam decided, *wouldn't* trust her, not if she were to swear her innocence on a stack of Bibles! She was deceiving bitch, a consummate actress. But there was one place where he was sure of her, one way he knew to exercise his mastery.

"Cam, what is it?" Uncertainly, she studied his set face. His eyes were deep blue and darkening. Passion, she thought, but with a trace of temper. She saw the relentless purpose and wondered what it might mean. And then she understood.

Abruptly, she rolled from him. She was wrenched back just as quickly. His fingers speared into her hair while his other hand clamped around her waist. "I warned you not to come in here." His voice was harsh, his breathing strained. "You wouldn't listen. You *never* listen. Damn you, Gabrielle! There are consequences to our actions. It's time you learned it."

It wasn't love that moved him. She sensed it almost immediately. Ironically, he was teaching her a lesson where she had hoped she could teach him. She wasn't afraid. She was heartsick. They might as well have faced each other with drawn swords. In the contest he was forcing upon her, there could be only one winner. And as it did in everything, his experience was telling against her.

But she would not have been Gabrielle if she had succumbed without a fight. She wasn't a complete novice in the contest in which she found herself. Like a duelist who had some knowledge of the strengths and weaknesses of her opponent, she went on the attack. Cam's passion was banked, his check on his emotions rigidly imposed. She tested that control with whispered words of endearment and velvet caresses. She rained open-mouthed kisses on his throat and shoulders, and with soft sighs and moans and murmurs of her need for him, she tried to slip under his guard. She felt him waver, but he rallied quickly before she could seize the advantage.

Cam captured her wrists in one hand and anchored them over her head. Control. He'd found it and he refused to relinquish it to her. He didn't want her love. He wanted her submission. Where he led, she would follow. She was totally his. He was going to prove it to her.

Slowly, he traced a path with his tongue from the pulse at her throat to her breasts, lazily, languidly laving her nipples till they hardened into pebbles. Her body jerked when he drew one peak into his mouth. He lingered and smiled his satisfaction when her breathing became labored. She tried to free her hands, but he wouldn't allow her to touch him. He sucked hard and she arched into him.

Without haste he moved lower, his lips and tongue skimming over each rib, neglecting nothing in their quest to bring her to surrender. With the flat of his hand he tested the muscles of her stomach. He lowered his head and his lips traced the thin silver thread of scar tissue on one thigh. And then his tongue dipped and touched her in that most intimate of all caresses. Gabrielle went rigid. He touched his tongue to her again, and she began to shake.

Cam brought his head up. She was moving spasmodically, fighting for each breath, incoherently protesting what he was doing to her. With his eyes locked on hers, he stroked his fingers into her. She cursed him vehemently. Smiling, he increased the pressure, moving rhythmically, stroking deeper into her warm flesh, forcing her to answer his demand. In her eyes, he saw resistance fight with passion the moment before she became lost to everything but the sensations he was creating.

When it was over and her body went lax, she looked up at him. Ignoring that hurt look, he pushed her knees high, positioning her to maximize his own pleasure. And for the first time ever he used her quickly and efficiently as nothing more than an instrument for his carnal appetite.

She didn't make a sound or try to resist him when he pulled her to his side. He had expected tears or recriminations, or even a bout of fisticuffs. She lay there like a stone, subdued and thoughtful. He felt empty and strangely dissatisfied.

He stirred and pulled up the bedpane to cover her

nakedness. She didn't seem to notice the solicitous gesture. Her eyes were focused on the canopy overhead. He wondered what she was thinking. Her silence unnerved him.

Turning into her, he anchored her more closely to him with an arm around her waist. She sighed and turned her head away, not in defiance but rather as if she was indifferent to his presence or simply didn't know he was there. He'd become used to her trying to draw him out of himself in the wake of spent passion. Now he missed the closeness and was coming to realize how much he might have forfeited.

"Gabrielle?" He searched his mind for something to say.

"Mmm?"

"Tell me about the scars on your body, the ones on your shoulder and thigh. How did you come by them?"

For a moment it seemed as if she wasn't going to answer him. "Please. Talk to me," he murmured, and he swept back her hair, touching her with the first tenderness he'd shown since she'd entered his chamber.

Surprise held her silent for a short interval. She gave him a searching look and then she began to speak. "I took a bullet in my shoulder when we ran into some *federés* outside Lyons. They were waiting in ambush for us." She paused, letting her mind drift back in time.

"When was this?"

"I don't remember. I think I was ten or eleven at the time. Yes, I must have been, because after that summer Goliath taught me how to use a pistol."

Under the covers, he touched his fingers to her thigh, and the underside of one breast. "And these other scars?" His voice was unnaturally quiet.

"More or less, the same story." She shrugged her

shoulders dismissively. "We didn't go looking for a fight, you understand. But when we were cornered, we gave as good as we got."

He eased away from her slightly, studying her profile. She returned the look. "You were only a child," he cajoled softly. "You ought to have been sewing samplers or copying your alphabet."

She laughed. "True. But in a fight, a rapier is of more use than a needle or a pen. You can take my word for it, Englishman."

Her levity brought a faint stirring of annoyance. "Your grandfather has a lot to answer for," he said.

"You know nothing about it," she retorted, drawing into herself when she heard the censure in his voice.

Only the wind rattling the windowpanes disturbed the silence. Cam edged closer and touched the backs of his fingers to her arm. "Talk to me," he said. "Tell me about it."

Her breathing quickened. "I don't like to remember those days, as you may understand. We were on the run. My world was very small—only Mascaron, Goliath, and Rollo. They were the only people I could trust. It was a rough life. I could not remain a female in this masculine society. It would have occasioned talk, suspicion, you know what I mean. I've told you some of this before."

"And so, to all appearances, you became a boy."

She nodded.

He squeezed shut his eyes, remembering. He'd been so hard on her, so open in his contempt of her lack of femininity and female accomplishments. He'd told her that she could never be a real woman. He knew how those words must have hurt her.

When he opened his eyes, they were very blue. "You never fooled me for a minute with that boy's getup," he told her.

She blushed with pleasure. "Not even for a min-

292

ute?" she asked.

He dragged the edge of his teeth along her shoulder. "Half a minute," he allowed. "But I was already half in love with you by the time Goliath spirited you away from Andely and back to the château."

She stared at him.

"It's the truth," he said softly. "I just wouldn't admit to it, not even to myself."

"But you said . . ."

"I know what I said," he interrupted. "I was a damn fool! I don't want you to change. I never did, not really." He gave her one of his lazy grins. "I've even become partial to your swear words. Now go on with your story."

Thunderstruck, she stared at him.

"Your story, Gabrielle," he prompted, gently.

"What? Oh, there's not much more to tell. As I told you, we were fugitives, always one step ahead of our pursuers. Someone, I don't know who, was out for our blood. We could never stay in one place for long. We were betrayed so many times we lost count. We were lucky to escape with our lives. The scar on my thigh? That came from the foil of a guard on the walls of Valence when we were trying to sneak away after we heard those murderers, the *representents en mission,* had come into the area. I fell off the wall and broke a rib. And the scar under my breast? That came from the knife of a *contrebandier* who objected to our taking away some of his business."

With a vehemence that surprised them both, he burst out, "What the hell was Mascaron thinking of? There must have been some other way to protect you—relatives, a convent, sanctuary somewhere, for God's sake."

"No," she contradicted. "You can't understand what it was like. Goliath agreed with Mascaron. They were afraid that whoever hated my grandfather would

293

not hesitate to make me an instrument of his revenge if I ever fell into his hands." She seemed to retreat to a place where he could not follow.

His arm closed around her protectively. "I'm sorry. Forgive me. I didn't know. I *couldn't* know."

She came to herself gradually. "I don't mind telling you about it," she said, "but only you."

Cam couldn't speak for the lump in his throat. He was thankful that she had misunderstood his impetuous words. He, of course, was the someone who had hated her grandfather. It was he, through his agents, who had tracked down Mascaron like a hunted animal. He wondered if he would ever forgive himself for the wrong he had done Gabrielle. He wondered how he would ever make it up to her.

His arms tightened about her, bringing her closer, and he dipped his head to take her lips.

Her hands strained against his shoulders, preventing him from completing the movement. "Now it's your turn," she said. "You've never told me what happened to your mother and sister. I know you went to France to bring them home. What happened, Cam? What went wrong?"

He lay very still, and his expression became shuttered.

There was a catch in her voice when she murmured at length, "I see."

He could almost feel her withdrawal. "Gabrielle," he protested softly. "We are so very different. It's what drew me to you in the first place. It's natural for you to reveal what you are thinking and feeling. I don't know if I can . . . reciprocate."

She gave him a clear-eyed look. "What are you afraid of?" she asked.

Without warning, he rolled over, pulling her with him, hugging her to him in a fierce embrace, as if someone or something were trying to snatch her away. And then, close-held in the sanctuary of a young girl's arms, he began to speak of the most painful episode of his life.

From time to time, he hesitated. He was choosing his words with care. He didn't wish to cause her pain. He didn't want her to know anything of the blame he ascribed to Mascaron for his mother's and sister's deaths. Mascaron's name was never mentioned. He did not even name the prison where his mother and sister had been held. But he told her enough to satisfy curiosity. What he could not know was that with every word he uttered he betrayed the frustrated rage and self-blame he had nurtured in the intervening years.

Ceaselessly her hands brushed over his neck and back, comforting, calming, until the story was told. When he finally lapsed into silence, she said in a curiously blank tone, "There was a madness in France in those days that no one will ever be able to explain." Remembering, she shuddered. "I wish I could forget. I wish *you* could forget. There's something there, I don't know what, a specter that makes me fear for the future."

"Hush love! Don't take on so," he soothed. "There's nothing there that can ever touch us. I wouldn't permit it."

She buried her face in his neck. "Then let Goliath go back to my grandfather. Don't you see? If you harm either of them, how can I be happy?" She began to weep uncontrollably, as if she had been storing all the tears of her short life for this moment in time.

He had to say the words several times before they finally registered.

Eyes brimming, she looked up at him. "What did you say?" she asked, unable to believe what she was hearing.

"I said that I agree. I've decided to let Goliath go

back to France. He can inform your grandfather of your changed circumstances. Mascaron is free, Gaby. Goliath will tell him so."

At his words, her face crumpled, and her sobbing intensified. It was some time before he managed to cozen a watery smile from her.

"That's better," he said, dabbing the moist spikes of her eyelashes with a corner of the bedsheet.

Her breath came out on a long, shuddering sigh, and she made a halfhearted attempt at a chuckle. He kissed her softly. She didn't object, but when he tried to deepen the embrace she protested weakly.

He studied her guarded expression, the pulse that leaped to life at her throat. "I want to make love to you," he said simply. "Not like the last time, but the way it should be."

Slowly, her arms went slack, no longer restraining him. He took her gently, carefully, filling her with all the tenderness and love of which he was capable. And as always, her generosity overwhelmed him.

It was not to be supposed that Cam's obsessive vigilance of Gabrielle would alter overnight. Nor did it. Though in his heart of hearts he knew that the girl loved him, and though he had come to accept that her explanation for Goliath's presence in Cornwall that night was too ludicrous not to be true, he was also sensible of the fact that she had come to him without choice, an unwilling captive of war. In weaker moments that thought intruded to a disturbing degree.

Having set his course, Cam was to discover, unhappily, that he could never be free of the suspicion that given her druthers and in spite of her love, Gabrielle would still not come to him willingly. Their countries were at war. Her loyalties, at the very best, must be divided. And if her loyalties to Mascaron were ever challenged, who was to say which of them she would choose? But time, he assured himself, was on his side. She was pregnant with his child. Once she was delivered of her babe and had assumed the mantle of motherhood, there could be no doubt that she would be reconciled to her fate. Then he need no longer play the cautious husband.

For her part, Gabrielle displayed a patience that would have amazed her intimates. She had not yet seen nineteen summers, and though in some respects she was ignorant of the ways of the world, she had matured into a woman of great depth of perception. She had always possessed a natural talent for judging character. Her grandfather was used to call it "Norman shrewdness." With love, that shrewdness converted to sensitivity. She loved Cam. She could be patient. And though she chafed at the restrictions he imposed, at the same time she understood the genesis of her husband's prudence. Like Cam, she also looked forward to the birth of their child, and for similar reasons. All Cam's doubts, she was persuaded, would then be resolved.

In the meantime, she was as happy as she had ever been in her life. And with Goliath's return to France and her grandfather's safety provisionally ensured, she felt free to love Cam with a whole heart.

Her happiness was infectious. Dunraeden's master had always shown a forbearing face toward his servants. The new mistress imbued that forbearance with a warmth that was irresistible. Servants went about their tasks whistling; laughter in the great, drafty halls became a commonplace; and jests flew back and forth on the new era that had been inaugurated at Dunraeden since Gabrielle had landed on Cornwall's shores.

"The second Norman Conquest!" exclaimed Cam,

laughing.

He was in his study and had yet to open the letter bearing the royal seal that his steward had just put into his hand.

The steward, who went, most appropriately, by the name of Mr. Stewart, answered dryly, "So I believe, Your Grace. In the servants hall, the word is that the little Norman maid had only to crook her little finger and Dunraeden's keep went down to defeat for the first time in its history."

Cam's lips quirked. "And what do they say of Dunraeden's master?" he asked pointedly.

Mr. Stewart coughed. He chanced a quick look at Cam. Discretion won out over an incipient confidence that had begun to manifest itself of late in his converse with his employer. "I'm sure I could not say," he offered politely.

The smile was still in Cam's eyes when Mr. Stewart made a dignified exit some few minutes later. Cam shook his head and opened the royal seal. When he set the letter aside, he was deep in thought, and frowning.

Her Majesty, Queen Charlotte, summoned him to Windsor for the express purpose of presenting his duchess. It was a summons that could not be declined.

Chapter Seventeen

Windsor Castle was not one of the favored residences of George, Prince of Wales. From the moment he had entered its draughty corridors, he wished himself at his own palace. Carlton House in Pall Mall was, in his opinion, by far the more worthy setting for the scion of the house of Hanover. It gratified him to know that Carlton House was coming to earn the reputation as one of the most magnificent palaces in the whole of Europe. Only Versailles, that monument of Louis XIV, now sadly fallen into neglect since the Revolution, stirred him to anything resembling envy.

As his valet laced him tightly into his corsets his thoughts roamed, as they often did, to the day when the mantle of sovereignty would fall upon his shoulders. The reverie was more than a little pleasant. In former times, other princes contemplating their ascent to the throne might have dreamed of glory on the field of battle. George, Prince of Wales, had long since relinquished any such fancies. His brother, York, was the acknowledged soldier, a leader of men. At one time he had envied him, but no longer. He had found his niche. He was an aesthete, a patron of the arts, a connoisseur of the first magnitude. His legacy to the nation would be as enduring as a Poitiers or an Agincourt, but of a different order. He esteemed beauty, elegance, refinement in brick and mortar, and his growing collections of works of art. One day, he promised himself, he would have a palace to rival Versailles.

"A penny for them, George." William, Duke of Clarence, lay sprawled inelegantly on the damask counterpane of his brother's commodious tester bed.

"I was wondering," drawled the heir, "what it is about Windsor that holds such an attraction for Papa. Mother has never been very happy here."

"No," concurred Clarence, surreptitiously comparing his own corpulent figure with that of his older sibling. "In spite of all the costly changes Papa has effected, Mama abhors the place. Well, it's not to be wondered at. It's the coldest, draftiest habitation that ever existed, if you want my opinion. We're well out of it."

The prince sighed. "Quite. And not to put too fine a point on it, Windsor is a museum piece, scarcely a habitation. In these modern times, who would choose to live in a draughty old castle? Only Papa."

"You're forgetting the Duke of Dyson," pointed out Clarence. "As I remember, he has a score of places from Land's End to the Scottish borders. Yet he chooses to make his seat in Cornwall, in that dreary fortress, I forget it's name."

"Dunraeden. I wonder if that's why I've always held Dyson in such dislike?" mused the prince rhetorically.

"Because he lives in a castle?"

"Mmm? No. Because he has our father's confidence."

Clarence chuckled. "What's your game, George?"

"Game?" The prince's pale eyebrows rose fractionally.

"To what purpose have you inveigled Mama into

summoning Dyson and his duchess to Windsor?"

The prince surveyed himself solemnly in the long cheval mirror. After dismissing his valet, he plumped himself down in a Louis XV gilt chair. "I've always had a partiality for this particular period of interior decoration," he said irrelevently. "What makes you think that I have anything to do with Dyson's presence here?"

"Then why are *we* here? We both know that nothing on God's earth would draw us back to Windsor short of the royal imperative. But here we both are, by choice, merely to be present at a very boring and private audience where only Dyson's duchess will be presented to our mother."

His Royal Highness made a steeple with his fingers. For a moment he contemplated the advice he had received from his closest friend, Charles Fox. Respecting the Duchess of Dyson, no one was to be taken into their confidence. He frowned in concentration, but could not bring to mind the logic behind such obsessive secrecy. Besides, he reasoned, William was not just anybody.

Finally, he said, "We're merely curious to make the lady's acquaintance."

"We? Are you employing the royal *we*, George, or the plural *we?*" asked Clarence quizzically.

"Both." His Royal Highness smiled. "It's Fox, if you really wish to know. He thinks there's something odd about this lady Dyson married." And he briefly outlined the circumstances that had provoked him into persuading the Queen to summon Dyson's duchess to Windsor.

Clarence yawned hugely. "If you ask me, Fox needs his head examined. 'Live and let live,' that's my motto. There's not many of us so virtuous that we may tolerate a close scrutiny of our private lives, Fox especially." He was thinking of his own dear mistress, Mrs. Jordan, and the bevy of little Fitz-Clarences she had presented him with over the years. A thought struck him. "George!" he exclaimed. "You've never persuaded Mama to receive Fox here! If father ever got to hear of such a thing . . ."

The prince waved his younger sibling to silence. "Don't be ridiculous, William. You must think that I'm a veritable imbecile. As if I would dare!"

As both gentlemen knew, Charles James Fox was *persona non grata* in the eyes of their father. If it had not been for the restraints of English law, the king would happily see the man go hang from the nearest gibbet. Fox's very name was enough to send His Majesty into one of his violent fits of madness.

Clarence visibly relaxed. "I beg pardon," he mumbled. "But if you don't mind my saying so, I don't see how your ploy can work. Dyson need only present the girl then carry her off to Cornwall before anyone's the wiser."

"He won't do that," drawled the prince, supremely confident.

"Oh? Why not?"

"Her Majesty will not permit it. Well, you know how Mama used to dote on Dyson's mother."

"Yes. They were bosom bows when mother came as a young bride to England. What of it?"

"Mama is Dyson's godmother."

"So?"

"I've put it into her head that his duchess is in need of a patron, that, in short, the girl faces social ostracism because of malicious and totally unfounded rumors surrounding their nuptials."

"I haven't heard any rumors."

The prince's lips thinned. "William, you're not thinking. Whether there are rumors or not is beside the point."

There was a stubborn set to Clarence's jaw when he doggedly replied, "If there is a point, I'd wish you'd get to it."

Sighing, His Highness explained, "With the best will in the world, Mama will compel Dyson to introduce his duchess to the ton. You know as well as I do that Dyson would never do anything to oblige me. And when she makes her bows to society, naturally Charles will be on hand to question her."

"Why does Fox have to question her? Why not you?" persisted Clarence. "If she wants to be rescued from Dyson, as you seem to think, she's just as like to appeal to you or to me if the opportunity presents itself. Why does it have to be Fox?"

The prince looked to be perplexed. After a moment, his brow cleared. "Lud, how should I know? Who can fathom the mind of a politician? There's a maze where their brains ought to be. Still, you've given me an idea. After the audience, let's see if we can separate Dyson from the chit. If she needs rescuing, what better time to make her gambit?"

His Highness hoisted himself laboriously to his feet and cast one last, admiring look in the long cheval mirror.

"I suppose we can't avoid looking in on Papa since we're here," remarked Clarence hopefully.

"If we didn't, Mama would never forgive it," was the crushing rejoinder. "Come along, William. It's time to meet Dyson's duchess."

Gabrielle tried to still her trembling fingers. Not even when she had been presented to the first consul, in Paris, had her nerves been so on edge. Cam's hand covered hers in an encouraging gesture, but he remained silent.

It was the waiting which was getting to her, she

decided. First, the long drive from Cam's house in Hanover Square. Windsor was a good sixteen miles from London. And then the interminable wait in the Queen's Presence Chamber. For almost an hour, Cam had tried to relax her by pointing out the distinguishing features in the rooms Charles II had created for his queen, Catherine of Braganza. In spite of its superb painted ceilings and Gobelins tapestries, the baroque interior was far too formal for comfort, in Gabrielle's opinion.

She abhorred the pomp and ceremony. It was to be an informal audience, Cam had chided her. Then why was she decked out in the most glittering gown that she had ever had in her possession? Her eyes dropped and once again widened as she took in the elaborately entwined pattern of vines and roses heavily embroidered in satin stitch and French knots. The gown, in tones of ivory and white, had formerly belonged to Cam's mother. Her wedding dress, he had informed her casually. And she had been too choked with emotion to say more than a bare "Thank you."

An army of seamstresses had been set to unpick the stitches and rework the material into its present, fashionable mode. Only it was not precisely fashionable. True, it had a low-cut, square neckline and puff sleeves. But beneath the cutaway gauze overdress was a satin hooped petticoat, and at its back was a gauze train that seemed to go on for miles.

"A simple, English frock," Cam had reassured her when she had protested that it was too elegant, too magnificent by far for her comfort. It was like no frock she had ever beheld. The gauze was embroidered so heavily that it gave the impression of Brussels lace.

It was the train that gave her the most trouble. She'd practiced walking with it for hours. As long as she remembered it was there she managed quite nicely. She couldn't see the point of a train. But Cam had assured her it was *de rigeur*. To please him, she continued to practise till she'd mastered the trick of it. Then Betsy had stuck those plumes in her hair, ostrich feathers, she called them, which made her feel a foot taller, and the practices had to start all over again. She could not help herself. Every time she went through a doorway, she found herself ducking.

It wasn't funny, but she giggled. She glanced sideways at Cam. The look in his eyes warmed her.

She made an effort to relax herself. Windsor. It was only a castle, she told herself, like Dunraeden, only grander. *What a whisker,* a little voice said in her head. From the moment the coach had driven through the Henry VIII Gateway into the lower ward, she'd been intimidated by the sheer size of the place. She was sure that the whole town of Andely could fit quite snugly within Windsor's walls.

"Is it a castle or a palace?" she had asked Cam as they'd been escorted through the state apartments to the outer chamber, where they were presently awaiting the queen's pleasure. There were towers enough for a dozen castles, in her opinion. But the luxury within surpassed anything she could have possibly imagined. It wasn't merely the rich tapestries on the walls, the gilt ceilings and frescoes, the priceless paintings and porcelain. Such things she had expected to find. But she had never before seen such intricately wrought silver chandeliers and silver tables. Even the chairs were studded with silver.

"It's both," Cam told her.

Gabrielle was very glad that she was not a member of the royal family. She shuddered to think how many irreplaceable treasures might have been lost over the years when they slipped through her care-

305

less fingers.

This luxurious setting brought to mind the *grande salle* in her château in Normandy. Gabrielle had never been comfortable in that room. It was Mascaron's room and reflected his taste. Such cold perfection merely intimidated her. She preferred the shabby charm of her own small sitting room, with all her treasures about her, or the pleasing aspect of Dunraeden's commodious and inviting private apartments.

The thought that she viewed Dunraeden in such a light arrested her for some few minutes. When, she wondered, had she begun to think of Cam's castle as her home and not her prison? She could not say with any certainty. Perhaps when Cam had begun to explain the personal history of each piece of furniture, and of each dent and scratch to have been inflicted by former generations of Colburnes.

He had given her *carte blanche* to do Dunraeden over to her own taste. At the same time, he had been boyishly eager for her to have some understanding of the pieces, some of them truly ugly, that he wished to retain. Laughingly, Gabrielle had told him that the refurbishing of Dunraeden was a project they would undertake together.

Of one thing she was certain. Their home would bear no resemblance to the exalted interiors of Windsor.

Clearing her throat, she leaned over the arm of her chair and whispered, "How much longer?"

"Soon," soothed Cam, and he embarked on a spate of anecdotes on some of the illustrious personages, beginning with William the Conqueror, who had founded, enlarged, and finally beautified the fortress over the centuries, till it attained its present splendor.

By degrees, Gabrielle became interested in spite

of herself, and her trembling ceased. When the door that gave onto the Queen's Audience Chamber opened, however, she almost bolted to her feet.

"Easy, girl," said Cam, smiling comfortingly. "There's nothing to fear." He'd said those words to her a hundred times over the last number of weeks.

She tried to return his smile, but her lips felt frozen. Someone, she was not sure if the gentleman was a servant in resplendent livery or a peer of the realm in magnificent ceremonial dress, bade them approach the chamber. Cam's strong hand on her elbow urged her over the long expanse of carpet.

"Breathe deeply," he told her, and Gabrielle obeyed.

He had done everything he could think of to lessen Gabrielle's fears. Queen Charlotte, he had told her, quite truthfully, was a provincial in outlook. Left to herself, the queen's preference was for a quiet life spent in the country. She hated ceremony and all the trappings of royalty. It was duty that constrained her to summon his duchess to her presence. What he had not told Gabrielle was that whatever the queen's preference, there was a tradition and protocol that must be observed to the letter.

As they reached the threshold, Cam's eyes flicked approvingly over Gabrielle. The formal court dress that he had had especially made for her was unsurpassable. Only he and the mantua maker knew of the gored skirt that would permit his wife, with her long stride and the obligatory hooped petticoat, a modicum of freedom that the fashions of the day otherwise precluded. The emeralds at her throat would have fetched a king's ransom — not that he had told her so. It would only be one more thing for her to worry about. He'd known, of course, how her eyes would absorb the color of the gems.

She was magnificent, he thought. There wasn't a woman in the world who was her equal. She could not know how the bloom of early pregnancy enhanced her looks. But Cam knew, and his heart swelled in pride at the sight of her.

As they moved into the audience chamber, Gabrielle's steps faltered. Her hesitation was scarcely noted by the several people who turned to study her, for Cam's fingers quickly closed around Gabrielle's gloved hand, and before she could think to object, she was swept forward.

They came to a halt before the seated figure of a diminutive lady dressed elaborately in grey satin. Several ladies-in-waiting hovered nearby. Gabrielle had no trouble identifying the two gentlemen who had stationed themselves on either side of the Queen. Cam had warned her to expect the Prince of Wales and his brother, the Duke of Clarence.

Gabrielle scarcely heard her husband's voice as he asked the queen's permission to make known his duchess. Highly conscious of the long train floating somewhere behind her, she sank in a deep curtsy, and held the pose, eyes downcast, until the queen's soft voice bade her rise.

It took ten full minutes before conversations finally began to register in her brain. Though afterward she remembered little of what the queen said to her, Gabrielle knew that she must have made appropriate responses, for there was a gleam in Cam's eyes that spoke eloquently of his approval. Still, she scarcely drew a breath until the queen signaled her attendants that she wished to retire. A touch on Cam's arm drew his attention.

"Ma'am?"

"Your bride is quite lovely, Cam. Bear with me a little. I wish a word with you in private."

There was nothing Cam could do but follow the

queen's lead. Before the Groom of the Robe shut the door at his back, over his shoulder, Cam managed to flash Gabrielle a reassuring smile. He noted that she was flanked by the Prince of Wales and Clarence. Two of the Queen's ladies-in-waiting were close by. Queen Charlotte was known to be a stickler for the proprieties. Cam was glad of it.

Once in the queen's withdrawing room, Her majesty waved her attendants away with a gesture of the hand. Obediently, they retreated to the far side of the room. Only then did the queen explain herself to Cam.

She meant well. Cam never doubted it for a minute. For some unfathomable reason, Queen Charlotte had always had a soft spot for him. True, he was her godson, but there were scores who could claim the same relationship to Her Majesty but who, to their misfortune, were not in favor. It never occurred to Cam that he had the queen's favour because she esteemed the man.

Her object, quite simply, was to put her stamp of approval on Gabrielle and so halt the ugly speculation that his nuptials had occasioned.

"Prince George has offered to lend his support," she said confidingly.

"Too kind," murmured Cam ironically. He suspected that the axe was about to fall.

"No doors of any consequence shall be closed to your bride."

"Perhaps, in the spring . . . ," began Cam cautiously.

"Too late," interjected Her Majesty. She was becoming fatigued, and looked around for her ladies. They hastened forward. "It's best to smother a fire before it has a chance to take hold." She rose to her feet and Cam rose with her. "George will tell you what's to be done."

There was nothing Cam could say but a simple "Thank you, Your Majesty."

"Charming girl," said the queen. "Your mother, I mean." She patted his arm in an absentminded gesture. "There was no malice in her, you know. When she went, and so young, I lost a dear friend."

As soon as the queen had quit the chamber, Cam was off like a shot. He thought he might very easily strangle the Prince of Wales if Gabrielle had suffered any insult. The sound of laughter, soft and intimate, hastened his steps. He found them in the Grand Vestibule, clustered around a magnificent suit of child's armor that had once belonged to Charles I. Gabrielle was in her element, and Cam did not know whether he was more relieved or annoyed.

"Cam," she said, catching sight of him. "What do you think? Windsor suffered the same fate as Versailles when the king lost his head."

"I beg your pardon?" Although he addressed his question to Gabrielle, his eyes quickly scanned the other occupants of the chamber. Nothing seemed to be amiss. By degrees, Cam relaxed.

Patiently, Gabrielle explained, "The Revolutionaries — in both England and France? They executed the king and then they had the temerity to sell off his private possessions."

"In England," said His Highness dryly, "Our revolutionaries went by the name of Parliamentarians."

Cam looked at Gabrielle blankly. Behind lace handkerchiefs, the ladies-in-waiting snickered. "Oh," he said, when enlightenment dawned. "You're referring to Charles I? Yes, of course. Cromwell sold off the king's Windsor collections to pay off his armies."

Turning to the prince, Gabrielle unthinkingly remarked, "My own grandfather was one of those who profited by the dispersion of Versailles treasures. In our château in Normandy . . ."

"Gabrielle!" Cam's voice, soft yet edged with a warning, cut her off in mid-stream. "The hour grows late. He smiled to soften the reprimand.

Gabrielle colored hotly. It was a careless slip. Cam's stepmother's family, the Valcours had no connection with Normandy. Furthermore, according to the story Cam had fabricated, Gabrielle had no recollection of relations, for she was an orphan raised by strangers. Inwardly she cursed her loose tongue. Outwardly, she pinned a smile to her face and said brightly, "Don't say we must leave so soon, Cam?"

Clarence immediately seconded her statement. "No. Don't say so, Dyson! I've promised to show your duchess St. George's. You know, the Knights of the Garter and all that. She can't conceive that England's premier order of chivalry is represented by an intimate article of lady's clothing."

Determined to lay a trail away from her near-fatal blunder, Gabrielle laughingly demanded of the younger lady-in-waiting, "Tell me these gentlemen are hoaxing me, Lady Mary. A lady's garter? It can't be true, surely?"

"It's true, Your Grace," answered Lady Mary. "Though whether it reflects to England' s glory or shame is a matter of opinion." The smile in Lady Mary's voice robbed her remarks of all censure.

"I don't think I understand," said Gabrielle.

The prince smoothly interjected, "Clarence loves to tell the story. Why don't you let your duchess go along with him, Dyson? It would be a pity to come all the way out to Windsor and deprive her of the sight of the banners and coats of arms of the Knights Companion. We shall crack a bottle of port as we await their return, if you like."

Cam made up his mind quickly. "Gabrielle?"

"Oh yes, please!" she instantly responded.

Clarence beamed a smile at Cam while offering

311

his arm to Gabrielle. "It happened like this," he said, leading her away. "At a ball given by Edward III at Windsor in 1347, or was it '48?, no matter, the date is immaterial. At any rate, the ball was to celebrate the capture of Bordeaux. No, no! Now I remember. It was to celebrate the capture of Calais. As I was saying, at this ball, a garter worn by an incomparable beauty, Joan of Kent, fell to the floor. The king . . ."

"The king picked it up," Gabrielle told Cam, an hour or so later. Their carriage was wending its way out of the small village of Windsor on the long leg to town. "But perhaps you've heard this story before?" she added as an afterthought.

"Remind me of it," said Cam generously.

Gabrielle did not need a second telling. The story had captured her imagination. "The king's courtiers and some of the ladies present made comments, not very nice ones, I should say."

"It was to be expected," pointed out Cam. "Legend has it that Joan of Kent was the king's mistress."

"You know the story," said Gabrielle. She could not conceal her disappointment

"I forget some of the details," responded Cam mendaciously. "Pray continue."

"Are you sure you've forgotten?"

"Perfectly."

Gabrielle settled herself more comfortably against the velvet squabs. "I hope she wasn't the king's mistress." She considered the matter for a moment longer, and said with more feeling, "I shall *never* accept that she was the king's mistress."

"Oh? Why?"

"Because the Black Prince, the king's son, married her, that's why. But all this is beside the point. King Edward picked up the garter, took one look at the knowing leers of his courtiers and said, *'Honi soi qui mal y pense.'*"

"Shame on him who thinks evil of it."

"You *do* know the story!" accused Gabrielle.

"It's coming back to me in dribs and drabs," allowed Cam.

There was a silence.

"And?" prompted Cam.

Snorting indelicately, Gabrielle quickly brought the tale to an end. "The king promised that one day those very same courtiers would be honoured to wear the garter. And so the Order of the Knights of the Garter was founded. What did the Prince of Wales have to say to you when I went off with Clarence?"

Stifling a smile, Cam smoothly responded, "This and that. Nothing for you to trouble your head over." After an interval, he went on musingly, "Gabrielle, I've been thinking. Perhaps we should stay on in town for a month or so. Since we've made the long trip from Cornwall, it seems like the ideal time to introduce you to society."

His words shocked her. "Oh, Cam, no! Please! I'm not ready for that!"

"Not ready? My dear, you're as ready as you shall ever be. Your performance this evening was masterly. I was proud to be your consort." He found her fingers and linked them with his own. "Angel, it's not in my power to leave London at present."

"Then send me back to Cornwall."

"What are you afraid of?"

"Nothing! Everything! You saw what happened tonight. I almost gave the game away."

"But you recovered quickly. You won't make the same mistake twice."

"But Cam, have you considered? Someone might recognize me! You have forgotten that those English gentlemen, Lord Whitmore and his aides, were presented to me at Vrigonde."

"I haven't forgotten. It's not important. I shall take Pitt into my confidence. He will know what to do." He laughed, and smoothed her frown with his knuckles. "It wouldn't surprise me if Lord Whitmore and company were sent to Ireland until our little escapade blows over."

"If only that were all!"

He heard the break in her voice, and his hand cupped her neck in a soothing caress.

"Oh Cam, I can never be happy in society."

"What's this?"

"A *lady!*" The word had the force of an oath. "I don't have it in me to be a lady. You said so yourself."

She squealed as Cam suddenly reached for her in the dimly lit coach and hauled her across his lap.

"I say too damn much," he said roughly, smothering her in a bear hug. "And it's not kind of you, Angel, to throw my foolish words back in my teeth."

"You meant them!"

"Idiot! Couldn't you tell that I was merely fighting your irresistible charm? My back was to the wall! You can't fault a fallen warrior for using whatever weapons come to hand. I swear on my honor as a knight of the garter, I never meant a word of it."

Arrested, Gabrielle murmured, "Cam? You? A knight of the garter? Is this true?"

"In a manner of speaking. I was thinking of my wife's garters." Under her hooped skirts, his hand stroked from ankle to knee. Gabrielle wriggled. Cam's fingers closed around one garter and pulled.

"Cam?" Her voice was deceptively sensual.

314

"Mmm?" His lips lingered on the sensitive juncture at the base of her throat and shoulder.

"It seems I *am* a lady! Unhand me at once, sir!"

"Not without my garter," said Cam, and suiting action to word, he removed Gabrielle's shoe. A moment later, he held up his prize.

"My stocking will fall down," warned Gabrielle crossly.

"Don't tempt me," responded Cam, throwing her one of his wickedly melting grins.

"What do you mean to do with my garter?"

She watched mesmerized as Cam slipped it over his wrist and smoothed it over his elbow until the garter would go no further. "There," he said, giving it one last pat. "I have just invented the chivalric order of Gabrielle's garters."

"I think all the English are touched with madness," said Her Grace in frigid accents.

"And now for the test." Cam gloatingly rubbed his hands together.

"Test?" echoed Gabrielle, eyeing Cam with marked suspicion. She had never seen her husband in such a playful humor.

Blandly, Cam avowed. "Didn't you know? A knight of the garter must be tested by, well, fire, or some such thing."

She was beginning to get his drift. With eyes twinkling, she stated, "Then I must be allowed to set my own test since it is my order of chivalry."

"That sounds reasonable," said Cam. "What is it to be?"

She leaned into him and whispered in his ear. Before she could pull away, he had grabbed her by the shoulders. "You're on, Angel. But I'm warning you here and now, there had better be only one knight who passes *that* particular test, and that's your very own lord and master."

315

Swiftly, he pulled down the shades.

"But not *here*, Cam," said Gabrielle, truly horrified. "What will the coachmen think?"

"*Honi soit qui mal y pense*," taunted Cam roguishly. "What else?" and his head descended as he took her lips.

The contentious issue of whether or not Gabrielle would make her bows to society passed without further comment. Only Cam was aware of it. Perhaps he should have taken Gabrielle into his confidence, but he did not wish to alarm her unduly. There was no question that they could remove from town when the queen had expressly intimated that she wished them to remain. And after his *tête à tête* with the Prince of Wales, it was very evident that the little season that loomed before them would be a memorable one, to say the least. The thought of it, he knew, would simply petrify Gabrielle.

Cam did not frighten so easily. He had no qualms about introducing Gabrielle to his peers. His one concern was that her true identity was certain to come out sooner or later. It could not be otherwise, unless he wished to keep her forever his prisoner at Dunraeden. The thought had merit, he reflected. He'd made the shocking discovery that his territorial instincts were as deeply ingrained as those he had observed in the animal kingdom. The woman belonged to him. He would hold her against all challengers. She was his possession. *Uncivilized,* mused Cam, and smiled to think how Gabrielle would chastize him if she could read his mind.

As the carriage rolled to take a bend, his arms tightened protectively around her sleeping form. Gabrielle sighed and snuggled closer. She was his possession, and at the same time she was infinitely more. He would let nothing and no one blight her happiness or cause her embarrassment.

His enemies had forced his hand. As a consequence, he had been compelled to alter his strategy. In a matter of weeks, the question of Gabrielle's identity would become irrelevant. He would take great pleasure in revealing it to the whole world, beginning with the Prince of Wales and Mr. Fox. In the circumstances, no one would fault him for the subterfuge he had been forced to employ in order to conceal the name of his wife's grandfather from French authorities. But that day could come only when Mascaron was safely on England's shores.

Even now, Rodier was setting things in motion to bring Mascaron out of France. Cam was confident that he would come willingly, for once his connection to Gabrielle became generally known, Mascaron would come under suspicion, at the very least. Only a stupid man would suppose that he could continue at the Ministry of Marine with no questions asked. And Mascaron was far from stupid. He must see that he had very little to gain by remaining in France. In point of fact, he had great deal to lose.

Some words of Lansing's came to Cam's mind. *If Fouché ever comes to suspect that Gabrielle has been abducted, he might put two and two together.*

Cam did not make the mistake of underestimating Fouché. There was a time when he had counted on him putting two and two together. There was a time when he intended the French authorities to discover Mascaron's complicity in passing information to British intelligence. But that was before Gabrielle's happiness had become paramount to him. Mascaron. He could never think of him without the bile rising in his throat. But for Gaby's sake he was willing to set aside his vendetta. There was no one else he would do as much for.

All in all, he decided, things were working out rather well. He had every confidence in Gabrielle's ability to make her way in polite society. And when the little season was over, he would carry her off to Cornwall, where, in the new year, their child would be born. Life had never been sweeter.

Later that evening, at Carlton House, the Prince of Wales entertained a few of his intimates. Fox and Sheridan had been expected. With them had come the young French *immigré*, Gervais Dessins. The prince eyed the young man's presence with disfavor, for reasons he could not quite name, even to himself. But since Mr. Fox had taken the liberty of enlarging their group of confidants, His Highness had insisted that his brother, Clarence, be one of their company.

"I shall never accustom myself to the penetrating cold of Windsor," said the Prince plaintively, by way of explanation for the roaring fire in the grate and every window shut fast against the draughts. "I'm chilled to the bone."

Charles Fox mopped at his perspiring brow with a large linen handkerchief. "What was your impression of Dyson's duchess, Your Highness?" he asked without preamble.

It was Richard Sheridan who found the decanter of brandy on the Hepplewhite sideboard. Having first topped up his own glass, he offered the decanter around. There were no servants on hand. The prince had earlier dismissed them in the interests of privacy.

The prince addressed the Duke of Clarence. "An unexceptionable girl, wouldn't you say, William?"

"Captivating," responded the duke. He could not

318

remember the last time anyone had so hung on his every word. "Silly Billy" they called him behind his back, present company included. The girl had made him feel like the wisest man in Christendom. His one regret was that, notwithstanding Mrs. Jordan, Dyson had seen her first. He had no love for the Duke of Dyson, but he liked Fox and Sheridan even less. "It wouldn't suprirse me if she takes the ton by storm," he added with malicious relish.

"That's as may be," said Fox, turning his penetrating stare upon Clarence. The duke slumped a little further into his chair. "But the whole point of the exercise was to discover why Dyson had been keeping her a virtual prisoner at his place in Cornwall."

"We don't know that for certain," offered Sheridan mildly.

Mr. Fox looked a question at Dessins. The Frenchman coughed delicately. It was at his suggestion, given by way of a jest, that Fox had prevailed upon the Prince of Wales to use his influence to bring the Duchess of Dyson into society. Fox and his cronies wished only to find a means of discrediting, or at the very least, embarrassing Dyson. His design was more covert. Fouché's instructions were that he was to befriend the girl. He'd done remarkably well, he congratulated himself, first by ingratiating himself with Mr. Fox, and second by rekindling the embers of Fox's suspicions just when it appeared the fire was about to go out. For his purposes, interest in the Duchess of Dyson must not be allowed to flag.

With affected negligence, he observed, "As you may remember it was Dyson's cabin boy who, inadvertently, was the source of our information. It seems that Dyson was extraordinarily brutal to the girl when he abducted her."

"He's never denied that the girl was reluctant to

leave France," pointed out Sheridan.

"And," continued Dessins, leaning forward in his chair as if to add emphasis to his words, "Louise Pelletier, Dyson's mistress, let slip a few things that made us wonder."

"What things?" asked Clarence.

"Oh, that the girl was as untamed as a wild animal."

"I can't believe that Dyson would shackle himself to such a woman," said Sheridan.

"He didn't," responded the Prince. "Gabrielle was . . . Clarence, you tell them. You spent more time with the chit than I. But if you want my opinion, gentlemen, I think we've been following a false scent."

As he lapsed into silence, the prince's eyes traveled around the interior of the chamber and came to rest on several exquisite pieces of Louis XV furniture that had once graced the Palace of Versailles. His agents had not been slow to capitalize on the dispersion of the French king's private treasure house. Dyson's duchess, he knew, would look askance when she first entered the portals of Carlton House. The thought amused him, but only for a moment.

He was becoming bored with the subject of the Duke of Dyson. There were far graver things on his mind, such as whether the state rooms at Carlton House should be on the street level or the floor above. The prince could never be satisfied with things as they were.

As Clarence's voice droned on, His Highness's thoughts drifted further afield, to Windsor. One day he would be king. He debated whether or not he would turn Windsor into the premier palace of all Europe. Should he decide to do so, he would begin by creating a room to rival the Hall of Mirrors in

Versailles. No. It must surpass anything created by a French king. He would not be content to take second place. But until such time he would devote himself to beautifying his pavilion at Brighton. Posterity would know how to judge him.

"A love match, you say!" The comment, laced with irony, came from Richard Sheridan.

"They were smelling of April and May," declared Clarence hotly.

"I think it smells rather fishy, myself," drawled Sheridan, smiling amicably.

"D'you know what I think?" asked Fox of the company in general. "I think I frightened Dyson into marrying the girl. And for some reason we haven't fathomed as yet, he is reluctant to show her in society. Is she to remain in town, Your Highness?"

"Hmm?"

"I'd like to give the chit a look over."

Prince George marshaled his thoughts with an effort. "To remain in town? Oh! The girl! Yes, of course. Dyson went so far as to thank me for my efforts on her behalf. He wasn't the least reluctant to fall in with Her Majesty's wishes. It's all been a hum, Charles. You'll have to find some other way to get to the duke."

It was to be some hours before the little party broke up, for His Highness insisted on showing his guests the most recent renovations to Carlton House as well as soliciting their opinions on his grand designs to turn Holland's rather severe interiors into something more opulent. No one dared gainsay him.

When his guests were finally released in the wee hours of the morning to go their separate ways, only one of their number regarded the evening as anything other than a crashing bore. Gervais Dessins was too elated to find sleep at once.

Dyson's duchess was not Gabrielle de Valcour. There was no such person, so Fouché had informed him in his most recent communication. It was suspected that she was Mascaron's granddaughter, the girl who had supposedly drowned. And the Duke of Clarence had innocently revealed in a private *tête à tête* that the girl's grandfather had a château in Normandy. Everything fit.

He lay motionless on his bed, staring up at the canopy. If he played his cards right, the first consul himself was sure to show his gratitude by bestowing honors he could not even imagine. He became involved in his favourite reverie — he would be the saviour of France. There was no telling what state secrets Mascaron, in his position as assistant minister of marine, had not passed on to the British. The girl was the key to unraveling the mystery. Fouché suspected that she was a hostage. That did not seem likely in light of what the Duke of Clarence had told him that evening. Either way, she must be returned to France.

Dawn was creeping over the rooftops before he succumbed to sleep.

The sun was beginning to set over the tiled rooftops of Paris, its muted brilliance bringing a sense of mystery and returning the most beautiful city in all of Europe to the secrets of the night. From the window of his office in the Ministry of Marine, Antoine Mascaron watched the play of light and contemplated life's ironies. His life, he reflected bitterly, had been one long irony after another. And this was the final irony of all, that the innocent should pay the penalty for the sins of the guilty. He thought of Gabrielle. He thought of Dyson. And he damned the gods for their caprice.

Once more, Providence or the Fates had taken a malicious delight, it seemed, in snatching the victory from him at the finishing line. Power had eluded him. Wealth had not helped him. The threat of disgrace had ever dogged his heels. The specter of death was no stranger. But he had taken to snapping his fingers in the teeth of the gods because, as he thought, Gabrielle was safely away in England and in the care of a man who had come to love her. Goliath had returned persuaded of that fact. Oh God, what fools they had been to trust the Englishman! And how ironic that he, Mascaron, should finally be careless when it most behooved him to be careful.

He could not believe how blind he had been. He could not believe how slow he had been to fit everything together, or how easy, once he had begun. Dyson. Héloise de Valcour. The Abbaye. The years of being hunted like animals. Gabrielle's abduction. It was all of a piece. And now the imminent threat of discovery. Had Dyson deliberately betrayed him, he wondered, or had Fouché ferreted everything out for himself? Either way, the end result was the same. He hoped, oh God how he hoped, that before he went in front of the firing squad, Goliath would get word to him somehow that he had succeeded in this last, desperate enterprise. If Gabrielle was to be saved, Goliath must eliminate the Englishman. He did not deign to pray for success to gods who had never before listened to his petitions. His hopes were fastened on Goliath.

The door opened, and his clerk entered. "Monsieur Fouché to see you, sir."

Mascaron smiled at the timid young man whose habitual air of preoccupation had converted to a harried unease. "Calm yourself Montaine," he said. "Monsieur Fouché and I have known each other a long time. This appointment is long overdue. Show him in."

Without haste, Mascaron seated himself behind his desk. Though he expected the worst, he had taken great pains to ensure that not a scrap of evidence was left behind to incriminate him. But such measures with Fouché meant little, as he well knew. When necessary, Fouché produced evidence from nowhere to suit his own ends. Then again, Dyson might very well have laid a trail straight to his desk. It did not signify. Only Gabrielle mattered now.

When Fouché entered, Mascaron did not offer him his hand. Thirty minutes later, Fouché called urgently for the clerk's assistance. When Montaine ran into the room, he found Mascaron unconscious and slumped over his desk. The young man tried not to let his dread show.

"I cannot understand it," said Fouché. "It happened so suddenly. One minute we were sharing a bottle of hock, and the next, he complained of a headache and fainted away."

Montaine did not know what to say. He picked up the empty glass at Mascaron's feet and set it on the desk. "Is . . . is he dead?" he asked uncertainly.

"Just a faint," replied Fouché with a hand on Mascaron's forehead. "He seems to have a fever. Fetch the porters. I shall look after Monsieur Mascaron and see him safely to his door."

When Fouché entered his carriage and dismissed the porters, there was no necessity to give his coachmen directions. They knew that they were bound for the Château de Vrigonde. What they did not know was that their master had bigger game in mind than Antoine Mascaron.

If it had been only Mascaron, Fouché was thinking, he would have taken him at once to the Conciergerie. And if evidence could not be found, it could be soon fabricated. But his ambitions were not so small. Mascaron was bait for the girl. The girl was bait for the English duke. And with these three aces, surely the first consul would relent and restore him to his former position.

But he must not become overconfident, he cautioned himself. It could be that Dyson cared nothing for the girl. The evidence on that point was uncertain. Fouché shrugged philosophically. In that case, he would still have two birds in his net. But in hopes that Dyson would come after his duchess, he had chosen his position with great forethought. The Conciergerie was impossible to penetrate. Dyson must not be made to think his task was hopeless. But the Château de Vrigonde . . . now that must invite a man to try his luck. And when Dyson acted, he, Joseph Fouché, would spring the trap.

Chapter Eighteen

From the moment Cam's eyes fell upon Louise Pelletier he knew that he had miscalculated. Badly. He had been overconfident. He had underestimated his enemies.

His first thought was for Gabrielle. In that crush of people crammed into the grand saloon at Devonshire House it took several minutes before he was able to locate her. She was with Gervais Dessins, a young man who formed one of the court she'd gathered around her in the fortnight since the small announcement that she'd been received by the queen had appeared in the papers. As was to be expected, the invitations had come pouring in and callers regularly beat a path to her door. Dessins was her most devoted admirer.

As his former mistress idled a path toward Gabrielle and her companion, Cam's eyes narrowed dangerously. He decided he didn't like Louise's smile. It was too confident, too intimidating, too knowing, and too superior by half given the fact that she was conversing with a duchess. He was on the point of putting a stop to her little game with Gabrielle when Louise moved away to join another group.

Cam felt some of the tension go out of his shoulders, but his back stiffened when his eyes collided with those of Mr. Fox. That gentleman was in conversation with the Prince of Wales and their hostess, Georgina, Duchess of Devonshire. The Devonshires were not only Fox's greatest admirers but also the greatest contributors to his purse. Cam was in a Whig stronghold, and though at ton parties and balls politics counted for little, he could not be comfortable surrounded by people who, to his way of thinking, spouted the veriest drivel.

On the other side of the ballroom, Fox raised his glass in a salute. Cam reciprocated, and let his eyes wander. Sheridan was making a fool of himself over Lady Bessborough, he noted, and her lover, Lord Granville Leveson-Gower was helpless to intervene. The lady's husband, the earl, hovered nearby like a vulture. Devonshire was strolling about, the picture of the exemplary host, but everyone knew that the lady at his side was not his hostess but his mistress, though to be sure, Devonshire House was her home. This interesting *ménage à trois* scarcely raised an eyebrow in these exalted circles.

They were all represented — the foremost Whig families of which England could boast, the Melbournes, the Hollands, the Oxfords, the Ponsonbies, and a plethora of lesser personages whose names, nevertheless, were household words. As Cam's eyes traveled the throng, absently remarking the various scandals that attached to many of his peers, he was struck with the thought that by some lights his own conduct with respect to Gabrielle would be roundly condemned. Again his eyes fell upon Louise Pelletier, and the suspicion that her presence that evening was far from innocent became a solid conviction. She was here to cause trouble. He could feel it in his bones.

"What the hell is she doing here?" he demanded harshly.

The gentleman at Cam's elbow followed the path of his gaze. "Louise?" asked Lord Lansing.

"Yes, Louise!"

"Haven't you heard? She's come up in the world. Rumor has it that she's the Prince of Wales's new flirt. She's invited everywhere. I thought I mentioned it."

"No, you didn't mention it. And I can scarcely believe that she's invited everywhere."

Cam's irascible tone surprised Lansing. He slanted his friend a curious look. "Louise may not gain admittance to Windsor and other such exalted portals, but there are few doors closed to her. If one wants His Royal Highness to accept an invitation, Louise's name had better be on one's guest list. What's wrong, Cam?"

Cam's eyes were trained on Gabrielle. On the dance floor people were assembling in sets for the quadrille. She caught sight of him and flashed him a grin. Not far distant were Louise and her partner.

Comprehension dawned, and Lansing clapped his friend on the shoulder. "What, Cam? Are your sins coming home to roost? I shouldn't waste any sleep over it, if I were you. Haven't you told Gabrielle that you're a reformed character?"

"No, I haven't mentioned it," he answerd absently. "But it's an omission I shall rectify as soon as may be."

He'd never denied that there had been other women in his life, thought Cam. On the other hand, he had never corrected Gabrielle's misapprehension that he'd reformed from the day that they'd wed. He remembered the house he had rented for Louise in Falmouth, in the early days of his marriage, and he damned himself for a fool. A harsh expletive burst from his lips.

But Lansing's attention had wandered. "She's here," he breathed.

"Who's here?"

"Lady Caroline Ponsonby, Bessborough's daughter." Cam's glance flicked to the far doors. A young girl

328

with a cap of blond hair, flanked by two young gentle-men, had just made her entrance.

"Lady Caroline and her two watchdogs," said Cam cynically.

"Her brothers," retorted Lansing.

Cam's eyebrows rose. "Simon! What the devil have you been up to in my absence?"

Lansing grinned sheepishly. "You're not the only who has been toppled by that mischief-maker, Cupid," he said.

Cam said nothing, but his look spoke volumes.

"I know what you're thinking," said Lansing.

"Do you?" murmured Cam.

"You're thinking that the Bessboroughs would never permit it, that they'll wed her to the heir of some illus-trious Whig title and fortune."

"There is that," agreed Cam. What he was really thinking was that Lady Caroline Ponsonby was too headstrong by half for someone of Lansing's gentle disposition.

"William Lamb is mad for her," said Lansing, his eyes never wavering from the girl's graceful form as she moved from group to group.

"I thought Devonshire's heir was in the running."

Lansing snorted derisively. "He's only a boy," he scoffed.

The Marquis of Hartington was about the same age as Lady Caroline Ponsonby, but Cam wisely held his own counsel.

"I don't think William Lamb has much of a chance," said Lansing. After a moment, by way of explanation, he added, "Their mothers, ladies Melbourne and Bess-borough, hold each other in marked aversion."

Again Cam held his peace. In his opinion, Lady Caroline Ponsonby would decide for herself whom she would wed, and there would be no gainsaying her. And in spite of Lansing's protests, William Lamb led the pack, as he'd heard tell.

Some few minutes later the last bars of the music brought the quadrille to a close. Lansing made his excuses and bolted in the direction of Lady Caroline. Cam, at a more leisurely pace, stalked his own quarry.

Gabrielle's smile faded when she observed Cam turn aside and deftly cut Louise Pelletier out of the crush. She observed their two heads together in an intimacy that excluded a third party. For a moment, she hesitated at the edge of the floor, her eyes scanning the crowds for a friendly face.

Charles Fox caught her look and inclined his head gravely. Gabrielle trembled and her eyes flew to Cam. She could not find him. A trill of laughter attracted her attention. Her head jerked round just in time to see her husband escorting Louise from the ballroom.

When the voice spoke at her ear, she started.

"Your Grace," intoned Charles Fox softly, "permit me to offer you my arm."

Gabrielle looked at the proffered arm as if the gentleman were offering her a snake. Gulping, she gingerly placed her gloved hand upon it. Cam had promised not to leave her side for the very eventuality that had overtaken her. She felt deserted. Worse, she felt betrayed, for he had left her to her own devices whilst he sought the society of a beautiful woman.

"Th . . . thank you," she stammered, and allowed Mr. Fox to escort her out of the ballroom.

"It's cooler here," he said as they entered the long corridor. Several couples were promenading. Others were seated *tête à tête* at chairs that had been conveniently set agaisnt the walls. Of Cam and Louise, there was nary a sign.

Gabrielle obediently seated herself at the place Mr. Fox indicated. She folded her hands and waited in some trepidation for the interrogation to begin. Her

330

story was well rehearsed. Cam had seen to it. And there was very little to tell. The less the better, was Cam's opinion. She was to say only that she was Gabrielle de Valcour and that Cam had forcibly removed her from France and made her his ward. And when, in the space of a few weeks, they had fallen violently in love, they had immediately wed. About her life in France she was to refuse to say one word with the excuse that to reveal names and places might jeopardize the lives of innocent people.

As Mr. Fox carefully lowered himself into a chair, Gabrielle drew on the remnants of her composure.

He studied her for a long considering moment before he said, "Mrs. Fox asked me particularly to thank you for the service you so kindly rendered the other day."

Gabrielle stared into his eyes in some confusion. "Mrs. Fox?" she murmured. To her knowledge, she had never met the lady.

"What! Did she forget to give you her name? Isn't that just like my Liz!"

"Mr. Fox," said Gabrielle diffidently, "I think there must be some mistake. I have never had the pleasure of meeting Mrs. Fox."

"On Thursday? You went shopping?"

There was a warmth about him, a certain consideration in his demeanor, which was totally unexpected. The man meant her no harm. Every instinct told her so. She stared at him wonderingly.

"On Thursday, you went shopping," repeated Mr. Fox gently.

"Yes. What of it?"

"Don't you remember?" he countered.

Gabrielle cast her mind back to the day in question. For the first time in days, there had been a let up in the rain. Even so, Cam had insisted that she take the carriage and one of the young maids since he was to be occupied with his man of business.

It was an experience to remember. Cam gave the coachman directions to some fashionable emporium on Bond Street. The coach had scarcely rolled to a stop when she was assisted to alight by the principal shopwalker. Having enquired what department Her Grace required, he then called another shopwalker forward who escorted her to the appropriate counter. He offered her a chair and, at the same time, summoned an assistant to attend to her needs. And when she had completed her purchases, the shopwalker returned and escorted her to the next counter. Gabrielle had found the whole process unnerving and had scarcely bought more than some needles and thread.

It was at the ribbon counter that she'd first observed that all customers were not created equal. The assistant was showing some ribbons to an older lady when the shopwalker called him to wait on the Duchess of Dyson. The original customer made a mild protest but was overruled. Gabrielle was embarassed that, merely because she was a duchess, she should take precedence over another customer.

"Oh!" she exclaimed, as the recollection came back to her. Her eyes flew to Mr. Fox. "Was that lady Mrs. Fox?"

"It was," he said and smiled knowingly.

Gabrielle's cheeks heated. She had not mentioned the contretemps to anyone, certainly not to Cam. It had started out so innocently. She had merely offered her chair to the customer who was ahead of her and advised the assistant that she would wait her turn. The shopwalker would not permit it. Gabrielle insisted. Some words were exchanged, but Gabrielle had her way. The lady was waited on. Gabrielle bought nothing. But she lectured the staff on the principles of fraternity, equality, and liberty. Having had her say, she offered her arm to the lady whose champion she had become, and they marched out of the shop. On the pavement outside, they parted company.

"I'm sorry if I embarrassed her," said Gabrielle in a small, contrite voice.

"Embarrass her! My dear girl, Elizabeth was positively charmed!"

"Was she?" asked Gabrielle, eyeing him doubtfully. She wondered what Cam would say if he knew she had espoused the catchwords of the Revolution, and in public too!

As if reading her mind, Mr. Fox asked, "Does His Grace know that he has taken a republican to his heart?"

There was amusement in his eyes, but Gabrielle recognized that there was no malice in it. Her smile was shy but clear.

"I thought not," remarked Mr. Fox. "Don't worry, it will be our little secret."

Gabrielle in no wise considered herself a republican, but she knew better than try to debate the point with Mr. Fox.

Abruptly turning serious, Fox said, "I'm no friend to your husband. You already know that. But for what it's worth, you may consider my friendship yours. I don't say that lightly, Your Grace. If ever you need a friend, you know where to come."

His eyes searched hers with an intensity that had all the force of an electric storm. In that moment Gabrielle was very glad that Mr. Fox had decided to be her friend, and she thanked providence for the chance encounter that had made it possible.

With an uncanniness that startled her, he again read her thoughts. "Mrs. Fox has little to do with it. Well, perhaps a little," he scrupulously amended. "There's not much I won't do to please my Liz. She likes you. I can see why. I've been watching you from a distance this last fortnight, but you know that.

You're a game little thing." He reached over and surprised Gabrielle by patting her on the arm. "I'm not going to ask you any awkward questions," he went on at length. "I'm sure your answers are word perfect. But mind what I've told you, Your Grace. I'm your friend. You may count on my protection if ever you need it. I won't try to embarrass Dyson again. At least," his bushy eyebrows wiggled roguishly, "at least with respect to his beautiful young wife. But let him put a foot wrong in the House, well, that's a different matter."

They conversed a little longer on generalities, but Gabrielle was relieved when Mr. Fox returned her to the ballroom, where she was again taken up by Gervais Dessins.

"You've made a hit with Mr. Fox," he observed as they waited for the orchestra to strike up.

"Is Mrs. Fox here? I don't think I've seen her."

"No. She doesn't go about much. To tell the truth, she's not received in polite society. The old notoriety still sticks, you see."

Gabrielle didn't see and said so.

"Last year," said Dessins, "the lady whom everyone thought was Fox's mistress was revealed to be his wife."

"I beg your pardon?"

"They'd been secretly married for years."

"But . . . I thought Mr. Fox was a libertine."

"That's what he likes people to think. In point of fact, he's devoted to Mrs. Fox. Oh, there's no doubt that she was his mistress at one time. But he married her long since. There's not many gentlemen would do as much."

Gabrielle did not doubt it. Mr. Fox's credit rose by a few notches.

"Is that why you've made a hit with Mr. Fox? Have you made the acquaintance of Mrs. Fox?"

Gabrielle replied suitably, but her thoughts were elsewhere. A moment before she had observed Louise Pelletier enter the ballroom. She was alone. When Gabrielle next saw Cam, Dessins was leading her into supper. They met on the stairs.

"Cam, your face!" Gabrielle cried out.

"I was trying to make friends with a cat," he replied ruefully. He dabbed at the wound with his folded handkerchief. Blood was dripping everywhere.

"Join us for supper, do," invited Dessins.

"Thank you, no. If you don't mind, I should have this seen to at once. Go ahead. I'll catch up with you later."

They watched in silence as Cam quickly ascended the stairs.

"I wonder who the cat was?" murmured Dessins provocatively.

"Do you?" responded Gabrielle. She was afraid that she had a very good idea. The vague feelings of despondency that had been plaguing her settled like a boulder in the pit of her stomach. She shook them off. She should be in high alt, not giving way to fancies.

In the two weeks they had been in town, she'd come through every test with flying colors. Cam had told her so. From her presentation to the queen at Windsor, through several parties, to tonight's gala event, she had conducted herself with all the aplomb of a duchess. Only the contretemps at the Bond Street emporium had been a small blot on her copybook, but even that event had turned to good account if it had won her the approval Mr. Fox. Then what was the matter with her? Pregnancy, she decided, but a small part of her brain refused to be convinced.

As Dessins went to fetch a selection of delicacies from tables brilliant with silver and crystal and laden with a plethora of exotic culinary delights, Gabrielle reflected on the humor that had gradually taken possession of her. She'd felt the first twinges when she'd turned to see Louise Pelletier bearing down on her like a hawk about to pounce on a sparrow.

She remembered that she'd been taken aback when Louise had intimated that she'd spent most of the summer at Falmouth. It was the first she had heard of it. Cam had never breathed a word. And what was the significance of the reference to her wedding night? It was mystifying. And it troubled her.

Louise troubled her. Cam troubled her. There was something going on and she meant to get to the bottom of it.

It was Dessins who carried most of the conversation throughout supper. Gabrielle's eyes kept straying to the door but Cam never appeared. She was startled into full alertness when her companion began on a tack she had never expected from that quarter.

"Where exactly on the Seine is your grandfather's château?"

"I beg your pardon?" she said, every instinct coming alive to her danger.

His eyes smiled into hers. "Is it close to Andely or Tosny or," he hesitated for a moment, "or Vrigonde?" His voice dropped on the last word.

When she stared at him blankly, he said cajolingly, "Gabrielle, you can trust me. I'm your friend."

For the first time, Gabrielle really looked at her companion. For two weeks he had attached himself to her quite assiduously. She had been flattered by his attention. He was young, handsome, and well connected. Cam saw no harm in him. But she discovered in that moment that she had never really liked Gervais Dessins, and she began to wonder why.

"Who are you?" she asked.

He laughed softly. "The question is, who are you?"

Her tone was level and deliberate when she answered, "Before my marriage, my name, as you well know, was Gabrielle de Valcour."

"Yes, yes!" he interrupted, not angry, not impatient, but as if they shared a private joke, "and Dyson abducted you from France and made you his ward."

"Yes."

"Then why did he marry you?"

"It was a love match."

"I take leave to doubt that."

Though they spoke in an undertone, and in French, they fell silent as liveried servants removed their empty plates and replenished their wine glasses. As soon as the servants were out of earshot, Gabrielle broke the silence.

"What makes you say so?"

"That yours was not a love match?"

"Yes."

He shrugged his shoulders in a deprecating gesture. "I'm not being unkind when I say this, mind you. You know it as well as I do."

It was Gabrielle who lost her patience. "*What* do I know?" she demanded coldly.

The smile left his eyes. "That on his marriage, for appearances' sake, your husband removed his mistress from his house. But he installed her close by. In Falmouth, to be exact."

For the longest time, she was silent. When the words burst from her, they were both shocked. "That's a lie!" Conversation in the vicinity abruptly died. After an interval, the buzz began again, but more muted.

"Gabrielle, you knew! You must have known!" said Dessins imploringly. "I know your marriage was a sham."

"It was a love match," she repeated, searching frantically for her control.

"He captured you! You were his hostage, for God's sake! He had to marry you. The Prince of Wales was about to give you his protection. Dyson could not let that happen, don't you see?"

"I was his ward. We fell in love. We were married." She said the words by rote.

"And, loving you, he kept a mistress on the side? Oh, I see what it is! Foolishly, you fell in love with *him*."

She shook her head, but her eyes betrayed her. She was coming to understand only too well.

"Dyson used you," said Dessins with brutal frankness. "It suited him to make you fall in love with him. It made you easier to manage."

She would have risen in her agitation, but he held her fast by both wrists. "Please! Listen to me! I would not have told you as much if I had not thought that you already knew the whole. I knew, you see, that he brought you to England against your will. I supposed that you'd wed with him to protect your grandfather. Mascaron, Gabrielle, Mascaron. I have a message from him."

She closed her eyes and tried to get a grip on her emotions. Her heart screamed that Dessins was a liar, that Cam loved her, that he would never betray his vows to her with another woman. At the same time her mind sifted through bits and pieces of half-remembered conversations and recalled scenes and impressions that gave the lie to her stubborn heart. The name of Louise Pelletier beat in her brain like a drumroll. By slow degrees, she forced herself to be calm. Only one thing Dessins had said was of any real significance. He had a message from Mascaron. The rest could wait.

She opened her eyes. "Walk with me, Gervais," she said, trying for a smile. "I should like to take a turn in the gardens."

He returned her smile, but with more fervor. "Good girl. I knew that I could count on you to do the right

338

thing."

From an upstairs window in Devonshire House, later that same evening, Gervais Dessins watched as Lord Lansing conducted Gabrielle to her waiting carriage. The English lord had not been best pleased to discover his friend's wife *tête à tête* with a French *immigré* in a secluded part of the gardens. He'd been looking for her everywhere, so he'd informed them, scowling at her escort. Dyson, it seemed, had long since departed. A physician had been summoned to tend to the annoying injury he'd sustained to his face. They were to meet up with each other in Hanover Square.

If Dessins had some misgivings about how Gabrielle would conduct herself after what he had told her, they were immediately laid to rest. Like a duchess, he thought, and could not help chuckling.

He was more than a little pleased with himself, he decided. In fact, he was elated. The Duchess of Dyson was, in truth, Mascaron's granddaughter. She had confessed it. And she was willing to return with him to France.

He thought of the performance he had just given and he could not help congratulating himself. He was sure it was the best in the whole of his acting career. As for Louise, by being her own natural self, unwittingly, she had helped him immeasurably. It had been a stroke of genius on his part to play Dyson's two women against each other. Above the hum of conversation in the supper room he had almost heard the click of Gabrielle's brain as she put two and two together. Dyson, he was sure, could swear his innocence on a stack of Bibles and his duchess would not believe a word he uttered.

She was a game little thing. He could not remember who had used those words in his hearing to describe her, but they were true. She was also cautious. Most of the ladies of his acquaintance would have been in a fever of impatience to exact retribution on an errant husband. Not Gabrielle. Like any trained agent, she had set aside personal considerations and had come at once to the crux of the matter.

"Who are you?" she had asked as soon as he had found a sheltered grove in the gardens where they could converse in private. No tears. No recriminations. Just a direct question. And he admired her for it.

He was Mascaron's man, he had told her, and had been from the beginning. It had taken him months to track down her abductors, and almost as long to find a way to meet with her on neutral ground.

She'd given him a few unquiet moments when she had asked after someone named Goliath. Fouché had never once mentioned anyone close to Mascaron by that name.

"I sent him back to Mascaron advising him of my changed circumstances," she had told him.

"Evidently he never returned," he hazarded.

She had turned deathly white and had stammered out something incomprehensible. It took him a moment or two to realize that his words had finally confirmed every suspicion she had begun to entertain about her husband's sincerity.

It was Dessins' considered opinion that the duke was indeed as unscrupulous as he had portrayed him. And it was the girl's misfortune that she was surrounded by rogues who used her shamelessly. He regretted that he must be one of them. He sighed, and after a moment's consideration went in search of Louise Pelletier.

Neither was very communicative in the short drive to her house. And when Louise invited him in for a glass of something to chase away the evening chill, he thought of Gabrielle and demurred.

"What happened to Dyson's face?" he asked, detaining her with a hand on her sleeve.

"He insulted me," she said, and shaking him off, hurried to her front door.

Dessins' eyes gleamed. Better and better, he was thinking. Laughing silently, he turned back into the coach. He wondered how the Duke of Dyson would try to talk his way out of that little scrape. He never doubted that Gabrielle would not be taken in.

The door had scarcely closed upon Louise Pelletier when she gave vent to her temper. Her eyes fell on a porcelain figurine of a Dresden shepherdess, a gift from Cam, that stood on the hall table. Going directly to it, she raised it high above her head and hurled it to the floor, where it shattered, gratifyingly, into a thousand pieces.

Servants came running. She screamed them away and marched into her bedchamber, slamming the door with such force that a piece of plaster fell down from the ceiling. She did not notice. She was beside herself. That Cam should speak to her in such terms! That he should prefer that hurly-burly hoyden who tried to pass herself off as a duchess! That he should mock her! That he should pity her! It was not to be borne!

She stopped in her agitated perambulations and stared at the reflection in her looking glass. She was a handsome woman, a woman in her prime. And yet she'd felt the pain of rejection, not once, but thrice, that very evening.

The Prince of Wales, she was relieved to be shot of. She could scarcely repress her shudders when he took her in his arms. Let him return to his dear Lady Hertford. Much she cared. When he made love to her she could not rid herself of the notion that she was

341

spawning with a whale. And for her pains she'd been given a diamond bracelet. *Delicate,* he'd called it when he'd snapped it on her wrist, *for a delicate rose.* Cheese-paring was a more apt description.

Dessins was another matter. He was young. He was handsome. And he was a knowledgeable and imaginative lover. He'd refused her gently, but it was a refusal just the same. No one had to tell her that there was another lady on his mind. She'd seen that look in a man's eyes before. Cam had looked just so on more occasions than she cared to remember before he had finally parted company with her.

She opened a commode that stood against the wall and removed a decanter of brandy and a small crystal glass. The first drink she bolted with a practiced movement of the wrist. Having poured a second, she carried it to the bed. She settled herself comfortably and began to relive the events of that evening.

Cam had scarcely taken his eyes off her from the moment she had come into his line of vision. She'd been elated. And when he'd spirited her away, under his wife's nose, to the privacy of the bookroom, she could not help the little crow of triumph that gurgled from her throat.

She still could not fathom how he had divined her game. But he had divined it. She'd had a rude awakening with the first words he'd said as he'd closed the bookroom door.

"I won't stand by and watch idly whilst you try to make trouble between Gabrielle and me."

She'd denied that she had any such intention. "I haven't said more than two words to her," she protested.

"And we shall keep it that way, if you please."

He wanted to know what had passed between Gabrielle and herself in the Devonshires' ballroom. She dared not tell him.

"Cam, we spoke in commonplaces about gowns and mutual acquaintances, and so on."

This was not how she had envisioned their reunion. She had been so sure that Cam would have come to his senses, that he would be regretting his hasty marriage and the loss of a woman who could give him so much pleasure. She'd practically offered herself for a night of dalliance. He would have none of her.

In the past she'd always suppressed her anger. A mistress could not afford the luxury of giving in to her sensibilities. In that moment, when she saw that her case was hopeless, there were no restraints, and the heedless words spilled over.

"You used me and discarded me like a filthy rag," she cried out.

He seemed to flinch at the words before quietly replying, "We struck a bargain. If I used you, I paid handsomely for the privilege."

The scene became uglier.

"You hypocrite," she raged. "You men are all the same. Women like me are good enough for your bed, but it's purity you marry."

He held out his hands in a calming, placating gesture. She thought he was relenting, that he meant to take her in his arms, but when he spoke his voice was quietly menacing. "You are right in this. Gabrielle did come to me a virgin. But if she'd known a score of men, or more, it would make no difference. I love her. There is no other woman I would have for my wife. I don't owe you an explanation. I am telling you this so that there can be no misunderstandings. Stay away from her, Louise. I won't let you hurt her."

"Cam," she pleaded, "how can you prefer that . . . that creature to me? Oh I daresay she can pass herself off as a lady for a few hours at a stretch. But don't you see, she's no better than a peasant, a common *poissarde*. She'll shame you, Cam. She'll make you a laughing stock."

For the longest interval he simply stood there staring. Then he made a sound that was halfway between a laugh and a sigh. "What more can I say?" he asked rhetorically. "You seem determined to misunderstand." Presently he went on, "Whether Gabrielle is a grubby peasant in boy's breeches or a lady in the high kick of fashion, it makes no difference. I love her because she is Gabrielle. It's as simple as that." And then he said those words which made her blood boil. "You don't understand, Louise, because you're a stranger to love. My dear, I feel sorry for you."

The action was purely reflex. She lashed out at him. She had no notion that in her agitation she had picked up a letter opener that lay on the desk. Cam dodged away, but not before the blade sliced the flesh of one cheek. When she saw what she had done, she was aghast. She dropped the knife and cowered away from him. But all that he said was, "Perhaps I deserved that. Let's say that we are even, shall we, and let it go at that?"

It was over. How could she have deceived herself into thinking otherwise? Long before, at Falmouth, she had suspected that Cam had fallen in love with the Norman chit. And she had accepted it. It was Dessins who had put it into her head that she could have any man she wanted—Cam, the Prince of Wales, even Napoleon Bonaparte. And she had basked in his empty flatteries. Fool!

But she was done with folly. She must consider her future. In the last week she had received two offers, neither of which excited her. One was from Mr. Robert Leslie, a middle-aged gentleman from the borders. He wanted her for his wife. The other offer came from Freddie Lamb, Lord Melbourne's younger son. He wanted her for his mistress.

With characteristic French shrewdness she weighed

the advantages and disadvantages of each offer. The last thing she did before retiring was write a note of acceptance to the gentleman she preferred. "My Dear Robert," she began, then chewed the end of her pen, debating the wisdom of her choice. If she married Robert her home would be miles from civilization. He would want children. Her conduct hereafter must be above reproach. But Robert was wealthy. And her position as Mrs. Leslie would be a respectable one. That must count for something.

She dipped her pen in the inkwell and continued, "It is with great pleasure that I write to accept . . ." Again she chewed on the end of her pen.

Freddie Lamb had a cruel streak, she reminded herself, and more often than not, his pockets were to let. On the other hand, he would set her up in London, and who could say whom she might meet on the morrow? Only that evening she had been introduced to the Marquis of Lorne, the heir to the Duke of Argyle. He'd been interested, she was sure of it. But if she removed from town, how was she to meet him again?

Discarding the first sheet of notepaper, she started over. "My darling Freddie, the answer is yes. Did you ever doubt it?"

For the third time she hesitated and chewed on the end of her pen. The unpleasant events of that evening intruded with a persistence she could not shake. Cam. She could not be sorry that she had disfigured his face. He had treated her abominably. She hoped one day she could serve him his just desserts. Shaking her head, she returned to her letter.

Chapter Nineteen

She felt numb. She felt betrayed. She felt used. Strangely, she was not angry. If there was one word that would best describe the state of her feelings, she thought that word would be *empty*.

In some sort, Gabrielle considered that she had got what she deserved. From the very first she had known that the Englishman was her enemy. To her cost, she had underestimated him. As it always did, his experience had told against her.

For a time she had held her own. His violent man-handling when he captured her, her subsequent incarceration, his blatant threats, even the boredom—nothing had subdued her or deprived her of her resolve to escape her captors and return to France. Not until he had used a weapon of which she had no experience—the seduction of her senses. If it had been only that! But Dessins was right. The Englishman had made her fall in love with him. She should hate him for it. If she felt anything at all, it was remorse.

Goliath. He had paid the price for her folly. Dessins was vague about Goliath's fate. Perhaps Mascaron had sent him on another mission. It was a forlorn hope, but she clung to it just the same. She would know more when Dessins returned her to France. Soon, before the month was out, he had promised. It could not come too soon for her peace of mind. There was no question that she could remain natural with Cam, no, she must think of him now as "the Englishman." As much as she was able, she must distance herself from him. It would not surprise him, surely, for she was a betrayed wife. They both knew it. In point of fact, to pretend to affection in the circumstances would only rouse his suspicions. She must play the hand she had been dealt carefully yet boldly. She had learned her lesson. She would not make the same mistake twice.

Mistake! The euphemism scarcely described the height of her folly. Out-and-out treason, some would call it. She was a citizen of France. He was an English spy. Their countries were at war. All along she had known that he had only one use for her and that was to coerce her grandfather into betraying military secrets. And knowing all this she had deliberately, stupidly, criminally, tumbled into his bed at his first sensual caress. Worse. His seed had taken. She was with child.

Her child. His child. She felt a faint stirring of emotion. At the edges, the numbness began to wear off. A choked sob caught in her throat. There was no one to hear it. She was alone in her chamber. Cam . . . the Englishman, she corrected herself . . . had asked her to wait up for him. He had something of a particular nature he wished to discuss. She had no wish to discuss anything with him in her present frame of mind. She was deathly afraid that she might betray herself into some indiscretion. Only a short while, she consoled herself, and then the charade would be over. Only a short while, and she and her unborn child would be out of his power forever.

To deprive him of his child was a form of retribution, she supposed. Not that her mind was bent on revenge. She had come to far too serious a pass for such a paltry ambition. It was imperative that she keep her wits about her if she and her grandfather were ever to escape the Englishman's coils. There must be no weakening, no more openings where he could slip under her guard. She must be as unscrupulous as he. In this final bout there would be no quarter asked or given.

She thought of Louise Pelletier, and another choked sob caught in her throat. Gritting her teeth, she fought against the tormenting pictures that flashed into her mind—Cam and Louise sharing the intimacies of lovemaking. She supposed that they had been laughing up their sleeves at her. She closed her eyes against the pain, remembering words Cam had flung at her so contemptuously, *You can never be the woman Louise is.* But she had tried to be . . . to please him. He had molded her to his every whim as if she had been a lump of clay. And she had blithely, heedlessly, conspired in her own downfall. Because she thought that he loved her. What colossal conceit on her part, to imagine that a man of his tastes and background could fall in love with the likes of a Gabrielle de Brienne! Hadn't she always known as much?

Let it go, she told herself. *It's over. Look to the future. Think of Mascaron. Think of Normandy.* She closed her eyes and tried to conjure the sights and scents of home. But what came to mind was the view of Cornwall's red cliffs and the screeching white gulls as they swooped toward Dunraeden's walls. Deliberately, she put the picture from her and concentrated on Normandy's orchards. Before long she could picture her grandmother's oak dresser, and the small sitting room where she kept her most treasured possessions.

When she returned home, her grandfather would be free of the hold the Englishman had over him. Cam had told her that French authorities would surmise what had been afoot if they ever discovered she had been his prisoner in England. Dessins had smoothed over that uncertainty. Mascaron, he had told her, had passed on nothing of a sensitive nature, and that the first consul himself had been in Mascaron's confidence from the beginning. She was greatly relieved to hear it, and at the same time, greatly distressed to discover how abysmally gullible she had been. Whatever the Englishman had chosen to tell her, she had taken for gospel.

She thought of Goliath again, and something deep inside her began to tremble. Only then did she begin to hate the Englishman.

"You were fortunate," said the physician. "The blade missed your eye with only an inch to spare." With a pair of small scissors, he clipped the ends of the sutures he had just made in Cam's cheek.

"It was a letter opener," Cam said dismissively.

Dr. Harlow's eyebrows came down. "The scar will fade in time," he remarked. He packed the instruments of his profession into a small case.

Cam remained silent as he pulled on a clean linen shirt. His valet was not in attendance. When Cam took his wife to bed, he abhorred servants hovering in the background. He preferred to undress her himself. He found his brocade dressing gown and shrugged into it.

It was Lord Lansing who took up the slack in the conversation.

"Very kind of you to come from your bed, sir, and oblige us in this matter." With an admonitory glance at his friend and a firm touch on Dr. Harlow's elbow, Lansing steered the physician from the room.

Belatedly remembering his manners, Cam added, "Yes, of course. My thanks to you, Dr. Harlow."

Dr. Harlow grunted and exited with Lansing. Lifting a candelabra from the mantel, Cam moved to the small mirror above his gentleman's dressing chest. He gingerly touched his fingers to the ugly black stitches.

"Handsome is as handsome does," quoted Lansing, entering at that moment. "Your valet should dispose of this." He picked up the shirt that Cam had been wearing earlier. It was crimson with blood. "The coat will have to go, too." He gave a cursory look to the bloodstains that had dried to a dark sheen down the front of Cam's black evening coat.

"My thanks to you, Simon, for fetching Gabrielle home." Cam's eyes flicked to the door leading to his wife's bedchamber, and he wondered how he could decently speed his friend on his way so that he could be alone with her.

Lansing threw himself into an armchair. "God, what a bloody awful night!" he said violently. "First you with Louise and then I with Lady Caro."

It was evident that Lansing was in no hurry to take his leave. Resigning himself to the inevitable, Cam returned the silver candelabra to its place. He gave Lansing an assessing look. "Lady Caro has turned you off, I take it," he said conversationally.

Glowering, Lansing retorted, "I'd rather not talk about it, if you don't mind."

Seating himself, Cam said, "As you wish," and preserved a diplomatic silence. After a moment he offered his friend a slim cheroot from a small ivory box. It was Lansing who fetched the candle to light them. Both men drew heavily and exhaled slowly.

At length, Lansing observed. "She didn't turn me off. I never made the offer."

"No?"

"No." He sighed. He caught something in Cam's expression and grinned. "She's a raving bluestocking, and I'm afraid I don't come up to her weight."

"Did she say so?"

"There was no need. I spent the most uncomfortable half hour of my life trying to converse with her in Attic Greek."

Cam choked on the smoke he had just inhaled. He coughed. Rasping, he said, "I shouldn't worry about it, Simon. Greek is a dead language. You're not like to have need of it in our circles."

"True," agreed Lansing, but with a complete lack of enthusiasm.

Cam stifled a smile.

"There's one consolation." Another sigh fell from Lansing's lips.

Cam waited.

"I don't think William Lamb will do any better."

"Does this mean you are resigned to your fate?" quizzed Cam.

Lansing laughed. "No! What it means is that I've had a lucky escape! And don't I know it! Shackled to a bluestocking! And I'm not forgetting Lady Caro's female relations. The whole tribe of 'em are tarred with the same brush."

"I see what it is," said Cam. "You've had a vision of what it would be like to entertain your in-laws should you marry into the family."

Lansing let his mind wander to the spectacle of the Duchess of Devonshire and ladies Spencer and Bessborough setting down at his estate in Ireland for a prolonged visit. He shuddered involuntarily. "Only the females of Lady Caro's tribe are clever," he mused. "I wonder why it is that the Spencer ladies are all so brilliant and the Spencer men are as thick as doors?"

"There's no accounting for it," agreed Cam.

Abruptly changing the subject, Lansing said, "How are you going to explain this night's work to Gabrielle?"

"I'll think of something," said Cam. At the mention

of Gabrielle's name, he glanced pointedly at the clock on the mantel.

Taking the hint, Lansing rose to his feet. "I wouldn't like to be in your shoes," he said, cheerfully offensive. "Take my advice. Before you become involved in explanations, sweeten her up a bit."

"What do you suggest?" asked Cam in his dryest tone.

"Lord, how should I know? Gew-gaws and such won't work with Gabrielle. There's no news from France, then?"

"Yes. I've had word. But nothing of a nature that I care to pass on to Gabrielle. Quite the reverse." To Lansing's questioning look, Cam replied, "Mascaron is incommunicable. It seems that he came down with a sudden fever and was removed to his place on the Seine. No one can get near him. The word is that he is gravely ill."

Incredulous, Lansing demanded, "And you've said nothing to Gabrielle?"

"No. And neither must you. Rodier is not convinced that things are what they seem."

"Good God! That *is* bad news!"

To Cam's way of thinking, the news from France was alarming, to say the least. Rodier put no credence in the story that was given out respecting Mascaron's illness and subsequent removal from the Ministry of Marine. Security at the Château de Vrigonde was so tight that Rodier's suspicions were roused. Either Mascaron was shamming for some reason known only to himself or he was a prisoner without giving the appearance of it. Either way, some plan would have to be devised to bring the man out of France, and as soon as possible. Cam was working on it. He said nothing of what he was thinking to Lansing, however, since he was impatient for his friend to depart.

When the front doors finally closed upon Lansing, Cam entered his study. He decided to fortify himself with a small brandy before facing Gabrielle. He needed it.

He'd made up his mind to confess the whole about Louise to his wife and beg her forgiveness. If it had been in his power, he would have followed Lansing's advice. He wished there was some way of softening the blow he was about to inflict. He wished there was some way to distract her or put off the evil hour. But he knew that he must either lie in his teeth or tell Gabrielle everything. Time had run out for him.

He didn't want to hurt her. Oh God, he didn't want to hurt her. He had no choice. Either Louise or Fox or someone who wished him harm had already sown the seeds of her distrust. He had seen it in the carefully averted eyes, the slump of her shoulders, and in the vagueness of her greeting when Lansing had fetched her home in the carriage.

He'd make it up to her, he promised himself. Naturally, she would lash out at him, call him every vile name under the sun that she could think of. It was to be expected. It was no less than he deserved. He would accept her vituperation meekly. And then he would worm his way back into her good graces with soft words of love and tender, voluptuous caresses. He knew how to get around Gabrielle.

The smile he attempted turned into a grimace. He touched his fingers to the wound on his cheek. And then he remembered the distasteful scene with Louise in Devonshire's bookroom.

When he'd first ushered her into the room, the impulse to murder her was almost irresistible. Not for a moment did he believe her protests that the words she had exchanged with Gabrielle were innocent. He knew Louise too well. But his anger had dissipated when it was borne in upon him that Louise really believed that she was the injured party. He did not think that he would ever forget those words, "You used me and discarded me like a filthy rag."

There was just enough truth in them to take the edge off his anger. He'd never before seen himself in that light. But dash it all, they had struck a bargain! Her sexual favors had cost him a packet. And Louise had received far more from him than Gabrielle ever had. But Gabrielle asked for nothing. At the same time, she asked for everything.

And she had it — his love, his fidelity, his esteem, his heart. He must convince her of it. He *would* convince her of it, he promised himself. She would give him another chance because she loved him. If their positions were reversed, he was sure . . . oh, God, he was sure he would murder her. But then, it was different for a man, wasn't it? And it wasn't as if he had really betrayed her. Surely she must see that?

He found himself clutching an empty glass. The hour was upon him. Squaring his shoulders, he strode from the room. As he slowly ascended the stairs he tried to shake himself of the conviction that his sins had indeed come home to roost.

For a moment, his hand rested on the doorknob to her chamber. He inhaled deeply, and pushed inside.

She was seated at the window embrasure, staring out at the square. Her head lifted as he advanced into the room. She had not waited for him to help her disrobe. She was in her nightclothes. The delicate, cream-colored lace clung to her breasts like a second skin, then fell to floor in folds. Her hair was unbound and brushed till it shone like satin. He looked into her eyes and read her complete knowledge of his affair with Louise.

Slowly, he let out the breath he was holding. He closed the distance between them and went down on his knees, pressing a kiss to the small swell of her abdomen. "I love you," he said simply. "Please believe that."

She was like a cold block of marble in his arms. Her voice was no warmer "Why, Cam, what has brought this on?"

She had set her mind against him. He could feel it in every rigid line of her body. Straightening, he captured her wrist and pulled her to her feet. She was silent as he led her out of the shadows to a corner of the room that had more light.

"That's better," he said. "I want to see your face when I talk to you."

"By all means," she replied, sinking into the chair that he held for her. "As I wish to see yours."

Cam leaned one hip against her escritoire and studied his wife thoughtfully. Her composure rattled him. He remembered a time when she would have lashed out with a string of curse words. He would have preferred that to this damning coldness.

With as much gentleness as he could manage he said, "Gabrielle, when I married you, I had a mistress."

"So I understand," she replied conversationally, as if they were discussing some commonplace. "And long after, as I've been given to understand."

Cam shifted uncomfortably. "I should like to know who has been carrying tales to you," he said stiffly.

"I'm sure you would," Gabrielle concurred noncommittally.

He forced his annoyance down. He was the guilty party here, and if this was to be the form of his abasement he was willing to accept it, up to a point.

"Our marriage was to have been one of convenience only," reminded her.

"And shall return to that happy estate from this night forward," she coolly informed him.

Cam smiled tolerantly and decided to let that provocation pass. He folded his arms and surveyed the small set face that was determinedly indifferent. "Gabrielle," his voice became husky, persuasive. "From the moment you became a true wife to me I have had no other woman in my bed. And long before, it was you and only you I wanted. For the longest time you held me at arm's length. You know I speak the truth."

"Englishman," she said softly, succinctly, "you are an inveterate liar."

"I have never lied to you!"

"What!" she feigned astonishment. "Were you telling the truth when you told me that I could never be the woman that your mistress was?"

"I already explained that foolish remark!" His voice had become louder, rougher as he felt the sharp rise of anger. She was fencing with him just as surely as if she held a foil in her hand. This was not what he wanted. He was going to make his confession. Gabrielle would forgive him and things between them would return to normal. Straightening, he came away from the writing desk.

"You've never lacked imagination in your explanations. I'll give you that," she said. "Explain this to me, then, if you would be so kind. Where were you, Englishman, on our wedding night?"

He groaned and swore vehemently on the same breath. "What difference does it make?" he asked savagely. "You did not want me. I went where I knew I would be welcomed."

"To Louise Pelletier, in fact. To the house you rented for her in Falmouth."

"Yes," he roared.

She stared at him in shocked silence. Her lips trembled. Her lashes lowered, but not before he had glimpsed the sheen of tears in her eyes.

"Gabrielle," he implored, and grabbed for her

356

hands. She jerked away from him. His grasp tightened, holding her steady. "You are too young, too innocent to understand. I know what you are thinking. No, don't pull away from me." He wrenched her back. His words were edged with impatience. "My relationship with Louise was carnal, and nothing more. Do you understand? She never meant anything more to me than . . . hell, my dinner, if you want it in its crudest terms. She was in my employ! She bartered her body for money! She wanted to make trouble between us tonight. When I would have nothing to do with her, she went for me with a knife." Gabrielle stopped struggling, and he let out a frustrated sigh. His voice gentled. "I've only ever loved one woman in my whole life, and that's you. Gabrielle, I love you."

His heart was in his eyes.

Her lip curled. He had chosen a new weapon in his arsenal of arms with which he thought to storm the citadel — patent, unadulterated sincerity. The man was a master of deception. Didn't she know it?

Lightly, tauntingly, her fingers brushed over the sutures on his cheek. "Is that what truly happened between you and Louise tonight, Cam? Or did you revolt her too?"

A dark tide of color rose in Cam's neck. Jealousy and anger he had expected. A stream of obscenities, he would have welcomed. But he had not considered how this open contempt would annoy him. She was looking down on him, intimidating him with that cool stare.

Words were having no effect on her. "Come to bed," he said abruptly, and pulled on her arm.

She wrenched herself from his grasp with such force that she went stumbling backward, falling against a chair. Steadying herself, she glared into his face. "You're mad if you think I'll permit you to

357

make love to me. I don't want you, d'you under-stand? Go back to Louise, if she'll have you. Or find some other woman who will welcome your atten-tions."

He smiled unpleasantly and he said, "Now that is more in your style."

Goaded, Gabrielle cried out, "Why don't you save yourself the trouble, Englishman? Cook will be de-lighted to prepare dinner for you." She scooted be-hind the chair as he advanced upon her. "You said so yourself—having a woman is just like eating your dinner."

With the force of one arm he swept the chair aside. "You weren't listening," he said, and grabbed for her.

"I'll fight you," she warned as he captured her shoulders in his powerful hands.

"You'll try," he agreed.

She didn't know how it had come about, but the power she had felt when he had first entered her chamber had slipped away from her. There had been a restraint about him, a humility, a meekness that had fueled her confidence. Just a few words and she would have him groveling at her feet, she'd thought then.

But he wasn't groveling. She looked into those reckless blue eyes and saw a wildness that ought to have frightened her. She'd goaded him to temper. She wondered if, unconsciously, it was what she had wanted to do all along. To chastise him about Goliath and Mascaron was not to be thought of. He must never know that she'd discovered his designs until it was too late to take action. But it was evident that to chastise him for the sins he'd committed as her hus-band was no more than he expected. She could give free reign to her temper with impunity.

The thought had no sooner entered her head when

her fury erupted like lava from a smoldering volcano. In a practiced movement she had learned from Goliath, she jerked up both hands and sent him reeling backward. He fell heavily to the floor, but made no move to rise. If she had not been so angry she would have laughed to see the shock that registered on his face.

"Lecher! Deceiver! Knave!" she raved at him, and threw in several eloquent French epithets that had Cam's eyes widen in admiration.

"Now this is the Gabrielle with whom I am more acquainted," he said pleasantly and rose on his elbows to get a better look as she circled him with her long, impatient strides.

"Who was it told me that he fell in love with me at Andely!" she raged.

"There's no explaining it, but it's true," he confessed, sighing theatrically.

Her voice vibrated with emotion. "Liar! Does a man who loves one woman take another to his bed?"

"He does if he thinks the woman he loves is beyond his reach," he pointed out reasonably.

"We exchanged vows before God," she shot back.

This was a new wrinkle, thought Cam, and one that deserved a thoughtful response. But not now. They would get to that later. In the same infuriatingly reasonable tone he said, "Vows that neither of us had any intention of keeping."

For a moment, just a moment, the wind was taken out of her sails. With arms akimbo, bosom heaving, eyes blazing, she regarded him in furious silence. Cautiously, Cam raised himself to sit crosslegged.

"Those nights you slipped away from Dunraeden?"

"What nights?" asked Cam, playing for time. He knew perfectly well to what she referred. Those were the nights he had slipped away to be with Louise.

She stamped her foot and stooped down till they

were nose to nose, "Where were you?" she hissed.

There was no levity in him when he answered, "You know where I was. And I've explained why."

Her lashes swept down to conceal her expression, but Cam heard the catch in her breath as she turned away. Very quietly, seriously, he said, "I've said it once, but I'll say it again. From the day you became a true wife to me there have been no other women. I'm sorry. I did not know that you were aware I was ever away from Dunraeden. Perhaps I was not very discreet . . ."

Her laugh stopped him.

Over her shoulder, she said, "If you were indiscreet, I never tumbled to it. Shall I share the joke? I thought you were off doing whatever it is spies do." She laughed again, not very convincingly. "Frankly, I was wishing you would stay away more often." Her thoughts seemed to wander.

Cam was not sure how to reach her. He remained silent, his eyes following her as she roamed aimlessly about the room.

When she spoke next, her voice was as brittle as fine crystal. "Those nights you left me for Louise? I was terrified that you would discover what *I* had been getting up to. What an irony!"

At her choice of words, he felt the faint stirrings of annoyance. "I did not leave you for Louise. You made it clear that you did not want me. And what were you getting up to?" Since her back was to him, he took the opportunity to rise to his feet.

"You'll find this hilarious," she said, and her voice cracked.

"Gabrielle," Cam pleaded, and raised his hand in a soothing, gentling motion.

She found her voice. "I was dangling from a rope over Dunraeden's ramparts, readying myself for the Grand Escape." A stray thought that she did not divulge flitted into her mind. She remembered that weeks before she had attempted to escape his nocturnal wanderings had come to an end, to her great regret. Had he stopped seeing Louise? She thought he must have done.

She sensed that she was weakening. In a flurry of motion, she sped to the door and flung it wide. "I'm bone weary," she said, "and my head is ready to split." It was no less than the truth. "Perhaps we should continue this conversation when we are both in a better frame of mind."

"I have no more use for this conversation," he agreed, surprising her.

He stalked pantherlike to the open door. Gabrielle tried not to flinch when he paused, towering over her.

"May I kiss your hand?" he asked softly.

Gabrielle's eyes swept over him, and her blood began to boil. He was the epitome of the English aristocrat—urbane, sophisticated, and as smooth as polished granite. She showed him her teeth and said dulcetly, "Englishman, for all I care, you may kiss my . . ."

She cried out in fright as Cam suddenly swooped down on her. With a great whoop of laughter, he dragged her into his arms and kissed her soundly. Gabrielle struggled madly. Stooping, he swept her up. With one foot, he kicked the door shut and carried her to the bed. She found herself falling, and cried out when she hit the mattress. In the next instant Cam was sprawled on top of her.

Gabrielle lashed him with her tongue as only she could do. Shocking, thought Cam, as a long string of expletives spilled from her lips. He threw back his head and laughed.

Her rage knew no bounds. With both hands she reached for his hair and yanked with every ounce of her strength. "Don't you dare laugh at me," she panted.

Cam easily disengaged her hands and pinned them over her head. "If I am laughing, it's only because I've found my wife again," he said. "You can play the duchess in public to your heart's content, and with my goodwill. But don't make the mistake of thinking you can play that role with me." His eyes bathed her with warmth and a tenderness Gabriellle could not sustain.

Averting her head, she murmured, "You're wrong, Englishman. You haven't found me. You've lost me. Forever."

At her careless words, Cam stilled. The silence seemed to vibrate with tension. Gabrielle was sorry she had said so much. She shivered when his long fingers splayed through her hair, bringing her head up.

"What is that supposed to mean," he asked, his voice so low, so precise, that she knew she had gone too far.

She had not known that she was holding her breath till she expelled it on a long ragged gasp. Trying to put him off the scent, she essayed, "I'll be your duchess and I'll be the mother of your child, but I can't, I won't be anything more to you."

His eyes grew hard, then flashed to anger. "You're overreacting," he told her. "You'll calm down when you've had time to think about it."

Pride dictated only one answer. "I don't want you to touch me ever again."

"And you think I'll be satisfied with that?" he asked incredulously.

"What choice do you have?" she recklessly countered, trying not to let the relief show in her expression. She had deflected him from the thought that she was about to take flight for France.

"I'll show you what choice I have," he said as his mouth came down hard on hers in a punishing kiss.

Too late she realized that Cam had read a challenge in her words. Frantically she pushed at the powerful shoulders that crushed her. With an iron grip, he manacled her wrists together over her head. She twisted and bucked, trying to dislodge him. He shifted, pressing her deep into the mattress, the hard weight of his body flattening her soft woman's contors.

Gabrielle changed tactics. She stopped struggling and offered a passive resistance. Cam took immediate advantage. He thrust her legs wide and settled himself into the cradle of her thighs. Only then did he release her from his grinding kiss.

He raised his head. The storm in his eyes battled with the storm in hers. Neither of them could speak, so labored and uneven was their breathing. Gabrielle shook her head. Cam ground himself intimately into the lower part of her body, blatantly demonstrating what he meant to do with her. She sobbed, but they both recognized it was a small sound of arousal.

Gabrielle was panic-stricken. She could not afford to forget that this man had betrayed her trust. He had used her shamelessly to further his own ends. The people she loved most in world had suffered because of her folly. To yield to him, now, when she knew him to be a faithless scoundrel, was to court catastrophe.

Cam released her wrists. His hands went to her shoulders to divest her of her nightclothes. But Gabrielle was not subdued yet. She clawed at him with her nails.

He swore furiously and slapped her hands away. He didn't think of what he was doing. He straddled her with his knees and held her down as he deliberately ripped the fragile lace of her gown from throat

363

to him. The violence of his action shocked them both.

"Has it come to this, Cam?" she cried softly. "Will you force me?"

"No," he groaned. "I just want to love you."

For a while it seemed that her words had brought him to his senses. He hesitated for the longest moment. But when he raised his eyes to Gabrielle's, she knew that she had lost.

He didn't know what was the matter with him. This was not what he wanted. He wanted Gabrielle willing and open to him, the way she always was. For the first time since they had become lovers she had rejected him, was still rejecting him. The pain of it tore at him. He didn't want to hurt her. He *wouldn't* hurt her. But he couldn't let her win this battle. He wasn't going to let her make a stranger of him. She loved him. He would prove it to her.

He controlled her desperate movements with his weight, one powerful leg hooked over her hips. And then he set himself to pleasuring her body. There was no barrier now to shield her bare skin from the brush of his hands, the rasp of his tongue, the caress of his lips. Ruthlessly suppressing his own desire, he exploited his secret knowledge. He knew just the right touches to make her writhe for him. Her fingers dug into his shoulders as he traced the peak of one breast with his teeth. He drew the swollen nipple hard into his mouth, and she arched helplessly. When he slipped his fingers into her wet warmth she went rigid, then lay quivering beneath him. He kissed her, and her lips softened and clung to his.

She wanted to hate him. She needed to hate him. She couldn't understand why she didn't. She knew that she wasn't thinking rationally. He'd started an ache deep in the pit of her belly. The heat of it was spreading like wildfire, consuming her. She couldn't remember consequences when every sense was on fire for him. She opened her mouth, protesting weakly, and his tongue swept in, thrusting and withdrawing in a slow erotic rhythm. She moaned, deep in her throat, and moved restlessly beneath the press of his weight.

He pulled back to study her. "Give in to me," he pleaded.

He had taken away her will to resist. "You've won," she cried out.

The flash of temper was back in his eyes. "Have I? Then if I've won . . ."

He crouched over her, shutting out everything but him. Calmly, with slow, deliberate movements, he arranged her limbs so that she was completely vulnerable and open to him. With his eyes locked on hers he began the torture. At each intimate caress, she jerked. Her breath grew heavy, thickened in her throat, then rushed out of her lungs. He kneeled between her legs, stroking his fingers deep into her body till she was mindless with wanting him.

It wasn't enough for him. His head dipped. With tongue and lips he took possession of her, permitting her no modesty in his sensual enjoyment of her body.

Gabrielle was past caring. She was a cauldron of seething sensation. With wanton abandon she offered herself for his every whim, reveled in the stroke of his tongue, the caress of his lips, the touch of his hands as they moved ceaselessly over her. She had never been more aware of herself as a woman. She had never been more aware of her body as an instrument of pleasure. She did not know that she spurred him on with words of blatant demand and praise.

When he pulled away from her, she moaned her protest. Quickly rising to his feet, Cam divested himself of his garments. The blood was thundering in his head. His hands were shaking. Her woman's scent was on his tongue, filling his nostrils, arousing him unbearably. He knew that she expected a fast and furious finish. That was not his intent. He closed his eyes, forcing back the hot rush of desire.

When he came back to her, Gabrielle sensed his control. Wonderingly, she turned into him. And then the torture began again. He lavished her with tenderness and gentle caresses, and those soft words of love against which her heart had no defense. It was as if what had gone before was of no consequence, that their lovemaking began only as she accepted him as her lover and gave her full consent for what he wanted from her.

"It's all right," she whispered, her woman's intuition sensing some battle he waged within himself. "It's all right."

He cupped her face, his hands strong yet gentle, and kissed her softly, then wildly as he felt the passion rise in her. His fingers curled around her hand and brought it to his arousal.

"Love me," he pleaded.

"I do," she whispered, and proved it by exploiting her own secret knowledge, forcing his control to the limits of his endurance. She rose above him, her hair falling about him like a sheaf of ripe wheat. With open-mouthed kisses she traced patterns from his shoulders to his groin, skimming every inch of him, tasting, wallowing in his scent and flavor. She demanded. He answered. With an age-old feminine instinct she molded herself to him, inviting him to that most complete act of love between a woman and her mate. Writhing, moaning, with her hands clutching his shoulders, Gabrielle urged him to take her.

Unchecked, he rose above her "Do you want me to?"

The rough urgency of his tone gradually penetrated the sensual fog that clouded her thinking. Her long lashes lifted. She tried to focus on him.

With barely restrained impatience, he threaded his fingers through her hair. "I want to be inside you," he groaned, his voice dark and heavy with arousal. "But know what this means, Gabrielle. It means you forgive me."

"Cam!" Her voice was weak and thin. She couldn't think. She didn't want to think.

"Take me inside you, Angel."

He forced her hand between their bodies, and thrust himself at her. Her fingers closed around him, caressing, savoring his virility. Obediently she guided him to the entrance of her body. She opened for him. Slowly he filled the emptiness. She didn't know that her cheeks were wet with tears.

Cam traced the path of one errant tear with his tongue. "You haven't lost," he whispered hoarsely. "We've both won."

Abruptly his mood altered. His hands cupped her hips, raising her to sheath him deeply, fully. His control disintegrated. And at the last, as she convulsed in the throes of rapture and he emptied himself in hard thrusts deep in her body, he groaned his love for her over and over. To Gabrielle, it was a bittersweet litany.

Chapter Twenty

Over the next several days, Cam had much to occupy his mind. His overriding concern was Mascaron, and how he was to effect his release from the
Château de Vrigonde. Security at the château had finally been penetrated. Mascaron was gravely ill, that
fact was incontrovertible. His own physician had
taken up residence to be near his patient. But to
what end the château was so heavily guarded had yet
to be discovered. It did not seem possible that Mascaron's activities on behalf of British Intelligence had
been uncovered, else the man would have been held
in Paris, at the Conciergerie or one of the other
prisons. And in very short order there would have
been a trial and an execution and the report of it
would have been blazed to the world.

Cam said nothing to Gabrielle, not wishing to
alarm her. She would know everything there was to
know in his own good time. One way or another,
Cam was determined to bring her grandfather out of
France. And since he had a vested interest in Mascaron's fate, he had resolved to take charge of the operation. If it had been Mascaron only, Cam would not
have lifted a finger to help him. It was Gabrielle's
happiness, and only Gabrielle's, that counted for anything.

He had hurt her more deeply than he would ever

have dreamed was possible. Her silence on the subject of Louise Pelletier, far from pleasing him, only tested the limits of his patience. A touch, a word, brought her into his arms. She denied him nothing that was his due as her husband. But there was a constraint, a reserve in her manner, and he did not know how to breach it. She had closed off some part of herself that she refused to share with him. It exasperated him beyond endurance. This was not the generosity he had come to expect from his Gabrielle. In some sort, he felt that *he* was the one who had been betrayed.

At first he was almost defiantly determined never again to raise the contentious question of Louise Pelletier. Then he reconsidered, and in the gentle aftermath of lovemaking, when Gabrielle was at her most vulnerable, he again broached the subject.

Gabrielle forestalled him. "This is not necessary," she said. "It's forgiven, Cam, remember? Put it out of your mind. I have."

"Then what is it? Why are you so different?"

She kissed him lingeringly. "You're imagining things."

He knew that he was not and refused to be put off. "Is it because I broke my vows to you?"

"Vows?"

"You said that we had made our vows before God."

"Did I? I don't remember."

"You said it. What did you mean by it?"

"Nothing." She stretched like a cat, and he adjusted his long body to the fit of hers. "I suppose I must have been thinking of the day we were wed."

"What were you thinking?"

"The strangest thing . . ."

"Go on."

"I felt a Presence. When I knelt with you before the altar? I felt a Presence. I wanted to pray, but I didn't know how. It's silly, really." She yawned and turned into the shelter of his arms.

"I don't think it's silly."

She raised herself slightly to see him better. "Do you believe in God, Cam?"

"Of course. Does that surprise you?" There was a smile in his voice when he said, "Do you think I'm such a disreputable character that I may not believe in God?"

"Oh, no," she answered, her eyes and voice heavy with drowsiness, "even the Devil believes." Her head drooped on his shoulder.

He had to shake her to get her attention. "If we were to renew our vows, sincerely, in the presence of God, would that satisfy you?"

"I'm satisfied, Cam, truly."

"Even so . . ."

She covered his lips with her fingers. "It wouldn't serve, Cam," she said. "God doesn't exist, or if he does, he doesn't listen to me."

He was truly shocked at this calm avowal and was rougher than he meant to be when he pulled her to a sitting position. "You've been duped by all that rot that Talleyrand and his cutthroats espoused during the Revolution. God exists, Gabrielle. Believe it. It is not we who should call the Deity to account, but the other way round."

Her eyes were huge and startled. "This . . . coming from you, Cam?" she asked. "On your own admission, an adulterer and God knows what else?"

He opened his mouth and closed it quickly, swallowing an angry retort. *Adulterer.* He tested the word gingerly and decided he didn't like it. He'd never thought of himself in those terms. He thought of it now and squirmed. Her innocent shaft had hit its mark. "God forgive me," he said, "I'm not perfect. But I swear to you, from this day forward I shall prove myself worthy of your trust."

She began to weep softly, then in earnest, with deep shuddering gasps. Cam felt helpless. She quieted when he pushed her into the depths of the mattress and covered her with his weight. But when he told her that he thanked God every day of his life for bringing her into his orbit, the weeping began anew. And there was no consoling her.

He was going to remove her to Cornwall the first chance he got. He was sick to death of London and the follies of the ton. He wanted his wife back, the girl who had captured his heart. A thousand times he damned himself for molding her to the role of his duchess. She had learned only too well how to play the part. Lansing applauded the new Gabrielle. Cam longed for the old one. He would give anything, he thought, for the saucy hoyden who didn't know how to conceal what she was feeling, at least not from him. And this new veneer she wore like a second skin — her charm, her grace, her beauty, pampered now to a sleek perfection — could not make up for what he thought he had lost.

In his mind's eye he could see her in her boy's breeches, swaggering with all the confidence of youth. She had never been afraid to show him her mettle. She had never turned aside from one of his challenges.

As clear as day he had a picture of her as she had been at Andely in their first encounter, when in fear and trembling she had raised her foil and warned him that she didn't want to hurt him. In quick succession, other impressions came and went. Gabrielle, in her boy's breeches, on horseback, riding hell for leather across the lawns of the Château de Vrigonde. Gabrielle, naked as the day she was born, cavorting in the waters of the Seine. Gabrielle, cursing like any common *poissarde* after he had kissed her on the stairs

371

at Vrigonde. Gabrielle, fighting him tooth and nail on that never-to-be forgotten day he had made her his captive.

What a blind fool he had been not to recognize that she was more woman than he had ever known. What arrogance, what colossal conceit on his part to judge her wanting because she did not fit his preconceived notions of womanly virtue. And how the fates must be laughing. She had become the epitome of everything he had once admired in a woman. And he wanted the old Gabrielle back.

And yet that was not precisely true. At Windsor, when she had made her curtsy to the queen, no man could have been prouder than he. His wife was not only beautiful but also a paragon of every virtue under the sun. He'd given her the challenge, and, as always, she had risen to it, surpassing every expectation.

God, it didn't matter to him! Boy's breeches or ball gowns, curse words or polite inanities, it was all the same. It was Gabrielle who made the difference. The essence of who and what she was—that was what he wanted from her. She had given it to him once. Because she had learned to trust him. He wondered what he could do to prove that he was worthy of a second chance. And the conviction that he had no one to blame but himself for his unhappy plight did nothing to improve his temper.

He took that thought with him when he called on Mr. Pitt at his rooms in Baker Street.

As was his habit, Pitt was nursing a glass of port. "You'll join me?" he asked as Cam seated himself.

Several minutes were taken up in discussing desultory commonplaces before Cam steered the conversation into a channel that was of more interest to him.

"My thanks for your assistance with Lord Whitmore and his aides."

Pitt eyed Cam from beneath lowered eyebrows. "It was relatively easy to arrange for their absence. Is that why you are here, Cam? As I remember, you said that when the time was right you would take me fully into your confidence."

"I had hoped that day would have arrived long since. Unfortunately, I must beg your indulgence for a little while longer."

"How much longer?" asked Pitt.

Cam imbibed slowly before replying, "A week. Two at the most."

Mr. Pitt said nothing. He knew Cam better than to suppose that this quiet *tête à tête* had been arranged for no other purpose than to pass on an intelligence of such paltry significance. On the other hand, in the last number of months he was beginning to wonder if he really knew Cam at all. He had found himself speculating more and more frequently on his younger colleague.

The first ripple of surprise had come with the report of Cam's hastily contrived nuptials. On reflection, Pitt had decided that the Duke of Dyson, like many men before him, had succumbed to a pretty face and form. Pitt put no credence in the story that had circulated respecting Cam's bride, namely that she had been browbeaten into submission. In point of fact, he'd done his best to scotch that ugly rumor.

He'd been on the point of advising Cam that it was in his best interests to introduce the girl to society when he'd been forestalled by Her Majesty. He had not given it another thought till Cam had arrived on his doorstep and made that strange request. The presence of Lord Whitmore, the former ambassador to France, and his aides could prove highly embarrassing to himself and his duchess at this time, he'd informed Pitt. And Pitt had found himself agreeing to arrange for their absence on the understanding that Cam would take him into his confidence in a matter of weeks. Idly, he wondered how Whitmore was getting on in Ireland.

There was no question of how the Duchess of Dyson was going on. Ton hostesses had not been slow to grasp the fact that her presence was a virtual guarantee of success. The girl was invited everywhere. And the latest shocking *on dit* to circulate, that Cam's former mistress had created a scene at Devonshire House, had, if anything, only added to the girl's popularity. As he'd heard tell, since the night in question the Duke and Duchess of Dyson were seen everywhere together and appeared to be on the friendliest of terms.

Mr. Pitt's reveries were rudely interrupted when Cam said consideringly, "I was wondering, Mr. Pitt, if I might beg the use of a couple of warships."

In the act of bringing his glass to his lips, Pitt's hand jerked, sending droplets of ruby red liquid in every direction. "What did you say?" asked Pitt, thunderstruck. He mopped at the front of his dark coat with a large white handkerchief.

"I have need of a couple of British warships," repeated Cam patiently.

Mr. Pitt glowered. "That's what I thought you said. Look here, Cam, I haven't the authority to put a rowing-boat at your disposal, much less a British warship. Have you forgotten? I'm no longer prime minister. And even if I were, your request is preposterous."

"It's a matter of national security," said Cam, and embarked on the story he had prepared. He told no outright lies, but he related just enough of the tale to serve his own purposes.

When Cam came to the end of his recital, Pitt repeated softly, "Antoine Mascaron. There's no telling what he might tell us if we can pull it off."

"Yes. He is singularly well placed in his position at the Ministry of Marine. But, as I say, no one can say with any certainty whether he will come willingly or not."

Mr. Pitt carefully set his empty glass on a side table. His eyes narrowed on Cam. "Look here, Cam, what's your interest in this Mascaron?"

"Surely everyone must be interested in national security," murmured Cam, his eyebrows lifting fractionally.

"Then how do you know so much? Where are you getting your information? I've heard nothing of any interest from France for weeks past."

"I have my sources," said Cam without elaboration.

For a long interval Mr. Pitt regarded the younger man in stony silence. At length he asked, "And you think that this is all the explanation I deserve?"

"Forgive me, no. In another week, two at the most . . ."

"Yes, yes," interjected Pitt testily. "I know. You will be in a position to take me fully into your confidence."

"Something like that." Under cover of raising his glass to his lips, Cam smothered a smile. He was thinking that his confidence had not been misplaced. Mascaron was a bird that Mr. Pitt would not with equanimity see fly out of his net. By the time he took his leave, Cam had what he had come for.

"Well, well, I'll see what I can do," said Pitt, "but I make you no promises."

"Thank you," said Cam, and tried for a smile that would not betray his sense of triumph.

But it was Mr. Pitt who had the last word. With a meaningful look directed at Cam's cheek, he purred, "Well, well, Cam. I see your pretty face has taken a beating. I'm sure it's no less than you deserve."

When he returned to his study, Pitt was thoughtful. His eyes fell on Cam's glass. *Blast the man!* he was thinking. *He had not even the decency to drink his glass of port!*

While Cam's plans went forward slowly, Gabrielle's proceeded at a faster pace. The eve of her departure for France saw her in somewhat of a quandary. Should she or should she not leave a letter of farewell for her husband? Dessins insisted that she should not. His arguments were persuasive. The duke was a formidable opponent. He had shown himself merciless in the pursuit of his ambitions. Mascaron had suffered almost as much as she. And then there was Goliath. Their chances of eluding such an adversary must not be compromised by even the slightest hint of what was afoot. If he were even to suspect, in those first few hours, that the bird had flown the coup, the game might be over before it had begun.

Gabrielle had resigned herself to accept Dessins's advice. But she did so with anguish. She did not know whether Cam loved her or not. She was inclined to think that as much as he was able to love anyone, he loved her. It was not the affair with Louise that troubled her mind. On reflection, she had absolved him from guilt in that transgression. But for his duplicity respecting Mascaron and Goliath — that could not, must not be over looked. And yet in spite of everything she loved him desperately. And though her heart balked at leaving him without a word, duty compelled her to caution.

If she had to think only of herself, she would have confronted him with her knowledge. Her own fate did not matter. But she recognized that to reveal what she knew was to court disaster. As long as she stayed with him, as long as he had her in his power, she was a tool that he would not hesitate to use against those whom it was her duty to protect. In light of what she owed Mascaron and Goliath, her love for Cam must not be allowed to count for anything.

She would never get over him, she decided. She never wanted to. Her grandfather would insist that she divorce the Englishman. It would be for the best, not for her sake but for Cam's. And the field would be clear for Louise. Cam and Louise. She'd thought of them as a couple from the first moment she had seen them together. If she had known that they were lovers she never would have agreed to marry him. And in spite of his protestations she thought that he liked the woman well enough. What man wouldn't?

Cam and Louise. It was a bitter pill to swallow. The thought of them together was like a knife twisting in her heart. But he was still hers for one more night. She wanted it to be a night to remember. The memory of it would have to last her a lifetime.

They were engaged to the Melbournes that evening. Lady Melbourne knew how to put on a good party. Her mix of guests was always interesting. The royal dukes were there in force, as were the foremost of both court and parliamentary circles. Gabrielle scarcely noticed them. She had eyes only for her husband.

If there was a more handsome man in Lady Melbourne's ballroom, Gabrielle was sure she did not know who it might be. Lansing was handsome but fair. Lord Paget suffered from the same failing. And Dessins, whom she had avoided like the plague all evening, though dark enough to suit her taste, lacked something of her husband's athletic physique. It was Cam, with his flashing blue eyes and tawny complexion, who outshone them all. And the small scar that stood out redly close to his cheekbone, far from detracting from his appeal only added a more dangerous, roguish cast to his unquestionable virility.

"Don't look at me so," Cam told her when he came to lead her into supper.

Dessins, a few paces behind, turned away with a pointed look at Gabrielle. She ignored it and presented her back. They'd already exchanged a few words earlier. Everything was set for the morrow. She didn't want to think about it, much less talk about it. Tomorrow was a long way off. Tonight belonged to Cam.

Placing her hand on the sleeve of Cam's dark coat she asked archly, "How am I looking at you, Cam?"

He inclined his head and lowered his voice to a husky whisper. "You've been ravishing me with your eyes all evening."

She gave him a bold stare. "And what do you mean to do about it?" Her eyes dropped to the sensual slant of his mouth.

Cam sucked in his breath, but before he could frame a reply, he became conscious that the noisy buzz of conversation in that huge saloon was gradually fading. In the next instant, he knew why. Louise Pelletier had just entered on the arm of Freddie Lamb. Cam felt Gabrielle stiffen, then begin to tremble at his side.

A deathly hush had fallen as interested spectators fell back to observe this encounter between the Duke of Dyson's erstwhile mistress and his young wife. Lady Melbourne was seen to slice her errant son, Freddie, a telling look that immediately summoned him to her side. Cam squared his shoulders and covered Gabrielle's gloved hand with his own, trying to convey in that one small gesture the sum of everything he was feeling—apology, regret, reassurance, love.

Louise Pelletier's eyes narrowed on the couple approaching. There was no one else in the vicinity. She blocked their path and knew it. The brilliant smile she bestowed on them as they drew level was at odds with the hatred blazing in her eyes. Ignoring Gabrielle, she said, very softly and deliberately, "Cam, what do you think? The roof of our house is leaking. Shall you take care of it, darling, or shall I approach your man of business?"

A murderous look crossed Cam's face. The color rushed out of Gabrielle's cheeks. Her hand tightened on Cam's arm as she felt him tense and ready himself to spring. It was Charles Fox, coming up at that moment, who placed a steadying hand on Gabrielle's elbow, and Richard Sheridan who distracted Cam from his murderous intent.

"Dyson," said Sheridan, "don't run off. I've been waiting for a word with you all evening."

Cam's eyes flickered momentarily, then moved to the gentleman whose hand manacled his arm.

"A word with you, Dyson," repeated Sheridan, and he exerted enough pressure to turn Cam aside.

"Alone at last," said Fox outrageously, and looked warmly into Gabrielle's dazed eyes. "There's a beautiful view from the long windows. You can see for miles over St. James Park."

Gabrielle obediently allowed Fox to lead her to one of the long windows. She gazed out blindly and saw nothing but darkness.

Fox chuckled. "The park is there, Your Grace. You'll just have to take my word for it."

Gabrielle looked up into those kindly, knowing eyes and she smiled faintly.

"That's better," said Fox. "You really mustn't let a woman of that ilk steal your composure."

Without thinking, Gabrielle answered, "If it were only my composure she had stolen!" At the betraying remark, she blushed rosily.

Fox's voice was very gentle when he said, "You're

wrong, you know. Though it goes against the grain to say anything in His Grace's favor, I must tell you that it's common knowledge that the affair is long over."

"Is it?" asked Gabrielle.

As if they had a will of their own, her eyes wandered to the woman whom her husband had once extolled as the epitome of perfection. Louise Pelletier stood alone. All backs were turned to her. As Gabrielle watched, Freddie Lamb moved toward Louise and escorted her from the ballroom. Gabrielle had no love for Louise Pelletier, but she could not help feeling sorry for the woman.

The orchestra struck up. In every corner of the saloon, the hub of voices resumed.

"Don't waste your sympathy on her," said Fox. "There's not a drop of the milk of human kindness in her veins!"

"You're reading my thoughts again!" exclaimed Gabrielle. "You must not be a very popular gentleman, Mr. Fox, if you play that trick on all your acquaintances."

"Strangely, I don't," he answered, then lapsed into silence as if meditating on that surprising thought.

Sheridan sauntered over with Cam and conversation became general. The two older gentlemen made their excuses to go to the card room. Cam stopped them with a few words of thanks for their timely intervention.

Sheridan's eyebrows rose drolly. "I don't believe I'm hearing this," he said in an audible aside to Fox.

Mr. Fox did not join in Sheridan's levity. Pinning Cam with a fierce stare, he said, "You're a very fortunate man, Your Grace. I hope you know it." His expression visibly softened as he made his *adieux* to Gabrielle. Cam was left staring.

It was not until they reached the privacy of Gabrielle's chamber that Cam tried to explain Louise's

380

vindictive reference to the house he had rented for her as part of his severance settlement. Gabrielle refused to listen. It was their last night together. She did not wish to waste a minute of it on useless recriminations and explanations.

She went into his arms and kissed him passionately. "Love me," she whispered and with her eyes holding his she captured his hands and deliberately molded them to her breasts.

"Gabrielle," Cam protested, groaning. His hands moved over her. "We must talk."

"No. It's not necessary."

"I want you to know . . ."

"I know everything I need to know."

She pressed her body against his hard length, enticing him with her femininity, making rational thought impossible. He wanted to resist her. He wanted to have everything out in the open. He went wild when she slipped her hands between them and caressed him voluptuously. Every touch, every soft word, seduced him from his purpose.

Moments later he was stretching out beside her on the bed. All that mattered was the present moment and the love she was offering.

Cam took it greedily, savoring her total surrender, her abandon to each whispered endearment and his words of blatant arousal. And as she clung to him as he moved above her. Just as surely as he filled her with the essence of his body he filled her with all that was in his heart. And he knew that everything that needed saying was said in that shattering act of love.

"More," said Gabrielle, turning into him a long while later.

Cam anchored her firmly. "No," he said, smiling. "Doctor's orders. I'm not to wear you out with my insatiable demands. You're more than two months with child, remember?"

"But, I want you," she pleaded. "I need you."

Cam's control slipped. "I shouldn't! I mustn't," he said, stopping her words with a kiss.

He had not the will to resist her entreaties. She could not seem to get enough of him. Her hands ran over him ceaselessly, as if she wanted to memorize every pore, every muscle, every tendon beneath his skin. At the last, when he refused to cover her body with the full press of his weight, he had to forcibly restrain her, showing her that there was an easier way to have what they wanted, that it was still possible to join their bodies and at the same time protect their unborn child.

Sated with pleasure, in the ebb of passion, Cam wanted to talk.

Gabrielle feigned exhaustion. "Just hold me," she whispered. "Just hold me as if you would never let me go."

"I never shall," said Cam fiercely, and, as if to prove it, kept her close held in the shield of his body.

The morning dawned bright and clear. Gabrielle breakfasted alone in her chamber. Cam gave her a warm but careless farewell before leaving the house on some vague and unspecified business. At ten o'clock, she sent for the carriage. Her Grace instructed her coachmen to conduct her to the emporium on Bond Street that she had visited once or twice before. To observe the proprieties, a young maid accompanied her.

Later, the principal shopwalker would tell Cam that Her Grace seemed in her usual spirits. He noticed nothing untoward when she first arrived. In point of fact, she had crowed with delight upon discovering an ell of gold satin that she thought might be the exact match for a fan she had recently purchased.

It was at this point that she had come face to face with a lady with whom she was acquainted. They had conversed amiably for a few minutes, whereupon Her Grace begged for a sheet of paper and a pencil from one of the sales assistants. This was soon procured, and Her Grace hastily scribbled a few words. Having folded the sheet of paper, she gave it into her friend's hand. The unknown lady departed. Shortly afterward, Her Grace decided to send her young maid home in the coach to fetch the fan in question so that she might match it to the gold satin before purchasing it.

Scarcely had the maid taken her leave to do her mistress's bidding, when Her Grace recalled that she had an urgent errand that she must execute at once. In vain had the shopwalker protested that it was more seemly for Her Grace to await the return of her coach. He had been overruled. Her Grace had stalked out of the shop and straight into a waiting hackney.

"You're sure that the hackney was waiting for Her Grace?" asked Cam, striving to hold on to his control.

"Quite certain, My Lord Duke," answered the shopwalker.

"What makes you so certain?" persisted Cam.

After a considering moment, the shopwalker replied, "I caught a glimpse of someone, I can't say if it was a lady or a gentleman, but there was someone in the hackney who expected her."

Cam slammed his balled fist hard on his desk, scattering papers. The other occupants of the room, his two coachmen, Gabrielle's maid, and the shopwalker, were startled into immobility.

"And this woman who met with my wife, does no one know her name, her direction . . . ?" His voice

383

trailed to a halt. He'd asked the same question a score of times in the last number of minutes.

The shopwalker gave the same answer, that no one at the shop knew the lady's identity, though one assistant thought her face looked familiar.

When he was alone, having found out all that there was to know from his minions, Cam leaned back in his chair and closed his eyes. He'd had a hellish day, from the time he'd met with Rodier's courier on the docks at Wapping to the moment he'd walked in his own front doors and found his house in an uproar. More than twelve hours had passed since Gabrielle had gone missing.

He didn't know what to think. None of it made sense. He could not believe that Gabrielle would wish to run away from him. No woman could have loved him as she had loved him last night and wish to be free of him. He could not believe that Louise's jibe at Melbourne House had sent her fleeing to God knows where.

On the other hand, it was evident that Gabrielle had left of her own volition. Had she been persuaded? or tricked? or bribed? or . . . ? His thoughts raced in every direction, bringing only more confusion. And that most alarming thought of all kept intruding. She'd been his captive once. Had she only been biding her time for the opportune moment before making her bid for freedom?

He shot to his feet and let out a roar like a wounded lion. He couldn't accept that that had been her design all along. She loved him. She was carrying his child. Gabrielle did not have a malicious bone in her body. Something untoward, something catastrophic, had happened. There was no other explanation.

An accident or an abduction—it must be one or the other. The former was highly improbable. In the

384

twelve hours since she had disappeared, someone, somewhere must have seen something and reported it to the authorities. Even now, the military who policed London's streets were on the watch for a lady fitting Gabrielle's description. If there had been an accident, it must have been discovered by now.

As Cam's thoughts shifted to the only other alternative, his teeth ground together. Abduction. He should have expected something of the sort. Once before Mascaron had sent his agents to find Gabrielle and return her to France. He'd been a fool to think that Mascaron would passively accept that Gabrielle was lost to him forever. Oh God, he should have taken better care of her.

Within minutes, he had all but discarded that conviction. Only that morning, he and Lansing had met with Rodier's courier. There was no question that Mascaron was gravely ill and in no position to mastermind anything, let alone an abduction that must take place in a foreign country. Cam's eyes narrowed in concentration as he tried to recall everything the courier had told them.

According to Rodier something sinister was afoot at the château, and that something went by the name of Fouché, France's unofficial though undisputed head of Intelligence. It was known that on several occasions he had visited the château under cover of darkness.

Fouché, thought Cam and let his mind revolve around everything he had ever heard about the man. Fouché was a grand master of espionage. He had a brain like a maze. No one could follow his thought processes. No one could predict what his next move might be. Had he discovered that Mascaron was a tool of British Intelligence? Cam discarded that thought as soon as it came into his head. If Fouché had proof of Mascaron's involvement, there would have been a quick trial and execution in Paris.

God, he didn't have time to sift through all the implications of that particular wrinkle. Mascaron was the least of his worries if he had no part in Gabrielle's abduction. In the circumstances, the whole enterprise to bring Mascaron out of France must hang fire until Gabrielle was found. He didn't care that two British warships were sailing to the coast of Normandy at that very moment. He didn't care that his own yacht was moored at Deal, and his crew waiting for his orders. Mascaron would have to look to his own interests. It was Gabrielle's fate that was of paramount importance.

With quick, impatient steps, he strode about the room. Lansing should have returned long since. He'd sent him to track down Gervais Dessins in the hope that Dessins might know something, anything, that could give them a clue. Not that he expected much from that quarter. He was aware that Gabrielle only tolerated the attentions of that young fribble because he was a compatriot. She did not look upon him as a confidante. To his knowledge, Gabrielle had no friends. There had scarce been the time or the opportunity to form any attachments, innocent or otherwise.

Suddenly stopping in his tracks, he inhaled sharply, and exhaled on a long, uneven breath. He was remembering the incident at Melbourne House and how Charles Fox and Richard Sheridan had stepped in to avert an unpleasant and embarrassing scene. One thought led to another. Charles Fox would stop at nothing to discredit him. It was at Charles Fox's instigation that the Prince of Wales had threatened to take Gabrielle under his protection. And when he had foiled their designs by making Gabrielle his wife, they had persisted in trying to make trouble for him. If it had not been for Charles Fox and his cronies, he and Gabrielle would still be safely at Dunraeden. The more Cam thought about it, the more certain he became that Charles Fox was the key to discovering Gabrielle's whereabouts.

By the time Cam was striding for the door, his fury could not be contained. His murderous thoughts stilled momentarily as he recognized that most hated of all voices raised in anger in his own foyer. With a roar of rage, Cam flung the door wide and sprang forward.

From the look on Charles Fox's face, it was evident that his fury was equal to Cam's.

"What the devil have you done to her?" roared Fox.

"Where is my wife?" bellowed Cam.

It was Lord Lansing, entering behind Fox, who averted a common fracas by expediently throwing himself between the two furious protagonists. Though it was touch and go, Lansing finally calmed both gentlemen sufficiently to persuade them to continue their quarrel in the privacy of Cam's study.

Visibly controlling his temper, Cam demanded, "Where is my wife, Mr. Fox?"

Fox scowled and in answer slapped a sheet of paper on Cam's desk. "Read it," he growled, "And your explanation had better be a good one."

Cam recognized Gabrielle's scrawl. He'd seen it often enough when he'd forced her to write to Mascaron. He picked up the sheet of paper. Across the top was the name and address of the Bond Street shop where she had last been sighted.

"Mrs. Fox met her by chance," said Fox to Cam's unspoken question. "They have a nodding acquaintance. On impulse, your duchess dashed off those few lines and asked my wife to deliver her note to me. It came to my hand not thirty minutes since."

One mystery had been solved, thought Cam, and

still bristling, began to read.

Dear Mr. Fox,
You said that you were my friend. Will you please tell
my husband that I am well and that he need no longer
concern himself about my fate? One day, I hope, when
our two countries are no longer at war, you and I may
meet again.

Adieu,
Gabrielle.

Cam's face was chalk white, and the scar across his
cheekbone seemed to stand out more starkly. She had
left him of her own volition. There had been no abduction. *When our two countries are no longer at war,* she
had written. The significance of that line was self-evi-
dent. Only when the war had ended could friends on
either side of the Channel come together again. He
thought of what she was returning to and his jaw
clenched.

Mr. Fox eyed Cam's bowed head thoughtfully.
When he spoke, the bite in his voice was muted. "I
promised the girl my protection, and I mean to stand
by my word. If she thinks she is better off in France,
then I won't let you drag her back under any circumstance."

Lord Lansing looked from one intent face to the
other. "What the devil is going on?" he demanded.
"Who said anything about France?"

Neither gentlemen paid him the least heed.

Cam's teeth snapped together. "My wife is my concern," he said. "I'll brook no interference from any
man, least of all from you, Mr. Fox, not even if I
have to drag her back from France screaming like a
banshee."

Lansing was almost beside himself. "Has Gabrielle
gone back to France?" he yelled.

388

"Yes!" snarled his companions in unison.

Slowly, Lansing sank into a chair. "But this is worse than anything," he said. "Cam, if Fouché were to get his hands on her . . . God, it doesn't bear thinking about."

Mr. Fox placed both palms on the flat of Cam's desk. His tone was silky when he said, "Dyson, I am not leaving this house until you explain that note to my satisfaction. And lest you think you may abuse that dear girl with impunity, may I remind you that I am not without some influence on *both* sides of the Channel? In short, Dyson, I have powerful friends you would be a fool to ignore."

The furious retort on Cam's tongue was never uttered. He picked up Gabrielle's note and toyed with it idly. Finally, he said, "How powerful, Mr. Fox?"

Fox knew exactly what Cam was getting at. "Talleyrand owes me a considerable favor," he replied. "Unfortunately, I think I may have forfeited the friendship of the first consul by that little speech I was forced to give in the House. Whether or not Bonaparte has forgiven me yet for my lukewarm support is anyone's guess."

Cam's eyes locked with Fox's, but there was no animosity now in the long look they exchanged. The stare was calculating, assessing, as each man took the other's measure.

Fox was thinking that in the last number of weeks he was seeing a side of the Duke of Dyson that he would never have believed existed. The man was actually human. There might be hope for him yet.

Cam was weighing the advisability of taking Fox into his confidence. There was no doubt that Fox held considerable sway in France, despite the war. Since the early days of the Revolution, Fox had proved to be France's most indefatigable ally. Nor was the reference to Talleyrand lost on Cam. It was suspected that Fox had warned Talleyrand of an assassination attempt on Bonaparte's life. What was known for certain was that the assassination plot of some hotheaded Royalists had been foiled by Talleyrand.

In France, Talleyrand was second only to Bonaparte. He was a useful man to know. And it was no secret that there was no love lost between Talleyrand and Fouché.

It was that thought which brought Cam to a decision. "Sit down, Mr. Fox. What I have to say may take some time. But first, I owe you an apology. I thought, you see, that you had lured my wife away." He stopped momentarily, then seemed to give himself a mental shake before continuing. "I don't know how it was contrived. There must have been someone there to help her. Be that as it may, there is no doubt in my mind that by returning to France, Gabrielle must place herself in a great deal of danger."

It was at this point that Lansing clapped his hand to his head and exclaimed. "Cam, what am I thinking? I meant to tell you when I arrived. Gervais Dessins? He left his lodgings without leaving his direction. Not one of his familiars knows what has become of him."

Into the silence, Fox said, "Gentlemen, time is wasting. Why don't you begin at the beginning, and then we'll decide together what's best to be done?"

Chapter Twenty-one

Gervais Dessins was restless. Fouché should have returned days ago. He swore softly under his breath, reflecting that he was as much a prisoner as the man and young girl who were locked in the chamber upstairs. He'd expected by this time to be sampling the fleshpots of Paris, not be incarcerated like a common criminal in some godforsaken house in the middle of nowhere.

God, but he hated Normandy! And he didn't much care for Normans either—a tight-lipped, sullen-faced, inferior breed of peasant, if the servants were anything to go by. And he particularly did not care for the Château de Vrigonde. It was a pigsty. But what could one expect when Fouché's men were virtually pigs, rabble he had enlisted from the gutters of Paris? They'd desecrated what had once been a thing of beauty and grace.

His head jerked round as the door opened. Mascaron's physician was framed in the doorway. Another peasant, thought Dessins, a sneer creeping over his handsome face. He watched idly as the old man shuffled into the room. Like a terrified rabbit, he glanced around him, his eyes bouncing from person to person. They came to rest on the fashionable figure of Dessins. After a moment's hesitation, with dragging steps, he approached the gentleman who had the least ferocious aspect of all in that room.

"Your honor," he said, his eyes fixed on a point below Dessin's chin. "I was hoping . . . that is . . . would it be permissible . . ." He stopped, and started over. "Mascaron's prize mare is about to foal," he said.

Before Dessins could frame a reply to this extraordinary observation, one of the men at the card table detached himself and came swaggering over. It was Savarin, a small, weasel of a man and Fouché's second in command. When his hand fell on the physician's shoulder, the old man visibly flinched.

"What, old sawbones? Are you pining for your sheep and goats already? Don't you like our company?" His jest seemed to amuse him inordinately. He bellowed with laughter.

The old man shrank into himself and said, whining, "I never pretended to be anything I wasn't. I'm not a physician, as I told you from the beginning. I doctor animals, not people."

The hand on the old man's shoulder tightened and he was roughly shaken. "You're a physician because I say so. Now go doctor the scullery maid or the stable boy, or better yet, go look in on your patient upstairs."

The doctor's Adam's apple bobbed alarmingly. "Someone must take care of her," he whined.

Dessins was moved to intervene. "Why don't you let the old man take care of the mare. Savarin?"

"He's not to leave the house. Fouché's orders," answered Savarin.

There could be no argument with that statement.

Dessins and Savarin were on the point of turning away when again that low, persistent whine trembled on the air. "I have two sons," said the doctor. "Good boys. I trained them myself. They could do it."

Savarin and Dessins looked a question at each

392

other.

"I don't see any reason not to send for them," said Dessins. He believed he was motivated by a kind heart.

"No harm in it that I can see," agreed Savarin. He knew the value of a good horse. He also knew the value of terror. Dragging the doctor forward by the epaulets of his coat till they were nose to nose, he snarled, "Send for your sons, old man. But one wrong move, mind you, and I'll cut their throats before I cut yours." And he threw the doctor from him.

The old man stifled a whimper and began to edge away. Bobbing his head ludicrously to every occupant in the room, he backed towards the door. When he felt the doorknob in his grasp, he spun around only to go sprawling in his haste to escape. A roar of laughter went up before men turned back to their occupations.

Dessins shook his head and looked around for the keg of Calvados. He would have preferred cognac, but there was none to be had. He replenished his glass and found a quiet corner where he might brood in silence.

He had nothing in common with Fouché's men, he decided, and in the week since he had delivered Gabrielle, he had scarcely concealed his disdain. He had thought to hand her over into Fouché's keeping. But Fouché was not there, and Savarin, his second in command, had insisted that Dessins remain until Fouché returned.

It was close to midnight before the crunch of carriage wheels on the driveway signaled someone's arrival, and another half hour before Dessins was sent for. Fouché was in Mascaron's bookroom and very much at home. He was seated behind the massive desk. The bookroom showed no signs of the desecration that had taken place throughout the rest of the

393

house.

With a curt greeting that bordered on incivility, Fouché indicated that the younger man was to take a seat. Dessins did so and waited.

"You arrived two days ahead of schedule," said Fouché abruptly. "Why?"

This was not the welcome Dessins expected, and he bristled. "I sensed a gradual softening in the girl toward Dyson. I didn't want to take any chances." His voice was as rigid as his posture.

Fouché nodded and smiled for the first time since Dessins had entered the room. "You've done well," he admitted. "It's unfortunate that it was impossible for me to leave Paris until now."

"Oh?" Dessins invited.

Fouché heard the question but ignored it. He wasn't in the habit of letting his right hand know what his left hand was doing.

He felt elated, and not only because his net was closing in on the English spy. The first consul had entrusted him with a very delicate operation. Mr. Charles Fox, that idealist without par, was in Paris for secret talks with Talleyrand. It was Fouché's task to ensure that no harm came to Mr. Fox for the duration of his stay. The honor had fallen to his lot because Talleyrand himself had specifically suggested it. Fouché did not think it a strange request. He knew he was the best. Evidently, Talleyrand knew it also.

In some things, however, Talleyrand was not very wise. Fouché could scarcely credit that the minister of foreign affairs still pinned his hopes on peace between England and France, not when it was evident that Bonaparte's designs were bent in the opposite direction. He'd come to the conclusion that poor Mr. Fox was on a fool's errand, and that the first consul was indulging his guest for reasons that were not hard to fathom. Charles Fox had been instrumental in saving the first consul's life. Bonaparte would not soon forget it.

Fouché's sense of elation dimmed somewhat when he recalled that it was Talleyrand and not he who had foiled that second assassination attempt on Bonaparte's life. It was to Talleyrand that Mr. Fox had secretly written. It was to be expected, thought Fouché, for not only were the two men on the friendliest terms, but he himself held no official position. But that would soon change.

His voice warmed slightly when he said, "I take it there were no difficulties?"

"Nothing of any significance."

"Oh?"

When Fouché wanted a report, he wanted even the most inconsequential details. Dessins shrugged negligently. "We were stopped on the docks by a detachment of guards. They were looking for the girl, all right. But Gabrielle, that is, Mascaron's granddaughter, was dressed as a boy. They let us pass without incident."

Fouché nodded his approval. "Anything else?"

"The girl mentioned someone by the name of Goliath."

"I know of him," responded Fouché. "He's not important."

Dessins had been on the point of explaining that it was anxiety for this man's fate that had been most instrumental in persuading the girl to leave England. He shut his mouth with a snap and merely said, "Oh?"

"He left Mascaron's employ some time ago." As an afterthought, Fouché added, "He's a known smuggler. Anything else?"

"No," said Dessins, and said no more.

Fouché absently picked up a pencil and began to drum with it on the flat of the desk. After an interval he said consideringly, "I wonder how soon we may expect Dyson?"

"Dyson?" A look of surprise crossed Dessins face. "You're expecting Dyson?"

Fouché permitted himself a short laugh. "My dear boy," he said, "the girl is merely bait. Surely you divined my purpose?"

"But he doesn't know where she is," said Dessins, a small frown pleating his brow. "I made sure we left no clues. Gabrielle didn't as much as leave a note. And I left my lodgings without seeing a soul."

Fouché's smile was infuriatingly superior. "My boy, you've done exactly as I wished. Come now, don't look so crestfallen. If we had left too obvious a trail for the Englishman to follow his suspicions would have been roused. From all accounts he's not a dullard. He'll work things out before very long. And when he comes, I shall be waiting."

"But the girl . . ."

"Isn't important."

"You're not going to question her?"

"Certainly not."

In quick succession the emotions of bafflement, disbelief, and finally fury registered on the younger man's face. His voice low and vibrant, he said, "Dyson won't come for the girl because she means nothing to him. Surely you read my reports?"

Fouché's eyebrows rose fractionally. "Of course," he said without heat. "And everything you wrote confirmed my hopes." He nodded sagely. "Dyson will come for her. I don't doubt it."

Dessins rose stiffly to his feet. "I wish you had taken me into your confidence," he said.

Fouché rose also. "I shall next time," he offered, with a hint of ingratiating apology.

Dessins was in no mood to be conciliated. "If I might impose upon you for a conveyance to take me to Paris?"

"Paris? Whatever for?"

"My job is done."

"And well done, too! But bear with me a little. You must see how I am placed. You know too much. Until Dyson is caught, I should prefer if you would accept the hospitality of the Château de Vrigonde."

It was an invitation that the younger man was not fool enough to refuse.

Mascaron stirred restlessly in his sleep. At the small sounds of distress, Gabrielle pushed back the blanket on her pallet and padded over to the prone figure of her grandfather. They were allowed no candles, but the cold light of dawn had already begun to penetrate to the corners of the small room.

Mascaron's eyes squeezed tight, then slowly opened. "Gabrielle?" he murmured, and reached a hand for her.

Gabrielle brought it to her lips. "I'm here," she said, her voice choked with emotion, then more urgently, "Mascaron, we don't have much time. The doctor will be here in a moment. You're drugged, darling. Do you understand? They've been feeding you an opiate. If you could only fight its effects, if . . ." Her voice broke. Everything was hopeless. She had been locked up with Mascaron for days, and she still did not know what was going on or what it was her captors wanted. She knew that Dessins had told her a pack of lies. She knew that her home had been taken over by a horde of cutthroats. And she knew, finally, that her grandfather was not deathly ill as she had at first supposed. But why it was necessary to keep Mascaron sedated and what they were waiting for was more than she had been able to fathom.

It was only in this short space of time, before the château came to life, that there was any opportunity of speaking freely to Mascaron. Soon the guards would arrive, and that awful, pathetic excuse for a doctor would pour another draught down Mascaron's throat.

"Mascaron," she said urgently. "Where is Goliath?"

Mascaron's eyes dilated wildly. "Get away while you have the chance," he said, his voice thin and hoarse at the same time.

It was all he ever said. He scarcely ever answered any of her questions. But this time she was determined to shake him from his stupor. There was a desperate edge in her voice when she said, "Concentrate, darling. Please, if you know, for God's sake, tell me! What has happened to Goliath?"

Something in her voice seemed to make an impression. His eyes narrowed and became more focused. It was a struggle to get out the words. "I sent him back to you."

"Back? You mean, you sent him to me a second time?"

He nodded.

Gabrielle felt as if a dead weight had been lifted from her heart.

"Why, darling, why?"

"Mustn't . . . trust . . . Dyson," he said through labored breaths.

"Why mustn't I trust my husband," she demanded softly.

"The Abbaye," he groaned. "He was at the Abbaye."

Gabrielle would have liked to unravel this new puzzle, but saw that Mascaron was growing weaker.

Laying aside the thought of the Abbaye, she implored, "No! Don't go to sleep! Why are they sedating you? Why?"

"Fouché's orders," he whispered.

"Fouché? He's here?"

Mascaron nodded, and his eyes closed.

But that dread name only added desperation to Gabrielle's entreaties. "Please, darling, you must tell me! Why are they sedating you?" She shook him gently.

His whole body trembled with powerful spasms as he tried to drag himself from the confusing darkness. In a hoarse whisper, he got out, "They know you won't leave without me. And how can I go anywhere? Save yourself, Angel, before it's too late."

His chest rose and fell with the exertion of uttering those few words. Gabrielle touched her hand to her forehead, and kneeling over him whispered, "I'll never leave you again, darling. Never."

She meant to comfort him, but Mascaron's agitation only increased. "Leave!" he gritted. "Leave, before it's too late."

"It's all right," she soothed. "My husband will come for us. He'll rescue us both."

His eyes went wide, then closed. "He's worse than Fouché," he said. "He hates me, and now I know why."

"What are you saying?"

He slipped into unconsciousness as the key grated in the lock. Gabrielle straightened and turned to face her gaolers. She knew she looked a sight in her boy's clothes. For a whole week she had lived and slept in them. No change of clothes had been offered, and she would not demean herself by asking for a favor. But in spite of her appearance, she drew herself up like a duchess. Her voice was as imperious as her expression when she said, "I demand that you tell me why I am being held here."

The men were big and brawny and might easily have been taken for rivermen. But their accents gave them away. No Normans, these, but dregs from the stews of Paris. In normal circumstances, Gabrielle would have been intimidated by their sheer size and fierce expressions, but in the week since her incarceration they'd shown her a deference that she surmised had been enjoined on them by a superior. She wondered if it were Fouché.

With a toothless grin, the bigger one lifted her by the waist and set her to the side. She did not make the mistake of struggling or trying to prevent what she knew must follow. She'd resorted to violence once, and for her pains had been kept from Mascaron for a full day. It was a punishment she would not again invite. But her eyes flashed daggers at the stooped figure who shuffled into the room cradling a tin cup in his hands. The physician had come to administer his poison.

Gabrielle's teeth clenched and she stamped her foot. "You miserable excuse for a man," she blazed at him. "I wouldn't let you doctor a cat, much less a human being."

The poor man paused and trembled, but he said nothing.

Goaded by his silence, Gabrielle raged, "You're not a doctor! You're not a man! You're a sniveling, craven worm! That's what you are!"

At her tirade, her gaolers laughed. Gabrielle turned her flashing eyes upon them. Scathing curse words, lurid, original epithets with which she might annihilate her mockers gathered on her tongue. She swallowed them, reminding herself forcibly that she was Cam's duchess. "Damn! Damn! Damn!" she said, and stamped her foot.

At that moment a muffled sound issued from the doctor as he all but fell over his patient. "No harm done," he said, and held up the tin cup. His hands were shaking.

In angry silence, Gabrielle turned away. She could not bear to watch Mascaron drink the sedative.

When they were left alone, she poured water from the pitcher on the washstand into a china basin and brought it to Mascaron. Talking softly as if to a baby, she washed the sheen of perspiration from his face and body and took care of his most personal needs. Only then did she tend to herself. She stripped to her drawers and chemise and quickly bathed. It was only as she pulled on her boy's breeches that she observed the wet stain at the knee. She touched it with her fingers, and sniffed delicately. *Cider*, she thought, *but acrid.*

Puzzled, frowning, she stood lost in thought. She returned to Mascaron's side and felt along the carpet beside the edge of the bed where she had been kneeling. She almost missed it. The carpet was the colour of wine. It was difficult to detect stains. But the pool of moisture was unmistakable. The clumsy doctor must have spilled most of his precious sedative on the floor but was too terrified to confess his incompetence. The significance of what she had discovered struck her like a thunderbolt.

She dressed quickly, then knelt at Mascaron's side. He wanted to sleep, but she would not permit it. She shook him gently, then with growing vigor. He groaned in protest but his eyes opened. Urgently, straining to keep her voice low, she bombarded him with questions, all the while her eyes darting to the door.

By slow degrees, as his haziness dissipated, Mascaron sensed her urgency. Hoarsely, stumbling over every second word, he strove to answer. In time, his voice strengthened and his eyes became clearer.

"Oh God," he whispered when Gabrielle sat back on her heels. She was lost in silence. "Angel, I'm sorry. I'm so sorry that it's come to this."

Tears were coursing down her cheeks, but she was smiling. "Don't give up hope, darling," she said softly. "In spite of what you've told me, I know my husband will come for us."

Mascaron's head twisted on the pillow. He raised his hand and Gabrielle clasped it. "Your faith in this man is touching," he said, "but I wish you would think before you give him your trust. He hates me. Haven't I explained it all to you?"

Quietly, she considered his words. At last, she said, "Yes, darling. You've explained everything. But love is more powerful than hate. And he loves me, you'll see."

He saw that her confidence could not be shaken. She was so young, he thought, and so innocent of the dark passions and powerful ambitions that sometimes drove men. Sighing, he closed his eyes and drifted into sleep.

Gabrielle was on her knees, motionless, her eyes fastened on her clasped hands. She had not adopted the pose by design. "Oh God," she said, "please keep him safe and give him good fortune."

Cam came for Gabrielle that very day. The light was fading in that twilight hour when the sun has set but darkness is still held at bay. Gabrielle heard the clatter of carriage wheels and raced to the window. Sounds of doors slamming below and raised voices roused Mascaron from drowsiness.

"What is it?" he whispered.

"A carriage. And not very welcome, by the sounds of things." Her breath caught in her throat as the carriage doors were flung wide and three gentlemen alighted. She would have known Cam anywhere. An animal cry of distress was torn from her throat.

"What is it?" asked Mascaron anxiously.

She could not drag herself away from the window. "Oh God," she said, "He's walked into Fouché's trap."

From the driveway, Cam quickly scanned the upstairs windows of the château. He had one glimpse of Gabrielle's white face before his attention was claimed by the jostling throng of men who rushed through the front doors. Before rough hands could be laid on him, however, an imperious voice from the doorway brought order to the mêlée.

Fouché, coming forward at that moment, faltered in midstride when he caught sight of the new arrivals.

It was Talleyrand who took charge. Limping forward, he said, "My dear Fouché, I am quite overcome by this welcome. You are acquainted, I believe, with His Grace, the Duke of Dyson, and Mr. Charles Fox?"

Talleyrand did not wait for an invitation but entered the doors of the château as though he were the guest of honor. "Dear, dear," he said when Fouché caught up to him, "a most unfortunate misunderstanding! Your gatekeepers? They mistook us for bandits or some such thing. But I gave my men orders to subdue them as gently as possible. Where may we speak in private?"

By this time, Fouché had found his composure and his tongue. He led the way to the bookroom. Smiling faintly, he opened the door and held it for his companions. Cam was in the rear.

"After you, Monsieur Fouché," he said.

Fouché's eyes sped to his men clustering in the grand foyer. Without his direction they were at a complete loss. Fouché shrugged and entered the bookroom. Cam closed the door gently at his back.

Not long after, the door was opened and Fouché stood on the threshold. "Get the girl," he said curtly, addressing two of the men who stood closest.

In a matter of minutes, Gabrielle was thrust into the room. Her first instinct was to rush into Cam's arms. But he blazed such a look that her steps faltered.

"Cam?"

Fouché came forward. "Duchess," he said with undisguised amusement. "I wish you would tell His Grace that you returned to France of your own free will."

"That's true, but . . ."

"And that no harm has come to you since you've been under this roof."

"That's true, Cam," said Gabrielle, thinking perhaps that Cam thought she might have been molested. "No one touched me! What . . . what's going on?"

During this brief exchange she had become conscious that Cam and Mr. Fox were not Fouché's prisoners. Her eyes darted from one gentleman to the other. Fouché looked to be amused, Talleyrand looked bored, and Cam's expression had become impenetrable. Only Mr. Fox's eyes conveyed any genuine warmth.

"We've come to fetch you home, Gabrielle," said Fox gently.

"I . . . I don't understand."

"The first consul has signed a *carnet* for your safe conduct."

"But . . . but our two countries are at war. How do you come to be here?" She felt her legs begin to buckle, and curled her fingers around the back of a chair for support.

Talleyrand's eyes locked with Fouché's. "It's quite simple," he said in that cold, smooth tone that never failed to bring goosebumps to Gabrielle's skin. "Mr. Fox and His Grace have diplomatic immunity, and Monsieur Fouché is charged with their safe conduct.

Is that not so, Fouché?"

Something flashed at the back of Fouché's eyes then quickly faded. Without inflection, he murmured, "Quite so."

Gabrielle could not make sense of this exchange, and her eyes flew to Cam. Ignoring that silent appeal, he made a point of examining his watch. "We shall miss the tide if we don't start soon," he said, addressing Fox.

"Tide?" Fouché murmured.

"Yes," replied Cam easily. "I'm conveying Mr. Fox home in my yacht. If I'm not mistaken, it should have reached Rouen by now."

"You must take care," said Fouché conversationally, "that you are not blown out of the water by French guns."

"It's not likely," said Cam. "We've been given French escort as far as the coast of Normandy. The first consul insisted upon it. He wants no harm to come to Mr. Fox."

If there was a warning in those words, Fouché seemed not to notice. Glancing from Talleyrand to Fox, he said, "I trust your meetings were fruitful?"

"Very," said Fox emphatically.

"And over so soon?" quizzed Fouché.

With matching irony, Talleyrand replied, "Diplomacy takes time. This is only the beginning."

Gabrielle had to force down the hysteria. She sensed the thrust and parry of each word, each raised brow and careless smile. It was a contest she could not follow, but there was one thing of which she had not lost sight.

"What about my grandfather?" she demanded.

Fouché looked at the paper in his hand. "This *carnet* makes no mention of Mascaron." His tone was polite and faintly bored.

"Cam?" she pleaded.

"Mascaron is a citizen of France," said Cam. "There is no reason that I can think of why he would wish to come to England. But even if there were, my authority does not extend so far."

Dumbfounded, Gabrielle stared at him. In a stifled voice, she said, "I can't, I won't go without him."

"You will," said Cam, in accents that Gabrielle knew only too well. She quailed as he went on in the same deadly tone, "The first consul himself has decreed it shall be so."

"You . . . you actually went to Bonaparte?" she stammered.

Cam held a chair for her and she sank into it. Only then did the gentlemen seat themselves. "Fortunately," said Cam, "the first consul's views on women coincide with mine exactly. It is his opinion that a rebellious wife should be soundly thrashed."

"Child," cut in Mr. Fox. "That you rushed off to be by your grandfather's side when word reached you of his illness was understandable but most foolhardy. A wife must cleave to her husband. The first consul understands this."

It was on the point of Gabrielle's tongue to blurt out the whole story, to cry that her grandfather was not sick but only sedated and that he had the best reason in the world for wishing to leave France. The warning look in Cam's eyes stopped her.

Cowed, she said, "I'll come with you, Cam, but only because I trust you. I won't say any more."

"Excellent," said Cam, his voice coated with sarcasm. "Docility and silence in a wife must always be welcome."

Fouché chuckled, Mr. Fox coughed, and Talleyrand angled his head to get a better look at the girl who had caused such a tempest.

He still could not understand why Mr. Fox had involved himself in the affair. Dyson, though a power-

406

ful figure, was a known Tory, and to all appearances the girl was no better than a street urchin. Through the shield of his lashes he surveyed the chit who had launched an undertaking that, to his knowledge, was without precedent in its scale. Diplomats at the highest level on both sides were involved. It did not seem possible that the fate of this child could provoke such a storm. She was no Helen of Troy, to his way of thinking.

A small frown came and went on his broad brow as one thought led to another. Helen of Troy's husband, Menelaus, had gone after his wife in much the same manner as this young English aristocrat. When he thought of it, the similarities were striking. Hadn't Menelaus summoned those heroes of old who were honor bound to help him, however reluctantly? Dyson had gone one step further. His reach, through men in high places, extended to both camps. And he had not hesitated to reach for what he wanted.

Talleyrand's thought drifted to the scene with the first consul. It was he, Talleyrand, who had requested the *carnet* that would release the girl into her husband's custody. Bonaparte had no fondness for the English at present. He had acceded to the request, but for only one reason. He felt honor bound to repay Charles Fox for services rendered. There had never been any question of asking for a safe conduct for Mascaron. His position at the Ministry of Marine made it impossible. Nor would he, Talleyrand, lend his support to any move which would spirit the man out of France. That act was too sensitive to be contemplated. His English friends had accepted that. Mascaron must remain in France for the time being. But there was no reason why he should be left to Fouché's mercies and many good reasons why he should not.

It was very evident that Fouché had no proof of

407

Mascaron's guilt, if he was guilty. But Talleyrand knew that such things meant little to Fouché. Men had gone before the firing squad on trumped up charges before now. Even the first consul was not above shaping circumstances to suit his own ends. Scapegoats were used as a matter of expediency. But Mascaron was no scapegoat. He was a stepping stone on the path of Fouché's ambitions. So was the girl and Dyson. But Fouché had overreached himself this time.

Charles Fox's pleasantly modulated accents broke in to Talleyrand's reveries. He was in conversation with Fouché. The subject of their conversation was Mascaron.

"I had the pleasure of meeting him when I was last in Paris," said Fox. "Those were happier days for our two countries. But, as you say, he's in no condition to receive visitors?"

"Regrettably, no," said Fouché. "Poor Antoine is delirious most of the time. He was laid by the heels by a most distressing fever. His physician scarcely leaves his side. A sad business! A sad business."

Gabrielle had to bite down on her tongue to preserve her silence. It was gradually being borne in upon her that these civilized gentlemen, far from being at each others throats, were determined to play out the farce as if they were on the best of terms.

"A sad business, as you say," said Mr. Fox solicitously. With a pointed look at Talleyrand, he dragged himself to his feet. "How fortunate for Mascaron that he has you for his friend, Monsieur Fouché."

Fouché was all smiles. "Oh, Antoine and I go back a long time," he said. "When he sent for me, naturally I dropped everything to be at his side."

"Naturally," returned Fox dryly.

As if on cue, everyone rose and idled towards the door. Gabrielle felt Cam's firm clasp on her elbow.

Fox was still speaking. "And may I say, Monsieur Fouché, how much I appreciate your efforts to preserve these old bones? I mean, of course, the measures you have so kindly taken for our safety."

Fouché's tone was equally charming. "Measures that you disregarded by coming here tonight, Mr. Fox."

Fox's bushy eyebrows rose. He paused with his hand on the doorknob. "By Jove, so I did! I tell you what, Fouché. I won't say anything to the first consul if you don't."

Stiffening slightly, Fouché intoned, "As you wish, Mr. Fox."

"Don't mention it," said Fox politely. "I understand how it is. You are very much in favor with the first consul at present. Any day now and I shall expect to hear that you have been appointed to your former position at the Ministry of Police. And I'm sure you deserve it." And mouthing many such polite phrases, Fox led the way out of the room.

Gabrielle hung back and turned to Cam, a spate of questions trembling on her tongue.

"Not one word!" he hissed.

In defiance of his command, she cried out softly, "I don't understand! Why is everybody so nice?"

"How far do you think we would get if we tried to take this place by storm? I want you out of here and safely away before all hell breaks loose."

"But . . ."

"Hush!"

None too gently, Cam propelled Gabrielle from the room. In the driveway, before she stepped into the carriage, Fouché took a very polite farewell of her as though she had been an honored guest and not his prisoner. Miserably, Gabrielle allowed Cam to bundle her into the waiting coach.

"*A bientôt*, Monsieur Fouché," she heard Cam say.

"Perhaps we shall meet again sooner than either of us expects," and he lightly followed her in.

I trust him, Gabrielle consoled herself under her breath, and tried to take comfort from that thought as the miles sped by and the Château de Vrigonde and her grandfather were left far behind.

Fouché watched Talleyrand's carriage until the night had swallowed it up. On entering the château, he practically fell over the doctor. Snarling, kicking, he shoved the unfortunate man out of his way.

"Am I always to be surrounded by wooden-headed clods?" he roared.

No one laughed as the hapless doctor fell over himself trying to get out of his way.

With undisguised contempt, Fouché viciously aimed a kick at the prone man. His action produced a terrified howl. Fouché smiled maliciously. In a night of unremitting humiliation, that one sound was like balm to a festering sore.

All his hopes lay around him in ruins. The English duke, the girl—both beyond his reach. And his hands were tied because he was the one who must guarantee their safety. Diplomatic immunity! he thought, and gnashed his teeth in rage. But he still had one bird in his hand. Mascaron.

Dyson would take his duchess to the safety of his yacht and return for him. Fouché was almost sure of it. For some few minutes he contemplated the pleasure it would give him to spring a trap on the damned Englishman. His pleasant reverie was short lived. If anything were to happen to the Englishman on French soil, his head would roll. Dyson knew it. He knew it. But he would not tamely stand by and let the Englishman walk away with his prize.

Coming to himself, he began to issue orders. "Make haste. We leave at once for Paris."

He might as well have said, *We leave for hell,* so lu-

410

dicrously terrified was the look that crossed the doctor's face. "P . . . Paris?" he stammered.

Fouché's cold eyes narrowed. It had not been his intention to take the doctor with him. But something in that look provoked him to suspicion. "You have some objection to Paris?" he queried silkily.

The wretched man began to shake. He lifted his sad eyes and looked forlornly from one stolid face to the next, as if seeking help from some quarter.

"Well?" bellowed Fouché.

The doctor was too petrified to say anything.

A cruel smile played over Fouché's lips. He had all the answer he needed. A few enquiries in Paris and he had no doubt that he would turn up something that would send this sniveling good-for-nothing to Madame Guillotine.

"Get your patient ready. You're coming with us." Catching sight of Dessins, Fouché instructed, "Dessins, go with him. I'll hold you personally responsible if he escapes." His voice dropped to an alarming whisper. "Well? What are you all waiting for?"

The suppressed fury in his tone set men in motion. They rushed off to do his bidding, too wise to tarry for further instructions or to voice their uncertainties about what it was exactly they were supposed to be doing. And when it was discovered that Fouché's coachmen were insensibly drunk and not fit to sit upright on a chair, much less the box of a moving coach, Savarin decided that he should not trouble his master with such a trivial intelligence. Two others, local men who knew the roads well, were pressed into service. They were the doctor's sons and cut from the same cloth as their craven sire. It was easy to terrif them.

The coach had not been on the road for more than ten minutes when its occupants seriously began to suspect that they were being driven by a couple of deranged madmen. It was a wild and reckless ride. Fouché cursed vehemently, the doctor braced himself against his insensible patient, and Dessins clung to the overhead strap for dear life. When the wheels hit a pothole and the coach bounced dangerously, throwing the occupants in every direction, Fouché's fury came to a boil. Lowering the window, he stuck his head out and screamed obscenities. The coachmen either did not hear or did not care. The driver cracked his whip and urged his team forward.

Fouché looked behind him and saw at once that the coach was outdistancing the riders who were there to protect it. "Fools!" he screamed, but the word was whipped from his mouth as the coach went tearing around a corner. As it went off the road, he was sure it would overturn. But by some miracle, there was a wagon track that led to the river. The lead horses charged along the track, faltered, righted themselves, and came to a shuddering halt.

Picking himself off the floor, Fouché stumbled from the carriage. He heard the drum of hooves and watched, helpless and aghast, as the shadowy forms of horses and riders went thundering past, unaware that his coach was on a side road. He was ready to do murder when he turned his livid face upon his coachmen. He could not believe his eyes. They were unhitching the horses. With startling clarity, he realized that he had been caught in a trap.

The night came alive with muffled sounds as men came out of the underbrush and surrounded the coach. Dessins descended, his hands high in the air. The doctor jumped down lightly, leveling a cocked pistol. Mascaron followed.

Fouché bared his teeth. "My men will soon realize their mistake and come looking for us," he stated.

"Oh I don't think so," said the doctor, motioning to two of his men to help Mascaron. "They're on their way to Paris, Mr. Fouché, following the wrong coach."

Fouché could scarcely credit that this man with the commanding presence was the same pathetic creature he had so despised. He seemed to be a foot taller and twenty years younger.

"What are you going to do with us?" asked Dessins.

"Why nothing," answered the doctor, faintly amused. "We're not butchers and murderers. Bind them. But don't gag them. If I know Monsieur Fouché, he is longing to vent his rage on someone. And what more fitting object than our young friend here?"

Dessins swallowed convulsively. His hopes had deceived him. The honors which he had dreamed about for months past faded quickly as fear took hold. He did not doubt that Fouché would make him the scapegoat for this night's work.

Trussed like chickens, Fouché and Dessins were deposited in the empty coach. With mock gallantry, the doctor bowed and bade them a fond farewell.

"When daylight comes, someone is bound to see the coach and investigate," he said cheerfully. "But by that time we shall be long gone."

Men and horses melted into the night. A small boat was moored by the bank. The two coachmen assisted Mascaron into it. The doctor stooped down to push the vessel into the stream.

"Wait!" said Mascaron. He was still groggy from the effects of the opiate. After a moment, he went on, "I should like to know the name of the man who rescued me." He extended his hand toward the doctor.

"I'm Dyson's man," said the doctor, clasping Mascaron's hand. "That's all you need to know."

Withdrawing his hand from Mascaron's clasp, Ro-

413

dier put his shoulder to the boat's stern. One heave and it slipped into the stream. Men picked up their oars and dipped them smoothly into the Seine's tranquil waters.

Rodier stepped back and watched the boat's progress. He was more than a little relieved that this particular adventure was over. For one thing, what he knew about doctoring could be written on the head of a pin. For another, he did not like tangling with Fouché, at least not face to face. And too many details had depended on chance. He preferred to order events where chance played no part.

Nevertheless, if luck had not been on their side there were other plans they would have fallen back on. If Gabrielle had refused to go with her husband, if Fouché had not decided to leave for Paris, if his own men had not been pressed to serve as coachmen, if . . . He broke off his thoughts and emitted a low laugh. Fortune had smiled on them, or someone's prayer had been answered. He would let it go at that.

Chapter Twenty-two

On board Cam's yacht there was a party atmosphere. Wine was flowing, toasts were unending, jests were flying. Even Talleyrand was seen to crack a genuine smile. If the Duke of Dyson and his duchess had not said two words together since they had come on board, no one remarked on it. That Gabrielle was sticking to her grandfather like a limpet seemed only natural. That gentleman had intimated that he had no desire to settle in England. In point of fact, he had made it plain that he had long since made contingency plans in the event that he found himself once again out of favor.

Gabrielle shook her head as if to clear it. She suspected that she was on the point of hysteria and she was sorely tempted to give in to it. The terrible hopelessness of the last few weeks, the relief of eluding Fouché, the worry over Mascaron, the despair of ever seeing Cam again—all had taken its toll. It was only the thought that they were not out of the woods yet that kept her sane. They were docked at Rouen waiting for the tide to turn. It would be days before they would reach Cornwall, if ever. She shuddered when she thought that before long they must shoot the treacherous bore. And if that were not bad enough, the English Channel must be crossed. Good God! Didn't these gentlemen realize that a war was in progress? Anything might happen! They might escape the bore only to be blown to kingdom come by a French warship. She could not understand these high spirits. It was almost as if her companions relished the perils to come.

Her eyes slowly traveled from one animated face to the next. It must be a dream, she was thinking, and she would waken to find herself still a prisoner at the château. She blinked to make sure that she was awake. Nobody disappeared. Mascaron, Goliath, Rollo, Mr. Fox, Mr. Sheridan, Lord Lansing, Monsieur Talleyrand, and dearest of all, Cam—they all looked remarkably real. And if she did not know better, she would take them for a crowd of school boys on a picnic. The thought was quite vexing.

Fuming, she listened in silence as Rollo related the mad dash in Fouché's carriage.

"When we hit that pothole," said Lansing, laughing, "I thought it was all over. And as for taking that turn, Rollo! I don't know how you managed it! I could scarcely make out the lead horses."

"I know the road like the back of my hand," said Rollo, coloring at this high praise. "That's the main reason I was sent for, wasn't it—that I'm familiar with the terrain?"

"So is Goliath," pointed out Lansing.

"You're forgetting, I was not here," said Goliath. Deliberately avoiding Cam's eyes, he chose his next words with care. "I'd gone back to Cornwall to look out for Gabrielle's interests, only to learn that she'd gone off to London."

"Then how do you come to be here?" asked Mr. Fox, handing around his snuff box. Only the older gentlemen availed themselves of this unprecedented honor.

Goliath shrugged. "When the Englishman sent for his yacht, I made sure I was one of the crew. It was simple."

"Incredible!" murmured Talleyrand, his voice shaded with envy. He shrugged it off, deciding that these capers were best left to younger men.

Picking up on that unspoken thought, Fox murmured wistfully, "I wish I were thirty years younger! What I wouldn't have given to be with you on that marvelous drive! And to see Fouché's face when he stumbled out of the coach!"

"That's if you hadn't broken your neck," said Gabrielle.

"It was wild," said Rollo, unrepentant. His eyes sparkled. "And just like old times! Remember, Angel? The only thing that was missing was you! I half expected you to appear on the scene with teeth bared and foil flashing."

"Those days are long over for Gabrielle," said Cam curtly, and gave the nod to his cabin boy to replenish his guests glasses.

Sheridan's alert eyes fastened on Gabrielle. "And thereby hangs a tale, I think?" he queried.

Gabrielle's cheeks went rosy. Before Sheridan could pursue that trail, she inquired, "And what part did you play in this rescue, Mr. Sheridan? You could have knocked me over with a feather when you reached down to help me on board."

Mr. Sheridan placed his hand on his heart. "Fair lady," he said, sighing, "forgive these old bones. In my younger days, I swear I would have slain dragons for you. As it is, convict me. I came along for . . . a lark."

Gabrielle snorted and all the gentlemen laughed. Mascaron patted her consolingly on the shoulder and by degrees her resentment melted. "I owe you all more than I can say," she said, smiling at each one in turn. "But . . . but isn't there someone missing?"

"Who, for instance?" asked Cam.

"The old doctor," replied Gabrielle. "I don't even know his name. I was sure, at least, I was beginning to suspect, that he was one of your men, Cam."

"I know of no doctor," said Cam.

Baffled, Gabrielle turned to Mascaron. "Grandfather, what do you think?"

"I remember him vaguely," answered Mascaron, his eyes fleetingly meeting Cam's stare before moving on. "An incompetent fellow if ever I met one. Half the time, I dribbled away the swill he tried to feed me and he didn't even notice."

"Oh," said Gabrielle, and lapsed into silence.

Her senses sharpened when Cam's dark head inclined toward Talleyrand. The Frenchman nodded, drained the last of his wine, and looked a question at Mascaron. As if on signal, Mascaron rose to his feet.

"You're not leaving!" exclaimed Gabrielle, clinging to her grandfather's hand.

He drew her up gently, "My dear girl, the tide waits for no man. Your husband must get under way or delay for another twelve hours."

"Then come with us!" she appealed.

He smiled whimsically and drew her into his arms. "I'm an old dog," he said. "I could never be happy in a new kennel."

"I shall never have a moment's peace knowing that you are a fugitive," she cried out.

"A fugitive? I?" Mascaron looked genuinely shocked. "My dear girl, you are far off! Fouché can't hurt me. Don't you suppose that I know enough about that old scoundrel to send him to the firing squad if I had a mind to?"

There was something not quite right about this logic, but Gabrielle was too overcome to detect it.

Mascaron made good use of her confusion to propel her into her husband's arms.

"Now kiss your old grandfather goodbye and show these damned English what we Normans are made of."

Smiling valiantly through her tears, she did as she was bid. Cam's hands tightened on her shoulders, keeping her captive, as Mascaron followed Talleyrand on deck. Rollo distracted her attention by taking hold of her hands.

"I had hoped we could all live in England," she said brokenly.

"I might have considered it," said Rollo, grinning ruefully, "but you see, Angel, there's this girl . . ."

"Not you too, Goliath," she whispered as the giant's beard scratched her cheek.

"I'll always be your man," he said, his rough voice not quite steady. "If I thought you had need of me . . ." His shrewd eyes swept over Cam. It did not take much intelligence to deduce that the Englishman was not best pleased with his young wife. That Gabrielle deserved a good tongue-lashing or worse, Goliath did not question. What he questioned was his own capacity to stand by and see someone else take over a role that had always been his. "I'm leaving you in good hands," he said, drawing some comfort from that conviction.

On deck, the crew were at their posts. A wind was getting up. Cam felt his spirits lift. The gangplank was raised. He gave the order to set sail, then turned back to the rail.

From the box on Talleyrand's carriage, Rollo gave him a wave. Goliath was mounted on a big roan. As Cam watched, he wheeled his mount and rode off into the night. Cam did not doubt that his destination was the Château de Vrigonde.

Inside Talleyrand's coach silence prevailed as the

419

two gentlemen considered the events of that night. Talleyrand was first to come out of his reverie.

"What you said to the girl, did you mean it?"

"What did I say?" asked Mascaron.

"That you had enough on Fouché to send him to the firing squad."

"Lord, no!" said Mascaron, passing a hand wearily over his eyes. "I had to say something, else she would have insisted on staying with me."

"Then what are your plans?" asked Talleyrand.

"I have none," said Mascaron. "I shall simply go to my office at the Ministry of Marine and wait for events to overtake me."

"I see," murmured Talleyrand, and became lost in private reflection. Several minutes were to pass before he broke the silence. "I could send Fouché to the firing squad several times over," he remarked.

Mascaron did not doubt it, and said so.

"And," went on Talleyrand in pleasantly modulated accents, "Fouché could do as much to me." He leaned over and said confidingly, "There are few of us who are entirely blameless, Monsieur Mascaron, and from what your son-in-law related, in your case, it seems you were more sinned against than sinner."

Surprise held Mascaron silent. Not knowing what story Dyson had concocted, he waited for Talleyrand to go on.

"Fouché and I are not friends exactly," said Talleyrand, "but neither are we enemies. I suppose one might say that we are colleagues of a sort."

Mascaron murmured something appropriate.

Softly, confidentially, Talleyrand continued, "It has occurred to me that France's future is very uncertain. It is to her benefit to have powerful friends on the other side of the Channel."

The thought was not original. It had been given

to him by the young Duke of Dyson when they had exchanged a private word on his yacht. Dyson was quite certain that his father-in-law had no contingency plans and he was loath to leave him in France to Fouché's mercies. Talleyrand had not been slow to take the hint.

"Leave Fouché to me," he had said. "I think I know how to twist his arm."

It was a favor that the young duke intimated would be repaid a hundred times over if ever it was in his power to do so. Talleyrand understood. Favors were a currency of exchange, and much more useful than money in the bank.

"Yes," he mused, "it never hurts to have friends in high places."

"Such as Charles Fox," suggested Mascaron.

"Precisely. And your son-in-law, Dyson."

A knowing look was exchanged.

"I can always use a good man in Foreign Affairs," observed Talleyrand. "If you are interested, I'd be happy to find a place for you."

Mascaron, as it happened, was very interested. "But what of Fouché?" he said. "The man is out for my blood."

Surprise registered in Talleyrand's face. "You are mistaken, Monsieur Mascaron. Fouché's ambitions transcend personalities. What he wants is power. And as it happens, I am in a position to be of some service to him." He leaned back against the leather upholstery, adjusting his lean frame to a more comfortable position. "It's settled then," he said.

Talleyrand's words had the ring of prophecy. Mascaron could not doubt them.

Dunraeden. From the deck of the *Marguerite*, Gabrielle surveyed its stout walls and soaring towers. High above, from perches in the rocky cliffs, gulls swooped down then circled, their lingering wails of lament carrying for miles around. The familiar tang of brine was in the air, and that pungent though not unpleasant odor of the secret things of the deep. Like a lover's caress, sunlight played over the scene before her, infusing the waters with that brilliant aquamarine that is native to Cornwall's shores, and embracing the protective walls of Cam's fortress with playful ardor, melting its coldness to an inviting warmth.

Gabrielle felt a sense of homecoming, and she laughed. Looking over her shoulder, she caught Cam's frowning expression. There had been very little laughter between them since he had taken her out of Normandy. Again and again she had tried to break through the wall of reserve he had erected since she had related all the circumstances surrounding her precipitous flight with Dessins. She had not been able to persuade him that it was only duty to Mascaron and fear for Goliath that had moved her to such extraordinary lengths. He saw it as a betrayal or worse—the culmination of a deliberate scheme to escape him that had been long in the planning. To Cam's way of thinking, Dessins had merely provided the opportunity and the means, and she had seized upon them.

She hoped there would be a final reckoning, and soon, for anything was preferable to Cam's cold and unfeeling civility. He was avoiding her with a deliberation that he had not troubled to hide since the *Marguerite*'s passengers, Mr. Fox, Mr. Sheridan, and Lord Lansing, had transferred by small boat to a British warship in the middle of the English Channel.

A cloud obscured the sun, and Dunraeden's aspect became instantly more threatening. Gabrielle shivered. Dunraeden and Cam. She thought they suited each other.

As Cam helped her into the small boat that was to row them to shore, Gabrielle tried to break the forbidding silence he maintained.

"We look a sight," she observed, her eyes sweeping over his coarse jerkin and stained breeches and her own boy's getup.

Cam said something polite and noncommittal.

She tried again when they passed through Dunraeden's two sets of massive doors and they were inexorably closed upon her. *"Déjà vu,"* she murmured.

No comment.

Reasonableness was having no effect, thought Gabrielle, and changed tactics. When they entered the great hall she looked around expectantly.

"What are you waiting for," asked Cam, urging her toward the stairs.

"Why, Louise, of course," she answered sweetly.

Cam's jaw hardened. Through his teeth he said, "Louise is not here."

"Oh?" said Gabrielle, all politeness. "Have you found some other lady whom you wish me to emulate?"

Cam grabbed her by the wrist and dragged her without ceremony up the stairs. Maids and lackeys who were going about their business froze in their places like marble statues. Cam ignored them. Gabrielle was all smiles.

Her smile faded somewhat when she was thrust into the circular chamber at the top of the south tower. Cam followed her in. She took a few strides into the center of the room and whirled to face him.

"Why am I here, Cam?" she asked.

423

Cam smiled unpleasantly. "Would you prefer the dungeon?"

There was no playfulness now in Gabrielle's manner. "Cam," she said softly. "Will you never learn?"

"I learned!" he said in a voice so savage that Gabrielle retreated a few steps. "I learned not to take any chances with you." His eyes heated, his jaw worked. "My God!" he said finally, "You would have robbed me of my child, and you did not care!"

"Cam, I cared!" Gabrielle cried out.

As if he dared not trust himself to speak, he spun on his heel and strode to the door.

"Please, Cam, we must talk to each other." She ran after him but halted when he turned furiously upon her. "Don't go, Cam," she pleaded. "Talk to me, please."

"Everything has been said," he answered and left her.

She heard the grate of the key in the lock and sank down on the bed, silent and thoughtful. Some few minutes later the key again turned in the lock and Betsy bustled in with towels and a pitcher of hot water. She sized up the situation at once. Clucking and muttering, she began on a long litany of her master's besetting sins, which were legion, by all accounts.

"He won't listen to me," said Gabrielle.

"Make him listen!" was Betsy's sage advice.

Easier said than done, Gabrielle was thinking as she disrobed and handed her boy's garments to Betsy.

"I'm to dispose of these," said Betsy, turning up her nose. "Master's orders."

Gabrielle wasn't listening. She was still mulling over Betsy's advice.

"Will there be anything else, Your Grace?" asked Betsy as she prepared to leave. She was not quite sure that she trusted the slow, cozening smile her mistress beamed at her.

"Betsy," said Gabrielle. "I need your help if ever that man is to come to his senses."

It was close to midnight before Cam retired for the night. He was in a curious humor. He felt spent, drained of all emotion. He could not decide what he was feeling. In the last several days it seemed that he'd run the gamut of every sensibility known to man. He knew he ached, and was forced to the reluctant conclusion that he was suffering from that silly idiotish known as a "broken heart."

A self-pity to which Cam would never have admitted crept up on him by degrees. With slow, absent movements, he shrugged out of his coat and pulled off his shirt, letting his garments drop in a forlorn heap where they fell. He might as well be a gelding, he was thinking, for he refused to exercise his conjugal rights with a wife who did not love him, and to commit adultery (supposing he could find any woman to tempt him) was not to be thought of.

Sighing, sleep the last thing from his mind, he stretched out on top of the bed and cupped his neck with both hands. He had meant what he told her. He wasn't about to take any more chances. She would remain at Dunraeden under lock and key for the rest of her natural life.

The notion was absurd and Cam knew it. Groaning, he rolled to his side. He didn't know how he was going to keep her. He did not know why he should even want to. She had deceived him, betrayed his trust and put him through hell. He must be a simpleton, he decided, to invite more of the same by hanging onto her against all reason.

She was his wife. That was the only reason he needed. He was an Englishman. This was his castle. He could lock her up and throw away the key, if he had a mind to, and no one would gainsay him. He had that right.

But that wasn't what he wanted. And what he wanted Gabrielle could keep from him till hell froze over.

A faint sound from the adjoining room distracted him from his unhappy reflections. He raised to his elbows. When the connecting door swung open, he rolled to his feet.

Gabrielle stood on the threshold. He saw in one comprehensive glance that against his express orders, Betsy had allowed her to retain her boy's clothes. Hell! Against his express orders Gabrielle already had the run of the place! His eyes narrowed to dangerous slits when he saw the flash of steel in her hand.

In a mocking salute, Gabrielle raised her rapier, then tossed it to Cam.

"What the devil!" he swore, and caught it in a reflex action.

Gabrielle quickly transferred the foil that she had retained in her left hand to her right, in the same moment, adopting a fencer's crouched position. *"En garde*, Englishman," she taunted, and came at him swiftly.

Cam never doubted for an instant that this was no feint, but a deliberate attempt to do him an injury. He had no choice but to parry her blade. He danced out of the way as she came at him again.

"What the hell do you think you're playing at?" he bellowed.

"You'll see when the tip of my blade is at your throat," she panted.

"Are you mad? You could hurt our child with

426

this foolishness."

He meant to throw down his foil, but she came at him with such deadly purpose that he was forced to use it to defend himself. They circled warily.

"I can't fight you in your condition," he told her.

"It gives me an unfair advantage," agreed Gabrielle cheerfully, and threw herself at him.

Cam parried her thrusts and dodged away. Like a kitten stalking a tiger, she followed him.

"I don't want to hurt you," said Cam, easily deflecting her glancing blows.

"Good," she said. "That's what I hoped you would say. You don't mind, I trust, if I don't reciprocate?"

Cam was swiftly losing his patience. "What's the purpose of this?" he demanded, and fell back a step as she came at him again.

"I want to talk to you. I want *you* to talk to me."

"I was not the one who kept secrets," he sneered.

"What about the Abbaye?" she queried.

Cam froze. It was Gabrielle who gasped as her rapier flicked along his naked torso, drawing blood.

"Don't you know any better than to drop your guard?" she asked crossly, examining the scratch she had inadvertently inflicted.

But Cam was suddenly alive to a graver danger than the point of her rapier. He discarded his foil. "What do you know about the Abbaye?" he asked hoarsely.

Preoccupied, she said, "It's only a scratch. No harm done," and she dabbed at Cam's bare chest with a far from pristine kerchief she'd found in her pocket.

Cam grabbed for her wrists, and her foil rolled to the floor. "The Abbaye, Gabrielle. What did you mean by it?"

Straightening, slanting him a troubled look, she said, "I know that you were there. I know what happened to your mother and sister. And I know that you blamed my grandfather for everything that happened that night."

"How do you know?" His face was a mask of coldness.

She faltered a little before that blighting stare. "My grandfather told me."

"How did he find out?"

"He . . . he just did, that's all."

He administered a rough shake to loosen her tongue.

"It was the judges, Cam! Over the years, every single one of those men who served on that tribunal fell foul of the law one way or another. They came to a bad end." She paused, marshaling her thoughts. "It was only recently that my grandfather began to see a connection. He was the last of that tribunal to remain at large. And he had known, of course, that for years he had been a hunted man. That's why we were always on the run. But he did not know who was behind it, or the reason for it, except, of course, that it was revenge." Breaking off, she let out a tortured breath. "I don't want to talk about this Cam. Later perhaps, but not now. I want to talk about us."

"But this conversation is so interesting, Gabrielle," he said ironically. "Pray continue." Turning his back on her he stalked to the window. From miles out at sea, the lights of a ship winked at him.

"I don't know what it is you wish to know," observed Gabrielle helplessly.

"When did Mascaron tell you all this?"

"The very day that you rescued us from Fouché's trap. He didn't want me to go with you if you came for me, you see."

"He would rather have left you to Fouché's mercies?" queried Cam bitterly.

"No, Cam. He wanted me to escape. I could have done so easily. But I couldn't leave my grandfather. And I knew you would come for me after I discovered that Dessins had told me a pack of lies."

"It's a pity you had not trusted me sooner," he said, and then with less heat, "Or was it always in your mind to leave me?"

Biting her lip, she looked away. "Cam, I have tried to explain all that. Don't you see? If it had been only me I would not have cared, but I couldn't take the chance that you would keep on using me to hurt my grandfather." Almost desperately, she cried out, "I didn't want to leave you. But I had a duty to Mascaron. And then Dessins led me to believe that you had . . . that something had happened to Goliath. I know now, of course, that Goliath had come back to Cornwall when we were in London."

"Why did he return to Cornwall?" asked Cam shortly.

"To . . . to protect me. By this time, you see, my grandfather had worked everything out. He knew about the Abbaye."

He swore viciously under his breath. Abruptly, he asked, "How did Mascaron discover that I was at the Abbaye? I made sure that he did not remember me."

"It was Fouché who told him that you had abducted your ward. The coincidence of two abductions at the same time seemed extraordinary. My grandfather knew that *I* must be that girl. He began to suspect that it was you who had hounded us for years. He knew your name at last. He made enquiries. It is a matter of record . . ." She broke off and stared miserably at the toe of her boot.

"Yes? You were saying? It is a matter of record?"

Exhaling slowly, Gabrielle went on, "It is a matter

of record that the Duchess of Dyson, formerly Héloise de Valcour, and her young daughter, were murdered at the Abbaye during the September massacres. He was sure, then, that you saw him as one of the executioners, and that my abduction was to be only the beginning of your revenge."

Spinning to face her, Cam said, "Well don't stop now. Go on."

"That's all I know."

"That's not all you wish to say, surely?" There was a mocking glint in his eyes that she distrusted.

Her look was uncertain and strangely forlorn. "I don't know if I can find the words to say it," she said.

He feigned incredulity. "My God," he said. "Think what a weapon your grandfather has put into your hands! Convict me! I confess! I was the one who hounded you from pillar to post. It was my agents who were set to track you down. Because of me, you were made to don boy's clothes and adopt the rough life of a vagabond." His voice grew harsher, fiercer, more menacing. "Those scars on your body? I might as well have put them there myself. Your broken ribs? Chastise me! I was the one who pushed you from that wall. It was because of me that you could never find any sanctuary. It was my thirst for revenge that made your life intolerable." His fists clenched at his sides. Overcome with the tempest raging inside him, he slammed them against the wall.

A wind was getting up. It ruffled the curtains at the windows and first dimmed then forced the candles to a brighter flame. Gabrielle did not notice. Her gaze never wavered from the broad back that was so rigidly turned against her.

Her voice husky with suppressed emotion, she said, "What I was trying to say is this. I'm sorry for

430

all the pain you were made to suffer. I'm sorry for what happened to your mother and sister. I'm sorry that I sang that stupid song. I didn't know what I was doing. The gaolers took great delight, you see, in teaching it to all the children. And most of all, I'm sorry that my grandfather ever came to the Abbaye that night and singled me out. Cam, I don't know what else to say. If only you could find it in your heart to forgive me!"

He had braced himself for her bitter contempt, steeled himself for her anger. What he heard, at first, made no sense to him. By degrees, her words washed through him, gently submerging him in the baptism of catharsis. But at the last he was more shocked than if she had uttered the foulest, vilest blasphemy.

That she should wish that Mascaron had not singled her out! Did she know what she was wishing for? *He* could not be sorry. He thanked God for it. Those women—his mother and sister included—they were doomed whatever the judgement of the tribunal. No one could have checked the murderous purpose of that mob. To save even one from the frenzy of their hatred was a miracle in itself. And, oh God, if only one could be saved, he was not sorry that one had been Gabrielle. He closed his eyes, remembering.

If only one could be saved . . . His breathing became constricted as the scene played out before his eyes. Against all odds, Mascaron had saved Gabrielle. If it had been in his power, he would have saved his mother and sister. He would have given his life for them. But Fate or caprice had decreed otherwise. He'd thought his own life forfeit until Rodier had intervened.

He grew still as the memory came more sharply into focus. Rodier had intervened. But it was Mascaron's silent communication to Malilard that had averted the sentence of death. He'd done it on a whim, and Cam had damned him for it. He had not wanted to survive if the people he loved best in the world were condemned.

He had survived. Gabrielle had survived. He did not know what it might mean. He did not care. He only knew . . . oh God . . . he could not be sorry for it.

"Gabrielle," he moaned, turning to face her.

She was no longer there. He did not know how long he stood there staring, paralyzed into inactivity. When he came to himself, he cursed himself for a fool. He knew only too well how quick Gabrielle was to seize on any opportunity that presented itself. He'd given her a head start. She'd had enough time to slip over the castle ramparts or walk through the gates or . . .

In two strides, he was through the door, shrugging into his coat, bellowing for his minions to rouse themselves and chase down his duchess. He had a terrible, awful vision of the night she had tried to outrun the tide. Like a madman he raced down the stairs, taking them two at a time. When he reached the bailey, he broke into a run. The gatekeepers had the gates open, answering his shouted commands before he came up to them, and men were dashing this way and that, unsure of what it was they were supposed to be doing. Some thought that a French attack was imminent, and were checking their firing arms.

Cam waited for no man. Careless of life and limb, he scrambled over rocks and boulders till his booted feet sank into the wet sands. She couldn't be far ahead of him. There had not been enough time. But where the hell was she?

"Gabrielle," he roared.

Silence.

The tide was coming in. He raced to meet it, his heart thundering against his ribs. "Gabrielle!" There was nothing but the muted roar of the breakers and the frenzied drum of his heartbeat.

He could see no trace of her. If he were on the ramparts, he would see for miles around. Cursing himself for acting without thinking and wasting precious time, he swiftly retraced his steps.

His lungs were almost bursting by the time he dragged himself back to the causeway. He pushed himself to the limit. He had to find her. God, he would never forgive himself if anything happened to her. Despair gripped him.

Entering the great hall, he found sleepy-eyed lackeys gathered uncertainly in groups. "Search the castle from top to bottom," he shouted, and went dashing up the stairs before thinking to tell them what or who it was they were supposed to find.

In his headlong flight to the door that would take him onto the castle walls, he almost missed it. He stumbled and turned back. There was a light coming from under the door to Gabrielle's tower chamber. He had to rest for several seconds to catch his breath.

Her door was unlocked.

When he pushed through, he sagged with relief. She was in a filmy nightrail in the center of the room, employed in nothing more dangerous than brushing out her long hair.

"Cam, what is it?" she asked, startled by his wild look and disheveled appearance.

"I thought you had gone," he said, fighting to control his breathing.

"Gone? Where?" She laid her brush aside.

His chest rising and falling painfully, he said, "Your door is unlocked."

"It's no great feat to open locked doors, Cam," she said quietly.

There was a wealth of meaning in those few words. No, thought Cam, it was no great feat for Gabrielle to open locked doors. If she really wanted to leave him, there was nothing he could do to prevent it. Besides, he had already made his decision. He wasn't going to take the chance that she'd put her life in jeopardy again.

His breathing had evened. Nevertheless, he was far from calm when he said, "If you want to leave, I won't try to stop you. In fact, I'll take you wherever you wish to go and see that you're settled." He tried for a smile. "I just want to make sure that you are safe, Angel. All right?"

It took a moment for her to find her voice. She swallowed and said, "Thank you for that, Cam. But it's not necessary. This is where I want to be. Oh, I don't mean Dunraeden. But wherever you are, that's where I want to be."

He closed his eyes until he could get a hold of himself. "Angel," he whispered. "Can you ever forgive me?"

"Forgive you? What do I have to forgive?"

She really did not know, thought Cam, and the weight of his transgressions pressed the more heavily upon him. His voice low and unsteady, he said, "Forgive me for making your life a misery, for setting my agents to hound you, for all that you were made to suffer when you were a child."

Her hand fluttered and her eyes went huge in her pale face. Swallowing, she tried to respond, but her voice failed her.

At her prolonged silence, Cam groaned. Imploringly, he said, "I don't blame you for hating me for what I did. But if you give me a chance, I swear I'll spend my life trying to make it up to you."

A choked whimper escaped her. "Oh, my darling, don't! It is I who should beg your forgiveness. And I never thanked you for what you did for my grandfather. Don't you think I know what it cost you to give up your hatred and save him, too?"

He shrugged helplessly. "I didn't do it for him. I did it for you. And I've discovered that I don't hate him. How should I when he saved you from the fury of that mob?"

She made a movement toward him, but he halted her with an abrupt gesture of one hand. "You must let me finish, Angel. There are things that must be said before I can ever again be right with myself."

Restlessly, he took several paces around the chamber before pivoting to face Gabrielle. "Louise Pelletier . . ." he began.

She cut him off without hesitation. "I assure you, Cam, I don't hold that episode against you. I never really did, my dear." She tried for a watery smile. "Well, perhaps for an hour or two, but no longer, I promise you."

He combed his fingers through his hair. On a harsh undertone, he exclaimed, "If that were only it!" Inhaling slowly, he went on in a more normal tone, "I hope you will believe me when I say that you, and only you, are the epitome of everything I admire in a woman."

Her voice was tremulous when she replied, "Thank you, Cam. I'll try not to disgrace you. It has not been easy for me, but with your help, I hope I may yet learn how to comport myself like a lady."

He groaned and cursed furiously on the same breath. "I don't give a damn for ladies!" he roared.

She fell back, startled at the sudden storm in his voice.

He shook his head and waited a moment before

continuing, "Don't you know it was a sprite in boy's breeches who captured my heart?" He laughed, a faintly self-mocking sound. "I was a fool not to admit to myself at once that everything about you surpassed anything I had ever encountered before in a woman. It has nothing to do with the clothes on your back. It's you, Gabrielle. It's who and what you are. And I would never forgive myself if you were under the misapprehension that I want you to make yourself over into something you are not. Angel, please, for my sake, stay exactly as you are."

Smiling through her tears, she said, "You must love me very much to ask that, Cam."

Cam was too deeply affected to hear the faint sally behind the words. Unsmiling, seriously, he began, "Is there . . ." He faltered, inhaled sharply, and went on, "Is there a chance that you could learn to love me, too?"

For a moment, her eyes fluttered closed. "No," she said and could not speak for the constriction in her throat.

Misunderstanding her silence, Cam looked at her in despair.

She found her voice. "No," she said, "There's no chance of that. You see, my darling, I could not stop loving you even if I wanted to."

For a long interval they stood very still, searching each others eyes. It was Gabrielle who made the first move. With a stifled cry she threw herself into her husband's arms. A torrent of incoherent words spilled from her lips.

Cam kissed her into silence. The embrace became rougher, then gentled as she responded to his demand. There was so much that still needed to be said, *must* be said, but he didn't know where to begin. He thought of a better way.

"We'll talk later," he said, and led her to the bed.

"Oh Angel, it's been so long, so damned long. Love me, just love me," he pleaded.

"I do," she crooned, and folded him in her arms.

He tried to be gentle. He tried to be kind. And if she hadn't responded to him so wantonly, he might have succeeded. But when skin slipped over naked skin they were both helpless to check the sudden mindless blaze of passion that flamed to flash point and was soon spent.

"We'll do better the next time," said Cam, and started over. Gabrielle wasn't voicing any objections.

Later, much later, when they had said everything that lovers say to each other in the deep of the night, Cam said, "We'll leave for London as soon as you like." He was reflecting that Dunraeden's aspect was too forbidding, that it held too many unhappy memories for Gabrielle's comfort. Perhaps she would always think of his castle as a prison. The thought troubled him.

Gabrielle rose above him. "That doesn't suit me," she said, and lightly, lightly, traced each dear feature with the tip of her tongue. "I don't want our child to grow up in the city."

Cam's hands stroked protectively along the small swell of his wife's abdomen. "I have an estate in Yorkshire," he offered doubtfully, "and a small manor house near Chester."

But that didn't suit Her Grace either.

"What do you want?" asked Cam. "I'll give you anything within reason." But if she mentioned Normandy, he knew he would throttle her.

"What I want," said Gabrielle, laughing, "is to lock you up in my castle in Cornwall and throw away the key."

Cam's bright eyes glinted up at her. "Will you be my gaoler?" he quizzed.

"Englishman," she said, tossing her head, "I'll

437

never let you out of my sight, and that's a promise."

"Careful," he warned, his eyes turning serious. "You'll be just as much my captive as I am yours. And I speak from experience, Angel."

"Devil," she whispered. "Don't you know yet that's all I've ever wanted?"

And nothing more was said till a long while later.

Epilogue

London: Two Weeks Later

Epilogue

Mr. Pitt was slightly mollified when he observed that his guests were imbibing his port with a proper respect for its character.

"You keep a very fine cellar, sir," said Mr. Fox, rolling the delectably sweet liquid over his tongue before swallowing.

"The finest," added Mr. Sheridan, and held out his empty glass for his host to replenish.

It was Mr. Fox who handed round his snuff box. The ice in Mr. Pitt's eyes melted a trifle. "Thank you," he said, gratified by the gesture, and sniffed delicately. "There's not many today who adhere to the old ways. The younger generation has no taste for port and snuff and such like."

"Pity," said Sheridan, and he too went through the elegant ritual flexing his wrist, then rubbing thumb and forefinger together after partaking of a pinch of snuff.

The companionable silence was broken when Mr. Pitt let out a long-suffering sigh. "Two British warships," he said, "and nothing to show for it."

Fox and Sheridan exchanged a quick glance. In the fortnight since they had returned from France and made as complete a report as they dared on Cam's behalf, the warships had become Mr. Pitt's constant lament. It seemed that whenever they

chanced to meet him, he could not refrain from
raising the subject.

Mr. Fox was beginning to regret that he and
Sheridan had ever taken it upon themselves to act
as Dyson's emissaries. At the time it had seemed
the least they could do under the circumstances.
Dyson wished to take Gabrielle to Cornwall at once.
Under no circumstance would he submit her to the
unpleasantness of ton speculation until the rumors
had a chance to die down. And Fox had encouraged
him in this course of action. He had forgotten how
irritatingly monotonous Pitt could be on occasion.

"Two British warships," intoned Mr. Pitt, echoing
his former lament "and nothing to show for it."

"Come, come, Mr. Pitt," said Sheridan pleasantly.
"It's not as if you lost the warships. They returned
safely. Dyson got his duchess back. And we are
here. That's something, surely?"

"It was Mascaron I was promised," said Pitt.

"Look at it this way," said Mr. Fox with an ingratiating grin. "By that small gesture you've made
friends for England in the highest reaches of French
diplomatic circles."

"You call two warships a small gesture?" asked
Mr. Pitt dryly.

"In the long run, yes, I do. And haven't we come
here today for the express purpose of passing along
a report that you should find highly gratifying? At
the risk of repeating myself, may I remind you that
Mascaron has taken up a position under Talleyrand
at the Ministry of Foreign Affairs? Think what this
will mean for England, Mr. Pitt. When this war
ends, we shall have friends in France in high places.
Don't forget, Dyson's duchess is Mascaron's granddaughter."

"I'm not like to forget," retorted Pitt with a flash
of temper. That Dyson had sent these gentlemen as

442

his spokesmen, and continued to do so when he should have had the decency to come in person, was a very sore point indeed.

Shrewdly guessing the source of Pitt's annoyance, Mr. Fox offered, "The duke had no option but to see Gabrielle safely to Cornwall. The poor girl had endured the most unspeakable hardships imaginable. He'll come to see you, all in good time, Mr. Pitt."

In answer, Mr. Pitt grunted. After a moment's considering silence, he said, "It's inconceivable that she would run off in that fashion without a word to Dyson." He was thinking that there were still gaps in the story he had been told.

"She knows that the duke would not have permitted it," Sheridan reminded him. "And with good reason. As we told you, Fouché had involved himself in the affair."

"I still can't understand what she hoped to gain," said Pitt testily.

Mr. Fox smoothly responded, "The girl was confused, naturally. She thought that by returning to France, her grandfather would be absolved of all suspicion, that no one would be able to accuse him of divided loyalties."

Pitt digested these words in silence. At length, he said, "It sounds plausible, I suppose, but . . . " He shook his head. "Mascaron's granddaughter and Dyson. I still can't believe it."

"Frankly, neither can I," mused Sheridan. "I would not have thought Dyson the type to fall madly in love with a young girl and carry her off."

"I don't know why you should not," said Fox. "Look at you." He was referring to an event that had occurred years before, when Richard Sheridan had eloped with a young beauty and secretly married her.

"That's different," said Sheridan.

"Oh? Why?"

"Because I'm me and Dyson is . . . well . . . Dyson."

"True," said Mr. Fox, stifling a smile.

Sheridan slanted his friend a keen look, but Mr. Fox was saying nothing. Of the three gentlemen present, only Fox had been made party to the whole of Gabrielle's story.

Mr. Pitt roused himself from his private reflections to say, "I don't think I understand this younger generation. They're certainly not what they appear to be."

His idle words acted powerfully on his two companions. As if struck dumb, they stared at each other for a long moment. Mr. Sheridan chortled. Fox soon followed. It was some time before their laughter had subsided. Mr. Pitt stared at them as if they were madmen.

Fox dabbed at his eyes with his pristine handkerchief. "I beg your pardon, Mr. Pitt. You could not know that you chanced to voice our most celebrated toast."

"Did I?" said Pitt.

Eyes twinkling, Sheridan raised his glass. "Gentlemen, I give you a toast." He waited till his companions had obligingly raised their glasses. "To the younger generation," he said, and looked to Fox for the expected retort.

Mr. Fox smiled expansively. He raised his glass higher. "To the younger generation," he repeated. "There's a lot more to them than we give them credit for." And he drank with gusto.

Author's Note

The description of the prison massacre in the prologue is based on an eyewitness account. There actually was someone standing at the turret window looking down on that frightful scene. To my knowledge, however, there were no female prisoners murdered at the Abbaye. But the fate of aristocratic women at some of the other prisons was appalling. I claim writer's license in placing some of those women at the Abbaye during the night of 2 September 1792.

I have used many factual characters and events in the background to Cam's and Gabrielle's story. Some things are a matter of record. The debate in the House between Pitt and Fox, for example, is exactly as I have described. The interpretation of why Fox took the position he did, however, and the circumstances that influenced him, come from my own imagination.

With respect to the two attempts on the life of Napoleon Bonaparte, Fouché was widely credited, from beginning to end, with engineering the plot that culminated in the execution of the young Duc d'Enghien in February, 1804. Talleyrand and Fox are known to have kept up a correspondence. In 1806, Fox did in fact write to Talleyrand warning him of an assassination attempt against Napoleon, and this when the war between France and Great Britain was in progress. What I have done, in the interests of my story, is invent two previous attempts that were discovered by Fouché and Talleyrand.

As far as possible, I have tried to portray historical characters and their points of view faithfully. This is particularly true of the depiction of Charles James Fox, the most fascinating, complex, and brilliant statesman of his generation, along with William Pitt.

For those readers who are interested, here is a summary of the fate of some of the historical characters who appear in the book.

WILLIAM PITT: returned to the office of prime minister in 1804. He died in 1805, largely unsung and unlamented, when his popularity was at its lowest ebb. He was buried in Westminster Abbey.

CHARLES FOX: finally, in 1806, over the vociferous protests of George III, came to office as foreign secretary in a coalition government. He died the same year, eight months after Pitt. He was buried with great pomp and ceremony in Westminster Abbey only inches away from his old adversary. The papers made much of this great man and dutifully noted the important personages who attended his funeral. There was no reference to Fox's widow, his beloved Liz.

RICHARD SHERIDAN: in the coalition government of 1806, he served as treasurer of the navy. He died in 1816, in his sixty-fifth year. Although we remember him best as a playwright, his political career spanned more than thirty years.

JOSEPH FOUCHÉ: was restored to his position as minister of police in 1804. He was notorious for his unfeeling efficiency, spy networks, and intrigues. In 1809, Fouché and Talleyrand, two men who had constantly intrigued against each other, conspired together to depose Napoleon. As ever, when discovered, they managed to extricate themselves without too much difficulty. Proscribed as a regicide in 1816, Fouché was exiled. He died in 1820 at Trieste.

CHARLES MAURICE DE TALLEYRAND: prospered under successive leaders in France. He became the French ambassador to the Courts of St. James in 1830. He died in Paris in 1838. Though it has never been proven, there has always been speculation that during the Naploeonic Wars, Talleyrand was in the pay of Austria, France's enemy.

MARIE JULIEN STANISLAS MAILLARD: the leader of the *sans-culottes* in the September Massacres. He disappeared after Robespierre was executed in 1794. The evidence suggests he was still alive, hiding behind an assumed identity, in the early years of the Empire. No one knows what became of him. My account of his death is entirely fictitious.

Finally, a word about the conduct of the war. Napoleon's designs to invade Britain were frustrated by first one thing and then another. As we know, that final confrontation for mastery of the seas was delayed until October 1805. At the Battle of Trafalgar, the British fleet under Lord Nelson won an engagement that crushed the naval power of France and Spain and established Britain as mistress of the seas for more than a century to come.